FRONT RUNNER

FRONT RUNNER

A NOVEL OF TEXAS POLITICS

ROB ALLYN

CROWN PUBLISHERS, INC.
NEW YORK

Copyright © 1990 by Rob Allyn

Published by Crown Publishers, Inc., 201 East 50th Street, New York, New York 10022. Member of the Crown Publishing Group.

CROWN is a trademark of Crown Publishers, Inc.

Manufactured in the United States of America

Library of Congress Cataloging-in-Publication Data
Allyn, Rob.
    Front runner : a novel of Texas politics / Rob Allyn. — 1st ed.
        p.   cm.
    I. Title.
PS3551.L525L66   1990
813'.54—dc20   90-30490
                                                                              CIP

ISBN 0-517-57762-3

Book design by Shari de Miskey

10 9 8 7 6 5 4 3 2 1

First Edition

For Monica

Politics are almost as exciting as war, and quite as dangerous. In war, you can be killed only once, but in politics many times.

WINSTON CHURCHILL

November
1988

Prologue

The candidate was dying.

His blood-sticky white hand gripped Johnny's tawny arm as they swayed through the busy traffic in the darkened rear bay of the ambulance. For the first time in nearly two years as a Dallas County paramedic, Johnny Rodriguez was scared. It wasn't the crimson-soaked sheets strapped tight to the crumpled body on the stretcher in front of him. Blood didn't bother Johnny. He'd seen plenty of it on the night shift: spilled over car seats, spattered on living room rugs, smeared on broken windshields and switchblade knives and garden hoes.

This was different. This wasn't some junkie gutted in an alley. This was a celebrity, a man Johnny himself had seen on television, in commercials that extolled his Honesty, his Experience in Congress. That scared Johnny Rodriguez, more than all the bloody corpses he had scraped off the county's asphalt over the past two years.

The sheeted figure on the stretcher gagged violently, writhing to avoid the stab of torn flesh and shattered bone.

3

"Come on, man!" Johnny urged frantically in his deep young bass. It was a big voice for such a small, slight Latino. The ambulance lurched right and left as they dodged erratically onto the freeway.

Using his left hand to flatten the patient's shoulder, Rodriguez tried desperately to control the contortions, struggling in vain to free his own right arm from the victim's death clutch. It was useless. Instead of growing weaker with loss of blood, the grip only strengthened, grappling Johnny's bony arm as if clinging to a feeble pulse of life that was slowly drifting away. The sour bile of fear rose again in the young paramedic's throat. This is my big moment, Johnny realized miserably. And I'm blowing it.

But what can I do? The blood flowed uncontrollably from the terrible maw of the gunshot wound. It bubbled sickeningly in the dark mass of the man's throat, drenching the soggy lump of compresses Johnny had wrapped around the patient's neck. The jerk and sway of the ambulance made things worse. The patient reacted to each sudden jar with another jagged series of contortions, ripping away bandages faster than Johnny could press them back into place.

The lithe young paramedic half stood, balancing himself with practiced ease. Concentrating his meager hundred and forty pounds to steady the shuddering figure on the stretcher, he peered out the little slit window on the left side of the ambulance.

Parkland Hospital! Johnny spotted its lights twinkling ahead to the right. "Thank God!" he gasped aloud, checking the thready pulse of his unhearing patient. At least the bastard hadn't died on him. Just let me get him inside alive, Johnny prayed. And I can duck the DOA tag.

The ambulance bounced onto Parkland's wide concrete emergency ramp. The flashing red lights cast an eerie intermittent glow over the faces of the doctors, nurses, reporters, and police officers gathered in front of the emergency room entryway. The policemen held back the reporters as two white-smocked interns rushed out to swing open the ambulance doors.

"He's lost a lot of blood!" Johnny shouted urgently, rolling out the stretcher. Its collapsible metal trolley legs snapped smoothly into place. Johnny hopped down to the pavement. A nurse took notes as Rodriguez shouted vital signs, pausing to check the straps for the patient's final trip into Emergency.

"How is he?"

"Will he make it? Has he said anything?"

4

"Excuse me! Hey, out of my way!"

"Did you see the gunman?"

The reporters and cameramen came alive at the sight of the bloody stretcher. They surged down the ramp, surrounding Johnny and the doctors, blinding them with the harsh glare of half a dozen mini-cams. An unending barrage of sharp, insistent questions jumped collectively from the snarling media pack as it closed in on the shattered victim. Smelling hard news, the slavering pack of news-hounds overwhelmed the hospital staff, barring the route between the dying patient on the stretcher and the neon-lit salvation beyond the metal-sheathed doors of the emergency room.

Johnny looked around at the faces of the medical staff. He saw six blurs of panic hovering above six frozen white-clad bodies. The young paramedic blinked twice at the flashbulbs, took a deep breath, and aimed the stretcher at the onrush of local journalists.

Then, he shoved. "Move it!" Johnny screamed. Spindly legs pumping hard, he barreled up the ramp and through the open doors to Emergency. Conditioned by countless brush-offs and push-throughs, the sea of reporters parted magically, then closed ranks and pushed inside behind the stretcher.

"Okay, Johnny. We got it," said one of the residents. The stretcher passed under the profusion of brightly colored directional signs pointing to Obstetrics and Pediatrics, Oncology and Surgery. The stretcher trundled down the long blue-painted hallway toward OR, doctors and nurses shouting orders and poking needles and jabbing tubes on the fly, TV crews trailing clumsily behind. Finally, the whole rolling contraption of white-coated arms, tense jawlines, and clear plastic IV bags disappeared through the impassive blue doors marked SURGERY, leaving the news-hungry pack baying outside.

As he watched them go, Johnny felt something like disappointment as the adrenaline drained from his veins. He unclenched his fists and fled. The blood on his smock would drive the reporters into a frenzy, and Johnny didn't want to spend the rest of the night trying to avoid making a mistake on television. He had done his job. The candidate was with the doctors now.

September
1962

1

It was a typical September day in Dallas, the enervating heat of that particularly oily summer of 1962 giving notice to all who dared think autumn might be on its way. The sun beat down mercilessly on the players on the practice field at Southern Methodist University's Ownby Stadium. I am still king here, said the blazing white ball in the sky.

"God, I hate this!" Andrew Sebastian gasped between breaths, flat on his back against the hard, bristly Bermuda grass.

"Placekickers," scoffed his fraternity brother, Tommy Butler. An aspiring linebacker since childhood, Tommy had sweated through more leg lifts than Bermuda grass has fleas. "No stamina," Tommy pronounced. "No wonder you're goin' nowhere with Tricia Farris."

Andrew, consumed with his own agony, ignored him.

"Thuhty-fo! Thuhty-faav! Thuhty-siiix!" droned the relentless Coach Chamberlain, a bantam rooster strutting scrawny tanned legs beneath dazzling white athletic shorts. Chamberlain's sunburned waddle of a neck flexed mightily above his open collar as he counted the cadence, sterling-silver whistle dangling beneath, Adam's apple jumping to deliver each new jolt of pain to the varsity squad. "Foaty-wun! Foaty-tooo!"

Andrew closed his eyes to keep out the sweat and tried to lose himself in the rhythm. The sun blazed through his eyelids, lighting his head red and yellow and orange. Fifty-one. Fifty-two. Andrew's rump ached. He wished the coach would wind up this nonsense and let him get to the crossbar.

"Fifty-naaan!"

At last, Andrew thought with relief. No one could do more than sixty leg lifts.

"Sixty-one! Sixty-tooo! Sebastian, stop draggin' ass!" Andrew blinked his eyes open, paralyzed. The muscles in his stomach refused to respond. Then, almost imperceptibly, his steel-cleated heels edged an inch off the ground.

"Gonna get any tonight?" Butler asked insistently. Tommy's mind nearly always ran down that narrow strip of track most traveled by college boys and prison inmates. "Y'all been going out for a year. When you gonna bag her?"

Andrew gritted his teeth. He hated it when guys talked of "bagging" girls. As though they were groceries. Or big game animals. Still, for all his locker room machismo, Tommy had a point. Tricia Farris was the last of that endangered species at Southern Methodist University: the popular virgin. Andrew twisted his head to avoid Butler's smirking black eyes. Across the field he could see a dozen or more would-be SMU Mustangs jogging halfheartedly toward the stadium, ready for second-string tryouts.

"Sixty-faav!" bawled Coach Chamberlain. "Sixty-siiix!"

James Brackler trotted out to the practice field behind fourteen assorted freshmen and sophomores. He slowed to a walk, lagging behind the eager beavers. The others ran all the way to the field. Showing off for the coach, Brackler thought balefully. "Jerks," he puffed under his breath as the distance stretched between him and the other tryouts. James sighed and picked up the pace, half jogging, half dragging his 280-pound bulk the second hundred yards to Ownby Stadium.

"Seventy-naan! Eighty!" Coach Chamberlain shouted. The coach specifically avoided glancing over at his last desperate chances for filling out SMU's second string. "All right, everybody to their units!" he ordered. "Move-move-move!"

Andrew heaved himself up on one elbow, tanned longish face flushed a deep rust, short brown hair black with sweat and tufted with a hundred yellow spikes of dead grass. His stomach burned deep down. For a second he thought he was going to throw up. Tommy was already sprinting downfield toward linebacker drills. Exhausted, Andrew lay on the stony Texas earth for an extra minute, waiting for the waves of nausea to clear.

He watched as a painfully overweight underclassman stumbled toward the rest of the group arrayed on the field. Poor guy, thought Andrew. The obese boy's shabby black street socks sagged down around a dilapidated pair of sneakers as he presented himself proudly to Coach Chamberlain. Andrew wished he could take the fat kid aside and talk to him, explain that he would never make the team, that he was only setting himself up for two weeks of ridicule and disappointment if he insisted on trying out: two weeks of brawny varsity lettermen like Tommy Butler snapping his big white butt with wet towels; two weeks of brassieres left hanging in his locker to mock the huge, udderlike breasts. People are cruel, the young crueler; young athletes the cruelest of the lot.

What the hell, Andrew thought. Maybe I didn't look like much three years ago either. Sebastian grunted and picked himself off the ground. He shambled to the uprights at the other end of the field, ready to begin another long, lonely, satisfying, frustrating afternoon behind the kicking tee.

Southern Methodist University is actually located not in Dallas, but in University Park, a fashionable inner-city suburb surrounded on three sides by prosperous North Dallas. Immediately to the south lies University Park's sister township, perhaps the most affluent, serene, beautiful enclave of residential real estate in the world: Highland Park, Texas. Every major American city has its own High-land Park. But none of them, from Detroit's Grosse Point to Los Angeles's Bel Air, is quite as insular, as complacent, as utterly self-confident as Dallas's Highland Park.

In Dallas, to be in business is to be in politics, and vice versa. Economic power is political power is social power; in one vast synergy of power elite, the same proud names dot the museum boards and the bank boards, the party-contributor lists and the best-dressed lists, the social registers and the check registers. In Dallas society there are no artists or athletes, no poets or psychologists; only businessmen and their wives, and the things at which they play.

The city's topography is such that all the interwoven fault lines of power find their epicenter among the lush green lawns and English country homes of Highland Park, this stately, incongruous suburb planted in the midst of an incongruous, bustling city that sticks out like a jagged rock formation on the barren tableau of the North Texas prairie.

Status in Dallas is roughly measured by the distance one lives from Turtle Creek, a waterway that meanders through Highland Park just quickly enough to keep the water clean, but sedately enough not to disturb the fabulous estates on its shores. It was here, along the eastern bank of Turtle Creek on status-studded Lakeside Drive, that Roger and Nan Sebastian guided their only son, Andrew, through a golden childhood as crown prince of a budding Texas dynasty.

All Highland Park children are born to affluence; most are weaned to ambition. Dallas rich is not an idle rich. It is a restless, competitive, burning, building rich. The Sebastians were no exception. Andrew's father was one of the wealthiest, most competitive men in the city. Roger Sebastian was the eldest son of a self-made East Texas wildcatter who dropped conveniently dead of a coronary at age thirty-nine. Young Roger walked away from Daddy's funeral with more than two hundred thousand dollars cash: an astonishing sum for a nineteen-year-old in Tyler, Texas, in 1930. Roger kissed his stricken mother on the cheek, shucked the dark gray jacket of his best church suit into the passenger seat of his 1928 Model A, and struck out for Dallas, a small but energetic city propped improbably on the banks of the sleepy Trinity River.

The Trinity was a swampy mess. With classic Texas disregard for the trivial caprices of geography, the city fathers were then in the process of moving the whole river some three miles west to avoid a recurrent flooding problem. Sensing opportunity, Roger launched an elaborate scheme to buy up reclaimed river-bottom land, with the idea of turning the whole ex-river into one big industrial park.

FDR's New Deal and World War II brought a boom of immigration and industrial relocation to Dallas. Roger Sebastian's spec-

12

ulation paid off thousandfold. By the late 1930s Roger was one of Dallas's leading real estate developers: a lean, jut-jawed young millionaire with a wiry stubble of short-cropped black hair and the extra measure of respectability that came with having his money slightly aged, at least by Texas standards.

In 1938 Sebastian laid the capstone on his reputation by acquiring the deed and title to one Elizabeth Ann Moore. The granddaughter of a pioneer dry-goods merchant, Nan Moore was a sprightly debutante with fresh blond looks and a bubbling personality. She was the perfect wife for the aggressive, hard-edged Roger: soft and genteel; outwardly unthreatening, inwardly ambitious.

Their home on Lakeside Drive was a wedding gift from Nan's parents. The year before Andrew was born, Nan created a bit of Dallas history by painting the mansion's entire facade a soft, glowing pink to match the stunning azaleas that carpet Turtle Creek every spring. In other hands it might have been gauche, but Nan's gamble paid off. In summer, fall, and winter the azalea-colored house was a striking counterpoint to the greens and browns of the seasons; for three weeks every spring, showcased by matching blooms, it knocked folks' eyes out. Through the years, the Azalea House became the mandatory Easter Sunday after-church drive for half the families in Dallas.

Nan's next big project blossomed on January 8, 1940, when she gave birth to Andrew William Sebastian. From the first, Roger made it clear: the acorn was expected to outgrow the oak.

Like many men of restless energy, Roger picked up and discarded countless hobbies over the years, from golf and mountain climbing to crossword puzzles. He reached competence and boredom quickly and simultaneously. The one game he never tired of playing was "makin' deals and makin' money," the Texas national pastime of high finance. By the time Andrew graduated from St. Mark's Preparatory School, his father had amassed one of the largest personal fortunes in a city of millionaires. Senanco, Roger's holding corporation, owned or controlled more than five million square feet of commercial real estate in Texas, 20 percent of the Port of New Orleans, and a network of apartment buildings and industrial warehouse parks in foreign countries. Were Andrew to become a billionaire, he would only tack another zero onto the long string of his father's digits.

Roger decided early on that his sport would not be Andrew's. He

13

pushed his son toward public life, rewarding the good grades in history, English, and languages; ignoring mediocre marks in math and the sciences. "I've taken care of all the numbers he'll ever need," Roger reassured his wife.

Andrew inherited a fair helping of his father's intuitive intellect, tempered with his mother's warm personality. There was about Andrew a great gentleness that endeared him to women and worried his father. "Boy's got no killer instinct!" Roger would growl as Andrew missed an easy tackle in a Friday-night game. "It's going to cost him." Nan just smiled.

Never a star in academics or team sports, Andrew nevertheless was always room monitor, the perennial team captain. His father took this as harbinger of great electoral victories to come. Never one to swim against the tide, Andrew accepted his dad's subtle prodding with slightly amused resignation. He went along with the group sports, the Boy Scouts, the speech classes. He was never the first to earn the next merit badge; always picked sooner for a sandlot team than his batting warranted. Andrew had the innate sense of the popular fellow: he knew that no one really likes an overachiever.

Andrew—apple of his mother's eye, extension of his father's will—took SMU as he did most things, in stride. He joined the best fraternity on campus, drove a mint-condition cherry-red 1958 MG Class E convertible, dated pretty girls. Mostly he courted Tricia Farris, a stunning Tri Delt he secretly thought he loved but told Tommy Butler he liked well enough.

Never a great football player, Andrew did enjoy the sport. Football is a little like sex: one doesn't really have to be good at it to enjoy it, especially when it comes with a shiny red-and-blue letterman's jacket. Besides, his father wanted him on the team. The trouble was, Andrew couldn't get halfbacks to fall down after he hit them. After a weak freshman season, he switched from defensive line to kicking punts and field goals. The placekicker's balance between team fellowship and solitude suited Andrew. Best of all, the first-string kicker was allowed to skip half the daily calisthenic grind.

That tryout day of his senior year, Andrew had to admit a certain secret glee as he watched the underclassmen struggle past his goal-post on their way around the track. He thought, Better get used to it, suckers.

"Oomph!" When James Brackler went down, he went down hard, slamming nearly three hundred pounds of bone and cellulite into

14

the rough red gravel. The sound shattered Andrew's concentration. He shanked the football five feet wide to the right. When the obese sophomore failed to rise, Andrew walked toward him.

"You okay?" Andrew called to the motionless heap collapsed on the track. James lay still, face pressed in the dirt between two white arms. "Hey!" Andrew yelled, alarmed. He jogged over and knelt beside Brackler, shaking the younger boy's shoulder gently. "You all right?"

James pushed blindly at Andrew with one arm, face still averted. "Go away!" he barked.

Andrew realized the boy's entire body was quivering in agony. "It's okay," he soothed. "Just take a deep breath."

"Go away!" James rolled his bulk over to face Andrew, teeth clenched, tears rolling down puffy, blotched cheeks. Andrew noticed how curiously *old* the boy's face looked. Though the underclassman was surely no more than nineteen or twenty, Andrew could see the shiny half-moon of a prematurely receding hairline, along with the kind of dark-jawed five o'clock shadow Sebastian secretly envied. Andrew himself was already twenty-two and never shaved more than twice a week.

As Andrew peered down, the fat boy's grayish face yawed open in anger. "Just leave me alone!"

"Look . . ." he apologized.

"Get the fuck away from me!" James hissed, voice coiling with sudden fierceness. Andrew lowered his eyes, measuring the oversize K mart gardening shorts, once white, now a dingy gray, smeared with the red dust of the track. A torn V-necked T-shirt clung tightly to each roll of the boy's belly; sallow white flesh gaped between shirt and shorts and the shapeless black socks that had fallen down again around a battered pair of Keds Hi-Tops.

James wiped his reddened eyes and nose with the back of his arm. "What are you staring at?"

Andrew tried to keep the creeping pity out of his voice. "Nothing, I just—"

"Bad knee, that's all," James snapped, regaining some composure. "Gives out on me sometimes. When I'm running."

Andrew thought he looked as though he was about to throw up. "I just thought you might be hurt." He offered his hand instinctively, with the confidence of one who never meets without befriending. "I'm Andrew Sebastian."

"I'm not hurt," James said. Ignoring the outstretched palm, he crawled shakily to his feet. "I'm not some chickenshit placekicker who cries every time he gets touched, Sebastian." James read the blank look in Andrew's eyes. He spat his contempt into the dust. "Yeah, I know you. I remember people's names. Read a book on it once. Andrew Sebastian," he pronounced half-wistfully. James hunched his shoulders around the sadness in his throat. "We all know how guys like you make the team, Sebastian." This time, the name was a curse.

"I don't understand," Andrew said slowly, backing away.

"No shit!" Brackler's voice rose sharply. "That's the understatement of the century." Again his voice grew quiet, melancholy. "Just get out of my face."

James staggered to the track as the pack came past on their second lap. Most were still running hard, scarcely out of breath. James moved after them, jaw set bitter and grim.

Suddenly he stopped. He fell to his knees and retched, loudly and horribly, on the gravel at the track's edge.

Andrew sighed and walked toward the heaving figure. He admired the guy's guts, even if he'd rather not see them spilled on the gravel track. He bent over the sick boy. "Hey," he said gently, consoling.

"Leave—me—alone!" James gasped between stomach heaves, spattering chunks of yellow vomit on Andrew's cleats. "I'm sick! The flu. My knee!"

"Sure," Andrew agreed, repelled more by the fellow's anger than by the gagging smell. "Take it easy."

James rolled over on his back. Slowly he wiped his mouth and watched Andrew jog back toward his kicking tee. "Screw you, Sebastian," he muttered almost inaudibly, between gasps of fresh hot air that revived the awful taste in his throat. Brackler staggered back to his feet. He wiped his hands on the dirty gym shorts and lurched dizzily to the track, gasping after the runners circling the far end of the stadium.

James was suddenly aware that the coaches and varsity players were staring at him from the center of the field, breaking away from workouts to gaze at him. In a sickening flash he saw himself as they saw him, an absurd vomit-smeared, sobbing hulk shambling slowly around the track. Sebastian, Brackler thought angrily. So transparent, simpering behind that thin, patronizing shield of pity. Nineteen years of experience had taught James Brackler to know when he was being mocked. The bastard had probably wrecked his chances of making the team. "Flu!" James gasped to anyone within earshot. "Bad knee!" He shuffled past the coaches.

"I can do it!" he cried desperately, tears streaming uncontrollably from his eyes. "Just got over the flu!"

The day had begun better than it was ending for James Brackler. Earlier that hot, muggy September afternoon, he had been in rare good humor, his usual bitter outlook toward the world in general, and Southern Methodist University in particular, laid aside in honor of the excellent promise of the day.

Today was special, because today he would begin an important step of the Plan.

James had puffed along the tree-lined mall in the middle of SMU's serene campus, cautiously throwing an occasional covetous glance at a sorority-sweatered figure. He was thinking of the Plan. The Plan would vault him into the smug world of these coiffed debutantes, pledging him to the exclusive fraternity of their buttoned-down beaus. One day, they would know James Brackler. Nobody at SMU knew it, and no one in the world expected it, but James Brackler was going to be president of the United States. The Plan was how he was going to do it.

The first step had been getting the scholarship to SMU, Dallas's most expensive college. Step two was making the football team, garnering the instant popularity that accompanied a Mustang varsity sweater.

On the surface, getting into SMU should have been tough for an East Dallas redneck like James Brackler. Unlike most SMU undergrads, James wasn't born to the well-watered lawns and Colorado ski trips of the Texas and Oklahoma upper-middle to upper to upper-upper class. On the day Jimmy Brackler was born, his father, a mostly unemployed trucker, threatened to walk out on Jimmy's momma: "Jesus Christ, Patty! My genes ain't that ugly!" One hot, sticky night four years later, Buddy Brackler gave his common-law wife one last beating. Kicking aside Jimmy and his little sister, he stomped out of their rented frame house on East Grand Avenue, never to return. Patty Brackler wiped the blood from her mouth and gave Jimmy a swat to stop his whining. Then she had another drink to toast the best thing that had happened in her life in a long, long time.

17

In Buddy's wake came a long succession of part-time husbands and live-in boyfriends. There was the inevitable string of half-brothers, half-sisters, and stepbrothers, a potpourri of facial features and last names. Jimmy, the oldest, was always expected to take care of the rest. This he affected to resent, but secretly he reveled in their attention. Especially that of Denny Frawley, the youngest, who toddled after him with an awe Jimmy repaid every day, kissing the skinned knees of Denny's childhood with a fervent affection he surrendered to no other. The Brackler-Dixon-Collins-Frawley kids were his only friends, a ragtag army that always let Jimmy play general.

At Dan D. Rogers Elementary, Jimmy's perpetual obesity made him a natural social leper. Like many grade school misfits, he became very good at schoolwork. Mama was inevitably drunk on report card day, so Jimmy swapped grades with Denny and the others. He cuffed their ears for every D or F, basked in their reverence for his steady A's. Jimmy thirsted for acceptance beyond his siblings, a yearning slaked only by the saltwater of teacher applause: he became that lowest of grade school outcasts, the teacher's pet.

Then, in the seventh grade, Jimmy discovered Mexicans.

While other boys his age were finding out about girls, unwrapping the power of desire in their taut adolescent bodies, Jimmy suddenly struck on the ore of brute strength buried deep amidst his bulk. He found an object for that irresistible force in Raul Martinez, a skinny, cowering twelve-year-old who sat uncomprehendingly through six classes each day taught in a language he couldn't understand. Jimmy's evolution from bookworm to bully was an accident. Rushing into homeroom with the usual armload of books, Jimmy tripped clumsily into little Raul's desk. The Chicano's carefully selected, utterly unused school supplies tumbled to the floor in a shower of razor-sharp colored pencils. Jimmy mumbled an apology. Raul cringed quickly to the floor, gathering up his scrambled notebooks in a babble of apologetic Spanish. Glowing suddenly, Jimmy gave a tentative kick at Raul's notebook. "Outa my way, Martinez," he growled, a bigot's sarcastic hiss on the Spanish final sibilant. A titter of laughter greeted Raul's second round of apology. Jimmy basked briefly in the unaccustomed warmth of class acceptance.

The next day, Raul opened the smooth brown paper cover of his math textbook to find obscene pictures scrawled rudely across the pages. As Raul's dark face flushed an even deeper cinnamon, the classroom erupted in hysteria. A popular football player—a ninth-grader, no less—even slapped Jimmy on the back.

He never became one of the crowd. But Jimmy did carve something of a niche as he bullied his way through high school. He still hated the drunken days and shrieking nights of his home life. He repelled the girls with his foul mouth and chunky, disheveled appearance. He nursed intense and bitter feelings toward the owners of the shining ebony Cadillacs he washed every weekend at the Kleen-Wash on Lemmon Avenue. But by his senior year at Woodrow Wilson High, Jimmy stopped minding all the setbacks.

By then, he had the Plan.

The jocks, the cheerleaders, the Cadillac owners from the north side of town: they didn't know it yet, but someday they would all hunch right over and kiss his ass. Someday he would be James Brackler: rich, popular, powerful James Brackler; "Jim" to the lucky few he deigned to call his friends. The Plan was James's mental rubric for the vague and ever-shifting schemes by which he saw himself marching down that aisle with Success on his arm. As he mopped the torn chamois across one gleaming black hood after another, he envisioned himself in somber cap and gown, graduating from posh Southern Methodist University and Harvard Law School. Squinting hard, he could already make out the big brass letters on his office door: JAMES BRACKLER, ATTORNEY-AT-LAW. He heard the crowds applauding as he declared victory: Congressman Jim Brackler, friends, at your service. He saw himself in John Connally's campaign posters, grinning from the steps of the Capitol: Governor Brackler, in a big long black limousine that would glide through the rolling brushes and carnauba hot wax of the Kleen-Wash like a cruise ship passing through the locks of the Panama Canal. Then there was the image he took out and fondled in his most secret moments, late at night, to shut out the incessant groan of salacious laughter through the paper-thin walls of his mother's bedroom: Big Jim Brackler, hero of the downtrodden, enemy of the rich, president of the United States of America.

Getting into SMU was easy for an outcast who had spent his life in the refuge of books—and the last two years getting to know the local Methodist minister. When the synod's annual scholarship came up in 1959, Pastor Brown thought acolyte Jimmy Brackler the perfect choice, especially considering that poor sick mother of his. Somehow her arthritis never allowed her to make it to services.

Getting through SMU was another matter. SMU is what college students call a "party school," a cozy haven where girls find husbands, and husbands "make contacts." Despite the cold comfort of his dreams, it still hurt James to stand outside in the rain. The Plan was no longer enough to overcome the sneers of upperclassmen as they barked malt orders at Hickey's. James worked there nights after classes, then trudged home, exhausted and red-eyed, to study until dawn in the tiny bedroom next to his mother's. None of the popular students ever said anything to James. But their voices mocked him in his sleep. Go back where you came from, redneck. Go back to your alcoholic mother, to your peeling-paint wooden shack on the other side of town. You don't belong. You'll never be one of us.

When his freshman year finally dragged to a close, James had a 4.0 grade average and a head-to-toe welter of painful social slights. Real or imagined, they begged to be salved. It was time for James Brackler to be noticed.

One day at Hickey's, James set a fourth milkshake in front of the biggest human being he had ever seen, a lumbering boy-man whose sunburned twenty-inch neck bulged threateningly against the white cotton ribbing of a Mustang varsity jacket. "Gotta make weight," the behemoth mumbled casually.

Make weight? Suddenly, James's limber imagination soared with the prospects. Football! Varsity sweaters. Cheerleaders. Homecoming games. Instant, total popularity: invitations to winter ski jaunts, spring break weekends at Daddy's beach house in Galveston. It was a perfect step two for the Plan, a clear conduit to the good ol' boy network of money and power via the Texas national obsession: Southwest Conference Football, where young men come as All-Americans and leave as fat-cat insurance executives with statewide connections. Sure, ol' Jim-Bob Brackler, I know him! Good man. Played against him when I was an Aggie.

Football. Of course!

James knew he wasn't cut out for the flashy positions. He had no speed or agility. The idea of submitting himself again to the humiliating locker rooms of his adolescence filled him with terror. But James and Failure were old friends; he feared him very little. Besides, in James's view, any idiot could play offensive line: most who did, were. He could smash and grunt and shove with the best of them. If there was one thing James Brackler was good at, it was pushing hard. As he plodded out to the practice field with the rest of the tryouts that day, James had seen his future all stretched out before him, grinning and glorious, like a taut-legged line of cheerleaders pom-pomming him on to victory.

Now, though James had staggered back to rejoin the pack, all his dreams lay in ruins, thanks to Coach Chamberlain and his cavalier aside: "Three quick laps, boys, then we'll get started." And a special standing ovation to Mr. Andrew Bigshot Sebastian, James thought bitterly, for making sure the entire SMU varsity squad caught the world premiere of James Brackler's 200-Yard Puke-Off.

Three laps in this heat. Might as well be three hundred, James thought. I'll never make it.

"Oomph!"

James went down hard again, this time for keeps. The other tryouts stood watching, running in place with knees high, unsure what came next. Coach Chamberlain trotted toward the crumpled hulk on the track.

Cold water splashed into his face. James blinked in the hot sun, his vision red and clouded. He barely heard the voices, couldn't make out the words. But there was no mistaking the tone: feigned sympathy; thinly veiled contempt.

Chamberlain shook the boy's shoulders. "Son, you okay?"

Great, just great, James thought. His mind reeled miserably, thinking of the Plan as the bile rose helplessly in his throat.

Then he threw up again, all over the little blue Mustang pony on Coach Chamberlain's starched white Bermuda shorts.

2

One of the good things about growing up in Highland Park is getting used to wearing ties at an early age. By age twenty-two, it didn't strangle Andrew to dress for dinner.

Seated across white linen in the cathouse-red opulence of the Pyramid Room, Tricia Farris could hardly believe her good fortune. Her mother had told her to concentrate on premeds: safe, professional, upwardly mobile. Ha! Tricia thought. I could teach Mama a thing or two.

Icy-blue eyes. Tall and fit, his gridiron-wide shoulders wedged perfectly into an Italian-looking sports coat. Tie knotted perfectly with a cleft in the middle, like an English butler in the movies. Skin smooth and tanned from summer tennis, deep brown tinged with red crests from his long afternoon on the football field, stretched tautly over even features: not movie-star handsome, but still one of the better-looking guys on campus. And rich? It made Tricia guilty to think about money, what with him sitting right there. Somehow the Sebastian millions kept jimmying open the back door of her mind.

Best of all, Andrew Sebastian was a gentleman. Opening car doors. Ordering for her in French, without asking. An evening with Andrew was a gallant contrast to the beer-guzzling, grabby-handed Friday nights of her youth, tussling in backseats out by the Texaco refinery. There were times when Andrew was just too much a dandy, when she wanted to reach over and muss up his flawlessly groomed head, when she felt a nostalgic ache for the beer breath and rough edges of Beaumont High School. But not tonight.

Because Andrew was willing to wait.

Long ago, Tricia had decided to save it for her wedding night. Really, she thought, it made things easier. With the ground rules firmly in place, she knew just how far to go before it was time to shut things down. Tricia knew other girls thought her a prude, but better a prude than Tommy Butler's girlfriend, Elma the Human Trampoline. And who was sitting in the most expensive restaurant in Dallas across from Andy Sebastian, whose dad had a freeway named after him?

"More wine?" Andrew asked. He poured a prewar French vintage he'd heard his father order here. He twirled the bottle around deftly to avoid spilling.

Seated across the Sevres china he saw, simply, everything he had ever wanted in a girl. A woman, he corrected mentally. Tricia was great fun, refreshingly down to earth, but she often seemed years older than the chattering sorority girls around her. Except in one way, Andrew remembered, thinking of Tommy's barbs. Tricia even looked older than other SMU girls, disdaining the white lipstick and bobby-soxer fads of the Tri Delta House for a fresh, seductive look all her own. Tonight, though dressed to the hilt, Tricia wore very little makeup. Her dark hair coiled loosely to slender shoulders, a carefully careless cascade that reflected the candlelight in soft, liquid arcs of brown and black. Tricia had enormous almond-shaped eyes of clear aquamarine that glowed, now green, now blue, above her high cheekbones. She had serious thick eyebrows; strangely hollow cheeks; full, sensuous lips that parted around small, even white teeth. When Tricia smiles, Andrew thought, it's a breath of cool wind on a hot, airless summer day.

Grinning, Tricia lifted her wineglass and said, "Thank you, sir." Unable to maintain the facade of adult nonchalance, she leaned forward and whispered confidentially, "I can't believe you brought me here! And for no special occasion."

"Any night with you is special." The stupid line popped out before he could stop it. God, he agonized, how could those words come from my mouth? I hope she doesn't gag.

"You have a way with words, Governor Sebastian."

"Ouch," Andrew said. "My ambitions are showing." He lit her cigarette off his, as he'd once seen William Powell do for Myrna Loy in a Thin Man movie. Andrew had started smoking last summer because she did. He was just now able to draw the smoke into his lungs without a fit of coughing.

"Don't be silly," Tricia corrected, matter-of-fact. "Everyone should have ambitions."

"No one should know what they are," Andrew said ruefully, trying to keep his eyes from straying to the tight bodice of her daring green silk gown, a sort of Roman wrap that wound around her inviting breasts like an adder, then slunk out of sight beneath the table. "You have to keep people guessing."

"Even me?" Tricia liked talking about Andy's future. It was a marriage-related subject.

"I'm probably too obvious about things," he admitted. Andrew poured more wine into the glass she'd just emptied, hoping she wouldn't notice he was trying to get her drunk. "I should lay back in the long grass sometimes, like my father," he went on. "Greatest negotiator ever. That's how he got, uh, where he is. He just sits there. The Great Stone Face. He waits for you to fill up the space by talking. You feel like you should rush in and give him a counter-offer. I go to his office, ask him for a raise in my allowance. He sits. I ask again. He sits. I ask if I can have a smaller raise. Silence. I end up with ten percent cut. He's faced down the biggest construction-union bosses in the country. Other countries, too. Am I talking too much?"

Tricia jerked out of her reverie. She loved it when Andrew talked like this, about business and his dad and when he was younger. And no guy had ever asked her whether he talked too much. They all talked too much. They were supposed to. Her mother had taught her to just sit there and listen, let him talk about himself. And never smoke a cigarette unless she was sitting down, under a roof.

"I like to listen," she oozed quietly. Am I overdoing this?

It's now or never, Andrew thought. "I love you, Tricia," he blurted.

There! He had said it. God, he realized sickly, that sounds stupid

24

when you say it in real life! At least he hadn't choked. Just belted it out, exactly like he'd planned. Straight up the middle. I love you, Tricia. In that moment, for the first time, he was absolutely, positively sure he did. He wanted to jump up and shout it to the whole restaurant.

"Andrew! Oh!" Tricia had not prepared for this. She wished there was some way she could sneak out and call her mother. To tell her in a restaurant! Didn't young men have mothers to instruct them not to tell a girl for the very first time that you love her in a public place stuffed with old penguins in formal clothes? She wanted to cry, and started to.

Which was perfect. If her mother had been there, she'd have cheered.

"Come on, Tricia," Andrew said, fumbling for his handkerchief. Were things coming off track? "What's wrong? Hasn't anybody ever said that to you before?"

What little mascara Tricia did wear dribbled down her cheeks. She took the handkerchief with its monogrammed "AWS" and dabbed at her eyes. She was really botching this. "Well, yes," she stammered. "But nobody, I mean, nobody I—I love you, too," she blubbered.

"Okay!" Now we're cooking, he exulted. "Let's dance."

They danced and ate French food they did not taste, and watched a floor show and danced some more, and drank champagne and pulled their chairs around the table for the second show. He loved the feel of Tricia beside him, fairly purred at the hot touch of her fingers against the fuzz on the back of his neck. Most of all, Andrew loved to dance slow with Tricia Farris.

At the Pyramid Room, every dance was a slow dance. The band switched smoothly into a serene "Blue Moon." Andrew pressed against her. Tricia never pulled back, even when telling him, "Far enough," like last weekend at his parents' lakehouse in East Texas. She had this breathtakingly sensual way of grinding into him when they danced. God, he wanted this girl. He knew that he would always be this much in love with her.

"Tricia," he said through a mouthful of her lush hair, muscling his chest into her stiffening breasts until his soft voice was half an inch from her ear. "Someday, after we get out of school"—his words were cautious, exact—"will you marry me?"

It was all she could do to let him stammer out the question. "Yes!" Tricia shouted, and kissed him violently, clutching hard at his shoulders and sucking all the air out of him. Then she pulled away from him abruptly and led him off the dance floor in silence. She plunked Andrew down in his chair, grabbed her clutch purse, and whirled to face him.

"I'll be right back," she said firmly. And headed for the pay phone in the lobby.

The wine sang Big Band melodies in Tricia's ears as she stared up at the tiny white stars above Lakeside Drive. Andrew was driving very, very fast along Turtle Creek. He was drunk, but then so was she. The crisp November air was exhilarating after the heat of their clinging bodies on the dance floor.

Andrew bounced the low-slung red MG into the driveway of the shuttered Azalea House. It looked forlorn and dark with his parents away in Acapulco. Tricia had been here before, but then it had been brightly lit and full of people, with squads of black valets hustling down the street to fetch the Caddys of the rich: smirking at the showy ten-buck tips of the nouveau riche; gritting their teeth at the quarters from the old-line respectables.

Andrew jumped out of the MG's seat, a scant four inches off the ground. He opened her door, boosted her out of the tiny roadster, led her inside. Their footsteps echoed in the cavernous three-story foyer. Here we go, Andrew thought. She trailed behind him into the living room. He started a fire, for effect. They snuggled on the wide white couch, trying out new things to say to each other, planning fifteen different lives to share. Gradually Andrew kissed her, softly and then urgently, his hands trembling and cold.

She was on fire with the feel of him. The strange sensation of a touch that was not her own made her moist down there, embarrassing her and making her wish he would stop. Except it felt so fantastic, like crawling into a warm, warm bath when she was cold and shivery. She pulled him even closer. His fingers pressed deep inside, tickling her. Tricia stifled an urge to laugh and scream at the same time. She dug her fingers into his back, her mouth and lips and tongue tearing at his, inviting the sweet pain of his teeth. Andrew fumbled with her bra strap with his spare hand. She wanted to help him but was sure she shouldn't. He finally managed, and

26

it was loose inside her dress. His hand found her breasts through a jumble of warm Playtex and cool green silk. His rough touch against her nipples made Tricia feel like reaching back and pulling her hair out. Aching for the feel of his bare skin against hers, she tore at the buttons of Andrew's shirt, pulling the tie clumsily from his neck.

Andrew backed away a bit to let her slide his shirt off and concentrated on the snaps of her dress. He ripped them loose in exasperation. They clung together for a long time, reveling in the sweet unfamiliarity of his bare cool muscles against her soft, smooth, warm flesh.

They wondered what to do next.

Andrew began kissing her lower and lower, a sensation better than anything she had ever imagined. His kisses reached her stomach. He pulled gently at her panties, already stretched and loose and wet from his handiwork inside. Tricia bent her head over close to him and whispered shakily, "I think it's time for me to go home."

"You are home," Andrew murmured, not taking her seriously. He could understand her not wanting to give in too easily, after all this time. Even if they were engaged.

"Andy, really."

He ignored her, easing the lingerie gently down her hips.

Tricia clamped her legs together and pressed her taut buttocks against the couch to stop him.

"Andrew, no!" More firmly now, she plucked at one of his wrists and eased it from between her thighs. One had to do this carefully, one step at a time. Her resolve grew stronger as the memory of his fingers inside her dimmed.

"I told you . . ." Andrew looked up at her mournfully. "I want to marry you."

"Come on, now," she soothed. This was tricky. She'd never gone this far with anyone. "We've talked about this before." She grabbed frantically for her dress, careful not to pull completely away from him.

"But Tricia—" Andrew winced inwardly at the whining note in his voice.

"Andrew, I love you." She was brisk, businesslike. "Tonight is the happiest night of my life. Please don't spoil it."

"What about the happiest night of my life? You don't think it's tough for me to wait?" he said coldly, "Some girls would—"

She leapt up from his arms. "Oh, the Big Man on Campus?" Fighting for dignity, she shuffled her disheveled clothes into place. "Money won't buy you everything, hotshot."

"Who said anything about money?" Andrew protested. "I'm talking about you and me! You know I didn't mean it like that!"

"No?" she shot back coldly. "Take me home."

The trip to her sorority house passed in stony silence, the autumn air chill and sobering. When they got there, Andrew reached rudely across the seat and wrenched at her door from the inside, flipping it open across the sidewalk. "Good night, Tricia," he said. "Let's do it again sometime, okay? Maybe we could play miniature golf."

The MG sped off in the dark. He was gone before she could deliver the retort she had worked out on the way over. Tricia burst into tears and ran upstairs.

A few minutes later, at 4:07 A.M., a telephone in Beaumont jangled Mrs. Adlene Farris out of the best night's sleep she'd had in a decade.

The lowest point in the bottomless pit that was James Brackler's job at Hickey's was the conversation he overheard while swilling the collegiate crowd. It was bad enough to be completely cast out from the mainstream of SMU social life. To hear about it daily, in effusive detail, was more than he could stand. He tried to tune it out, but he was like a man who reads the sports pages while trying to ignore his wife's soap opera. Before long he can't help but think Veronica really ought to go ahead and dump Alphonse.

James knew nothing of double dates and homecoming dances and Chi Omegas and Corvettes and God, isn't he the cutest! It was a universe in which he had never been welcome. The irritating closeness of that rosy world merely made his own bleak planet all the more inhospitable. James struggled to ignore the sneering rich boys and their haughty girlfriends as they gossiped and plotted and cackled within his earshot, as though he were part of the furniture, like the cracked red vinyl of the booths or the gray plastic bus trays he used to clean their greasy ketchup-splattered plates. Sometimes, on bad days like today, it hurt so bad his throat grew tight, and the prickling shame of tears heated his eyelids. Then James sought refuge in his dreams, where he sat at table and laughed with them and ordered in their offhand way, without glancing at the menu to check the price. Or even raising their languid eyes to meet those of the lonely young man who stood behind the counter in a stained white apron, order pad in hand.

At the periphery of his vision, James saw two girls plop down on red vinyl stools. He recognized them as old hands at Hickey's. James barely looked up from his miserable reverie at the grill, scooping hot messy Hickey's Hick'ry Specials and splattering them down again. As he mashed down his spatula on top of the cheese, he couldn't shut out their shrieking tones.

"So what'll she do?" Elma Heitmeier, James thought. Wonder if she ever got that new car?

"Not go, I guess." Carrie Blackwell, James guessed. He started to check but remembered he didn't give a damn.

"Just because of what happened Saturday?" Elma was incredulous. James wondered who they were talking about.

"Because of what didn't happen, if you know what I mean." Both girls broke into stifled peals of laughter. James slapped another Hick'ry Special onto one of Mrs. Baird's Homebaked Hamburger Buns, Baked with Family Pride.

"What's so funny?" a new voice asked. James turned around with a tray full of greasy burgers just in time to see Tricia Farris arrive, an unsuspecting smile affixed to her jaw. Carrie and Elma greeted her with guilty, empty smiles. Suddenly it hit James. Tricia Farris! He missed a few seconds after that, to deliver orders to the other end of the counter. James was back at his stove in record time, craning to hear Tricia's voice.

"—know what to do," she quavered miserably. "I've already got my dress and everything." James, though inexperienced in such matters, thought Tricia sounded upset about a great deal more than her dress.

"Can't you get somebody else?" Elma asked solicitously.

"This late?" Tricia scoffed. "Are you kidding? I'd give anything. I'd go with a freshman."

"It's just a dance." Carrie Blackwell, despite a love of good gossip, really was Tricia's best friend.

"I can't believe I was so stupid," Tricia moaned.

"What about—" Carrie began haltingly, sorting through her mental catalog of unattached upperclassmen.

"Don't even bother," Tricia snapped, clearly uncomfortable at being the object of a friend's pity. Couldn't Carrie understand this was more than just pride? That she was worried about losing him?

29

Andrew certainly wouldn't have any problem getting another date. Tricia could see them all at the Baker Hotel Saturday night, dancing and laughing and talking about her, even as all her dreams for the future shattered.

"I've been racking my brain all afternoon," Tricia confessed. "I might as well forget it. Everyone in the damn school has a date to Welcome."

Not everyone, James thought, throwing four more rock-frozen patties into the grease.

Carrie picked up the phone from the little white wicker table in the downstairs foyer. "Tri Delts, best in the West," she announced brightly. A pause as she listened. Then she bawled, "Tricia! For you!"

A patter of feet sounded above on the hardwood floors as Tricia came to the top of the stairs. "Who?" Tricia asked in a loud stage whisper.

"Not Andrew," Carrie whispered back hoarsely, hand clapped firmly over the mouthpiece.

Tricia threw down the 1959 SMU annual she had been inspecting and raced down the stairs. "I haven't done anything yet. Did you?"

"No," Carrie said blankly. She thrust the phone toward her.

Tricia seized the receiver. "Hello?"

"Uh, Tricia?"

"Yes, this is Tricia."

"Well. This is James Brackler. You don't know me, but I'm, uh, a friend of Andrew's. From the football team. Actually, he hardly even knows me. I'm new on the team. Actually, that's not true. I didn't, uh, I had an injury. My knee." Tricia wanted to help him forward but knew it was best to let him stammer on. She felt sorry for boys at times like this. Tricia was glad she would never have to call someone for a date and pick through the cold silence. "Anyway, I heard around campus," the voice trailed on, "about you and Andy. Look, you don't know me or anything, but I was wondering if you might like to go to the Welcome Dance. With me, I mean."

She hesitated a flat, still moment. "Yes!" Tricia burst out, puncturing the balloon of his suspense and swelling her own, as she wondered what she had gotten herself into.

3

Friday night's autumn thunderstorm had been what Texans call a real frogstrangler, dousing the parched yellow grass of Ownby Stadium with thousands of gallons of rain. The skies had cleared by midday, when Tricia, Carrie, and twenty-eight thousand screaming partisans gathered at Ownby to watch the Welcome Day game against Texas Tech.

It was one of those sloppy, muddy, glorious football games, with great gouts of gritty sludge that slid into the players' eyes and mouths and ears, mud that made the wet leather ball slippery to catch, impossible to hold. By the end of the third quarter, Tech was ahead 7–0.

Andrew dreaded these mud games. He cowered under the big blue canvas rain poncho, hating the way his sparkling white jersey stood out from the mud-spattered, bloodied warriors along the sidelines. It blared that his role in this battle was embarrassingly safe and trivial. He wanted to sneak behind the bleachers and roll around in the muck.

Andrew had been on the field only once. He couldn't

31

fault the coach's lack of confidence: his practices had been terrible all week. He had shanked kicks right and left, his mind focused on Tricia, the harshness of her silence, the scramble to find another date so she wouldn't think he was dependent on her. Finally, he had resolved to forget all about going to the damn dance and worry about the damn game.

As the fourth quarter began, SMU's quarterback lobbed a pass into the end zone: SMU 6, Tech 7. Chamberlain, bandy legs pumping in sodden bright blue stretch pants, strode to Sebastian. "Well?"

"Sir?" Andrew blinked.

"Well?" Chamberlain repeated.

Andrew stared back at the coach, refusing to flinch. "I'd say it's up to you, sir," he said evenly, respectfully.

Coach Chamberlain was a cautious man by nature. The field was drying up, his offense was coming together, and he felt sure they'd score again. "Tie it up," the coach barked, slapping the side of Andrew's rain-soaked head so hard his ears rang for a brief second. Andy grabbed his helmet and ran to the field, feeling absurd in his Mr. Clean jersey. Was that Tricia up to his left, in the grandstands? He took a deep breath and paced back from the holder, counting his steps. One, two, three. As the ball hiked back, Andrew swept forward and swung his right foot skyward, slipping in the mud just as his toe made contact with the ball. He went down hard on his tailbone. Andrew glanced at the scoreboard. SMU was still behind, 6–7. He picked himself up slowly. He was now as muddy as his teammates.

For Andrew, the remaining minutes of the game stretched into agony. He stood alone on the sidelines, feeling the silent, baleful eyes of his teammates. Late in the fourth quarter, Tech went up 13–6. With less than two minutes to go, Tommy Butler snagged a Tech pass in the end zone and ran it back to the SMU forty-two. On a deftly executed trap to the left, SMU scored a touchdown with only a minute left in the game.

Chamberlain never even looked at Andrew. Behind 13–12, the coach sent the halfback back in to attempt a two-point conversion. The halfback made it to the two and slipped in the mud.

"Sebastian!" Chamberlain bellowed. Andrew jogged up the sidelines to the coach. Chamberlain's eyes were cast iron: he was goddamned if he was going to watch his ticket to the Cotton Bowl trickle away in the muddy residue of a North Texas gulleywasher. "On-side kick, Sebastian," Chamberlain growled. "Can you handle it?"

"I'll do my best, Coach," Andrew said, his heart pounding. "Right side or left?"

"You pick."

"Right. The right."

"Okay." The coach grabbed both of Andrew's bulky shoulder pads. It was as close as he could come to a plea: "I'm counting on you, Andy."

Andrew trotted out and joined the huddle. "Coach wants to go for the on-side," he said, ignoring the doubt on ten muddy, sweat-streamed faces. "I'll drill it to the right. You all just be there to cover."

An on-side kick is one of the trickiest maneuvers in football, a sleight of hand to keep the opposing team from gaining possession of the ball after a kickoff. It's a delicate business: the ball must travel at least ten yards to qualify as a kickoff. If the kicker boots it much more than that, the opposing team will recover it at midfield. Andrew had run the on-side drill a thousand times. Under the cautious Chamberlain, he had never tried it in a real game.

The whistle blew. As his teammates ran parallel to the scrimmage line, Andrew concentrated all his energies on a perfect kick: hard, fast, hugging the ground, a bullet to the right-hand sideline. Amazingly, mystically, it worked just as in practice. The Mustang players sprinted down to clutch their last shot at an undefeated season.

Forty yards to go. On the sidelines, Andrew sat on his helmet and watched SMU's quarterback work the two-minute drill. With three seconds left on the clock, SMU stalled at Tech's twenty-four-yard line. The coach strode again to Andrew. Wordless and grim, he yanked Sebastian roughly to his feet.

The weak autumn sun had hardened the mud at this end of the field. Andrew reached down to feel the earth as he set up for the field goal. He gazed upward at the stands, oblivious to the now constant roar on both sides of the field. He searched in vain for Tricia among the vast sea of shouting faces. He knew right where his folks were: front row, fifty-yard line, behind the SMU bench. He did not look there. Andrew signaled to the referee and tried to stop the thumping in his chest.

Three running steps. Midway through the third, Andrew pulled

33

hard with his right leg. His toe collided solidly with the ball and sent it sailing upward, spinning lazily, end over end, straight ahead, as though guided by a string toward the exact middle of the uprights.

It fell short. On target, Andrew realized light-headedly. But not enough gas. Sputtering inches below the crossbar, the football plopped harmlessly into a puddle.

Andrew dropped to his knees in disbelief, howling as if in physical pain. He thought crazily of running up to the referee and asking for another chance. The ball was perfectly on target. Perfectly! Just a little more height! Andrew ripped off his helmet and slammed it into the earth, looking around to face his teammates. None looked back.

Her first glimpse eliminated any doubt. Tricia had made the mistake of her life.

At 8:50 P.M. she made her usual Scarlett O'Hara entrance. Layered pink skirts of shining satin swirled down the spiral staircase of the Tri Delt house in a practiced maneuver designed to stun whoever had been kept waiting for the past twenty minutes. Chin high, eyes forward, she descended gracefully and slowly, as she'd been taught in Mrs. Taylor's School for Etiquette.

Below, James sprawled uncomfortably on a white wicker chair. More than a little awed by the vision above, he dabbed quickly at the stubbled cheeks he had spent the day shaving again and again, plucking away the last tuft of white toilet tissue he had used to stem the bleeding. He shook his head visibly, to clear the fumes of the Southern Comfort he had drunk to slow the pounding jitters in his chest. His mind skated effortlessly on a pond of liquor and exhilaration. So many times, James had gazed at the white columns of Greek Row, loaded down with books, trudging toward the bus stop. Now here he sat, in the inner sanctum of the sleek and the happy. Picking up a date! He staggered eagerly to his feet, not so much incapacitated by liquor as he was unable to escape any low chair with a degree of grace.

Tricia reached the bottom of the stairs, lowered her eyes carefully, and caught her first panorama of James Brackler. Her first thought was, Oh, my God, he's wearing a suit! Not a black tuxedo, as every other young man would wear to the dance. A shiny, light blue suit with pale white stitching around the lapel. A dark blue shirt to match. To keep things consistent, a medium-blue tie hung loosely

34

around his neck, collar unbuttoned above the dark red stain—
ketchup?—on the tie's bulky knot. She could not have done worse,
Tricia decided. He was terribly overweight, sloppily dressed, and
he stank of liquor.

Still, there was *something:* a certain raw heat, a hunger in the
eyes, a rough cut to his jaw. He was not appealing, but he looked—
strong, Tricia decided. A man, not a boy.

"Trish?" James said, broad and blustery. She saw in an instant
how nervous he was and decided she liked him for it. He wiped his
hand on the seat of his pants and extended it for a handshake.
"James Brackler," he said, too loudly. "You can call me Jim. Or
James, if you like. Whatever. I, uh, I'm glad to meet you." His
sweaty hand enveloped her tiny one, crushing her fingers together
and smearing the dress-matching pink polish she'd spent the last
hour applying to her nails. James pumped her hand up and down
and launched into a nervous narrative about himself, his studies,
his trick knee, his car: "Sorry, mine's in the shop. We'll have to go
in this old thing."

"This old thing" was a baby-blue 1951 De Soto, with ripped-up
blue plastic upholstery that stabbed Tricia in the back, ripping the
hem of the lustrous pink gown her mother had sewed for her last
summer, when they both had thought Andrew Sebastian would be
her Welcome Dance date. James chattered to cover the noise as
the car shuddered through the busy Saturday-night traffic toward
the Baker Hotel. Where, thought Tricia miserably, everybody I
know will be lined up, waiting to view my entrance. With a fat guy
in a blue suit.

"Quiet, are ya?" James shouted over the agonizing moans of the
De Soto's engine. He belched slightly under his breath and giggled.
"'Scuse me! Repeats on you, you know?" Tricia was surprised to
hear her own laughter. She wished Andrew would cut loose a burp
once in a while. She was always happy with Andrew, but rarely
comfortable.

James looked at her sideways. "Listen, did I tell you my great-
grandfather fought at the Alamo?" He knew how hollow it sounded,
but somehow he just couldn't help himself. She was so beautiful,
and his mother's car was so shabby.

The De Soto lurched forward to the hotel entrance. Tricia banged
her head on the broken dashboard clock, knocking her hair askew.
She felt James's huge, moist hand clamp down on her bare back

35

above the low-cut evening gown. "You okay?" he asked solicitously. His breathing was strained, Tricia realized, as if he had bronchitis. His other hand was suddenly on her left knee, inching quickly thighward.

It was going to be a long night.

"I'm fine, James," Tricia said politely, beaming an etiquette-school smile. She pulled away from him smoothly, kicking open the sticky passenger door with the heel of her dyed pink pumps. "Really. Thank you. Shall we go in?"

"Sure," he agreed. The feel of her warm, smooth skin was positively electric. James released her knee, hauled himself out from behind the steering wheel, and tossed the doorman the keys to the De Soto. Suddenly it seemed to him a Cadillac. "Careful with that car," he ordered curtly, winking at the elderly black man. "We're gonna need it later." His light-headedness was only partly the whiskey: James knew this was the finest night of his life.

Carrie met Tricia at the door, whispering the news: Andrew wasn't coming. Tricia endured all their mocking eyes. "Hi, Carrie, Elma. Have you met James Brackler?" They hadn't, and made no effort to pretend they had. Tricia was embarrassed at her friends; she even squeezed his arm with a smile as James did his best to ignore the upturned noses. "Guess I'm the only one with a sense of style," he said ruefully, eyes roving around the tuxedos. "What's the deal, all these guys shop at the same place?"

James did not ask Tricia to dance; he didn't know how. He seemed content to catch up with her every thirty minutes and be introduced to another couple as "Tricia's date." Tricia began feeling less sorry for herself and more guilty about this silly spite date. James was fat and boasting and crude, but she could recognize the Cinderella outsider trying desperately to look at home at the ball. And he'd had the decency not to attempt to touch her since the incident in the car, thank God. They stood together now, the spangled reflections from the revolving globe above the dance floor jumping up and down Brackler's broad chest. His eyes raked up and down the front of her dress incessantly. Do men think we don't notice? James had been staring fixedly at her bosom for three minutes now, silent and brooding. She stifled an urge to slap him silly.

A tap on her shoulder. "Tricia?" She turned to see Andrew's best friend. Tommy gazed into her eyes with slightly tipsy seriousness. "Wanna dance?"

"Please," she said, grabbing his hand and threading quickly to the other side of the ballroom.

"Trish, what's going on?" Tommy said, the rum-sweetened punch loosening his tongue. "That guy!"

"He's not so bad," she shot back defensively. They both looked at each other squarely, pausing in the slow swirl of clinging, rustling, sweaty formalwear. Simultaneously, they burst out laughing. "Okay, he's bad," Tricia admitted. "I shouldn't have done it. Stupid, and mean. But Andrew deserved it."

"Maybe," Tommy said doubtfully. "I'm just sorry he's alone tonight. He should be here, with his friends." He grinned unevenly. "Drunk, like me."

"I don't understand," Tricia said. Tommy eased her through a classy combination. Drunk or sober, Tommy could outdance anybody, even Andrew.

"Didn't you go to the game?" Tommy asked.

"The first part," Tricia admitted. "We lost. So what?"

"Andy missed an extra point," Tommy explained slowly. "Then he blew a field goal that should have—could have—won the game. When he came back to his locker after showers, someone had written 'CHOKE' all over it."

Tricia snorted in disgust. "It's just a—"

"Game. I know," Tommy said, then gushed on with a sudden sober intensity: "Look, why don't you dump him and ride back now with Elma and me? I bet Andy's still sitting there with the lights off. You know how he gets."

Tempted, Tricia peered across the dance floor. James stood there alone, swaying slightly from side to side, his brilliant blue suit a beacon of poverty in an elegant black sea of formality. In the dim light, he looked like an overgrown child, twisting his head this way and that, squinting small eyes searching in vain for the wondrous pair of breasts he had brought in his 1951 De Soto to the Welcome Dance. "I can't just leave him here," she said abruptly. "Tell Andrew I'll call him later, okay?"

"You're the boss," Tommy said simply. He led her back to James. Nodding to the heavyset boy, he went to find Elma.

"May I have some punch, please?" Tricia asked James with strained politeness. Let's make this quick and painless, she thought.

"Sure," James said. He smelled of the damp whiskey flask in his

37

right suit pocket. "Help yourself." He smiled patiently, wondering why she thought she had to ask his permission. "I'll wait right here."

Tommy Butler was higher than a kite, especially after the smooth symphony of fellatio Elma conducted as he drove them back to campus at seventy miles an hour up the new North Central Expressway. Tommy came just as they veered off the Mockingbird Lane exit. Jamming his foot down on the brakes, he inhaled the sickly sweet bread aroma from Mrs. Baird's bakery across the freeway. "Elma," he gasped, fondling her long blond hair as she dabbed at her lips with a hanky. "You really are something, you know that?"

"Green," she replied, applying her lipstick and smiling.

"Huh?"

"The light," she said, matter-of-fact. "It's green. Let's go. You owe me."

Outside the fraternity house, Tommy buckled up his tuxedo trousers and leaped out to open her door. Elma arose slowly, a tall, statuesque girl from the German hill country town of New Braunfels. Elma was maybe a shade hefty, Tommy acknowledged. But always ready for more. They planned to get married right after graduation. When they reached the top of the stairs, Tommy said, "I'll be right there." Elma reached over her shoulder and unzipped her dress in reply, not looking back as she walked down the hall to his room.

Andrew's room was pitch black. Andrew lay on top of the covers. Still wearing his postgame jacket and tie, he stared sightlessly at the ceiling. "Hey," Tommy said, unsure whether to intrude.

"Hey," Andrew answered quietly, immobile. They sat that way for a while, in the manner of those who've been friends nearly all of their lives.

Then Andrew broke the silence. "Was she there?" he whispered, voiçe husky. Tommy realized Andrew hadn't been thinking about football at all. If the roles had been reversed, Tommy thought, Andrew would have picked up on that.

"With some guy," Tommy said bluntly. "But she was having a terrible time," he stumbled on. "She said she'd call later."

"Come on, Tommy," Andrew said insistently, louder now. "Who?" His hair was unusually mussed, eyes reddened and bloodshot. Butler thought, Has he been crying?

"It was that guy. You remember the first day of tryouts?" Tommy could not seem to string his words together. "He was real—he had a weight problem. You talked to him. Something about his knee. He fell, remember?" Curiously, Tommy felt he should build Brackler up. If Andy could remember Brackler as somewhat less of a geek, he reasoned, maybe it wouldn't hurt so much.

"Brackler?" Andrew sat bolt upright, recalling the strange scene by the track. Brackler's hostility, his eerily knowing bitterness.

"Yeah," Tommy replied, confused.

"Are you sure?" Andrew swung his feet to the floor and grabbed Tommy by both shoulders. "James Brackler?"

"Yeah, James Brackler," Tommy said, hastening forward. "Tricia admitted it was just a spite date. She picked the fattest, dorkiest guy she could think of."

"Damn!" Later, Andrew could never explain to himself why he jumped up and grabbed his keys off the desk. Brackler's unwarranted belligerence, perhaps. Or just the need to escape from Tommy's cloying sympathy.

"I gotta go," he said shortly. Tommy watched his friend disappear down the stairs. He consulted his watch, then shrugged.

A voice came from his own room down the hall. "Tommy?" Tommy opened his door to see Elma Heitmeier, Class Favorite Girl of 1959, dangling upside down from the plywood ladder of the loft he'd built in his room. She was naked, plush silky legs hooked around the top rung, fleshy body stretched taut.

"Help me," Elma said, giggling. Her arms gyrated wildly, her face was turning red. "All the blood is in my head."

"This," Andrew said aloud to himself as he cut the ignition in the parking lot of the Baker Hotel, "is stupid." He and Tricia had had a stupid fight. She went to a stupid dance with a stupid sophomore who did not like Andrew. And here he was, rushing to her side like some stupid Lancelot.

"Andrew?" The voice sliced into his reverie.

"Huh?" Andrew looked up and saw a vaguely familiar youth, one of five hundred he knew by sight but not by name. He stared at Andrew curiously, his head bobbing above his sleek black formal attire, a girl out of focus over the fellow's shoulder. "Wake up, Andrew!" The youth laughed. "What's going on? I saw Tricia walking out a few minutes ago. With—" The voice paused and changed timber. "Y'all aren't together?"

"I was just, you know," Andrew said, embarrassed. "Out for a drive."

"In the parking lot?" the anonymous voice persisted. What *was* his name? Andrew puzzled. Brian Maroney? Bill Monroe?

"Come on, Brian." The girl tugged at her date's arm, corsage wobbling on one thin wrist. "G'night, Andrew."

"Yeah . . ." Brian moved away, eyeing Andrew curiously. "Sure. Good night."

"'Night," Andrew said with relief. He had parked around back, hoping all the other kids would leave by the front. I guess Mulrooney's too cheap to use the valet, Andy thought aimlessly. He gunned the engine to life and tore out of the lot, toward campus and bed. It had been a stupid day and a stupid night. All he wanted to do was end it.

Trapped alongside James in the car, away from the protective environment of her friends, Tricia's unease returned in force. Maybe I should have gone with Tommy and Elma, she thought. James pulled a second pint of Southern Comfort from under the seat, cracked the seal with his big teeth, and unscrewed the cap. The De Soto weaved wildly. Brackler sucked at the bottle like a baby at his mother's breast, eyes floating backward, left hand loosely guiding the car up the expressway.

"This is it," Tricia said.

"Huh?" James spluttered, spilling whiskey down the front of his shirt.

"Mockingbird," she said. "The exit. You passed it."

"I can take University, can't I?" he said a trifle scornfully. He yanked at his tie, threw it in the backseat.

"Sure, James," Tricia said, her voice shaking ever so slightly. "Whatever you like." She breathed a sigh of relief when he aimed the car at the University Drive exit ramp and threaded his way through the quiet streets around the campus. If they crashed now, at least they wouldn't be going more than thirty.

James's driving was not the only thing that scared her. Mr. Hyde was back again, his sweating, groping hands juggling between bottle and steering wheel and aggressive forays at the naked back above her low-cut, designed-for-Andrew gown. Tricia resolved to bolt from the car the minute he pulled up to the sorority house.

"Well, here we are," James said, noting how the snotty bitch had cooled to him now that the dance was over. Eyes narrowing, he looked briefly into hers and saw exactly how he had been used. The car slowed nearly to a halt, then slowly picked up speed as James jammed his foot down on the accelerator.

Tricia's hand fell from the door handle to clutch her knees. "What's going on?" she snapped. The car lurched to a halt at the end of the dark street, beside the deserted science building.

James smiled playfully. "Just kidding," he said, wondering where people went to "park." He had heard it discussed often at Hickey's, always with a giggle and a leer, but he had no idea what was expected of him, how to begin. He eased his right arm across the seat behind her and locked her door. "Tricia, I know we just met . . ." He looked at her wetly. "But I really like you."

"I like you, too, James," Tricia replied nervously. "Really."

His hand crept down around her bare shoulders. His forearm was big and hot and sticky to the touch. The fabric of his sleeve clung unpleasantly to her back. His left hand tossed the pint bottle to the floor, the dregs spilling out on the floorboards. Then he started pulling off his jacket, one-handed. His right arm clenched tighter around her shoulders.

"I really like you," Tricia rushed on. "But it's late. Really, James. I'd like you to take me home."

Not knowing how to reply, he said nothing, just shrugged halfway out of his suit coat and began unbuttoning his shirt with his left hand. He shoved his right hand down farther around her, below her arm, so he could reach his fingers around and brush the soft outer swell of her breast.

A chill of fear struck deep inside her, urgent and primal. It was time to switch tactics. "James," she said sternly, pulling away from his arm. "Take me home. Now."

James shucked his jacket and slung it awkwardly onto the backseat. "Ah, you don't wanna go home yet, honey," he drawled. The more he drinks, she noted, the more Texas he gets. He put his hands on her shoulders and pulled her to him. "The party's just begun, right?" His breath was pungent; an explosion of whiskey fumes turned her stomach.

Suddenly, Tricia was scared. Bad scared. She twisted her head about wildly, looking for hope through fogged-up windows. No one in sight. Just James overwhelming her with his size and bulk and strength, pressing forward, as silent and menacing now as he had

41

been talkative and harmless before. Tricia grabbed his hands and tried vainly to push him away. He was much, much too strong for her. He grabbed the back of her neck and pushed her down in the seat, pressing the flat of his left palm down hard on her shoulder. He was trying to force her to lie horizontally on the De Soto's wide front seat.

James seemed lost in his own world, methodically acting out a fantasy he had played many times. "Come on, baby," he murmured almost inaudibly, as though talking to himself. "Come on, now." His hands kneaded her breasts, sliding Tricia's trembling body beneath him.

Once he had his weight on top of her, Tricia knew she would be helpless. She had been trapped like this before, with the gropers back in Beaumont. But it had always escalated naturally, from kissing to fondling to, "Okay, that's enough!"

This was different. It happened suddenly, but with no passion, no human nature. Just a sudden, bizarre onslaught, as though he'd planned this all along. James's hands clenched her breasts, hurting her, crushing her beneath yards of tangled satin and hundreds of pounds of Hickey's hamburgers.

Panicking, she did the only thing she could think of. She jammed her right knee into the archway between his legs, as hard as she could.

"Aaagh!" James screamed in high-pitched agony. "You fuckin' bitch!" He released her and clapped both hands over his groin, shrieking in pain. She squirmed quickly under his doughy, half-naked chest. Wiggling free, she reached up and popped the lock on the passenger car door, hurling herself against the splintered vinyl. The door flew open with a loud squeak of unoiled springs. She fell out of the De Soto and into the gutter, skinning her knuckles in the gritty mud. She rolled over the curb, onto the withered grass in front of the science building.

James's mind reeled from drink and pain and nausea. Son of a bitch! Everything had been going perfectly, according to plan. The Plan. Now everything stood in jeopardy. He lunged out of the car toward Tricia, grabbed the pink hem of her gown, and pulled hard on her skirt. Tricia pushed away from the car, trying frantically to get up, to turn, to escape. James yanked with all his might. The heavy pink satin ripped free, tearing at the waist as Tricia fought to get away. The icy wind whipped at her bare legs as she kicked free

42

of the cumbersome fabric. One of her shoes flipped into the air and hit James in the eye.

"Ow!" he grunted in anger and surprise. He swept the torn gown aside and heaved himself out of the car. Tricia pushed herself up, out of the muddy gutter, white garters showing beneath what was left of her gown. She got shakily to her feet, stumbling on one spiked heel. Then she lost that shoe, too. Her feet touched the cold, hard sidewalk, and she began to run, pulling up the top of her gown to cover her exposed nipples.

Then she stumbled and cried out, ripping her stocking as she fell to her knee, her palms slapping into the concrete. James fell upon her from behind, slamming her body into the pavement, driving the breath from her ribs. Pinned beneath his bulk, all she could do was sob silently.

"Listen to me!" he hissed angrily into her ear, closing his huge hands tight around her throat. He squeezed hard, his powerful thumbs punching deep into her throat, strangling her. God, he's strong, Tricia realized in terror. A reddish mist swum before her eyes. She gagged for breath. She clawed at James's eyes. Her will to fight began to ebb. Soon, she wanted only air.

"I'm gonna poke you," James enunciated slowly. He pressed his thumbs deeper into her throat. "I know what you think of me. I'm gonna stick it in, and you're not gonna say a thing. Or I'll hurt you. You understand?"

Tricia felt herself nodding mutely. Consciousness slid slowly away. He was killing her, didn't he know that? James pulled her to her feet, one arm around her waist. The other still clutched her throat, less tightly now. She gasped in a shallow draft of frozen night air as he propelled her back across the lawn. Not to the sputtering De Soto, but back, away from the lonely street, deep into the pool of darkness that surrounded the empty classrooms fifty feet away. He tossed her down on the edge of the path between the science building and the laboratory, pressing her head back into the gravel. His right hand was clamped over her mouth, and he pinched her nose shut with his left.

"I'm not gonna hurt you. You understand me?" he whispered urgently, unclenching her mouth.

"Yes," she wheezed. "Ohpleaseohplease—"

He clapped his hand back over her mouth. "I'm gonna make you a deal. Okay?" He slackened his grip imperceptibly. He felt himself

43

beginning to panic. Everything was wrong, out of control. He knew he had gone too far, pushed too hard. It frightened him, and excited him. "You gimme what I want. Quietly. No trouble, no screaming, nothing." He reached one arm behind her, allowing Tricia another gasp of air as he grabbed the back of her dress and ripped it open. He pulled off the remnants of her gown and flung them into the hedge. "Give me what I want. I won't hurt you. I promise."

"Oh, please," she gasped. "No, please. I—"

"Shut up!" James grabbed her face, squeezing her cheeks into her mouth. "Shut up and listen!" He clawed furiously at her body with his free hand. He pinched her nipples, tore away her bra, then ripped her panties from her hips, shredding the thin fabric effortlessly. He flattened her body beneath him on the ground and covered her with his bulk, working his belt loose and easing the baggy blue slacks down his legs.

"You'll never tell a soul," he predicted with that odd, sage wisdom, so much older than his years. In a sick flash, Tricia knew he was right. "You'll make up some bullshit story about getting drunk and takin' all your clothes off after I left, and running naked down the street as a joke. You'll sneak in the window of that sorority house, so none of your rich girlfriends'll ever know."

"No!" Tricia protested. He was reading her mind. Her head spun wildly, irrationally. All she could think was: How can I fix it so no one will know? James could kill her. Tricia could see it in his eyes. He had almost done it, strangling her back on the sidewalk. He was a monster and she hated him, but he was right. She would never tell a soul. Is this what she'd saved it for, through all those difficult nights with all those sweet, thoughtful boys she'd really cared about?

James jammed his left forearm against her neck, using his right hand to slip his tattered, yellow-stained underwear down over his rump, pulling his erection away from the elastic band. He spread her legs with his knee and collapsed on top of her. Tricia felt his horrid thing, pulsing warm against the icy goose bumps on her thigh. She bit back the tears and rocked her head back against the gravel. Her bare bottom scraped painfully into the grit as James ground into her.

He had trouble at first. She was scared and cold and angry and dry, and it was his first time, too. For a second he thought he would come all over her thighs without ever penetrating the unforgiving door between her legs. Tricia stared up at the black night, trying to shut it all out, to cut herself off from what was happening to her. A sudden flash of pain below brought her back to reality. James heaved hard against her, forcing his way in, grunting and biting at her neck. Help me, God, she prayed. Then she traveled far away, looking for a place to hide in the darkest caverns of her mind.

Andrew wasn't sure why he decided to turn off Airline Road two streets below Fondren and cruise Tricia's sorority house. Maybe he thought her light would be on. Maybe he just hated to go back to the darkness of his own room, alone with his black thoughts. He drove slowly past the gloomy Tri Delt house. Her room was unlit. He sped up, then slowed for the stop sign at the end of the street. He didn't need another ticket from Campus Security. He was about to shift into first and make a right turn when he noticed an aging, rust-spotted monolith of a car parked at an odd angle to the curb, the engine thumping noisily. The passenger door gaped open, the car's interior light spilling out onto the grassy shoulder. Andrew started to pull away, then backed his car parallel to the De Soto and put the MG in neutral. There was no one inside. He shut off his ignition and got out of the roadster.

He walked around to the passenger side of the old car. There, lying in the gutter, lay a long tangle of muddy pink cloth, torn raggedly at the edges. Andrew stooped to pick it up. He heard a faint rustling in the distance.

"Hello?" he called out into the dark, sure he had heard something. There was a stifled cry. Cat, maybe? A hard slap. Andrew ran toward the noise. "Hello?" he yelled, running faster as he heard scuffling. "What's going on back there?"

Andrew's shout reached Tricia just as James thrust himself deep inside her. Gritting her teeth at the sear of pain swelling around his violation, she felt the warm blood trickle down her thighs, tasted the salty tears rolling down her cheeks into her open, gagging-dry mouth. She tried to scream, but James shoved his fist into her mouth, pinching her tongue with fat fingers and thumb. She retched slightly. Taking courage from Andrew's voice—it was Andrew, it had to be—Tricia tore at James's loose shirt with her fingernails. Oblivious, James rammed his huge body into her again and again, ten times, more, deaf to the footsteps behind him.

Andrew rounded the side of the building and saw two dark forms wrestling in the moonlight. At first he thought them two college lovers. He nearly turned away in embarrassment. But his eyes adjusted quickly.

James, pants clumped at his ankles, shirt flopping in the breeze, exploded inside Tricia, a sensation beyond his most daring fantasies, dazzling all the sweat-soaked wet dreams and bathroom autoerotica of the long, agonizing adolescence he had thought might never end. Feeling him geyser inside her, Tricia bit down furiously on his right hand, tasting blood. James screamed aloud, in triumph and in pain.

Andrew dragged at James's broad shoulders, hauling him off Tricia's naked form. He threw Brackler's huge figure into the prickly bushes surrounding the red brick building. Then he gazed down stupidly at Tricia's pale white body in the moonlight, at the blood smeared between her legs. Her hands flew to cover her nudity. She sobbed for breath. Grief and humiliation scored her cheeks with patchy blotches, shiny tears.

Andrew whirled on James, who was trying simultaneously to pull up his pants and extract himself from the brambly yaupon holly. "You piece of shit!" Andrew said slowly, crossing the grass to grab James's shirt front.

"I-I-I," James stammered. His hands waved and pointed wildly. "I didn't, she was—she *wanted* to, Sebastian! I swear to God. I swear on my mother!"

Andrew tackled him hard, a mad rage taking over where physical strength left off. They tangled in the bushes, thudded heavily to the ground. Andrew's fury gave him the edge over the bigger youth's heft. Quickly he was astride James, bony khaki-clad knees pinning down naked meaty shoulders. Andrew paused to catch his breath, fist drawn to pummel the sophomore's face.

Then, cursing himself for letting this happen, Andrew hit him. Again and again, until his arm was too wrenched and leaden to hit him anymore.

December
1971

4

W ell, Andy, what do you say?" asked Bill Crawford, the new county Republican chairman. Crawford, managing partner of Dallas's second-largest law firm, leaned his slender frame forward in the antique cherrywood rocking chair in Roger Sebastian's private study. The chair's long, curved wooden sliders creaked downward, narrowly missing the gently flicking tail of Shivers, the family's last surviving housecat. The elderly black tom scurried out of the room, claws savaging the thick red Persian rug.

Smiling, the party leader lit his oversize meerschaum pipe and studied Andrew's surprised grin through intense glacier-blue eyes. He was a man who chose his words carefully, like a job applicant selecting just the right tie for an interview. "I'll be straight with you," Crawford continued, picking his way cautiously across the thin ice of local politics. "You probably can't win. Not this time. John Masters has held that seat for twelve terms. He's won by over sixty percent ever since the second Eisenhower landslide. Including last year. What'd he do last fall, Austin?"

Austin Peters, the party's treasurer and self-appointed statistician, leaned his beakish nose forward from the row of party chieftains arrayed on an endless yellow couch. "Masters took 88.7 percent against Amberton, the black activist, in the Democratic primary," Peters reported, consulting the manila folder stuffed between his knees. "He carried seventy percent against our guy in the general."

"I know." Andrew nodded briefly. "I voted for Masters."

"So did I," added Andrew's father, walking back into the room with the oddly hurried nonchalance of one who doesn't want to miss a word. Roger carried drinks to two of the nine Republican leaders crammed into the cozy oak-paneled study of the Azalea House. The others were already nipping at their Scotch and nodding at the fiery blaze in the small grate of the marble-edged fireplace, shivering off the unusual chill of that December Saturday afternoon.

"Half the men in this room voted for Masters," Roger commented, running one hand through the steel-wool brush of hair perched high atop his stooping frame. "John Masters is a solid Texas conservative. One of the last good Democrats left, except for my damnfool son here." Roger matched the disapproving words with an unabashed fawning glance at his son, who sat twiddling his thumbs nervously behind Roger's big brass-edged oak desk. Warming his hands at the fire, Roger added bluntly, "Why would Andy want to fight a losing battle against a good man like that?"

"Because Masters is going to retire after one more term," Crawford shot back.

Roger's bushy gray eyebrows lifted in surprise. Since when does Bill Crawford find out things before me? he wondered. He made a mental note to call John Masters first thing Monday morning.

"So?" Andrew asked.

"John Masters is getting old," Chubb Howard put in. An independent oilman, Chubb had bolted the Democratic party with Roger Sebastian, Austin Peters, and many of the other downtown business leaders, after Kennedy "stole" the nomination from LBJ back in 1960.

"Masters is practically senile," Howard said, ignoring the awkward silence. "Let's put the cards face up on the table, Bill. Masters finally got enough seniority for the appropriations chair last year, and he doesn't want to give it up yet. Okay. So he gets one more term, assuming he beats Andy here." Chubb glanced at Andrew, rubbing one fat cheek as he measured the young man behind the desk. "After that, Masters retires."

"What we need is an heir apparent." Crawford drilled his words one by one into Andrew's receptive eyes. "Someone who can put on a good show this time around. Set himself up to replace Masters when he steps down. Someone who can raise a lot of money." Crawford could not help but glance at Roger, who seemed more interested by the minute. He went on in an impassioned tone, a final charge to the jury: "A bright, attractive young candidate who can help turn out votes for the president." Crawford looked around the room and saw nine gray heads nod in support of his summation. "You're young, Andy," said Crawford. "But you've paid your dues in the Rotary and the Chamber. Working for your dad's company like you do, you've got freedom. You could create some excitement in the Fourth District."

Roger cleared the phlegm from his throat and started to reply. Andrew held out his hand.

"There's only one problem, Mr. Crawford," he said.

"Bill," Crawford corrected quickly, a politician's first-name instinct.

"Bill," Andrew corrected cautiously, obeying the rule his father had taught him as a young adult: Call them mister 'til they tell you otherwise. He gulped, his mind reeling with the possibilities. "I'm a Democrat," he reminded them. There was a long silence.

"Hell, so were we," Howard said, chuckling at Andrew's naïveté. "But times have changed. The Democratic party just ain't what it used to be."

"I'm not crazy about where the Democrats are headed," Andrew replied doggedly. "But I've got to be honest with you. I don't care a whole lot for your president. Vietnam, wage and price controls, more taxes. We ought to get in there and win the war, or get the hell out. And the economy! Republicans are supposed to stand for free enterprise, less government. He doesn't stand for anything, except himself."

Roger sipped his Scotch and stared at the ceiling, enjoying the shocked look on the other faces.

"No offense, of course," Andrew said hastily, realizing he'd gotten carried away. "I'm flattered, really. I like most of what the Republicans stand for, on paper. I just wanted to be straight with you. To

51

tell you the truth, Dad didn't even tell me what this meeting was going to be about." It was a small white lie. "Heck, I'd love to be a congressman," he added with a flash of white teeth. "I think I'd do a good job. You'd like where I stood, even if I didn't always walk your party line." He trailed off. He was nervous, babbling. *What am I saying? They're offering me a shot at Congress.* He needed time to think. He looked to his father for help. For once, Roger kept his own counsel.

Crawford rocked forward, perching his spindly elbows on his knees. "We agree on more than you think, Andy," he said carefully. "Our party is the right place for you. We know what kind of man you are. After all, you and I have been together on a few things. Like that mayor's race last year?" Crawford had a lawyer's nose for the common ground. "You'd make one damn good congressman for Dallas. That's all we care about."

"Party labels don't mean shit, Andy," Chubb Howard added, stuffing his 320-pound frame deeper into the red leather love seat. "And you know the Democrats'll never give you a shot at that district. You're too rich, too young, too goddamn independent. Look at the way you mouth off to all of us old farts. So where's the problem?"

"If I were to run," Andrew said slowly, his thoughts racing, "and I really need to think about this, and talk to my wife, my folks—"

"Of course!" Crawford said. "Take all the time you—"

"If I were to run," Andrew continued as though Crawford hadn't spoken, "I'd run my own campaign? With your help and advice, of course."

"Hell, yes!" Howard replied.

"And if I could beat Masters this time, this year, that would be okay with you?" Andrew persisted. "There are no deals behind my back with the congressman?"

"We don't fix elections!" Crawford said stiffly, biting back his anger.

" 'Course you do, Bill," Roger said mildly, swirling the ice in his glass. "That's why we made you county chairman."

Laughter broke the tension. Roger rubbed his hand again through the short iron stubble of his crewcut, then pinched the bridge of his nose: an old man who wished he had worn his glasses.

"Let's not play games here," he said in a soft voice. "What Andrew's asking is, can he be his own man on this? Have you indicated to Masters in any way that we'll go easy on him next fall?"

"Absolutely not, Roger." Crawford looked the old man in the eye. Andrew could see that Roger believed him.

"Gentlemen," Roger said abruptly, stepping forward into the middle of the room. "It's a great honor for Andy and me. You know we've got some thinking to do. I appreciate you coming here on a weekend. I'm really flattered."

Andrew watched his father usher out the party mandarins, one by one. The younger Sebastian was left sitting alone in the chair beside his father's big desk, staring at the dregs of whiskey in glasses scattered around the empty room.

"Me, too, Dad," Andrew muttered quietly. "I'm flattered, too." He gazed thoughtfully through leaded-glass windows at the brown winter landscape, watching the curling yellow leaves blow into the motionless black water of Turtle Creek.

It was even colder in Washington. An icy Canadian wind crusted over the slush in the gutters of Independence Avenue, along the massive white marble pile of Rayburn House Office Building. James Brackler slipped on the worn leather soles of his scuffed brown shoes as he hustled across the broad plaza toward the building's main entrance. James checked his watch hurriedly. He had dawdled too long over his hamburger at the Hawk 'n Dove.

In the two years James had worked as a legislative counsel on Capitol Hill, he had never before been summoned to an actual meeting with the congressman. "Meetings" were for constituents and colleagues in the House. Staff members scrambled for the occasional leftovers: walking down a hallway at his side; leaning over his shoulder in a hearing room; a quick rush of words over the intercom. James pushed through the revolving door, into the arid warmth of the lobby. He signed in and nodded to the guard, wondering about the curt note he had discovered on his desk this morning. "Brackler," read the congressman's spiky handwriting, scrawled in the usual blue felt-tipped pen on a small sheet of House notepaper. "Meeting. 2:00 today."

The brisk young aide who strode down the wide marble hallway was, in some ways, a very different James Brackler from the awkward, ungainly boy who had attended SMU a decade earlier. James was still in no imminent danger of making *Gentlemen's Quarterly*. His chest and stomach bulged against the vest of his cut-rate blue suit. He had not yet mastered the fine art of knotting his tie much smaller

53

than one of his hamlike fists. He still didn't realize that a professional man never, ever wears brown shoes with a blue suit. But he was no longer fat. He had grown up, slimmed down, fit in. After five years in the long stone hallways and arched domes of state and national Capitols, he was in his element, acclimated to the ever-changing winds of the Washington power structure. Sloppy or not, he was a young man on the way up.

But why this unusual summons? James felt like the child called without explanation to the principal's office, who instantly begins to catalog all possible sins. Cutting gym classes? Starting a fire in that locker? James's mind clicked at high speed as he pulled open the sixteen-foot-tall wooden door with its ornate congressional seal. He stepped into the office foyer, where gigantic stacks of twine-bound Saturday constituent mail sat piled on the receptionist's desk, waiting for the Monday-morning clerks to attack with little black-handled letter openers adorned with the blue congressional eagle, as were all the coffee cups and desk clocks and every other item in a congressional office.

A gruff voice called out from the inner office. "Brackler?"

"Yes, sir," James replied. He made a vain attempt to mash down his windblown black hair, now fringing back with frightening speed to reveal a half-bald pate. He walked into the congressman's office, the big meet-the-constituents office festooned with maybe three hundred framed pictures of the congressman with every president since FDR; the congressman with Warren Beatty; the congressman with John Glenn; the congressman with other congressmen; and the congressman with gawking constituents, posed in front of all the other pictures in the congressman's office.

The congressman was on the phone. Politicians' lives are an exercise in time management. Each second is a precious chance to stroke a fellow legislator, intimidate an unruly freshman, renew a long-standing friendship with a contributor. Just now, the congress-man was talking football with the chairman of the largest bank in Texas. Rolling his eyes, he waved James to a chair.

"Jarrett, I jes' don't believe your Aggies got a prayer," he prodded teasingly. Brackler tuned out the sports chatter, pacing the photo-graphs. He liked the game of putting a name to each of the faces. When he had come here three years ago, he had known only the presidents and a couple of senators. Now he knew them all, from the scoutmasters to the most powerful figures in the home district. James bent to the bottom row to look at an old photo he'd never noticed before: the congressman as a young man in his World War II marine uniform. Had it always been there?

He straightened up as his employer lifted his feet off the desk and squeaked forward on his swivel chair. One shirt-sleeved arm dropped the phone into its cradle. The old man launched the meeting with his usual abruptness. "You came to us straight out of the service, didn't you, boy?" asked John Masters.

"Yes, sir," James said with pride, drawing his head back the way they had taught him at Officer Candidate School in Virginia. "Advocate General Corps. At the Pentagon."

"Pentagon." The elderly politician spat the word back with distaste, as if a Norwegian water rat had somehow climbed into his mouth. "Desk soldier, huh?" The congressman glared malevolently at the sloppy, physically intimidating young man who had recently become his most valuable aide.

Masters had disliked Brackler from the first interview, despite the five-star recommendation from Hank Talmadge. Talmadge had run Masters's first campaign for Congress, back when Masters was a maverick young war hero who seized Dallas's oldest congressional stronghold away from the downtown establishment. The pair of upstarts won again in 1950, electing Henry Talmadge state senator from Masters's district. Talmadge's Austin office became a training ground for aspiring young liberal apprentice politicians like Brackler, who signed on with Talmadge while a scholarship law student at the University of Texas. The old fighting liberal had died just recently, a useless old relic who had no more windmills to fight.

Masters's career had been different. He set out to work within the Washington system, trimming sails enough to steer his bills through the committees and lobbyists and more committees. After nearly twenty-four years in the House, John Masters was the dean of the Texas congressional delegation, titular head of the conservative Tory wing of the Texas Democratic party.

But the congressman's steady drift to the right had not been without cost. He had alienated much of his old support from liberal elements of his increasingly working-class and minority district. That was why he had found a spot for leftish young Brackler, and it was the reason for this private meeting today.

55

"I never liked desk soldiers," the old man announced after a moody silence. Masters's lizard eyelids slitted shut in disgust. "And I never liked you. You know that, don't you?"

"Uh, yes, sir, I guess so," James stammered, taken aback by the man's brutality.

"But I need you," Masters continued. "In politics, it's much better to be needed than to be liked. Believe me. Politicians throw away people they like. They never get rid of anyone they can still use."

"Yes, sir." James sat down on a polished burgundy leather visitor's chair, nervously picking lint from his suit jacket.

"I heard from Austin late last night." Masters paused, thinking that the young man's perennial five o'clock shadow reminded him of the president's dark jowls. "We lost the first round on redistricting," he said sharply. "The feds got their way. The Moore plan is a done deal."

James's heart sank deep into his belly. Texas's twenty-four congressional districts were being redrawn along new lines based on the 1970 census and the Supreme Court's "one man, one vote" decision. The Moore plan took most conservative white voters out of Masters's Fourth District, reshaping it into a polyglot of minorities, union voters, and Republicans—none boosters of Masters.

Shit, James thought, he called me in to tell me he's retiring. I'm out of a job. "How can they do this to you?" he said in despair. "You *are* the Fourth District. You are—"

"Old," Masters said heavily. His face suddenly showed it. "They know I'm fixin' to retire in a couple years," he acknowledged ruefully. "They've decided the district is unwinnable in the long run."

"So they stab you in the back and use your constituents to save the other districts," James finished. "Damn. I can't believe it."

"Hold on, boy." Masters frowned. "Don't bury me yet. I was winning campaigns when that Lieutenant Governor Moore was pissing his bed every night. I'll win that district," he grated. "No matter how they draw it up. But I need your help."

James's spirits soared. The congressman had never taken him into his confidence like this.

"You've done a good job for me up here, Brackler," Masters said grandly. His thin lips twisted into a sardonic smile. "You work harder for sixteen thousand a year than anybody I've ever seen. You been up here only two years, and you've got every black activist and Ralph Nader kook in town in your back pocket."

James, unused to such praise, panicked. *Is he saying I've been too liberal?* He was getting tired of Ping-Ponging back and forth between insults and backhanded compliments.

"I know what I get out of you." The congressman rocked forward suddenly, thrusting his weathered face into James's blinking eyes. "What do you want out of me?"

The question caught James off guard. "Experience, I guess," he said lamely.

"Bullshit," the old man shot back. "Don't snow me. You think you're the first ambitious lil' fucker who ever came up here wanting my job?"

"N-no sir," James stuttered.

"'Course you do." Masters coughed, contentedly spitting green scum into the monogrammed handkerchief he kept especially for that purpose. "Or you wouldn't work sixteen hours a day, and take shit from a withered old peckerwood like me. You're creaming your jeans to run for office." Despite the old man's biting tone, James felt a thrill of excitement. "You've learned most of what you can learn up here," Masters wheezed on. "I want you to move to Dallas and run my reelection campaign." The congressman nodded wearily at the fire in James's eyes. "Joe Cawther's been running my district office, and my campaigns, for almost twenty years now. He's had it," Masters pronounced. He shrugged and added a trivial footnote: "Besides, he's dying of cancer."

"I didn't know," James said with studied concern.

Masters ignored the crocodile tears. "I want you to go down there and do a number on the coloreds, the union boys, the pinks," he rushed on angrily. "That's my seat, goddammit! Nobody's takin' it away until I'm good and ready."

"Yes, sir!" James replied emphatically.

"Pay 'em off. Sweet-talk 'em. Rat-fuck 'em. I don't care what you do," the old man emphasized slowly. "Just make damn sure they don't find some good-looking white Baptist family-man bastard to run against me in the primary."

"No problem, Congressman," James said.

"It damn sure is a problem," Masters countered snappishly. "But you're gonna take care of it. I'm making you a deal," he added in a soothing voice. "Win me the Democratic primary without me having to come home to campaign, and I'll give you a raise. Beat the Republicans next fall, and I'll let you take my place in two years."

James was stunned. Masters, choosing him as heir? Actually winning the seat would be another story, of course: the Republicans were feeling their oats in that district. But Masters's endorsement would vault James directly into the Democratic nomination: a gigantic leap forward for the Plan.

There has to be a catch, he thought suspiciously. "Are you kidding?" he almost shouted.

"Son, I never kid about politics." The congressman smiled his most grandfatherly damn-the-constituents smile. "I may not like your left-wing politics, but you've got balls, and you're meaner'n a junkyard dog. I want you—heart, soul, and *cojones*—for another year. Then you can spend my last term setting up your own campaign. I'll even endorse you. I'll be damned if I leave anyone but my own man sittin' on this toilet when I crap outa here."

"You bet," James said, thinking that there was more than a little of the maverick left in the old man. James suddenly loved him more than anyone he had ever known.

They stayed in Masters's office for the most wonderful four hours of James's life. A curious youthfulness overcame Masters as they talked of precincts and boundaries and neighborhood leaders, of phone banks and direct mail and endorsements: all the weapons and tactics of modern political warfare. When James finally shrugged on his overcoat and walked down the echoing marble hallways to the elevator, he felt uplifted, ennobled, inspired. For the first time since he had left that city of bad memories, he couldn't wait to get back to Dallas.

Outside, the frigid night wind sliced into his face. His car was parked across the street on a lane winding up the West Front of Capitol Hill. As he scuffed the ice off his windshield with the orange plastic scraper, James gazed up at the broad white expanse of the Rayburn Building. More than a few windows were still lit, yellow beacons of power in the early dark of a December Saturday in Washington. He felt a tingling sensation deep inside. The next time I work late up there, he thought, I'll be a congressman!

He laughed aloud in glee.

"Dad thinks I should pass it up," Andrew said from his usual perch atop the kitchen stool later that evening, watching his wife bustle around the kitchen, preparing an elaborate Saturday-night dinner.

Tricia enjoyed cooking on Louise's nights off. She was glad she had started the roast beef early. It was hard to concentrate now that Andrew was home, bringing news of this curious proposal.

"He says I'm not ready. That I shouldn't go into a fight I can't win," Andrew mused, his gaze wandering across the little chain of hand-painted ducks dancing gaily about the ceiling molding. "What do you think?"

"I think," she began slowly, trying to time the green beans and mashed potatoes and gravy and rolls and roast beef so they would all be ready at once, "your dad has a point. Do you really want to lose your first race? You've put in so much time on other people's campaigns. It's much worse for the candidate."

"And the candidate's wife," he added.

Tricia burned her finger on the oven rack. "Damn!" she whispered, popping her finger casually into her mouth. "Sure, Andy," she said carefully, concentrating hard on saying it just right. "I've always known this was coming. But it scares me a little," she confessed. "You'd never be here. If we went to Washington, it'd be even worse."

"I don't think we'll have to worry about that. This time, at least," Andrew said ruefully, running his hand through the long brown hair sprinkling over his eyes. If he did decide to run, the first order of business would be a haircut. "Masters is practically unbeatable." Andrew took two bundles of silverware and napkins from her outstretched hands. He finished the thought as he laid the dining room table: "But Dad thinks he can get Masters to back me when he retires. Even if I run now as a Republican."

"But Masters is a Democrat," she said, confused.

"He's a conservative, and he owes Dad a lot of favors," Andrew said. "If I can keep from hacking him off this fall, I could be his chosen successor. It's becoming a Republican district." Tricia's mind quietly unhooked from Andrew's dissertation.

It was not that she lacked interest. She was vitally interested. She had always accepted, since their wedding day, that her role in life would someday be that of a politician's wife. It had sounded glamorous, thrilling. But now, she knew the other side of politics. Long evenings knocking on doors. Barbecues and rubber-chicken dinners. Those endless, endless speeches. All weekend every weekend, working the phone banks, waking people up too early on Saturday morning and having them slam down the telephone in your ear.

All-night strategy sessions where wives were neither needed nor welcome. Tricia had come to dread the inevitable day when Andrew would step up from bridesmaid to bride.

Now the party leaders had come wooing, and she was jealous. The truth of it was, she didn't want to share Andrew Sebastian with half a million constituents. Things were strained enough as they were.

Tricia took a deep breath and focused on her husband's eager words. "I really think I could surprise them."

"But you're a Democrat," she put in, voice trembling with innocent hope. Take this cup away from me, Lord. I'm just not ready yet.

"Not anymore," Andrew said frankly, setting one last fork on the smooth green baize of the small table where they ate together most nights, childless and alone. "The New Frontier? The Great Society? It's a flop. All it's brought us is more government, more welfare, more poverty. Not that this administration is doing any better," he rambled on, wrapping his long legs around the red-checked vinyl stool where he liked to sit and talk to Tricia while she cooked. His hands waved in the air, words singing along musically in an easy, pleasant cadence that put complicated political issues into simple, coherent language. Usually she enjoyed these talks. But right now she wished he would stop talking about politics and focus on what was really at stake.

Their eight years of marriage had been difficult. They never spoke of it, had tried with some success to blot it out of their collective marital memory. But that September night lurked always in the background, an early childhood canvas not quite painted over by the adult artist.

Tricia had refused to go to a hospital that night. She had insisted she was not hurt, that Andrew had come "just in time." Andrew had gone along. He'd driven Tricia straight home through the night, all the way to Beaumont, she dressed in his blue blazer, trying vainly to hide the bloodstains between her legs.

When she came back to school that January, he tried to tell her it didn't matter to him, even pushed her to press charges. She just shook her head and smiled tightly, explaining that it was in the past, that she never wanted to talk about it again.

Andrew had been gentle and caring; Tricia, jumpy and irritable. She recoiled uncontrollably at Andrew's touch. When he kissed her after a date, all she could taste was James Brackler's foul tongue in her mouth. When Andrew held her, the strength in his arms scared her; she would ask Andrew to please let her go and take her home, now. Andrew seemed to understand that she had to be treated gingerly for a while, like a fragile Japanese paper sculpture that would crumple if held too tightly.

They were married two weeks after his graduation. It was a big family ceremony at SMU's Perkins Chapel: a perfectly choreographed ballet in glowing Kodachrome. But the scars inside refused to heal. On their wedding night, alone in the honeymoon suite at the Adolphus, their facial muscles aching from hours of smiling, the glow faded. When Andrew came out of the bathroom wearing nothing but a towel and a foolish, expectant grin, he found Tricia folded up in the fetal position on the bed, fully dressed in her green linen traveling suit. Her arms clasped her ankles, her knees shuddered against her chin; her shoulders quivered in helpless sobs. Andrew eased the champagne bottle down on the bedside table and sat beside her. Somehow, he had known this was coming.

"Hey," he said lightly. "What's wrong?"

"I, I can't! I'm so sorry," Tricia cried. Andrew clambered gently behind her, the cool strength of his arms encircling the sweat-soaked fabric plastered to her small, shuddering form. He held her that way all night, telling her that he understood, that everything would be all right.

But it was not all right. In the snapshots pasted in Tricia's big white scrapbooks, they grinned in front of Eiffel Towers and Alpine peaks: the loving couple on the perfect honeymoon of every girl's dream. But the photos did not show the nightmares. Andrew tried everything. He got Tricia drunk on French wine. He took her skinny-dipping in the warm Mediterranean. He kissed her, stroked her, cajoled her. Once, gently but firmly, he even tried to force her, which ended in Tricia screaming her head off until the hotel porter hammered at their door, leaving them embarrassed and remote all the way through the endless flight back to Love Field.

Andrew was baffled. Tricia was not the exuberant girl he'd loved and courted, the one he thought he'd married. In her place was a listless young woman fighting off constant bouts of melancholy. Her highs were muted, dampened. Her lows were lower still, leaving her sitting alone in front of a dark television set for hours at a time or lying in bed until two o'clock on a Sunday afternoon when they had made plans to go to church, have lunch with his parents, take in a movie.

Finally, grudgingly, they began to consummate their marriage: a dutiful, spiritless biweekly coupling that was always subject to cancellation on the most specious of grounds. No matter how many times she clamped her muscles together and sobbed him away, Andrew kept on trying. Because he felt sure she must have loved him once.

And because he felt guilty.

The rape had been his fault. Because he'd had a fight with Tricia. Because he had somehow made that crazy Brackler hate him enough to rape his girlfriend. And the whole damn thing had happened because he'd tried to push Tricia into sex. No matter how hard he hit James after it was over, pounding until his own fists were shattered and bloody, Andrew would always feel as much a rapist as the unconscious youth he had left stretched half-naked on the gravel-strewn path next to the science building.

The years passed quickly. The draft lottery missed Andrew. The pregnancy lottery missed Tricia. Andrew's business and politics absorbed him, giving him some of the satisfaction he couldn't find in bed. Tricia was left lonely and bored, scrambling to fill her time with charity work and shopping and playing league doubles at the club. They stayed in the Lakewood house his parents had given them as a wedding present, turning what was to have been a nursery into a studio for Tricia's arts and crafts. Andrew wanted children desperately, and so did she. It was another in a long list of ways she felt she'd let him down.

In public, they still grinned and patted each other's knees, filling Tricia's scrapbooks with endless snapshots of the Loving Young Couple. If, in private hours, Tricia and Andrew mourned their life without love, by their eighth year of marriage they had accepted it, a punishment for sins they could not remember and never really understood.

As Tricia laid the hot dishes on the table late that December Saturday afternoon, Andrew followed her around like an overeager puppy, supplying her with salt shakers and Waterford crystal and a cornucopia of data about the Fourth Congressional District. Tricia fidgeted with wisps of her new shag haircut, the brown edges frosted ever so slightly, and waited for him to ask.

It came after dinner, with the coffee and peach cobbler. "Tricia, if I do this . . ." Andrew thought of all the politicians he knew. And their wives. "It's a long haul. We'll be on display. The way things are," he said limply, "with us, I mean. Could you go through with it? All the way?"

"All the way where?" she shot back, irritated as always when he alluded to their sex life. "To Washington? It's what we've always wanted." The sarcasm was unmistakable.

"Haven't we?" Andrew looked hurt.

"You have," she said archly. She took in the hurt expression on his face, and her voice softened. "That's not fair," she admitted. Dampening a yellow napkin in her water goblet, she dabbed distractedly at a tiny grease spot on her sleeve. "I want it for you, too. For us. Really."

"Are you sure?" Andrew asked, blue eyes piercing and hard. He added flatly, "You don't seem happy."

"You know me." She smiled brightly. Heart thundering inside like a jackhammer, she thought of how much she cared for this good man, and how frightening and lonely the world would be without him. "I don't show it so well. But I'm with you, all the way. I promise."

He broke into a huge grin. "That's great, honey," he said, digging into his dessert. "But we've still got a lot of thinking to do. Lot of talking to people. Before we decide." He jabbered through a mouthful of cobbler, "After all, this may not be the one. But whatever we do, I've got to have you with me."

"Okay, Congressman," she replied winningly, wondering if they really knew what they were getting into.

As usual that first Sunday in February, James Brackler rose at 5:30 A.M. Glaring briefly at the screaming brown plastic travel alarm, he sighed, recalling the sleep-in mornings of his slothful youth. Then he snapped robotically out of bed. He jumped into a gray-and-burnt orange University of Texas sweatsuit. Then he bolted out for four quick miles of roadwork through the black, hung-over stupor of the Village Apartments, threading his way through parking-lot rows of macho-red Corvettes and baby-blue Datsuns.

James chugged resolutely down Greenville Avenue, careful not to glance toward SMU. As the first sweet pains of running swelled his chest, he recalled that other Sunday morning. Nearly a decade later, his head ached with the memory.

The first rays of September sunlight had stabbed him into consciousness, searing James's slightly concussed skull. Then, far worse than now, every breath was an agony, raking against ribs that had turned a faint purplish color in the night. He had squeezed open one swollen eyelid to survey the shattered ruins of that bizarre night. It had been cold then, too, that autumn morning, with an icy dawn wind that bit into his naked torso. With his muddy underwear tangled around his ankles, James had propped himself up on his elbows. He'd gritted his teeth at the agony in his head, trying to stem the seep of images from the night before. Tricia, recoiling in horror, scratching at him, screaming. Sebastian, shouting, pounding, tearing at his face.

James glanced about. He forced his arms past broken ribs to pull up his pants and hide his shrunken member from the world. Was that a face, behind the window? He rolled into the prickly bushes, gathering his blood-splattered blue shirt around the clawed pads of flesh of his belly and chest and back. Fighting waves of pain and nausea, he staggered out toward the De Soto, still parked at a crazy angle to the sidewalk. He heaved himself into the car, wrenched the key in the ignition. Nothing happened. The idling engine had run out of gas hours before.

It had been the lowest moment of his miserable two decades on the planet: a battered, sickened hulk of a boy collapsed over the steering wheel of a battered, useless automobile. For the moment, neither was going anywhere.

After he got out of the hospital—where he'd told some silly story about getting jumped "by a couple of nigras"—James eased his clothes over stitched ribs, checked his reset nose in the mirror, and crept fearfully back to campus. He quit the job at Hickey's in favor of a similar post farther from school. On campus, he skulked from class to class, carefully avoiding Andrew or Tricia. He did bump into a few of the "in" crowd he'd met at the Welcome Dance. "I'm James Brackler," he would say feebly. "Remember me?" Their blank stares depressed and reassured him, all at once.

If by day James was damply glad they had forgotten him, by night he played that evening over and over again, dreaming of how different it could have been. Lying in the sagging twin bed where he had slept since infancy, he fantasized about Tricia, sobbed at the revulsion he had seen in her eyes, rewrote the scene with a hundred dreamlike endings where she gave herself to him, loved him, and her friends embraced him, too, because they really would like him if only they would let him *in*, and then he wouldn't have to do things the hard way.

Then he would remember the truth, her anger and her fear, and he would grow hard at the thought of her blood-smeared thighs, and he would rub fiercely against the tattered sheets and bite down hard on his pillowcase, until the tender flesh was red and raw and he would convulse in spasms of lust and pain, and imagine it hers. Then he sobbed silently into his sweat-sour pillow, cursing his desire for things that would never be. There was only one consolation.

James had been her first!

He had been shocked and elated and a little terrified by the revelation, by the telltale blood and pain of Tricia's virginity. Surely guys like Andrew only dated girls who put out like gumball machines. But I did it! James Brackler, he of the wrong side of town, was the very first to get into Tricia Farris's pants! It bred in him a new vision. If he could somehow change, start over fresh, maybe there could be another Welcome Dance. Even another Tricia.

Slowly, arduously, James Brackler began to make himself over. He transferred to the University of Texas in Austin, whipping through his final two years of college in only twelve months. He started jogging. He rose early each morning, burning off two or three pounds a week; then he ran to keep it off, jogging and working and slugging his way up into the top 10 percent of his law school class. He left the old James Brackler in Dallas, rebuilding the Plan with hard physical exercise, all-night sessions in the law library, forty hours a week clerking in Senator Talmadge's office in the red granite replica of the U.S. Capitol perched on the banks of the Brazos River. A lawyer by the time his deferment ran out, James automatically rated a captain's rank and the opportunity for soft duty in Washington. He spent his Pentagon years making contacts on the Hill and helping the sons of rich Texas Democrats avoid combat duty in the Mekong Delta. Now, John Masters had set the new James Brackler on the brink of everything he ever wanted.

Breathing hard, James staggered the last few steps across University Drive into the parking lot of the Park-It Markit. He leaned his back against the store's brick wall, inhaling deeply with his head down, staring at the mosaic of blackened chewing gum and aluminum pop-tops on the cement. Then he pumped three quarters into each news box and grabbed the fat Sunday editions.

Half an hour later he burst into his sparsely furnished living room, his face beet red and frozen. Dropping the sweat-soaked newspapers on a coffee table, he collapsed on the floor. He lay on his back against the rough auburn carpet for a full five minutes. Then he began the annoying task of separating all the classifieds and travel sections and movie pages and sports news, so he could immerse himself in the only news that interested him, beginning as always with the Weathervane column in the *Morning News*, where the fishers of men in local politics dangled bright, shiny lures to hook the attentions of others in the trade. What James read there made his heart pound anew:

> Insiders say Andrew Sebastian, son of real estate developer and GOP financier Roger Sebastian, may follow in his father's footsteps and switch parties soon. The younger Sebastian had been thought a likely candidate for Democratic County Chairman or State Representative next fall. Now, sources close to Sebastian said the 31-year-old Democratic activist may switch to the GOP, challenging John Masters in the newly redrawn Fourth Congressional District.

Sebastian! James boosted himself up and went to the telephone, dialing the number by heart.

"Hello," answered Julian Mendoza in a sleepy voice. Mendoza was the congressman's home district press secretary.

"This is Brackler," James barked. "We've got a new opponent."

"James, it's seven-thirty on a Sunday morning!" Mendoza said bitterly. "Can't we deal with this tomorrow?"

"It's Andrew Sebastian."

"Rumor," Mendoza scoffed. "Come on, James. He was a co-chair for our dinner last year."

"Don't count on him for any more contributions," James said sarcastically. "He sent up a trial balloon in today's Weathervane."

"Jesus . . ." Mendoza's visions of an easy reelection skittered away with the last vestiges of sleep. "He could be trouble."

"I know Sebastian," James snapped. "I went to school with him." He rasped a shallow echo of one of Congressman Masters's favorite threats: "We're gonna pinch off his head and shit down his neck, you understand?"

"But all that money!" Mendoza moaned.

"We got more money'n we know what to do with," James said, a curious tinge of anticipation mingling with the dread in his belly. "We don't get the usual Republican sacrificial lamb. So? Downtown'll still go with Masters. We're the incumbent, and we're gonna win."

"He's so young," Mendoza protested, a slight Hispanic whine just audible in his careful diction. "That's *in* right now. Just think how old our guy is going to look, side by side with a pretty boy like Sebastian."

Mendoza had a point, James thought. Masters looked like a withered caricature of the aging Southern pol he had become. They would have to stay off television. No debates. And hire a makeup artist.

"Sebastian's got zero experience," he said, wishing he felt as certain as he sounded. "We'll kill him on that. Besides, I've got that guy's number."

"How so?" Mendoza harbored an abiding belief that all things turned out badly, in the end.

"He's weak," James replied. "No throat instinct. He'll never make it in politics." He had lost track of his old nemesis over the past ten years, though James always kept his spirit close at hand: a talisman for all the defeats and rare, costly victories of his savage youth. "Meet me at the office," he ordered. "Pronto." Mendoza hated it when James mocked his Hispanic origins.

"Sure," Mendoza said coolly. The middle-aged Mexican-American, fifteen years James's senior, had expected to get Joe Cawther's job when Masters's old district manager had gotten cancer. "If it's necessary."

"It's necessary." James smiled. "It's time to start the opposition research file on Andrew Sebastian."

In Austin three days later, James stared moodily at the six-foot blueprint map of Dallas County spread on the long beige table. The room was beige, too, and drab, like all the back rooms of the Texas Capitol: beige linoleum, beige walls, beige straight-backed chairs that knifed into a man's back after five solid hours. The only attempt at decorative relief was a long brown band striped around all four walls, inscribed at ten-inch intervals with dates of great events in Texas history. THE BATTLE OF SAN JACINTO, 1836. TEXAS ANNEXED, 1845. TEXAS JOINS THE CONFEDERACY, 1861. James arched his neck in distraction, idly memorizing the dates for some unforseen occasion when he could impress a constituent by knowing the year of the PETERS COLONY REBELLION.

When his turn came again, James said nothing, just stared down at the map's pale blue boundary lines, squinting at the street names, at the tiny population figures etched in blue below each precinct number. He had never been much at higher mathematics, but he could add votes in his head faster than one of those new Texas Instruments desktop calculators.

Across from James sat two middle-aged legislators in identical gray suits, their enchilada-swollen bellies pressing up against the ragged edge of the flaking, pencil-scarred conference table. Senator Roman Paige, Democrat of Lufkin, chairman of the Texas Senate's Select Committee on Redistricting, looked as though he were about to belch. State Representative Albert Haney, Democrat of Texarkana and chairman of the House's redistricting panel, did so. Loudly.

James jerked his head up at the sound, smirking slightly.

"Excuse me, son," Haney said, bloating his cheeks to swallow another minor gaseous explosion. "Have to tell Rosita to cut back on the jalapeño."

"Senator," James began, wondering when these good ol' boys would stop calling him "son." "Mr. Haney. I think I've got something that will work for everybody."

"What might that be?" Paige said with mild sarcasm.

"If we drop Precincts 1104, 1105, and 2116, that gets rid of Amberton, Haslow, Morton, and Cadillo," James said crisply. His stabbing finger spattered taco grease over the tissue-thin blue paper of the huge map. "We'll keep 1341. We're not worried about Snowdon, he has no following."

"Maybe you weren't listening, son," Haney said menacingly, reaching into his pocket for an antacid tablet. "We ain't moving those precincts into the Seventeenth. Buck Drake would never go for it. Six thousand more black and Mexican votes in his district? He'd never make it through the primary!"

It was the final round of the redistricting process. The game was called Draw the Opponent out of the District. Haney and Paige had been playing it for weeks in this conference room, as nearly two dozen Democratic congressmen begged the legislature to excise precincts containing potential troublemakers and graft them onto neighboring congressional districts. After gutting John Masters's district last December, Haney and Paige had dumped "undesirable" elements from surrounding areas into Masters's district: blacks from South Oak Cliff and Fair Park; unionists from Pleasant Grove; Hispanics in Oak Lawn; Republicans around White Rock Lake and the suburbs. The Fourth District now crawled farther east and south, springing tentacles that coiled out to suck in unfriendly areas, gaping unsightly holes where bordering congressmen had ripped out huge hunks of choice voter flesh.

James understood the party's reasons. In the long run, the seat was untenable for the state's conservative Democratic hierarchy; eventually either the liberals or the Republicans would take it. Masters was due to retire, and the party needed the Fourth's safe votes in neighboring districts.

But James's own political future was now bound up with that of Masters and the Fourth Congressional. The immediate threat was the primary. Half a dozen candidates had lined up to the left of Masters, ready to take advantage of the new boundaries. As the legislature made its final decisions on exactly where the boundaries would fall, block by block, house by house, James's mission was to make sure credible primary opponents were "drawn out" of the district. Whatever it took.

It was taking a lot. Paige and Haney were at great pains to let James know: they did not like dealing with an underling. Still, James and the congressman had worked out a strategy, and James was determined to stick to it.

"Those two colored boxes will have to stay," Paige said fiercely. "Drake doesn't want more nigras. That's final."

"The same goes for Cadillo and his precinct," Haney added triumphantly, knowing the party would back them on this. The minorities stayed in the Fourth. That was final.

"We'll even agree to keep Morton and his union people in 1105," James pleaded desperately. "I've already agreed to take Snowdon and the homeowner nuts in 1341. But we can't handle that much minority vote, plus Snowdon and Morton."

"You'll have to," Paige snapped back. "What's John been doing for twelve terms, if he can't hold his own seat?"

It was time for James to play his final card. "I probably shouldn't be telling you this," he said, voice low and ominous. Paige and Haney sat forward, knowing full well they were about to hear the real reason for this meeting.

"The congressman is tired," James continued, sotto voce. "He is not interested in fighting on so many different fronts in the primary, then fighting another battle against the Republicans next fall."

Each legislator gave that politician's nod that comprehends, without committing to agree.

"Congressman Masters will not take on the white liberals, Snowdon and Morton"—James paused, holding up two fingers on one hand for dramatic effect—"and the minorities, Amberton, Haslow, and Cadillo." He ticked off these three on his other hand. "He will, if forced, take on one group or the other, preferably Snowdon and Morton. He's sick of dealing with minorities."

"What do you mean?" Paige, intrigued, rolled a cigar between pudgy fingers.

"If you insist on leaving all five of these troublemakers in our district"—James leaned his broad shoulders forward boldly—"the congressman will retire now, and endorse Willie Haslow as his successor. And Dallas will have its first black congressman."

A shocked silence filled the room. Paige paused in the act of lighting his cigar, letting the match burn out without touching the fat brown tip. "Bullshit," he said calmly, fumbling in his shirt pocket for another match. "That's about like Curtis LeMay endorsing Jane Fonda for U.S. Senate. This meeting is over."

"Listen, Senator!" James cried loudly. "You cut Haslow and the rest out, or have lunch with 'em at the Congressional Club next year. Understand?" He knew he had overplayed his hand, but their smugness was more than he could handle.

"I tell you what we're gonna do, boy," Haney said, his tone dark and somber. He cast a concerned glance at his colleague, whose face was reddening behind the white haze of cigar smoke. "We're gonna take a break now. You're gonna go outside and sit on a hard wooden bench, and learn some manners. Then we'll start over, for John Masters's sake, and see if we can resolve this like gentlemen."

Two hours later James strode exultantly into the lobby of Austin's venerable Driskill Hotel, adjusting his eyes to the perpetual gloom. This must be where they coined the phrase "lobbyist," he thought, peering through the darkness to pick out familiar faces at the huge black oak bar. A couple of arm twisters and two—no, three—legislators looked up from their respective huddles and waved the standard halfhearted flips that signaled only recognition, and not necessarily friendship, in Austin's oldest and most popular political watering hole.

James hustled upstairs, up the creaking elevator, down the faded red carpet of the labyrinth hallways, to his room with the window facing out on a brick wall. The room had the faded elegance of a grand hotel gone to seed. It also held the telephone James coveted and, at the other end of the line, an impatient congressman.

"Well?" Masters demanded with a cough.

"It worked," James said, still out of breath. "Exactly like you said."

"Well?"

"They were real pissed off that you sent me. As predicted," he said excitedly, collapsing on the bed. "I gave 'em your ultimatum, and they made me sit outside. Then I went back in, and they did just what you said they'd do."

"They kicked your ass," the congressman rasped with relief. "Taught you a lesson."

"You bet," James said in triumph. "They told me Amberton and Haslow and Cadillo were staying in the Fourth. Period. Then, right before they kicked me out, they said I was a little shit, and they didn't understand why John Masters was sending a boy to do a man's work, but as a favor to you, they'd draw Snowdon and Morton out of the district. Just the two of them—I mean, their houses! You won't believe the crazy map we drew. Two tiny little fingers, one street wide, sticking right into the middle of East Dallas. I liked to die laughing."

"We got the blacks and the Mexicans, who don't mean shit." The congressman chuckled. "Instead of Snowdon, who could kill us, and Morton, who's got the unions. That's a good day's work. We just won the primary. Go downstairs and let the lobby buy you a drink."

"Yes, sir." James smiled, thinking of Br'er Rabbit and the briar patch, and how much he admired the crusty old Uncle Remus at the other end of the line.

5

ndrew, in dusty blue jeans and faded denim shirt, leaned over the bright metal Pearl Beer keg and pumped the handle. The heat-reflective aluminum scorched his sweaty palm. The heat was stifling, insufferable, incinerating: as it is every day of every summer in the Lone Star State. Andrew took the judge's empty plastic cup and held it under the spigot to catch a few ounces of pale yellow drizzle. The beer puddled in a wad of spiritless foam, barely covering the base of the politician's cup. Judge Hansen accepted the dregs gratefully. His vaguely pompous sunburned jowls quivered as he spoke: "How's it feel to be the only other man in the county fool enough to run on our ticket?"

"Feels great," Andrew said without hesitation. "Besides, you and I aren't so alone. You may even get some help down at the Commissioner's Court next year."

"Mebbe," Judge Hansen said doubtfully. Hansen wasn't a real robes-and-gavel-type courtroom judge. The only Republican in county government, Hansen technically ruled over the political-hack circus of the County Commissioner's

Court and Sheriff's Department and Tax Collector-Assessor's Office, and all the other Democratic strongholds of the turreted Old Red Courthouse overlooking Dealey Plaza and the grassy knoll downtown. The tall, stentorian-voiced county judge rather liked his distinction as the lone Republican at the courthouse.

Politician that he was, Hansen put it more politely to Andrew. "I'd give up all the local races just to get you into Congress." In Washington, the judge thought wryly. Where you can't muddy up the water I drink. "How's it looking?"

The bantering tone was gone; the judge wanted a serious assessment. Andrew dropped his voice and launched into his standard insider spiel about his race against Masters, mindful that the bar association's Fourth of July barbecue at Rock Creek Park was packed with Democrats.

There are dozens of political barbecues in Texas every summer. But there is only one Rock Creek Barbecue. The bizarre tribal ritual of local politics has two distinctive features. First, like the exclusive top-floor dining clubs perched in each of the tallest buildings downtown, the Rock Creek Barbecue admits no women into its citadel. One lady politician, a city council member from Irving, had been ejected last year by off-duty sheriff's deputies after she was caught sneaking into weedy old Rock Creek Park dressed in a man's business suit: a dead giveaway among the pols in Levi's jeans squatting on the edges of weatherbeaten pale green picnic tables.

The no-women rule exists to protect the barbecue's second and most celebrated tradition. Every year, as beer flowed freely and bladders filled to bursting, judges and lawyers and senators and precinct captains would strut grandly to the dry, poison-ivy-choked gully known as Rock Creek. Then they would pee majestically into the dust fifteen feet below, neutralizing the acid of last year's political grudges as their urine mingled in the spirit of togetherness on the way down. It is the kind of pointless, barbaric, ornery tradition Texans love. Andrew wondered if, year after year, all these old pros looked forward as much as he did to pissing on the creek bed.

"It's going good, Judge," Andrew said with heartfelt enthusiasm. "Masters can't run against me the way he ran against the minorities last spring."

"I've never seen a dirtier campaign." Hansen led them away from the buzzsaw babble of lawyers and cicadas, to a quiet clearing by a cement barbecue pit. There, stuck in a big cool dark green trash

73

can full of ice, a fresh beer keg was just beginning to draw a few hardy prospectors. The florid, statesmanlike county official stooped and did the honors, filling Andrew's cup to the brim. "Sending literature to Mexican neighborhoods that looked like it came from Cadillo, featuring Juan as the Friend of the Negro," he said sadly. "Same thing in black boxes with Amberton. I never realized how much the Mexicans and the blacks had it in for each other. Somebody on Masters's team sure had it all figured out."

Andrew changed the subject. "Masters is going to endorse the president," he said quickly, quietly.

"No."

"Yep," Andrew said, eyes sparkling. "Masters is feeling the heat, Judge. McGovern's going to hurt him."

"Have you endorsed the president, Andy?" The judge's clever eyes narrowed to two shrewd olive-green slits.

"I'll tell you what . . ." Andrew clapped Hansen on the shoulder and stared him seriously in the eyes. He needed to end this on a positive note. "Next time you see the president, you tell him this," he said, trying to push Tommy Butler from his thoughts. "The minute he ends the war, I'll back him one hundred percent."

The judge smiled broadly and moved away toward the western-shirted politicians' backs along the creek. "You tell him, Andy," Hansen called. He flapped one big hand loosely in Sebastian's direction. "I got a feeling you'll be in Washington soon."

Andrew sighed in relief, wondering if the judge had asked about Nixon because he wanted to know where Andrew stood or just to find out how well Andrew handled the tough ones.

"Andrew!"

Sebastian whirled to run smack into John Masters, knocking the elderly man's beer out of one liver-spotted hand. The plastic cup smacked into the hard-packed dirt, splashing amber liquid on the congressman's expensive rattlesnake boots.

"Jesus—" Andrew cringed, his face a shade redder than the August heat warranted. "Oh, Jesus."

"Call me John." The old man smiled. Masters glanced over his shoulder, where a younger, beefier man scurried to keep pace with Masters's feisty piston legs. Masters barked quickly at his shadow: "Get me another beer. Andrew?"

Andrew glanced at his own empty cup. "That would be great. I really apologize, Congressman."

"Call me John," the old man repeated emphatically. Masters steered his aide toward Andrew's outstretched hand.

The big man snatched the plastic cup wordlessly, eyes smoldering above the dark jaw. It took Sebastian's scattered mind a minute to realize: I know that face. The features were modestly thinner; the body fitter, stronger. But the eyes still burned with some unquenchable indignation. The congressman's gravelly voice broke in, "Andrew, my district manager, James Brackler." They shook hands awkwardly, two quarreling schoolboys forced by the principal to make up.

"We've met," Andrew said, staring with frank amazement at Brackler's new physique. The former college outcast now seemed capable, sure of himself. "We went to SMU together. At the same time," Andrew corrected himself quickly.

"I'll get the beer," James said dully. He stalked over to the keg, shielding his eyes from the glittering white flashes of sunlight bouncing off the silver barrel.

The congressman's stooped figure doubled suddenly in a fit of laughter or coughing, Andrew wasn't sure which. "Let's get out of the sun," Andrew said abruptly. He grasped a skinny elbow and towed the old man's frail figure to a crowded picnic table under a hail-beaten tin awning.

Out of breath, the congressman nodded, absently shaking a few passing hands. They found an empty bench and sat down on the prickly peeling paint.

"Saw your wife at the Daughters of the Texas Revolution," Masters said. "Still pretty as ever."

"Yes, sir," Andrew said dutifully. He remembered how Tricia, who once liked Masters, had exploded upon hearing who was running the old man's campaign. When it came to James Brackler, they didn't believe in coincidences. As it turned out, Brackler had been employed by Masters for years. Besides, SMU was a lifetime ago. Andrew would never forgive James Brackler, but they were all different people now. Or so he told Tricia.

James pumped bitterly at the keg, watching his boss chatting happily at the picnic table with his worst enemy. To James's envious eyes, Andrew had not altered a bit. The tousled brown hair was a little longer, perhaps: this was the seventies. But it still held the same annoying glints of gold, the kind they airbrush on male models in after-shave ads. Nothing else had changed. The smooth, unlined

75

good looks, the flash of white teeth, the bright blue eyes setting off the smooth tan: even in faded jeans and tattered blue cotton work-shirt rolled up at the sleeves, Andrew exuded a casual elegance that set him apart from the sweaty political hacks jabbering and slapping backs under the awning.

Juggling three cups of beer, James hurried toward Masters and Sebastian, spilling great gobs of white foam along the way. He paused behind them.

"I want this to be a clean campaign, Andrew," Masters rasped. "I know you'll work hard and fight fair. We'll do the same."

"Yes, sir," Andrew said, meaning it. "And if you'll just agree to debate me?"

"I don't know about that." Masters smiled slyly. "I don't want to get on television with a good-lookin' Boy Scout like you. But I do want us to still be friends when this is over."

Eavesdropping, James felt a hot iron in his stomach. He had spent the past three months trying to convince Masters to take a tougher line against Sebastian. Masters had forbidden it, insisting on the standard campaign tactic of incumbent politicians: Ignore the Opposition. The congressman was not about to end his career with a smear campaign against Roger Sebastian's son.

"Here you go!" James announced shrilly. Mustering a grim smile, he pushed between them to set the trio of beers on the flaking wooden planks.

"Thank you," Andrew said, suddenly sans charisma. He rose awkwardly to his feet. "Good talking to you, John."

Andrew strode into the crowd. Masters tallied the quick, firm handshakes Sebastian received from his former Democratic comrades: a little chummy for Masters's taste. The old man cocked his head perceptively at James. "There bad blood between you two?"

"A little," James admitted, smirking brightly. "We were, ah, on the football team together at school. We didn't get along."

"You keep that out of this," the congressman said sharply. "You'll be up against Sebastian yourself in two years. But as long as my name's on the ballot, I don't want any rough stuff."

James nodded, anger flushing his face.

"Unless things change, of course," Masters added thoughtfully, wondering how long he could sustain the huge lead his polls were showing. "You never can tell."

✳ ✳ ✳

By the cooler afternoons of mid-October, the storefront office down the street from the old Lakewood Theater bustled with Sebastian volunteers. They folded and stuffed and licked and stamped, glancing subconsciously at the big handmade wooden clock in the shape of the state of Texas to watch time run out before the November 8 election. Tricia had been there since they opened the headquarters the previous summer, supervising the eager hordes that surged into the remodeled beauty salon in greater numbers each day as the Sebastian effort caught fire.

Tricia hated the long days among metal trash bins and gray desks, organizing phone banks and neighborhood walks, orchestrating mass mailings, recruiting more and more volunteers to recruit more and more volunteers. Some days she didn't see how they could lose; surely every voter in East Dallas had enlisted in "Andy's Army." I ought to know, Tricia thought. I'm the quartermaster general.

She finished the list for her next Safeway run: twenty red felt-tipped markers, a box of lapel stickers, three cases of Diet Pepsi. She didn't mind the routine labor. It was being the Candidate's Wife that grated on her, smiling that idiotic smile for hours on end, until her cheeks hurt and she wanted to go home and frown her head off.

"Mrs. Sebastian?"

Tricia looked up to see two girls in SMU sweaters and sorority pins. One was a Tri Delt, she noted with satisfaction. Both girls wore silly straw hats with Sebastian bumper stickers wrapped crookedly around the crown.

"Yes?" Tricia smiled stupidly, as if she had no idea why they were there. Mrs. Sebastian just wasn't ready to go into her hello-and-welcome routine.

"We're done with our route," Tri Delt chirped enthusiastically, unloading armloads of literature and walk cards and small slips of paper telling the canvassers what to say at each door. "We met some really sweet people."

"Not many Republicans," the other said disapprovingly. She added with pride, "We argued with some folks, but they seemed set on Masters."

Tricia sighed inwardly. When would these airheads learn that the walks were just to identify Sebastian voters and not to rile up the opposition? Then she remembered how long it had taken her to grasp all of this and smiled her best volunteer smile.

"Girls, you have done just terrific," she said, shuffling the canvass cards to see they had missed two-thirds of their route. "Andrew will be so pleased. Can you work tomorrow?" She despised ever having to ask people for more than they had to give.

Tri Delt hesitated, thinking of impending midterms and a sort-of date with that swimmer.

"We really need you," Tricia said quickly, turning the screws. She really did need the bimbos, now that someone else would have to go out and finish their rotten little precinct.

"We can make it," Best Friend answered, elbowing Tri Delt. "Anything for Andy. Uh, Mr. Sebastian. Ma'am." The girls waved good-bye to the blue-haired Republican ladies clustered around the worktables.

The veterans nodded absently, their trembling withered hands dancing well-rehearsed steps over the piles of glossy red-white-and-blue campaign flyers with that sappy mug shot Andrew hated. Bold type bannered: SEBASTIAN. THE INDEPENDENT CHOICE.

Tricia looked up at the white alarm clock on her desk and sighed. Second shift, she thought. She rose to begin making her rounds of the volunteer tables. When she'd finished thanking each soldier, she walked wearily back past the borrowed Xerox machine to the campaign manager's office. She tapped on the door and poked her head in, smiling genuinely for the first time that day.

Ron Callahan's tie flew at half-mast, one shirttail hanging out over baggy trousers. As always, he looked like a pile of dirty laundry alongside the trim figure of his boss.

But for a few gentlemanly wrinkles in his tailor-made powder-blue Oxford shirt, Andrew looked just as he had at six-thirty that morning, before breakfast with two black Baptist ministers and the drive back to Lakewood in her silver Buick to pick up Tricia and help her fire up the morning shift at headquarters. Andrew could not drive the Mercedes while campaigning; congressmen had to buy American. Then it was brownies and Hi-C punch at the Casa Linda Republican Women's Club and chicken-fried steak with the Garland Rotary, and the three o'clock shift change at the Neuhoff meat packing plant, and a door-to-door trek through eighteen winding blocks of hilly Lake Highlands. Plus this meeting with Ron to go over the new survey, about which Tricia was dying to hear in detail. But there absolutely wasn't time.

"Let's go," Tricia said briskly. "Fund-raising reception downtown at six, then the Hispanic banquet at seven. But we can be late."

"Aren't we always?" Andrew grinned. "Ron, tell her." She slipped inside eagerly and pressed the door shut.

Callahan's slightly pudgy frame bobbed up and down uncontrollably on his swivel chair. At twenty-nine the transplanted Boston politician looked forty, his hair and face gray from the ten years of work he'd invested in this campaign alone. Of all the people Tricia knew in politics, she liked the beer-drinking, thoroughly déclassé Callahan the most.

"It's too good to believe," Callahan said, using one cigarette to light another. Tricia ached for her Winstons. Andrew had made her quit when the surgeon general's warning came out. "Two weeks ago, Masters had fifty-two percent to our twenty. Since we went back on television with the new spots, we're up to thirty-eight. Masters is steady at around fifty."

"We could come close," Andrew enthused. "Really close."

"It's all television," Callahan said, swiveling back around to flip through the yellow survey sheets. "Voters just plain like Andrew. They feel a younger man will do a better job. Among women, we're actually leading Masters by over five points. But we're hurting with men."

"Vietnam," Andrew said ruefully. "My fault, that one." Early in September Andrew had been asked at a VFW meeting whether he believed in amnesty for Vietnam draft dodgers. Certainly not, Andrew had replied. Never, unless they agreed to come back from Canada and serve in the armed services. Or perhaps, he'd ad-libbed, draft resisters could be required to do a couple of years of public service. Looking at the cold blank faces beneath the blue sergeant's caps, Andrew knew he had said the wrong thing.

In the next day's paper, Masters's response was crisp and effective: "No, I do not support my opponent's proposal to give amnesty to draft card burners after two years working at some national park. I don't think the mothers of boys who died for their country support that, either." The *Morning News* had crucified Andrew, calling him "young, naive, and irresponsible"—and, ouch—"the draft dodger's best friend."

The worst had been Elma Butler's icy voice over the phone, piercing through Andrew's I-was-quoted-out-of-context denials. "How could you?" Tommy's widow had cried in anguish, evoking guilty memories of Andrew's best friend. Tommy Butler had only wanted to laugh and dance and screw his way through life. Instead,

Andrew thought, he had been slaughtered with sixty thousand other guys by that prick in the White House.

"The amnesty thing is eating us alive," Callahan said flatly. He squinted through a cloud of smoke at the computerized figures. "But Vietnam is a big part of your popularity with women. They want out, and they think guys like you can get our boys home."

"They're right," Andrew said seriously, jaw tight.

"Before you bring peace to the land, we need to raise some money at the Petroleum Club," Tricia said dryly. "You've got twenty volunteers to thank before we can leave."

Andrew worked the ladies quickly, efficiently, leaving each aglow. This was the part he liked best, the simple, rewarding task of making people happy. He praised the attention-starved old ladies on their progress, asked after their grandchildren by name, gave them the quick sugar cube of pride they had slogged all afternoon to earn. Tricia literally dragged him out the front door. The volunteers glared jealously, despising her monopoly on their hero.

He chattered excitedly the whole way home, up the front walk between the white columns, through the front door with its massive brass gargoyle knocker. The monologue echoed with their footsteps on the hardwood steps, past the lacquered Oriental furniture and dark green walls of a home that was a mirror of their marriage: beautiful to admire, uncomfortable to inhabit. Andrew recounted anecdotes about the people he'd met, the hundred tiny victories and defeats of a politician's day. Tricia smiled thinly at the punch lines, chuckling when he mimicked all those petty local kingpins he knew by heart and she could never quite place. The whole time she was thinking, Will it always be like this?

Back in college, Tricia had loved the idea of being the wife of Andrew Sebastian, Famous Politician. But the roller coaster turned out to be a ribbon of endless highway across a flat prairie where the faces and names changed, but the routine was always the same. She was with Andrew constantly: at headquarters, at the receptions and rallies and photo sessions. But they were never really together. Even now, as they whirled through another runway-model's wardrobe change, Andrew was miles away. Planning his next moves. Whom he needed to see tonight. What he ought to say.

"You look great," he said automatically. He stood behind her in the mirror, his hands touching the cool blue silk of her cocktail dress.

"So do you." Tricia squirmed out of his grasp, trying to control the revulsion she always felt at being held too tightly. She spun to face him, picked at the perfectly straight knot in his burgundy tie, flicking an imaginary speck from the lapel of the navy suit she'd bought him at Neiman's.

"We match," Andrew said, holding her clumsily in his arms again, blue on blue. She wriggled free and grabbed a hairbrush.

"Your hair is perfect," he mouthed in her mirror, a tiny glint in his clear blue eyes. Tricia was surprised to find herself liking that. He still noticed her, wanted her. His lips bent down, caressing her long, warm neck.

"Andrew," she objected mildly, fidgeting nervously with her shoulder pads. "I'm trying to get dressed."

"I'm working on the opposite," he declared softly, toying with her zipper.

All of a sudden she thought, Why not? For once, just leap into it! Like a swimmer who knows the water is freezing, Tricia took three steps and dove in, and was surprised to find that her heart didn't stop.

"Hey!" Andrew was taken aback as she whirled and stripped the green malachite studs off the pleated front of his starched white tuxedo shirt. "I thought we had to go."

"We do," she mumbled, yanking off her own suit jacket with one hand as the other pulled his shirt away from his broad chest. But for a small trickle of hair down the middle, the muscles of Andrew's chest were bare and taut. They rippled subtly up his rib cage as he raised his arms in bemused surrender, allowing her free rein to unhook the forest-green cummerbund. Her face industrious and grim, Tricia had their clothes off in seconds. Andrew stood in astonished silence as she stripped him to his white skivvies. Tricia stood back in her tight black brassiere and lace panties, appraising his well-sculpted body in the awkwardness of the brightly lit bathroom. She felt a chill down her spine, a blend of shivering fear and sexual excitement and the icy tile against the bottoms of her feet. Then she stretched her palms toward him and ran them down his chest. How strong and comforting and hard he was.

Closing her eyes, she moved to him. Her fingers slithered down his sides, noting the way his waist still tucked in, slim and firm, before it reached the hard buttocks. She hooked her fingers in the taut band of his underwear and slipped them down to his knees. She still couldn't bring herself to look at his private parts. She could feel him pulsing upward now, warm and trembling and scary against the pointed, straining nipples of her cool breasts.

Andrew stumbled to his knees on the bathroom floor.

"No," she said, shivering a little. She cupped his ears in her hands, drew him unsteadily back to his feet. He kicked the white shorts off with one foot and followed her, naked, mute, painfully erect.

They fell on each other in the bristly shag carpet. Andrew probed at her with his fingers first, giving her time. She pulled urgently at his flanks. He arched his body above hers, planting his knees on the thick mint rug, spreading her thighs with his hands. She grappled his chest with her arms and sucked his torso down to her own, feeling strange and disembodied, as though this were some other woman lying here on the carpet with her bra still lashed tight and the yellow glow streaming in from the open bathroom door, etching the firm round curve of Andrew's butt, swelling cold and smooth like a Greek statue, gyrating up and down as she bit deep into his shoulder and held back the tears and felt him filling her inside.

Later, she would wonder why. The quickness of it all, giving her no time for dread? The fact they were sprawled on the floor, his heels thumping into the bottom of her cedar closet? Whatever the reason, she felt a rocket explode inside her, for the first time ever, shattering up between her legs to transmit fiery shock waves through her chest and arms and thighs and head.

Then, before she could lock into the shuddering sensation, Tricia felt his lukewarm ooze leaking out of her onto the carpet, and she realized how awfully trapped she had become and how dirty and unpleasant and oppressive it really was.

She wriggled furiously from beneath him. There was a sickening plop between her thighs. Then she ran into the bathroom and slammed the door, leaving Andrew confused and hurt and wondering what exactly he had done wrong.

Julian Mendoza ran one thick brown hand through his wiry salt-and-pepper hair. It was saltier than ever now and starting to fall out. Thanks to the ogre perched on the edge of Mendoza's desk, across the cluttered office on the eighth floor of the Earle Cabell Federal Building in downtown Dallas. Every month, Julian's wife measured the distance from his left eyebrow to his hairline, to prove to him that it wasn't really receding. But Julian knew better. It was all Brackler's fault. Mendoza looked up at him blankly, trying to remember the last time he'd seen a bald Mexican.

"Well?" Brackler demanded.

Mendoza, on his knees among the reams of computer printouts, shrugged helplessly. "We've dropped since September," he said, wondering where he would find another job in politics at his age. "Sebastian's up a lot. Fifteen points, maybe more."

James bored in, "The demographics?"

"The blacks are voting straight Democrat, or planning not to vote." Mendoza pushed at his black horn-rimmed glasses until they hurt the bridge of his nose. "We're winning among union voters, and white men as a whole. But Sebastian's killing us with women and independents. And young people."

James stood up and hitched his pants, stretching with a loud groan. It was time to get dressed for the banquet. "Sounds like everybody's made up their minds, except—"

"The barrio." Mendoza felt a twinge of ulcer as he regarded the printouts. "No doubt about it. Whoever gets the Hispanic vote wins. And they're all waiting to see what Cadillo does."

"The Mexicans were supposed to be your problem," James berated him. "You were supposed to fuckin' lean on him!"

"You left a lot of bad blood," Mendoza shot back. "The Cadillos believe in revenge, man. It's all I can do to keep Juan from coming out for Sebastian."

"For a Republican?" James bellowed incredulously.

"It's not Republicans and Democrats," Julian said, shaking his head at Brackler's insensitivity. "It's pride. Old man Cadillo told me to my face: 'John Masters treated my son like a dog in the primary.' Even the congressman thinks you went too far."

"He didn't object when I won the primary for him," James snapped. There was a hostile silence while tempers cooled. Then James spoke again in measured tones, remembering how much he needed Mendoza to get Mexican votes for future Brackler campaigns.

"I'm sorry, Julian." James shook his bearlike head from side to side. "It's just. . . ." He paused, taking a deep breath. He hated having to eat shit like this. "The pressure. My first big campaign. Okay?"

"Sure, Jim," Mendoza said dully, picking at the dandruff that plagued his burly shoulders. He tried to wear light-colored jackets so it wouldn't show, but the Hispanic Chamber banquet was black tie. He had changed too early: his dark satin lapels were already covered with tiny white hailstones. "The word is, Juan Cadillo is going to endorse Sebastian tonight," he added damply.

"He couldn't pick a better time," James mused. "The press'll be there. Be tough for us to reverse momentum before election day. We've gotta head this off." He wrapped his purplish paisley tie mindlessly around his fingers. "What do I tell old man Cadillo tonight? I'm meeting him at the hotel before the banquet," he added casually.

"Goddammit, James!" Mendoza protested. "You should have told me. Does Cadillo know it's you he's meeting with? Or does he think the congressman will be there?"

"The congressman told me to handle it," James admitted. "He decided not to make the trip down just for this."

The two aides stared at each other, wondering why they were working so hard to elect an ornery old politician too lazy to fly home and save his ass three weeks before election day. James shifted his gaze to the shiny congressional calendar on the wall, with its red-leafed October view of the Jefferson Memorial. Sighing, he stepped carefully over the pale green computer sheets. "You're no help," he said, not looking over his shoulder. "There isn't anything Cadillo wants?"

"Yeah." Mendoza laughed bitterly. "He wants his son to be a congressman."

James halted in the doorway. "Yeah," he said softly.

Mendoza saw James staring down at him intently. What was the arrogant Anglo thinking? James ran quickly into his own more spacious office. And shut the door behind him.

"No." The congressman's reedy voice was firm over the WATS line. "Absolutely not."

"What do you care?" James blurted. He was tired of fighting with his hands tied behind his back. "This could lock it up for us. After that, Cadillo's my problem." Rebuked by a long silence, he took a deep breath. "I'm sorry." He spoke hurriedly. "I was out of line. But if Juan endorses Sebastian tonight, we could be facing a disaster."

"For me, or you?" Masters put in none too gently.

"For us!" James said urgently. "Trust me. I won't promise. I'll just imply it."

There was a pause on the line. John Masters always did enjoy a good compromise. "Your implications are your own business," he croaked slowly, spacing each ambiguous word. "But I warn you, this will come back to haunt you."

"I'll cross that bridge when I come to it," James said confidently. The congressman hung up on him in midcliché.

"I can't tell the waiters from the guests," Tricia whispered caustically into Andrew's ear as they took their places, rolling her eyes at the tuxedoed diners seated around the blue-and-green-carpeted ballroom.

"Shhh," Andrew said coldly, embarrassed. "These people are friends."

Tricia ignored the reproof, sipping more cool white wine. She strained hopelessly to catch sight of anyone she really knew, as opposed to the five hundred total strangers to whom she nightly exclaimed: "So good to see you again!"

It was strange, really. When she first glimpsed him, Tricia felt the normal little kick of recognition one always feels when encountering an old acquaintance. When it finally came to her, his name and how she knew him, it was like stubbing her toe. Wham, her foot would smack into a chair leg. There was a pause while she thought, Damn, that's gonna hurt. Then the pain folded over her.

She tugged at Andrew's sleeve. "I know," he said quietly. "Just try to forget it."

"Okay," Tricia said shakily. She was glad the room was dark, the program under way. She nodded and smiled, picked at the limp lettuce and watery chicken. But all she could think about was that night, and there he was, my God, sitting right there at that table. She had a fleeting fantasy of standing up and demanding the spotlight. When it streaked away from the podium and blazed on her, she would thrust an accusing arm at Brackler: "He raped me!" And two stout, honest, hardworking, Catholic Mexican family men in black tie would grab Brackler and drag him out the—

"This is it!" Andrew's excited whisper knifed into her reverie. He grabbed her thin wrist, squeezing until her eight-carat diamond bracelet cut into her skin. Andrew's gaze never flinched from the podium, where a tall, toothy young man with wispy sideburns stooped to address the microphone.

"Thank you!" Juan Cadillo showed an even bigger flash of white teeth in his olive face, clasping a plaque above his head like a prizefighter. He began formally, "To receive this award is the fulfillment of a great dream."

Twenty feet away, James Brackler mopped the sweat from his forehead with his Thousand Island–smeared napkin, the uncertainty wearing on him. Catching sight of Tricia Sebastian hadn't helped. For a second there, he had this crazy premonition that she was going to leap up and holler rape. He shook it off, trying to concentrate on young Cadillo's rococo oration. How his candidacy for Congress, while not victorious, had been a major step for Dallas Hispanics. How he wanted to thank his mother, his brothers, his supporters. Come on! James thought, drumming his fingers impatiently on the tablecloth. Thank God they had started the speeches with the salad. Otherwise they'd have missed getting this on the evening news.

"In watching this general election campaign," Cadillo droned on, "I've learned a lot about a man who's here tonight: Andrew Sebastian."

Tricia put her arm around Andrew, patting his shoulder reassuringly. Coming face to face with James for the first time since college, she felt abruptly suffused with love for her husband's intense face.

"He's going to do it!" she hissed, wanting Andrew to know that she was on his side, that maybe tonight was something they could build on, that she was aware and involved and knew why they had come here.

"Wait," Andrew said tensely, struggling to keep his expectations down.

Cadillo broke the stagy pause, speaking directly to Sebastian. "Andrew," he said hesitatingly, "you are a fine man. But I cannot endorse you."

Andrew let out his breath in a quiet whistle.

"John Masters has been a good friend to our community," Cadillo continued haltingly, looking terribly unsure of himself. "And as a Democrat . . ." He looked again to his father. Manuel Cadillo sat oblivious, cut from stone.

Cadillo continued, "I have decided, *we* have decided, to endorse Congressman Masters for reelection. John Masters supports our dreams. He has personally assured us," Juan ad-libbed, pleased to see his father nodding in agreement, "that he will work actively to promote Hispanic candidates at all levels. Including the United States Congress!" He was improvising freely now, finding that he rather enjoyed it. Averting his eyes from Andy Sebastian's crestfallen face, he clasped his hands over his head and stared hard at the back of the ballroom, smiling and nodding at the crowd's ovation.

"What happened?" Tricia whispered loudly.

"I can't believe it," Andrew replied, stunned. "Old man Cadillo called just four hours ago to say Juan would endorse me. He's not the kind of man to go back on his word."

"Masters got to him?" Tricia asked, a little frightened at how quickly she was beginning to comprehend all of this.

"You bet," Andrew growled, jumping to his feet angrily. "That bastard. Masters offered him the only thing I can't give! Why didn't I figure that?"

Andrew practically pulled Tricia's arm out of its socket as he yanked her through the crowd, ignoring the proffered handshakes. Tricia's last glimpse of the dais revealed Brackler bounding up the steps to congratulate the Cadillos. Tricia wondered, What does *he* look so worried about?

By election day, the Sebastian trend had reversed itself. Hispanic leaders were falling neatly in line behind the incumbent, and things were breaking Masters's way.

If money is the mother's milk of politics, momentum is the spank on the bottom that brings victory to life. Voters get caught up on the bandwagon. The media accelerates its speed and direction, exaggerates its impact. On November 8, momentum indicated a big win for John Masters.

Still, election day spirits were high at Sebastian headquarters. The party spilled into the parking lot of the Lakewood Theater, Andy's Army mingling freely with the teenage couples streaming out of an early-evening showing of *The Godfather*. Grinning volunteers milled around with white paper cups of beer and wine, eating potato chips and watching the assortment of TV sets that sat atop cardboard boxes marked VOTER LISTS and WALK PACKETS.

As dictated by both tradition and common sense, the candidate was secreted with his wife in the campaign manager's office, watching returns on Ron Callahan's little black-and-white. Callahan was doing the play-by-play. Andrew did color commentary. Tricia had been there for hours, her stomach curled in knots that she tried to untie with the lukewarm bottle of Gallo Chablis on Callahan's desk. The glamorous world of politics, she thought, draining another Styrofoam cup of the sickly-sweet stuff.

The voice of the TV announcer droned on, "From early results just in, we now predict that the president will carry Texas."

"Wow, stop the presses," Callahan cracked.

Andrew nodded. "Can you imagine Texas going for McGovern?" The candidate propped his feet on Callahan's desk and rocked backward dangerously.

"Quiet," snapped Tricia, leaning over to adjust the volume: "There, challenger Andrew Sebastian is running suprisingly strong. With two percent of the vote counted, Sebastian has fifty-six percent of the vote to forty-four for the incumbent."

Tricia jumped up, screaming, "My God! Fifty-six percent!"

"Ssh," Callahan hissed. "Let's find out where the votes are from. Probably our boxes up by White Rock Lake. Those come in early."

The news anchor's counterpart cut in, "What's interesting there, Bob, is that President Nixon has only fifty percent of the vote counted so far in that district. It's very early, but John Masters could be in for a long night."

"Now that," Callahan said, "is interesting. We're running six points ahead of Nixon." He snatched the phone off the hook. "Hello?"

"Who is it?" Tricia demanded, wondering if Callahan could see through the calm set of Andrew's jaw. Aren't we cool tonight? she thought, noting the way her outwardly placid husband quietly tore little chunks of Styrofoam away from the rim of his cup.

"Okay," Callahan said quickly, flipping open a notebook full of precinct numbers with columns of blank space. Each blank column was marked at the top: AS. JM.

"Precinct 1503, got it." Callahan began scribbling furiously. "Sebastian 385. Masters 322. Precinct 1541. Sebastian 325. Masters 391."

"Who is he talking to?" Tricia asked. The confusion was making her shrewish.

"We've got a guy downtown," Andrew said distractedly, not removing his eyes from the figures marching steadily down Callahan's notebook. "He'll call in every five minutes with new numbers, as the county releases them. This way, we know which precincts the figures are coming from. That's all that matters."

Callahan hung up the phone and began punching a calculator.

"Well?" Andrew said quietly. "Do we have a chance?"

"Yeah," Callahan wheezed, his pudgy fingers flashing across the Texas Instruments desk model. "We have a chance."

The Masters campaign had taken the penthouse suite at the Adolphus Hotel, its curved Palladian windows flanked by the huge stone gargoyles of the hotel roof. A pale, elderly waiter cowered in the far corner of the room, unsure whether he should approach these busy, shouting men or wait for them to come to him.

"Damn!" James slammed down the phone. He shoved a yellow legal pad across the desk. "We're already a thousand votes behind," he lamented. "Eight hundred votes behind McGovern."

Masters surveyed the precinct list. "Mostly boxes along Central," the old solon pondered. "College vote. I thought we had those people."

"We should be able to make it up in the barrio," James stammered uneasily. How could they be so far behind? With 20 percent of the vote already in! "Our precinct chairmen say the Mexicans turned out in record numbers."

"They turned out," Mendoza said quietly. He sat alone on a plush blue velvet sofa with ornately curved wooden legs. "Let's just hope they're with us."

"After all we've done for them?" James blustered. "Old man Cadillo better keep his word."

Masters's head jerked up. "You gonna keep yours?"

"Quit while you're ahead, Jim," Mendoza interjected boldly, casting a knowing look at the congressman. James suddenly realized that Mendoza was closer to Masters than he'd ever realized.

The phone rang again. James seized the receiver in his left fist, drawing the precinct list back across the table. He listened in silence for a moment, then took up a ballpoint pen. "Yeah. Got it," he breathed in relief. "Keep talking, Mike. Music to my ears."

By nine Andrew's Styrofoam cup was shredded into a hundred tiny pieces, floating in little golden globs of wine splattered across the campaign manager's desk.

Andrew had been through this in other campaigns. The heart raced so hard one could hardly catch breath, the mind working overtime to keep track of all the vote counts and precincts and trends. With his own neck on the line, the waiting was horrendous. The worst were those dreaded five minutes out of each hour when Andrew was forced to saunter calmly out to the parking lot, smiling

89

and shaking hands, when all he wanted was to rush back into Callahan's office and find out which side of the roller coaster they were riding now.

Andrew ignored the knock on the door, concentrating on the television set. During the last half hour, Callahan had gotten quite piggish with his notebook. As the vote counts belatedly hit TV, Andrew began to understand why Callahan was shielding the numbers.

"It may be morning before we know who will win that hot race in the Fourth," the commentator chattered brightly. "The latest returns show Masters neck and neck with his Republican challenger. With almost half of the vote in, Sebastian has fifty-one percent; Masters, forty-nine percent."

The door flew open. An elderly woman, one of a breed Tricia called the Republican Blue Hairs, burst into the room. Her gnarled hand grabbed Andrew's sleeve with that surprising, pinching strength of the old. The other claw groped for Tricia.

"You all simply must come outside!" she ordered sternly. "And Ron, we must have more numbers."

"Fair enough, Maudie," Callahan conceded. Putting his hand over the mouthpiece, he scribbled on a scrap of paper. "Put these up. They're not good, but they'll hold everybody off."

As Andrew and Tricia craned their heads to read the numbers, Maudie dragged the two of them out into the parking lot. The street lamps were shrouded in an unusually warm, foggy November night. Andrew talked with his father and mother and shook hands with the volunteers and all the big contributors Roger had lined up. Andrew grinned fatuously into the cameras and tried mentally to add up the long list of precinct totals as Maudie Phillips chalked them onto the blackboard on the makeshift stage.

It was nearly impossible to fight their way back inside. "The trick to it," Tricia whispered into Andrew's ear, "is to start trying to escape the minute we get out here."

"You grab me and pull," Andrew murmured. "Then I can go reluctantly. Miz Brodersen! Peter, good to see you!"

Tricia blocked six tackles on their way back to the goal line, slapping away a couple of particularly feisty Blue Hairs as Andrew backed into Callahan's office.

Andrew yanked his wife inside and swept the door shut. He leaned his back against the door and sighed in relief. "East Dallas come in yet?"

Callahan sat upright in his swivel chair, the telephone silent, his notebook still littered with blank spaces. "It's over." He half smiled. "We lost."

"Very funny, Ron," Tricia said tensely. "Where are we?"

"I'm sorry," Callahan said simply. "We just got the rest of East Dallas. Our best boxes. Plus the barrio. They're ahead three thousand votes. We can't make it up." His eyes drooped in exhaustion. "What the hell?" he said weakly. "We never expected to win this one, right?"

"Right," Andrew said softly, his stomach heaving.

"We'll come a helluva lot closer than anyone thought. They'll be disappointed." Callahan gestured outside. "But the big boys'll be impressed as hell. We'll get forty-seven, maybe forty-eight percent. That's a good five points ahead of Nixon in our district."

"Wait a second!" Tricia pointed at the television set and shouted, a little more loudly than she'd intended. Too much Gallo Brothers, she thought light-headedly. "Look! They've got us at fifty-fifty!"

"Channel eight is an hour behind Ron, honey," Andrew soothed. "He's right. We lost." He scanned Callahan's notebook with care, trying to envision the people and faces and neighborhoods that went with each precinct number. "Jesus, they killed us in 1462. All the Hispanic boxes."

"Cadillo," Callahan said gloomily. "They were pushing these in the precincts today." He held up a pale blue card reading: MASTERS '72, CADILLO '74.

"Subtle," Andrew said. "I guess it's time to go face the music." His tone was brisk, businesslike. "I need to call John and concede as soon as possible. Stay on his good side. Right?"

Ron nodded. Andrew glanced over at Tricia, who was dabbing at her mascara. "Hey," he said quietly. "We knew this was coming, right?"

"Right," Tricia said, trying not to gag as she gulped another swallow of wine.

It had been a mistake, Andrew realized, letting Tricia think they might win this one. But unavoidable. Because he had thought so, too.

6

James lay back on the mattress he had flung on the black linoleum of his Capitol Hill apartment, screwing his eyes shut against the harsh winter sunlight that streamed through threadbare mustard-colored curtains. The sun made him want to throw up. Everything nauseated James that February morning: the sickly-sweet fish smell of Vietnamese cooking on the ground floor; Jimi Hendrix screaming on the hippie stereo upstairs; the barking grind of rush-hour traffic as it surged into one of Washington's dreaded roundabouts outside.

Normally James drank only on Saturday nights, by the flickering light of his black-and-white portable TV. He was a busy, lonely man: liquor was the date that wouldn't reject him, the Florida vacation he couldn't afford. He was a miser of sorts, as much as one can be on a government salary. He lived in the cheapest apartments he could find, no furniture, no bedframe when the floor would do just as well. That left enough to pay for Denny's junior college and five or six hundred bucks a month to sock away in the savings account that slowly, ever so slowly, widened the distance between James Brackler and the ever-present poverty monster that hovers always behind the child of a welfare mother.

She called him once in a while, for money: on the weekend; on Mother's Day; at Christmas. James rarely gave in: he didn't owe her a nickel of the $32,805.56 he had saved through the long years of scrimping on government salaries. Besides, she'd just drink it up. It did occur to him once that Patty Brackler invested far more in long-distance charges than she ever recovered, that perhaps the maudlin Saturday-night calls, both of them drunk and alone, might just be her excuse to talk to her son. James pushed the thought away. It complicated his clear picture of who he was and whom he had to rely upon.

James hadn't seen his mother's face since he'd invited her to his college graduation in Austin, because it was in the morning and she wouldn't be too smashed, and because the university allowed nothing but flower petals in the raspberry punch, and because even James needed someone in that mass of faces to appreciate his years of struggle against long odds, even if she did look horribly out of place in her tight-hipped lime pants suit, amidst that sea of genteel fathers in button-down shirts and matching mothers in long white gloves and pale lavender dresses. That was his last image of his mother, standing proudly in the sun, clapping too loudly when his name was called, breathing gin fumes in his face at the reception. Where did she find the stuff? James had taken her home and dropped her off, out of his life, and gone on to law school and the state Capitol and the army and Washington, and tried never to think of her again.

During the campaign last fall, she'd found out he was back in Dallas. Denny must have given her his number. It was a strange time for his mother to call, a Tuesday night in early November. James had just walked in from the Masters victory party at the hotel, floating pleasantly on an ocean of booze and congratulatory back-slaps. Good job, Jim, the big boys said. Jim, the contributors said, you really pulled us through. We got plans for you, Jim. He decided he would tell everyone to call him that from now on. Jim Brackler: he imagined it on his campaign signs. Basking in the afterglow, he'd no sooner poured himself a nightcap and collapsed on his bed when the phone rang. Now, months later, lying sick and sorry on his bed in Washington, her cracked voice haunted him.

Jimmy, you there, honey?

93

Yes, ma. How are you, ma.

Just fine, but where you been, honey? I been havin' a time with my back.

Suddenly James had felt sorry for her. He couldn't bear to hear her catalog of grievances against the welfare and the Medicare and the AFDC. He'd hung up quickly, grabbing for a checkbook and scribbling out the figure and stumbling out to the mail slot before he could change his mind.

James had spent the holiday season twiddling his thumbs in Masters's office, waiting for the congressman to conclude an endless vacation as the guest of some South American dictator. Now, as he lay in his frigid room, fumbling to turn up the controls of the electric blanket, his head throbbed to remember the old man's grim face as he'd tottered back into the Rayburn Building yesterday, looking unusually frail and withered under the veneer of Latin suntan. The scene replayed over and over as James drifted in and out of hangover dreams, the temporary bliss of alcohol pierced by arrow-sharp darts of rare February sun slanting in through the cracked window.

The first danger sign had been Julian Mendoza, sitting in the corner, his mahogany eyes half-closed to avoid James's curious gaze. What was Julian doing here? Not wanting to alienate either man, James sat down and jabbered blithely, spewing all the ideas and questions he'd stored during the long hibernation since election night.

James's booming voice trailed off as the congressman held out one trembling, sun-wrinkled hand, using the other to cover a spasm of racking coughs. "Hold on!" Masters rasped, recovering enough to speak. "What the hell you talkin' about?"

"My campaign." Suddenly unsure of himself, James glanced at Julian. Mendoza stared intently at a photograph on the wall: Masters with his fatherly arm around the beehive-hairdoed Cotton Bowl Queen of 1963.

"Your campaign?" Masters expectorated into a phlegm-spotted handkerchief wadded into one hand. "I called you in to talk about your job!" The tone was jagged, cruel. "You're not playing with a full deck, Jim." Masters shook his head. "After that stunt you pulled with the Cadillos, you're lucky you still work for me."

"I don't understand," Brackler protested urgently. "You promised!"

"Like your promise to Cadillo?" Masters leered. "I gotta keep my

94

word, don't I? I'm stuck with that, uh, character." Brackler knew Masters meant to say Mexican or spic but had remembered just in time that they had one in the room. A single glance told Brackler that Mendoza knew it, too, and didn't care.

"But you said," James said limply, every fiber in his body melting into the chair. "Right here in this room."

"Congressman James Brackler?" Masters snorted, Brackler's beautiful dream words foul and ludicrous on his tongue. "Can you imagine, Julian?"

At first, James had groveled. He'd begged for any crumb: a state representative seat, a spot on the city council. "Maybe someday, Jimmy," the congressman counseled sagely. "You jes' slow down a little, learn from guys like Julian. Maybe he can help you get elected to something. Someday."

It was all painfully clear to James. He was out, Julian was in. James's only fault was success. In negotiating the critical deal to reelect the congressman, James had given the old bastard an excuse to escape a distasteful promise.

The most savage aspect of a hangover is not the nausea. It's the remorse: watching yesterday's performance from the awkward twenty-twenty hindsight of a never-ending instant replay. Like a wide receiver who rewinds the film to watch himself drop the ball again and again, James lay in bed, accusing himself, wondering how he could have fumbled things so badly.

James had turned on the congressman, swearing revenge, shouting over Masters's quavering voice, calling him a liar and a cheat and worse, until the old man's eyes had bulged impossibly huge and white and yellowish spittle had frothed at the desiccated corners of his ancient, quivering lips.

Dimly, bleakly, James remembered storming from the room, Masters gasping breathlessly behind him: "No one—talks to me like that! You're—fired—you white-trash sumbitch!"

James had flung himself out of the Rayburn Building, half walking, half running the four long blocks up Independence Avenue to Capitol Liquors. He remembered little after that. He had driven a bit in his claptrap red 1965 VW bug. Had he gone to 14th Street, to that scary, thrilling strip of downtown D.C. where hard-faced men with skin hued blue and green and red by the neon stepped from the shadows and clapped him on the back in their hearty, friendly way, and offered him—

A wave of guilt trembled through him. Oh, God, he thought. James staggered up out of bed and ran to the bathroom. The memory of last night's final episode rose up in his throat, spilling out with the whiskey-flavored vomit and sweat and tears.

Three hours later James emerged on the cement porch steps of the town house. He felt shaky and drained inside his best brown suit. At least he was done throwing up. Hopefully.

He walked briskly down the steps to the sidewalk that sloped gently toward the Capitol. Fuzzy-headed black children scampered in the unusually warm winter sunlight, popping little wheelies on their banana-seated bicycles. Why aren't they in school? James wondered idly. And where the hell do they get the money to buy bicycles? He hadn't had a bike until he'd stolen one from the schoolyard in seventh grade.

He glanced at his watch: 1:15. Not bad. The congressman wasn't due in the office until after lunch. He turned down Independence and strode the next eight blocks quickly, inhaling great drafts of fresh air to lighten his aching head for the crucial meeting ahead.

Would Masters agree to see him? Doubtful. He might have to settle for Julian, who would already be ensconced in James's old office, drinking out of Brackler's favorite coffee mug. That was okay. James had done Julian a few good turns. He would have to crawl in front of Mendoza. James didn't mind, as long as it served the Plan.

James didn't think of the Plan in the same silly schoolboy way of ten years before, as though it were some well-orchestrated schedule that would advance him, step by step, to the top. He now knew politics to be a fluid, short-term game where the teams and strategies and even the rules changed constantly. Yesterday had been a disastrous setback, one that would move James's timetable back a bit. But Masters had been right about one thing: thirty was outrageously young for Congress. If he could just smooth over last night, get his old job back: the possibilities whirred in James's fast-loosening head. Wouldn't old man Cadillo see James as the kingmaker who had crowned Juan Dallas's first minority congressman? If Masters wouldn't have him back, maybe James could manage Juan's campaign next year! Then the Cadillos could support him for state legislature. Maybe even the state senate!

His head full of district maps and election calendars, James neglected to take his usual glance at the Capitol facade, a sight that still struck awe even in his cynical heart. Nervous, oblivious to the sleek white marble glittering in the sun, he risked one of the city's notorious jaywalking tickets and scuttled across the busy midday traffic.

Stuck in a crowd of pedestrians waiting for the lights to change, James glanced to his right. The trees of the Capitol lawn blocked most of the view. But he could still see the dome and the flags flying above the parapets over the House chamber.

Wait a second, he thought curiously. Not flags. Flag*poles*. Why were the flags at half-mast?

"Jim, I am so sorry." A husky female voice penetrated his concentration. It was Mary Lord, the middle-aged librarian type who ran the staff on one of Masters's subcommittees. "He looked so good last fall." She sighed, dabbing needlessly at her cheek with a crumpled handkerchief. "Such a gentleman he was. And you two were so close!" With a brief, insincere pat on James's elbow, Mrs. Lord launched herself into the crosswalk.

James whirled around to face the Capitol again, thinking of how many times he had glimpsed those flags at half-mast for some dead member. Standing dazed on the jostling street corner, he felt a strong hand clamp his shoulder.

He turned to face Howell Champlin, the octogenarian Georgian who was Masters's closest colleague. "Jimmy," the hump-shouldered member croaked, his eyes streaked red with compassion, "I still can't believe it." Champlin grieved with the practice of one who was very old and must do so often. "None of us knew about the cancer. Well, goddamn, I guess we should have. You must be in shock." He shivered an old man's hatred of even the mildest winter day. "Come in out of the cold," he offered, steering James by the arm. "You must be sick about this."

No, old man, James thought, his suddenly clear mind spinning anew. I'm not.

Ron Callahan shifted nervously on the plush leather seat as Roger Sebastian's new Lear jet began its gentle descent over Acapulco Bay.

Callahan had logged countless hours in private planes during eight long years in Texas politics. A King Air or a Cessna was the only way to make a Rotary breakfast in Brazoria, a luncheon in Lubbock, a press conference in Austin, and a black-tie fund-raiser that night in Houston. But this was his first time in a Lear. The

97

slender silver tube was Roger Sebastian's latest toy, an elegant little rocket ship that streaked through the air at six hundred miles an hour. The Lear gave the five occupants of its cramped doeskin seats an almost spiritual sensation of flight. Callahan felt as though he were sailing through the atmosphere without an airplane at all, his body soaring up and down with each smooth adjustment made by the soft-spoken men in the cockpit just five feet away from his short, stubby legs. This is a real kick, he thought. But he was more comfortable in a storefront headquarters in East Dallas or downtown El Paso, shouting at people on the telephone, living on cold cheeseburgers and raw political adventure.

The wheels touched down with a gentle screech. Callahan fidgeted in his chair and stared out at the palm trees surrounding the low whitewashed buildings. He wondered how many more minutes would pass before he could politely light the single cigarette he craved more than all the resort vacations he would ever take.

Andrew leaned across the carpeted deck. "Not long, Ron," he said sotto voce, nodding at Callahan's fingers drumming on the armrest. "Thanks for humoring Dad."

Callahan smiled weakly. The jet eased to a stop near the terminal, where a black Mercedes 600 waited patiently. A thick-set Mexican lounged on the front grille of the limousine. The plane jolted to a complete halt, and the co-pilot flipped open the hatchlike door.

"Here we are!" Nan Sebastian said brightly, gathering a flowing pink-and-purple cotton muumuu about her as the co-pilot helped her down the short aisleway. A warm, steamy Mexican smell flooded through the sterile interior. Callahan helped Andrew and the pilot pass luggage out to the phlegmatic chauffeur, whom Andrew introduced as Jesus. Callahan stretched out his hand. Jesus ignored it politely, grabbing for two more suitcases.

Callahan shrugged and lit a cigarette, walking a few feet away from the chattering family. Andrew walked with him. Callahan took a deep drag, feeling warm little tears of relief in his eyes. They watched the others walk leisurely toward the terminal. "Not sure which I want more," Ron said, "a cigarette or a piss."

He was dying to talk politics. He tried to appear interested in the small talk during the twenty-minute drive along the twisting clifftop roads, but his mind drifted back to last night's unexpected phone call.

Andrew had jumped in breathlessly: "Guess what?"

"Andrew?"

"Who do you think?" Sebastian had barked. "Sorry I haven't called. There hasn't been much to say."

"What's up?"

"Masters is dead."

"What?"

"John Masters died early this morning," Andrew had said, trying to weed the enthusiasm out of his voice. "Dad just heard at the country club. They'll have to call a special election to fill the term. When, in May?"

Callahan's head had tumbled quickly, the political hack's ever-recurring worry of seasonal unemployment abruptly dispelled by visions of next year's election calendar. "June thirteenth," he'd said, leaning over to turn on the evening television news. "Unless the Democrats want a quick campaign. They could go May eighth. You are going to run?"

"What do you think?" Andrew had replied. "Dad wants us to have a little strategy session, just the three of us. And Mom and Trish, of course. Can you meet us at Love Field tomorrow morning? Say around, uh, five-thirty?"

Callahan had given Andrew the groan he'd expected. Why did rich people always get up so early? He knew there was a connection, but he'd never wanted the worm badly enough to be the early bird. "We're going to Dad's villa in Acapulco," Andrew had added quickly. "Bring your trunks."

As the big black limo negotiated another hairpin twist, Callahan wondered, What exactly is a villa? Is it like a house? A condo? The Mercedes worked its way down a narrow, rock-walled lane cut into the face of a promontory above the bay. He caught glimpses of Mediterranean bungalows, with lush tropical gardens planted improbably amidst scorched brown underbrush.

Each villa was half-hidden by stone gates adorned with sappy names: EL PARADISO. VILLA SUZETTE. HARVEY'S RETREAT. Finally Jesus made a sharp turn into a long gravel driveway near the bottom of the hill. It was marked with an inconspicuous wood-burned sign bearing a mock cattle brand: THE SOUTH FORTY. The limousine scrunched to a stop. So this is a villa, Callahan mused, thinking just how far this was from his parents' modest frame cottage in the slushy backwash of their working-class Irish neighborhood in South Boston.

99

It was a fantasy, a sudden splash of white glistening at the edge of a brown cliff shooting fifty feet up from the gentle waves slapping the rocks along the northern shore of Acapulco Bay. To the left lay a tennis court, its high gray-clad fences overgrown with bright red hibiscus. To the right, a heavyset Mexican woman emerged from an elaborate formal garden. The house itself was stunning, a somehow harmonious jumble of stark white perpendicular levels interlaced with six different roofs and decks, all stitched together by short, sharp spiral stairs that ran at odd angles. It was vaguely modern Monaco Moroccan, a bright, sun-bleached palace kept flawlessly clean by Jesus and his wife for those rare occasions when their Texas sultan would descend from the sky for a long weekend.

Andrew grabbed Callahan by the arm. "Ron, this is Rosita. And this"—he flung open the front door—"is Dad's place."

Callahan had never seen so much marble. Terrazzo staircases spiraled to hidden rooms. Cold brass furnishings were warmed by an enormous wash of sunlight through the two-story curtain of solid glass that composed the entire rear wall of the house. Once inside, Callahan saw that the villa's seaward edge actually jutted out over the cliff, giant stone pillars anchoring it to the flinty shale of the hillside.

He looked over his shoulder at Andrew's beaming face and couldn't help himself. "Wow," he said.

Andrew nodded, gazing out across the crystalline bay at the jumbled pastels of the city of Acapulco. "Right," he said briskly. "Your room's upstairs, second door to the left. I'll meet you at the pool in ten minutes."

"I talked to a friend in the governor's office last night," Callahan said, settling into a lounge chair on the hot white poolside cement. "They're going for a snap election on May eighth."

Andrew's father joined them, pulling up a chair under a navy-blue-and-red Cinzano umbrella. "Is that good or bad?" Roger shucked a tattered Hawaiian shirt to reveal a tanned chest matted with silken gray hair.

The older man's lean muscles, sagging only slightly despite his nearly seventy years, made Callahan embarrassingly conscious of his own fish-white belly, which now served as a tray to hold a freshly uncapped bottle of Carta Blanca beer.

"It's good," Callahan replied. He shielded his eyes from the sun

100

and stared at the two Sebastians, seeking but not finding a resemblance. Andrew's looks were smoother, softer. More like his mother's, thought Callahan. He explained, "We're much better organized than any of the Democrats. And we can raise money faster. I hollered like hell last night, of course, to make them think we needed more time."

Roger smiled impishly. He liked this part of the game best. He particularly liked the way young Callahan played it.

Callahan's lips sucked quickly at his beer. "The truth is, our whole organization is still in place," he added. "May is much better for us than June."

"Especially if this Watergate business gets any worse," Andrew put in from his lounge chair by the railing.

"Who knows?" Callahan said. "That could be a plus. You were the only Republican in Texas who refused to endorse Nixon. Maybe we ought to play that up now."

Roger was silent. Callahan knew why: the elder Sebastian had served on Nixon's finance committee. Roger had quarreled bitterly over his son's refusal to back the national ticket. Andrew had been adamant. Thank God, thought Callahan, who had been on Roger's side at the time.

Through the gaps between the hibiscus that intertwined the wrought-iron deck railing, he could see a few whitecaps out in the ocean. Inside the bay, the blue-green water was still as glass, etched here and there by a frothy white double line of wake spreading from the water-skiers looping lazily around the barren, looming rock of El Morro.

Wincing from the glare, Callahan surreptitiously slid his gaze to the painfully beautiful woman who, having rubbed Coppertone onto every luscious inch of her near-naked anatomy, cautiously eased her black-bikinied body onto a blue inflatable raft near the steps at the shallow end of the pool. He couldn't help watching as Tricia plucked at her bikini bottoms and snuggled her skimpy top around those brown, pear-shaped breasts. How did that strap stay on?

"Ron?"

Callahan started guiltily at Andrew's voice, spilling a dash of icy beer on his baking chest. Andrew and Roger were both staring at him.

"What about the Democrats?" Andrew asked intently, his eyes straying subconsciously toward the pool. Tricia now floated toward them, her hands sliding thin black spaghetti straps down over her shoulders to avoid tan lines.

Callahan focused. It was the most important question at this stage: Who would their opponents be?

"You both know how it works," he lectured, in case they didn't. "In a special election, there are no party primaries. All the candidates run against each other in a free-for-all, Democrats and Republicans. If anyone gets more than fifty percent, he wins."

"But that never happens," Andrew prompted. He wondered whether Tricia, floating three feet from his sandaled toes, was even remotely interested in all of this.

"Exactly," Callahan continued. "The top two vote-getters usually go into a runoff, held five weeks after the original election."

Roger leaned forward, bony elbows on bony knees, his sharp blue eyes boring intelligently into Callahan's face. "So why don't the Democrats try to rally behind one fellow before the first election in May, to avoid dividing their strength?" he asked. "Couldn't they beat us outright?"

"Sure." Callahan laughed. "But they won't. You know what Will Rogers used to say."

"I don't belong to any organized political party," Andrew quoted. "I'm a Democrat."

"Exactly." Callahan smiled indulgently, a teacher patting an apt pupil on the head. "The Democrats have their panties in a wad. Nobody expected John Masters to drop dead, even though he was almost seventy."

He stopped suddenly, aware of Roger's amused gaze. Jesus, he realized. Masters was probably the same age as Andrew's father. He hurried on: "My contact in Austin tells me the Hispanics are pushing the big Democratic leaders to rally behind Juan Cadillo. They say Masters promised to back Juan as his successor."

"Will they?" Andrew queried.

"Some of them," said Callahan. "But some are looking in other directions."

"Where?" asked Roger. The older man walked slowly to poolside and sat down on the scrolled marble edge, dangling his thin, hairy legs in the cool water.

"There may be only one other. He was already making phone calls yesterday." Callahan paused, his eyes again wandering toward the gently rocking figure on the long blue air mattress.

"Are you gonna tell us his name?" Roger said irascibly. "Or just let us die in suspense?"

"You've never even heard of him, sir," Callahan said, grinning at the old man. "A total unknown. He ran Masters's last campaign. Young guy named Jim Brackler."

Then Tricia fell off her raft into the heavily chlorinated water, drenching her carefully coiffed ash-brown hair, throwing the men into paroxysms of laughter. Except Andrew, who stared soberly at the little funicular railway that plunged down the steep rocks, connecting his family's hilltop paradise with the sun-bleached dock fifty feet below.

"You can't!" Tricia hissed through clenched teeth. "I won't stand for it!" The bitter dagger of her voice sliced across the quiet of their bedroom on the villa's top floor.

"Ssh," Andrew said, closing the door. "They'll hear you."

"So what?" Her glare defied him.

Andrew crossed the room and clicked on a bedside lamp. He and Tricia stared at each other for a moment, two chessmasters trying to anticipate their opponent's next move.

Andrew eased open the sliding glass door that separated their room from the stucco-walled balcony. The ocean breeze swept in to chase out the stifling heat. The fresh striped polo shirt Andrew had donned before dinner was already soaked with a fine sweat. He pulled it off his long, sleek torso in a single quick motion. His chest glowed brown and pink from the afternoon by the pool. He tossed the shirt in a straw hamper next to their bathroom door. Then he stretched himself out on the bed, folding his arms behind his neatly combed hair, stretching the long legs wrapped in loose white painter's pants. It irritated Tricia: Andrew always liked to get comfortable before an argument, as though it were a late-night movie on television.

She tried to calm herself, to be as cool and rational as he always seemed. "I—can't—do it," she enunciated slowly. "I've always gone along. My whole life is built around your career, your family. I work hard. I do all the things you want me to do. All those meetings. Dinner parties for your political friends. Trips with your parents. Christ, we live in the house they picked for us."

"Now hold on!" Andrew said suddenly, a referee blowing the whistle. "We love that house."

103

"*You* love that house! Your mother loves that house," Tricia cried. "I never had a choice!"

"I never noticed you complaining when all of our friends were living in grubby little apartments, and you were running around furnishing a five-bedroom house out of *Architectural Digest*," Andrew said coolly.

"That's not the point." Tricia sat down on the stool next to the vanity table and poured herself a glass of bottled water. "I shouldn't have brought it up. We're talking about *him*."

"You still can't say his name?" Andrew shook his head. "You've got to learn to deal with what happened to us."

"It didn't happen to us!" she shouted. "It happened to *me*, goddamn it! I was the one who was, was—"

"Raped." Andrew spoke softly, gently, not unclasping his hands from behind his head. He barely even moved his lips. "You were raped, Tricia, by James Brackler. It happened eleven and a half years ago."

"I know damn well when and where and how it happened!" Tricia whispered hoarsely. "How can you even think about getting involved with that animal?"

"I am not getting involved with him," Andrew said clinically. "He's running against me in an election."

"You think it's a coincidence?" She wanted to scream at him, hit him with her fists, shock him out of his insufferable complacency. "Why do you think he's doing this? Surely he has no chance. He just wants to hurt us!"

Andrew swung his legs to the floor and sat upright. "Tricia, you don't know what this means to me," he said quietly. "It's all I want. All I am. And you're making way too much out of this. It's circumstance. Brackler was Masters's right-hand man. At least that's what he's telling everybody," he added parenthetically, with the politician's automatic resistance to giving an opponent any edge. "It's a natural move for him. Just like this is a natural move for me. For us."

Andrew stood up and walked to her, slipping his long fingers around the softness of her upper arms.

Tricia shrank back, turned her head away. "You do what you want, Andrew," she said icily. He dropped his hands to his sides. She continued tonelessly, "Just like always."

104

The debate, like the campaign, was over before it began.

Tricia's dire predictions failed to materialize. As February blurred into March and April, James Brackler was too busy fighting Juan Cadillo for Democratic votes to lay a glove on Andrew.

Tonight will change all of that, Brackler thought, his mind caressing the explosive missive in his jacket pocket.

His ancient red Volkswagen rattled into Channel 13's parking lot. The VW was Brackler campaign headquarters. On the floor rested stacks of black-and-white brochures with an enormous photo of "the late Congressman John Masters and his strong right arm, Jim Brackler." In the trunk under the front hood lay a stack of yard signs: JIM BRACKLER FOR CONGRESS IN THE MASTERS TRADITION In his lap were a Mapsco book of cross-referenced street maps, his Rolodex, a pile of hand-scribbled notes, the day's schedule. Behind the wheel sat Brackler's press secretary, scheduler, aide-de-camp, and campaign staff: Denny Frawley.

"You're sure?" Brackler inquired closely, inspecting his stepbrother's acne-scarred face for signs of a screw-up.

"Absolutely," Denny replied fervently, his lanky knees banging the steering wheel as the two tall men, one skinny and one bulky, clambered out of the tiny automobile. Denny scooped a handful of brochures from beneath the pedals.

"I called the producer twenty minutes ago. It's just the two of you." He grinned knowingly, proud that Jimmy—Jim, he corrected himself—had let him quit school to help.

"You're sure Sebastian doesn't know?" Brackler growled, knowing Denny wouldn't let him down. It was going to work!

"Positive." Denny held the plate-glass door so Jim could stride confidently into the air-conditioned lobby of the public television station, free to shake hands with the receptionist, two technicians, and the moderator. They worked their way down the hall, Denny answering the unspoken question in their eyes: "He's Jim Brackler." He stuffed a brochure in each hand: "Democrat for Congress."

Brackler stopped suddenly, jerking his head back to whisper in Denny's ear, "There he is." He nodded to a door slightly ajar on the left. Blocked by Ron Callahan's short, stocky back, Denny could just see Andrew Sebastian, in front of a makeup mirror ringed by two dozen white light bulbs.

"Mr. Baxter?" The makeup artist looked up uncertainly, her wrinkled brow measuring the two ungainly young men. "Will you come with me, please?" She gestured down the hall.

"Jim Brackler," Denny explained, pressing a flyer into her hand. "Democrat for Congress."

Brackler followed, unconcerned. His trap was set. Andrew Sebastian had just taken the bait.

"What's he grinning about?" Andrew asked nervously, picking at the white cotton sheets pinned tightly around his neck.

Callahan leaned his back against the door to press it shut. "He's just playing with your head," he advised. "Let's talk about what to say tonight."

"I know what to say tonight." They had gotten here much too early. The waiting made Andrew irritable. "If your poll is right, he's got nothing to be smiling about."

"My poll was taken by the president's pollster. It cost your father's buddies nine thousand five hundred dollars. It's right," Callahan said shortly. "Andrew, we may win without a runoff."

"Hush." He held a finger to his lips, smiling tensely. The makeup lady had finished; they could talk. "You tempt the Fates."

"The Fates aren't registered," Callahan jeered. "Andrew, we have fifteen thousand votes identified off these phone banks. Fifteen!"

"Masters pulled twenty-four against us last time," Andrew cautioned. Callahan's overconfidence was beginning to spook him.

His campaign manager waved airily. "In a presidential year, Andy. This is a special. We're the only race on the ballot. Who's gonna vote in a special election for Congress on a balmy day in May?"

"Brackler and Cadillo—" Andrew began warningly.

"That's two votes," Callahan snapped. "Will you stop? All they've done is piss on each other. Watch them tonight. They'll tear each other to shreds."

"I want to see the stage," Andrew said stubbornly. He boosted himself out of the low-slung chair, stripping the sheet carefully from his starched button-down shirt. Callahan was pleased to see the candidate had worn blue, as instructed: white shirts blurred on television.

"Aw, Andy," he soothed. "Sit down, huh? You're making me nervous."

106

"Are you coming?" Andrew asked. "They always put my microphone too low on the podium." They walked down a short corridor to a door marked by unlit red letters: QUIET. ON AIR. "It makes me stoop," he added petulantly.

"You'll be sitting down," Callahan said laconically. Andrew had never debated on television before. "They hang the mike around your neck."

Huddled together like fraternity brothers on a panty raid, they peeked through the thick glass panel in the stage door.

"There's three chairs." Andrew frowned, perplexed.

"You, Brackler, Cadillo. So?"

"Me, Brackler, the moderator," Andrew rejoined quickly. His eyes darted down the hall. Suddenly he knew why Brackler had been smiling.

"Where's a phone?"

"Andrew, it's forty-five minutes to air," Callahan soothed. "They probably haven't finished setting up yet."

"The phone," Andrew ordered, his tone brooking no argument. "Is my Rolodex in the car?"

"Five, four, three . . ." the technician droned over the loudspeaker.

Brackler, crossing his legs awkwardly on the swivel chair, looked over the young black moderator's shoulder, straining to read the note Ron Callahan had just handed Sebastian. His opponent seemed agitated, incessantly flicking his fair hair away from his forehead.

What a chump, he thought jubilantly. He's just now figured it out!

Desperate to slip past Cadillo and force a runoff with Sebastian, Brackler had called in an old favor.

"I can't," Channel 13's public affairs producer had protested.

"That's not what I said when your grant came before Masters's subcommittee," Brackler cajoled. "And I won't say 'can't' next year, when I get to Congress."

The producer sighed, afraid to call his bluff. "But Juan Cadillo's a known name," she objected. "How can we leave him out of the only televised debate in the campaign?"

Brackler laughed humorlessly. His suggestion was more like an order: "Simple. Don't send him an invitation."

And here they sat, before the eyes of the district and the reporters Denny had called that morning, ready to go one on one with Andrew

Sebastian. The press, quick to spot a trend, were already scribbling the leads for tomorrow's front-page news: "Democrat Jim Brackler, former top aide to the late Rep. John Masters (D-Dallas), yesterday made the Fourth District congressional battle a two-way duel between himself and Republican Andrew Sebastian."

Brackler literally licked his lips as the camera dollied forward. He reached into his breast pocket for the tenth time. It was still there, the ammunition he'd hoarded so long, awaiting this moment.

The moderator turned to Andrew. "Mr. Sebastian, your opening statement?"

"I have nothing to say," Andrew said, looking flustered.

"I'm sorry?" the moderator replied.

"We can't proceed with this, Mr. Saunders," Andrew continued, his voice growing bolder. "All the candidates aren't present. It's not right."

Now it was the moderator's turn to be flustered. "Mr. Sebastian," he said coldly. "We are live."

"You guys go ahead," Andrew replied calmly. This was going to work! Even if Callahan was standing in the back of the room, eyes bugging out of his head as he glared out the stage door. "I'm going to wait for Juan Cadillo."

"Mr. Cadillo won't be here tonight," the moderator barked. Realizing from the press gallery's agile scribble of pens that news was being made, the broadcaster softened his tone.

"In the interests of time"—he looked into the camera, dewy brown eyes begging the viewers' indulgence—"the station decided to invite just the two leading candidates to debate—"

"Whose idea was that?" Andrew cut him off. "His?"

Brackler thrust his head forward at the accusation. "I resent that." His voice trembled a bit. "Are you ready to debate or not?" It's time to heat this up, he thought urgently. I don't want to spend the whole night arguing over why Cadillo isn't here.

Suddenly, Cadillo was. There was a small commotion at the stage door, and Juan Cadillo burst up the aisle, storming confidently up three carpeted risers to the stage.

"Thank you, Andrew," he puffed, literally out of breath. Callahan had reached him in the shower forty minutes ago. His hair still wet, the drama of the moment shining in his eyes, Cadillo uttered the sound bite that would lead all three newscasts at ten: "Where's my chair?"

Andrew grinned in triumph, beaming at the sight of reporters scratching new leads in their long spiral notebooks.

Brackler sank back heavily in his seat, feeling his cheeks flush red. The envelope in his pocket was useless now. He had lost. I'll hold on to it, he thought rebelliously, avoiding Denny's crushed face in the back row. There's always next year.

7

Please stand right there, and still!" Gunther Rettmer commanded, setting a glass of champagne on a rosewood sideboard in the crowded, jade-strewn hallway of the embassy of Thailand. Rettmer, a minor West German cultural attaché, made little shooing motions to urge Andrew and Tricia closer to each other, positioning them beneath the foyer's massive brass Buddha. "Good! *Eins, zwei, drei!*" Andrew smiled into the flash, trying to arch his eyes wide open as Tricia advised, so he wouldn't look squinty in the picture.

Rettmer was a popular fixture on Washington's diplomatic circuit. His social cachet owed less to his hearty gemütlich personality than to the small Kodak pocket camera that dangled eternally about his neck, ready to shoot party snaps of any upwardly mobile couple who caught his eye. Rettmer then mailed the snapshots to Washington's famous and would-be famous, at his own expense. No one knew why he went to the trouble, unless maybe it was to get invited to more parties.

"What an odd little man," Tricia said quietly, watching the German bob away.

Andrew noticed an earnest young fellow in a blue pin-striped suit who was trying to catch his eye. Pinstripe shot between two Africans in voluminous dashiki. He stretched out his right arm in greeting.

"Whew!" The young man drew his left hand through short blond hair in mock relief. "Congressman, I'm Philip Stuart, and I'm very glad to meet you. And you, Mrs. Sebastian. I work for the White House."

Instinctively Andrew drew back a bit, then caught himself. Had Stuart noticed the gesture?

"How wonderful!" Tricia covered quickly. "What do you do there?"

"Congressional Relations," Stuart said diffidently. "I fetch drinks for freshman congressmen who are, ah, a little dubious about the president. What'll it be?"

Andrew laughed. "Champagne for me. Tricia?"

"Vodka tonic, please," she stammered. She shot Andrew a look: Careful, honey, let's not offend the White House. Any more than you already have.

"I'm not dubious," Andrew told Stuart when the young man returned, juggling three glasses with an ease that bespoke practice. "I've never even met the man," the Fourth District's new congressman added. "But what I've seen lately makes me nervous."

Andrew looked at Stuart's unfazed bright eyes and couldn't help but ask, "How old are you, anyway?"

"Twenty-six," Stuart replied. His voice dropped a little. "Actually, that's a lie. I'm twenty-five. I added a year to get the job at the White House. I've been twenty-six for so long, people are getting suspicious."

"Have a birthday, and tell them you're twenty-seven," Tricia suggested. "In Washington, consistency is more important than truth, right?"

"Touché." The young presidential aide smiled winningly. "Let's change subjects, shall we?"

"How come?" Andrew shot back with a cat's joy at slapping an injured mouse around the kitchen. "Is honesty in government not the favorite topic of this administration?"

The young White House official dropped his bantering party facade and leaned closer to the young Texas congressman. "All kidding aside, you are with us on the big things, aren't you, Congressman?" he asked.

"The big things?" Andrew looked at him curiously.

Philip Stuart gulped at his Scotch. "Well, the issues, I mean, nobody cares how you vote on that stuff," he allowed. "Defense, foreign policy, taxes. That's between you and the district."

"Without a doubt," Andrew said blandly. "But what about the big things, huh?"

"Exactly," Stuart said earnestly. Tricia stared at her first White House aide. She wondered, Can he get us invited to a state dinner? Stuart went on quickly, "Are you with us, sir? On the trust issues?"

"You mean Watergate."

"Sure. Watergate, executive privilege, the power of the presidency," Stuart listed. "It all boils down to whether the president is going to be allowed to govern."

"I'd say that's up to him," Andrew said shortly. "Nice meeting you, Phil."

"What's that supposed to mean?" Stuart snarled. His party mask fell away. "Are you going to start more trouble?"

"How would I know?" Andrew said jocularly. "I just got here."

Tricia looked her husband sharply in the eye, a little frightened by Stuart's vehemence.

Andrew gave Stuart a friendly wave and began to steer away. "He's wondering if Phil Stuart will be able to piss all over the president of the United States by the time he gets to be thirty-two," he said cockily. "Or will he be thirty-three?"

"Very funny," Tricia said worriedly. "Is that what you're doing? Pissing on the president?"

"A figure of speech," Andrew said. "Not pissing, exactly. Just a little cold water on their heads. They'll drag the party down next year. Maybe the whole country."

Tricia sighed wearily. She was tired of hearing about Watergate. They had been in Washington six months now, and Watergate was all anyone wanted to talk about.

Congress was in outright revolt. The city was alive with seditious talk of impeachment hearings and special resolutions and curbing the "imperial presidency." The normally cautious Andrew was right in the thick of it, leading a band of eight newly elected young House Republicans who had rebelled against the party leadership.

Together, the eight upstarts were sponsoring a "Sense of the

112

House" resolution calling for the president to resign and step down voluntarily, rather than dragging the country through the agony of an impeachment process. Haldeman had dubbed Andrew and his group "Snow White and the Seven Dwarves." The handle stuck.

At first, Tricia rather liked all the fuss. It showered prominence on her husband, who was more famous as "Snow White" after six months in Congress than were most members after six terms. But it scared her, too. Though she was new to Washington, she knew Andrew was going too far, too fast. She worried about what would happen if her husband and his seven young colleagues lost the dangerous game of chicken they were playing with the cold-faced men at the other end of Pennsylvania Avenue.

Things had not started out this way. Tricia remembered how warmly the Republicans had welcomed Andrew to Congress last May, lauding his knockout 58 percent victory over Brackler and Cadillo. For the first month or so, Andrew kept his head down, studying the House rules, learning the ropes, acting out the quiet modesty the House requires of freshman members. It was a role that came easily to a young man who had achieved everything he'd ever wanted by smiling brightly, paying his dues, and getting along with others.

The trouble began when the White House refused to allow Andrew's Asian Affairs Subcommittee to interview State Department officials. Incensed over the abuse of so-called executive privilege, Andrew joined his Democratic colleagues in voting to subpoena the administration.

Suddenly, Andrew was frozen out of GOP party caucuses. His name was no longer requested as a co-sponsor of Republican legislation. Andrew came home each night of that agonizing summer in bitter frustration, pouring out his anger to Tricia over reheated suppers in the mottled gray town house she had picked out for them in Georgetown.

Late last August, as they hosted a dinner party for GOP freshmen, Andrew had heard the same complaints from others who sensed something rotten in the White House barrel. Eight of the new congressmen met later that week, several times, in secret session at Andrew's house. Tricia interrupted frequently to serve coffee, anxious for them to break up so Andrew could crawl into bed and tell her the whole story.

"Hello?"

113

The voice cut into Tricia's reverie. She looked up into the wry smile of Kitty Kellerman. Her husband was one of the rebellious Dwarves, a thirty-four-year-old congressman from Wisconsin.

"Kitty!" Tricia said. "I'm sorry. I was lost for a second. What's going on?"

"Where's your husband?" Kitty's green-gold eyes sparkled.

"Hell if I know," Tricia admitted, feigning the callous indifference of the seasoned Washington wife. They laughed brightly, two attractive women with important young husbands on the rise.

"Thank God they got that bloody resolution in the hopper." Kitty sighed. "I had no idea Washington would be quite this exciting. Even if we won't ever get invited to the White House."

"Did you see our guys on *Meet the Press?*" Tricia lamented. "We're lucky to get to an embassy party." She tried not to listen to herself. She sounded like a typical Washington socialite, clattering on about party invitations, wondering aloud what "the men" were up to, like some inane Edith Bunker. Her mind wandered. Where was Andrew, anyway?

Andrew sipped his eighth—ninth?—glass of champagne. He felt very loose, cat-footed, sure of himself. He sensed the insiders' eyes as they caressed his face, which had graced the pages of *Time* and *Newsweek* twice this year: once as the upset victor in a congressional race with "national implications"; more recently in those simulated eyeball-to-eyeball photos with the ski slope–nosed president Andrew had never met. And now probably never would.

This was fun, much more fun than he'd ever thought it would be. Andrew knew he was risking his career by refusing to play by Washington's rules. But for the first time in his life, he had stepped out of his father's shadow, out from under the protective umbrella of those who expected him to wait in line and take his turn. Suddenly he was rocking the boat a little. He liked the way it made him feel.

"Here in Washington, you have to go along to get along," Jack Longley, Texas's senior U.S. senator, had counseled during their tense meeting last week. At five feet two, the diminutive senator was living proof that everything wasn't bigger in Texas.

"Slow down," the senator advised, primping the tie-matching handkerchief in the coat pocket of a dandyish English-cut suit. "You're going to burn out awfully fast up here."

The little senator, whom Capitol Hill secretaries had voted "The

Man We'd Least Like to Meet Alone in an Elevator," wasn't present at tonight's party. Andrew was glad. It left the field wide open for him.

He had decided that tonight would be It. The Night.

It had been building up for months. For years, perhaps, through all the loveless nights and frustrated "mornings after" of his sexless ten-year experiment with marital fidelity. Andrew's determination to stray redoubled after each of those fruitless occasions when, once every week or two, he cuddled and cajoled and caressed his way into the dead-fish body of his frigid wife, her only reaction an infrequent groan or sigh that Andrew almost welcomed, signifying as it did indisputable proof that Tricia might in fact be alive and not another victim of Death by Sexual Contact.

Divorce was not an option. That would just hurt Tricia, his parents, his career. Especially his career. Besides, he still loved Tricia. She was loyal, beautiful, intelligent. As a politician's wife, she was a stunning success. As a politician's lover, she sucked. Or rather, she didn't, Andrew thought, giggling aloud at the prepos- terous notion of Tricia Farris Sebastian giving head.

"Thank you," a cultured feminine voice said near him. "But I haven't said anything clever yet."

"Ah," said Andrew, rounding on the voice to encounter a blond lawyer-lobbyist whose name he couldn't remember. "I read your mind."

It wasn't very good party repartee, but it was amusing enough after a few drinks. Lady Lobbyist had had more than a few, so she laughed. Besides, Andrew thought exultantly, she thinks I'm cute.

"Amanda Roberts," the lobbyist announced suddenly, thrusting her paw at Andrew in a way he found mannish, at odds with the soft, lace-edged cocktail dress of winter-white silk, with the nice long slit along those very fine skinny legs. She coaxed him, "We met at the Philippines hearing last week."

"Right, Philippines," Andrew said. "Can I get you a drink?"

"I have a drink."

Their eyes were almost level. Amanda Roberts was very tall, almost six feet. Which might account, Andrew thought, for the very feminine clothes. Washington career women usually turned him off, in their boxy blue blazers with brass buttons, sincere white starchy shirt-blouses, and severe navy-blue bows. This one was different. Very sexy, long and thin, a little on the flat side, but a very interesting face with huge brown eyes that drank in a man's romantic interest and swirled it around deep inside.

Andrew had spotted Amanda earlier, recognized her hazily, been attracted to her. But he had moved on past, embarrassed not to recall her name, leaving her with two Asians who touched her elbows slyly as they spoke. Now here she was, smiling a frank invitation. "Refresh my memory, Amanda," he said firmly, grabbing another glass of champagne from a passing tray. "About Philippines. For whom do you lobby?"

"Oh, the bad guys," she said in a sexy-hoarse cheerleader voice that Andrew liked a lot. "I work for the big fat generals with the cigars and the sunglasses."

"And the triple rows of medals on their chests," he added, smiling briefly at a passing flashbulb.

"Exactly." Amanda nodded vigorously. "All in need of foreign aid to pay their dry cleaning bills. Marcos in Manila, Somoza in Nicaragua. That's where the money is."

"In foreign aid?"

"No, from the regime, of course," Amanda replied. "You don't expect a big Washington firm like ours to lobby for the guys in the hills with the girls in their sleeping bags, do you? They have bad credit ratings."

"Besides, they've already got Ernest Hemingway."

"Exactly."

Andrew stared at her. On impulse he whispered, "Want to go for a drive?"

"Whoa." Amanda literally backed away. "You do like to make things happen, don't you? Slow down a little. Have another drink."

"I have a drink," he mimicked her.

The lobbyist looked at Andrew for a long minute, a little frightened by the raw hunger she saw in his eyes. And a little turned on by it.

"Okay, cowboy," she said lightly, setting down her empty glass on another passing tray. "But no drive. Let's go for a walk."

They strolled for what seemed like hours in the frosty October night, down Embassy Row to busy Dupont Circle, crowded with nightclubs and buses and members of Washington's gay population cruising in little clusters through the best-known of the traffic-circle parks that dot America's capital city.

At first, they talked politics. Guerrillas in the Philippines. Wa-

116

tergate. The governor's race in Texas. Watergate. Agnew. Water-gate. They wandered past the Circle Theater on Pennsylvania, where *Casablanca* and *The Maltese Falcon* played next to a lively pub called the Twenty-First Amendment. Standing side by side, they stood silent, staring across the street at the ornate hulk of the old Executive Office Building, the White House annex that once, incomprehensibly, had housed the entire federal bureaucracy of the United States. It was now infamous as the building where the "plumbers' unit" had set up shop in the basement to sabotage the president's political opposition.

Andrew and Amanda walked slowly around the black iron fence of the Executive Mansion itself, two political scientists trying to understand the curious political animal caged inside, no doubt prowling the historic hallways at the midnight hour.

"They say he gets smashed every night," Andrew mused.

"Martinis." Amanda nodded authoritatively. "I hear he breaks down and cries in front of the Lincoln bedroom, on his knees, in front of Old Abe's portrait."

"No."

"Have you heard about the childproof caps on the aspirin bottles in his medicine cabinet?"

"What about them?"

"Teethmarks."

"No!"

"No kidding," Amanda said. "Of course, you can hear any damn thing. When I first got to Washington, they said LBJ was dressing up in ladies' underwear to play volleyball with the Secret Service."

They laughed and gossiped. Amanda was with one of the city's best-known power brokerages, a law firm that specialized in representing foreign governments, selling influence at four-hundred-dollar-an-hour consulting fees. She knew who was sleeping with whom, which White House officials would be subpoenaed next, which foreign ambassador was about to be recalled.

Andrew slipped his right hand into her icy fingers as they crossed into the Mall and circled the eastern edge of the Washington Monument. Amanda squeezed his hand gently to show him his touch was not unwelcome. Then she drew their cold clasp into the warmth of her full-length Blackglama mink coat.

They stopped and looked eastward, down the vast tree-lined sweep of the esplanade connecting the alabaster monuments to the huge

117

domed Capitol Building, which glowed an impossible white from ten blocks away.

"I'll never forget the first time I saw it," Andrew began quietly.

"Nobody ever does," Amanda interjected softly.

They stared at each other for a minute. When the unsaid became uncomfortable, they looked back at the dome.

"My father brought me here," Andrew continued. "Right where we're standing. We walked toward the Capitol. He rode me on his shoulders most of the way. I must have been at least seven or eight, and heavy. But my dad was the strongest man in the world. Wasn't yours?"

She nodded.

Andrew smiled. "He held me up so I could see better. As though you could miss it!"

They moved toward the gleaming marble magnet that had drawn Andrew and Amanda, like so many other ambitious young people from distant and common places like Texas and Illinois. Andrew could still hear his father's booming voice. *There's no limit to what you can do, Andrew. You can be anything. A congressman. Senator. President. Wouldn't you like that, Andy?*

Yes, Daddy. Youthful eyes sparkling at all the huge sights and sounds. *I'd like that, Daddy.*

"Must be nice, having parents who appreciate what you do." Amanda sighed. "My dad is a cop in Glen Forest, just outside Chicago. I'm pretty sure he thinks I'm a legal secretary."

She paused. "No, that's not fair. The proudest day in my folks' lives was the day I became a lawyer. They're very proud. But they live on a different plane, you know? They come here every year, and I introduce them to congressmen, Cabinet members. The names don't really mean anything. They're proud, they're just not sure why."

"Maybe they want their little girl to get married and move back to Glen Forest," Andrew said softly.

"Their little girl did get married, and it didn't work out," Amanda said bluntly. As they skirted the reflecting pool and mounted the series of steps up the Capitol, she spoke of her brief marriage to a Senate committee lawyer, a match based more on intellect than passion.

"His idea of romance was staying up late to watch election returns," Amanda recalled. "How can you make love to the sound of Walter Cronkite?"

They reached the Capitol's uppermost balcony and stared back down the Mall at the twin avenues spreading away from them in a V. The synchronized traffic lights switched in tandem from red to green on the empty midnight streets. Andrew withdrew his hand from Amanda's silk-lined pocket and sneaked it around the back of her coat, sliding it into the right-hand slit in the fur. He felt like a teenager trying to get things going in a parked car. Amanda curled into him like a housecat in need of stroking. Slipping her arms around Andrew's back, she stared frankly into his eyes.

Andrew kissed her, hesitating at first, then exploring her. He was a little shocked by how easy it was, how simply you could be pulled inside someone who wasn't your wife. The warmth of her mouth brought tears to his eyes, to know that she wanted him. Her sweet, gentle curves shifted boldly into his pelvis, a sensation he hadn't felt since that bittersweet night a million years ago, when he had proposed after a sweet, sensuous dance in the Pyramid Room.

The steady rhythm of footfalls jerked them apart: a Capitol Hill policeman, making his rounds.

"Evening, Mr. Sebastian," the tall black cop said quietly, trying not to intrude as his belt jangled past them. Andrew had a theory. He figured the clerk of the House circulated photos of all new members to the three thousand cops, cooks, barbers, trolley-car operators, and elevator men who comprised the Capitol's permanent infrastructure, so they could be sure to give members their proper due. Andrew knew he should be used to it by now, but the ease with which the cop had recognized him made him uneasy. Considering the circumstances.

Amanda regarded Andrew steadily for a moment. Then she took his hand and led him down the walkway to the steps leading toward the West Front.

"Let's walk a little farther," she said, not looking back at the strapping congressman who trailed behind her.

Amanda's apartment stood on the first floor of a renovated row house three blocks from the Capitol. On the glossily stained hardwood floors, barely visible beneath scattered remnants of last weekend's *Washington Post* and *Washington Star*, Andrew glimpsed lush green Oriental rugs with pale cream-colored geometric symbols.

"Sorry," Amanda muttered, pulling the key out of her door. "I wasn't expecting guests. Want a drink?"

"No thanks," Andrew said. He eased the heavy mink off her shoulders and laid it over the back of a white courduroy sofa. Quickly the fur was joined by his own tan cashmere overcoat and, seconds later, his black Pierre Cardin dinner jacket and red satin tie. They sat down, close together.

Moments later Amanda pulled Andrew to his feet. They stumbled awkwardly from the couch to her dark bedroom. Andrew unzipped her dress. It slid effortlessly down her long silky body, his trembling hands smoothing the lacy fabric past her taut breasts and flat stomach. He sank to his knees in front of the stunning figure, kissing her thighs lightly as he took off her shoes. He reached up to pull down the tight panty hose, burying his lips in her silken ecru, pushing her gently back onto the mattress, crawling up beside her. Amanda worked at the studs of his shirt.

Then they were both naked. Andrew was terribly excited by the cold satin veneer of unfamiliar skin against his own heat. Soon he was inside her, crying out in wonder at the forgotten sensation of entering a woman who was warm and juicy and moving. The feeling shocked him, and he came much too quickly, like a boy on his first time or a man who'd been away from home too long. But it didn't matter because he felt so good, all the electricity from his toes to his head plowing out of him in one big rush.

Andrew barely slowed. His muscular hips gyrated for another angle. He dug inside her, this time more deeply and for longer. Amanda cupped her hands behind his rock-hard buttocks and drew him in, crying out in surprise. Andrew kept on, again and again, until they were spent and groaning and laughing, and then he rolled back on the cool pillows and wiped the tears of joy from his eyes, and wondered how he would ever be able to leave.

Bored, Jim Brackler flipped through the magazines spread out on the institutional-brown coffee table. *The London Economist. U.S. News and World Report. Forbes. Fortune.*

The same business magazines covered the same bland foyer tables of every rich man's lobby in Dallas. Brackler had read them all that winter, paying court to the beleaguered nobility of the city's once omnipotent Democratic party oligarchy.

He'd had no time to contact all these petty feudal chieftains before

120

the last election. The big boys just sat back and waited it out, figuring they could always come back this year and groom someone to win. Theirs was the ideology of victory. Their test of a good politician was not so much what he believed, but whether he could get in— and how quickly he returned their phone calls once he got there.

Jim Brackler needed these men. Not all of them; to get them all, he'd have to give too much, and he'd lose the unions and blacks and blue-collar whites he had rallied so easily last year. The trick was to give just a little, to compromise here and there, on trivial little matters that put cash in the pockets of the old-line kingmakers he needed to win the seat.

He had spent four hard months canvassing the tenants of Interfirst Tower and Southland Life Building and Exchange Park and One Main Place and One Dallas Centre, riding elevators until he couldn't remember which floor he was after or whom exactly he should see once he got there. They had been hard, endless days of pointed questions and brusque secretaries. Mr. Haskell was so sorry, and could Mr. Haskell call Mr. Brackler when he got back in from Houston?

Brackler had been about to give up when, earlier that week, he had called on a hotshot young trial lawyer, a Democratic precinct chairman. Dan Mullins surprised him with a warm welcome.

"You're Jim Brackler!" the black-bearded thirty-year-old had exclaimed, ushering him into the plush conference room of Mullins and Partners, Attorneys-at-Law.

When Brackler commented that he and his partners must be doing well, Mullins boomed a hearty laugh. "Partners! You're looking at 'em, Jim. The furniture's all rented, every stick. So what can I do for you?"

Brackler rattled into his standard pitch.

Mullins raised a hand to cut him off. "You're preaching to the choir, Jim," the lawyer cried. "I saw you on the stump last spring. Unfortunately, nobody's gonna do shit in this race until they see what old man Hart does. I'm with you," he added quickly, as though that were a given. "But that and two bits'll buy you a cup of coffee. When did you last talk to Mr. Hart?"

"I don't think he likes me very much," Jim admitted. "I saw him at a dinner last year. Asked him for his support. He walked away without a word."

"You asked at a party?" Mullins asked incredulously.

"Sure," Brackler said, faltering. "You know, the way you do. Hello, sir, I'm Jim Brackler, glad to meet you, love to have your help."

"Oh, man, you got a lot to learn."

Mullins then carefully explained: Brackler needed banker Jarrett Hart's backing before any of the other big Democrats would come in. Prospective candidates had to come see him personally and ask for his support. Hart had to like what he heard in the first five minutes enough to write a check on the spot. Hart's check, explained Mullins, was the down payment Jim needed to open an account with the downtown oligarchy.

Brackler, thinking back to the wordless glare he'd gotten from Hart at the dinner, panicked aloud. "Have I already blown it?"

"Let's find out," Mullins said. The attorney had reached across the table and dialed a number from memory. "Penny? Dan Mullins. Listen, I've got Jim Brackler here. Used to be John Masters's right-hand man. Yes, ma'am, that was a terrible loss, very sad. Jim is running for the congressman's seat now. I thought Mr. Hart might like—"

Within seconds Brackler had the appointment, and Mullins was ushering him out of the office. "Hey"—Mullins looked at the name-plate on his front door—"you a lawyer?"

"Sure," Jim replied.

"Want to join Dallas's fastest-growing practice?"

Brackler hedged, realizing he'd never actually practiced law. "I don't have much trial experience."

"I didn't say you have to do anything," Mullins said almost scornfully. "I don't have to pay you. You could hang your hat here, use my secretary. People like a candidate to have a job. You could do a little research, a little lobbying. Chip in on the office expenses, and you can keep whatever you make. Who knows, maybe my partner will get elected to Congress next year." He grinned, teeth shining wolfishly through the black bristle surrounding his lips. "Wouldn't be the worst thing to happen to an up-and-coming young law firm."

Now, thanks to Dan, here Jim was, thumbing through *Business Week* in the small foyer separated by glass walls from the white tile of the Hart Building northwest of downtown. His best gray suit held his new business cards from the Kwik-Kopy on Greenville Avenue. It seemed a big expense. The campaign against Sebastian and Cadillo had drained nearly every dollar he had hoarded so carefully since his army days. But the cards gave him new confidence. The old-fashioned black lettering covered his shaky career situation with a patina of downtown respectability: JIM BRACKLER. ATTORNEY-AT-LAW.

"Mr. Brackler?" the honey-voiced secretary glanced down at the card he'd placed proudly on her desk twenty minutes earlier. "Mr. Hart will see you now."

Jim rose eagerly, expecting the secretary to get up and lead him through the door behind her desk. Instead she made a practiced gesture to the left. "Just press the button, Mr."—she glanced downward—"Brackler. The elevator will take you upstairs."

When the elevator slid open at the top, Jim's mouth gaped open in surprise. The entire floor, rambling a hundred yards in every direction, was one huge office. He could barely see its sole proprietor at the far end of the cavernous space. Hart's feet were propped up on a massive antique wooden desk, phone cradled between his ear and one huge shoulder.

Directly in front of Jim, a tiny, birdlike woman sat at a delicate little desk. She looked even older than the septuagenarian Hart. She smiled sweetly at the new arrival.

"Mr. Brackler," she said, "I'm Penny. Go right over. Mr. Hart is ready for you."

Jim walked hesitantly across the extraordinary office. He passed overstuffed settees and dining room ensembles, kitchenettes and wet bars and tiger-skin rugs, moose heads dangling over gun racks and thirty-foot conference tables lit by rows of green-hooded lamps. It looks like the inside of Gabbert's Furniture, he thought in awe. He crossed a broad expanse of red Persian rug that served as demarcation line between the lunatic terrain of some interior designer's nightmare and the home territory of Hart's office proper.

The elderly Texan behind the desk flipped his telephone receiver from shoulder to cradle in one rehearsed maneuver. He heaved his bulk skyward. The banker's wrinkled once-white shirt encompassed a rangy six-foot-six frame running to fat. Hart blotted out a fair portion of the sunshine shimmering through the endless windows. Beyond the massive panes, the icy-sharp February skyline served as fitting backdrop for the tycoon whose bank had financed half the jagged peaks piercing the blue sky south of the huge oaken desk in the rooftop field where Jarrett Hart played ball.

"Mr. Hart," Brackler began. He proffered his second business card, hoping the fresh ink wouldn't smear.

Hart's bovine face cracked in a smile. The businessman ran one hamlike hand through his thick white hair as they sat down. "Tell me about yourself, Jim," he said simply. The old man's big brown eyes were soft and kind. His gentle nods put Brackler at ease, drew him out. He was tempted to try a joke and ask Mr. Hart for cabfare back to the elevator, but thought better of it. Instead, Jim Brackler talked politics. Skipping the usual spiel about qualifications, he went straight to the heart of the matter.

"I'm here because I'm the only Democrat who can beat Andrew Sebastian next year," he said. "I've got the old Masters supporters because I worked for Masters. The blacks and the blue-collar voters like what I stand for. Unfortunately, not too many folks make it to the polls for a special election. It'll be different this November," he emphasized, moving on to the next point on Dan's list. "I've got name ID, sir. Fifty-seven percent of the voters know who I am."

He took a deep breath and plunged forward, "What I don't have is your blessing. Or money. They go hand in hand. I need you, Mr. Hart. And I can win for you."

Without batting one big cow eye, the banker shifted the silver-and-turquoise scarf ring below his Adam's apple and peered intently at the awkward, stocky young man sitting at the edge of his chair.

"You do get right to the point, don't you?" Hart said.

"Yes, sir." James nodded vigorously. "I didn't want to waste your time. I'm a Democrat for life, Mr. Hart," he continued, watching the old man's eyes light up. Mullins had said party switchers were Hart's pet peeve: the old man considered them traitors who had abandoned the Democratic party to northern liberals. Going for the kill, Jim added, "I don't switch causes according to the prevailing political winds."

"I encouraged Roger's boy to wait for John Masters to retire and seek that seat as a Democrat," Hart mused quietly. "Andrew's just like his dad. Pushy. Look at that boy up in Washington, already too big for his britches. He's gonna wear out his welcome real fast."

The aging banker glanced moodily westward, toward the eight-lane ribbon of concrete below. "Know how Roger got that piece-a-shit freeway named after him?" he asked gruffly. "He gave five hundred acres of useless swamp to the government. Gave another

124

fifty thousand dollars to LBJ's reelection campaign. Then Roger made a good fifty million developing the land on either side!" Hart's rheumy chocolate eyes bugged open wide. He chuckled, embarrassed by his own vehemence. "He built this building," Hart said approvingly. "With my bank's money, then sold it back to us. Best damn customer we have."

"Yes, sir," Jim said levelly.

"You couldn't beat Sebastian last year," Hart zeroed in. "What makes you think you can beat him now?"

"Several things, Mr. Hart." Brackler was prepared for this. "This November, there'll be five times as many votes as the special election last May. Whole new ball game. This time, we won't split the Democrats between Cadillo and me. I'll beat Juan hands down in the primary. In the general, Sebastian's incumbency is going to kill him. I'll hang Watergate right around his neck. This will be a great year for us, sir. I can feel it out there, at the homeowner's meetings, in the union halls, at the Kip's Big Boy on Mockingbird. I know those people in East Dallas, Pleasant Grove, Mesquite. I grew up there. I'm one of us, you know? Not one of them: the Nixons, the Rockefellers, the Sebastians. That's what politics is all about. Us and them. I'm us."

"What does that make me?" Hart shot back.

"Oh, you're them, sir," Jim replied earnestly.

The old man barked sudden laughter. His voice was a sonic boom in that airplane hangar of an office.

"I like you, Jim," Hart said, wiping a tear from his eye. "I really do. But I just don't think you can beat Roger Sebastian's boy. It's nothin' against you. You've got a future. I can tell. But I'm gonna have to pass on this one."

"What if I had a surefire issue?" Brackler said in desperation. He hadn't planned to go this far. But Hart was slipping away from him. He'd have to trust the old bastard.

"Like what?" Hart said.

"Like this." Jim drew a dog-eared Xerox copy from his inside jacket pocket. He unfolded it quickly, spreading it flat on the green desk blotter.

The old man grabbed a pair of rimless spectacles off the desk and slid them on his big hawk nose, the legacy of distant Cherokee ancestors. The banker peered down at the document, noting the

125

familiar letterhead of Senanco, the Sebastian holding corporation. When he finished reading, he whistled soundlessly between coffee-stained false teeth.

"I'll be damned."

"Nobody knows about this, except you and me, Mr. Hart," Brackler said slowly, carefully. "And them, of course."

"I'll be damned," Hart repeated softly, toting up the credits and debits of this particular balance sheet.

Brackler plunged in deeper. "Frankly, sir, I'm committed to this race. I spent everything I had on the last campaign. With this in my back pocket, I can beat Andrew Sebastian," he said seriously, boldly, without a trace of arrogance. "And I'm going to do it. With you or without you, sir, with all due respect. It'll be tough without you, but I've got the votes in the primary. And I've got this"—he pointed to the document—"for next fall. Either way, I win. But I sure need your help."

Unhearing, Hart stared at the document. Then he swirled his chair to face the long wooden credenza against the window. The banker slid open a drawer and hauled out—Brackler's heart skipped a beat—a giant black checkbook.

Hart flipped open the big ledger in his lap. He picked up a silver Cross pen from the blotter where the damning letter lay, creased and folded from two years following Brackler from Dallas to Washington and back again: often fondled, lovingly contemplated; never before revealed to another. The old banker scratched his pen across the topmost of three yellow business checks perforated together on one sheet. This is how real money changes hands, thought Jim. He watched anxiously as Hart filled in the date and an amount Brackler couldn't read upside down.

The banker paused, pen hovering over the signature line. "Is it true what I hear?" the old man asked abruptly, hesitating a moment. "That your mother is an alcoholic?"

"Yes, sir," Brackler said deadpan, his heart stopping momentarily. The old man was awfully well informed. "But she ain't nothin' compared to my pa. Now he could drink!"

The old man chuckled softly and signed the check. Then he rose to shake Brackler's hand. "Good luck, Jim," he said, adding a pointed, "Keep in touch."

Brackler nearly sprinted the hundred-yard dash across the vast obstacle course. Remembering to nod politely at Penny, he punched the knob that closed the elevator doors, so he could breathe a sigh of relief and peek at the yellow check clutched in his sweaty fingers.

My God, it can't be, he thought, staring. Ten thousand dollars! He wanted to holler out loud. The elation of acceptance flooded over him, and with it, a sure and sudden scent of the victory to come. I'm *in*, Jim thought exultantly. Jarrett Hart is behind me. *I am in!*

He burst out of the elevator and ran out into the parking lot, making a mental note to thank Dan Mullins for the solid advice about Jarrett Hart. Don't bullshit him, Dan had told Jim. Be honest. Stress party loyalty. Above all, be yourself. Hart wasn't always rich, Dan had said. He was born dirt poor in Tennessee. His mother drank; father ran off when Hart was just a boy.

Jim pried open the door of his rickety VW and shoved himself behind the wheel. He slammed the door shut, made sure the windows were rolled up tightly.

Then Jim Brackler screamed aloud, tears of joy running down his cheeks, spattering down to smear the still-moist ink of the wonderful yellow ticket trembling between his fingers.

8

on Callahan puffed out of the crowded elevator into Rayburn Basement. Not breaking his hurried short-legged stride, he shoved back one wrinkled shirtsleeve to reveal the watch strapped too tightly around his hairy left wrist: 2:25. No sign of Andrew.

Callahan sighed, hustling through the little knot of Capitol Hill staffers gathered around the vending machines where he ate dinner most nights. He rushed through the pneumatic *whoosh* of the sliding glass doors that led to the small subway platform. Then he boarded one of the two miniature open-car trolleys that shuttled back and forth under Independence Avenue, ferrying members and aides between the domed Capitol to the House Office Buildings, or HOBs. A creaky old conductor nodded his black cap to two even older congressmen who had boarded the front car. It was marked with a small white sign: MEMBERS ONLY.

Watching the bald heads bob and mutter just inches from his nose, Callahan was struck as always by the incredible openness of the American democracy. He remembered the first time he had ever ridden the Capitol Hill subway in 1967, when he had been called back from some hopeless congressional crusade in Iowa to accept a big new job with the Republican Senatorial Committee.

The chairman, a tall, bespectacled senator from Illinois, was briefing Callahan in his office when three short bells rang, lighting three of the five red bulbs on the clock above the senator's head. "Got to vote," the senator said, jumping to his feet. "Walk with me?" It was raining outside, as it does nine days out of ten in Washington. They rode the elevator down to the basement of the Senate Office Building (the SOB, in the delightful alphabet soup of Washington) and hopped on the little trolley. Together, big-league senator and rookie from the farm team, they had ridden the secret little power train through the long dark tunnel. The senator got caught up in debate on the floor. Callahan spent all afternoon riding back and forth alone, marveling at how close he could get to the famous politicians, a die-hard fan suddenly allowed backstage with the band.

Now Callahan was on top, a producer who had finally discovered his star. Andrew Sebastian was a campaign manager's wet dream: toothy, smooth, high-minded, rich. If Andrew had a failing, it was that things had come to him a tad easily, which made him a little soft, a shade too trusting. Politics will knock that out of him soon enough, Callahan thought.

The trolley bumped softly into the Capitol terminal. Callahan stepped down to the slick gray concrete of the Capitol cellar. He spotted Andrew immediately, on the escalator from the House floor elevators, laughing with a tall, smart-looking blonde Callahan didn't recognize.

He waved at his boss, who parted suddenly from the woman and strode swiftly through the surging mass. The slim young congressman grinned broadly as the train carried them back toward Rayburn.

"What makes you so happy?" Callahan snapped. "You're a half hour late. Cadillo's fuming by now. What was so important?"

Andrew's smile vanished self-consciously, like a man who suddenly realizes he's been talking to himself. "Nothing," he said with studied nonchalance.

Callahan felt like a nagging wife. "Christ, Andrew. Why should I be the only one living on Pepto-Bismol? We're in trouble, and you know it. You saw the poll."

Andrew sobered abruptly. Last week's *Dallas Morning News* poll showed Andrew well behind Jim Brackler. Sebastian's three-year-old conversion to the Republican party was looking like the worst mistake of his life. The party's scandal-ridden administration was teetering on the brink of collapse. Washington's soupy August heat was rife with wild rumors. The president would resign tomorrow. The president would never resign, had sworn to barricade the White House with army troops if Congress dared impeach him.

It was a dangerous and wonderful time, and Andrew was right in the thick of it. Callahan's candidate was flush with Potomac fever, that most deadly political disease, its symptoms a swelled head from too much exposure on network TV, a sudden loss of contact with the folks back home.

"Andrew . . ." Callahan leaned close so no one could hear. "People up here know you're a knight in shining armor. Back home, people aren't so up on things. They've lost track of all the Haldemans and Ehrlichmans and Siricas. I've seen the party's numbers from two dozen congressional districts all over the country. They look like hell. Nixon lied to the voters, and they're gonna throw out everybody connected with him."

"Come on, Ron!" Andrew hissed in soft frustration. "Who connects me with him? All I've done is fight the White House. I've been in *Time*. On *Meet the Press*. Twice."

"How many people in Mesquite watch *Meet the Press?*" Callahan cut in. "Polls don't lie. People vote the party label. Right now, 'Republican' means crooked."

The subway bumped to a stop. They rose quickly on cue, talking in quick undertones as they hustled through the now quiet Rayburn basement.

"Big Jim Brackler," Callahan said. "Remember him?"

Andrew groaned.

Callahan persisted, "Okay, it's corny. But the voters are lapping it up. Big Jim, man of the people. Big Jim, fighter for the little guy, meaner'n a junkyard dog. I'm telling you, it plays! They like a guy like Brackler. Rough around the edges, roll up the sleeves, take some names and kick some ass up in Washington."

"I'll show him kicking ass," Andrew mumbled gruffly, punching the elevator button.

"Big deal. Big talk," Callahan gibed. He was riling Andrew. Good, he thought. At least I have his attention. "Brackler's everywhere, Andy. Mixing it up with the Lions. Raising money at Jarrett Hart lunches. Shaking hands at barbecues."

"Yeah, he's a good eater," Andrew said lightly.

"So he's a little heavy, and he's got chili stains on his tie," Callahan remonstrated. "So do I. So do most of the guys that work in auto parts warehouses, and down at Sears. Don't be such a snot, Andrew. That's part of his appeal. He's one of us, you know?"

"What's that supposed to mean?" Andrew said. The youthful congressman pressed resentfully at the elevator button. Nobody talked to him like this anymore.

"Never mind," Callahan said, annoyed. "If you don't get it by now, you never will. Point is, you're going back to Dallas. Now, and for good, right through to November."

"Now?" Andrew said incredulously. "With all that's happening?"

They fell silent as the elevator arrived, smooth silver doors sliding open to reveal a young aide in a seersucker suit. Andrew and Ron glared at each other, observing the old Washington rule: Never talk politics on elevators, because you never knew which side your traveling companions were on. "Information is power, and power is this town's universal currency," Callahan had warned. "Talking on an elevator is like handing out hundred-dollar bills."

"What about this deal with Juan?" Andrew said as they stepped out, neatly tabling the going-home debate.

"Juan hates Brackler's guts," Callahan replied curtly. "But old man Cadillo's too smart to allow Juan to get in bed with you for nothing. You didn't help things any by being forty-five minutes late," he added, unable to resist one last shot.

They paused briefly outside a huge oak door bearing the simple legend they'd worked so hard to win: MR. SEBASTIAN. TEXAS. Andrew turned abruptly to his administrative assistant, speaking with unaccustomed awkwardness. "Ron, this business with Cadillo," he said hesitantly. "He isn't going to ask for—"

"Money?" Callahan said brightly. Funny, he thought, how rich people have trouble with the word. "Possible. Whatever he wants, the meter's ticking."

Tricia slammed down the antique-looking enamel phone into the ornate brass cradle on the tiny escritoire. The kitchen nook was her workbench. The bookshelf to her right held her tools. The Green Book, Washington's social register. The Congressional Directory.

A *Guide to Protocol*, which told new congressional wives how to address thank-you notes to princes and ambassadors and postmasters general. And the sexual self-help best-seller she'd bought on Dupont Circle, which had been utterly useless in re-creating another interlude like the one that had given Andrew rug burns on his knees that night in Dallas. She purposely left the book in plain view so he could at least see that she was trying. He hadn't noticed it.

Now she knew why.

A tidy clutter of sticky yellow slips of paper marched up and down her bulletin board, above the vast alligator-bound folder where she kept her own daily schedule. Tricia updated the enormous notebook twice weekly down at Andrew's office, in clipped, efficient meetings with Darla, the sweet, ugly little Alabama gal Tricia had personally selected as Andrew's secretary. Together they annotated the calendar with a concordance about the people and places and politics that she would face: "Lunch w/Sen. Kelly's wife, Susanna (not Suzanne!). Kids Bert (Navy) & Billy (Yale) & Paula (drugs, don't ment.)."

She'd sat like this for the past hour, on her tiny rolling stool in this wee corner of the great dappled-gray battleship of a town house, glaring at the fastidious blue-inked entry. February 20, no doubt there. She compared it with the damning scrawl on the postcard she had plucked from that day's mail. "Found this in my files. I knew you and Mrs. S. would want it!" read the backward-slanting European script. "The two of you look so happy!—G. R." Tricia remembered the beaming portly German, his silly social climber's camera popping away at party guests.

And since when did her hotshot husband not return his wife's calls? It was one thing for a politician to cheat on his wife, she thought bitterly. Half the pols in D.C. do that. But not to keep in touch: *that* was breaking the rules.

Now, that mush-mouthed southern trampette said he was "in a meeting." With whom? An awful sick thought trickled into Tricia's brain. Her? She snatched the dainty instrument off its cradle and began dialing once again.

Andrew couldn't concentrate on what the slender young Mexican-American was saying, despite stern looks from Callahan that meant "Pay attention, stupid, this is important." He was getting tired of the way Ron pushed him around, arranging his schedule, interfering with what little time he was able to siphon off without anyone noticing.

Time stolen for her.

Andrew had finally found something for himself, a secret pile of miser's gold, and all he wanted was to go into the vault and run his fingers through it. He wanted to see her, be with her, make love to her, talk to her. When they were together, in those five or ten hours a week he could slip between the crisply typed lines of the agenda Ron laid on his black walnut desk every Monday morning, Andrew simply reveled in her, burying himself alive in her sweet earth, losing consciousness of the whole outside world even as they spent their stolen minutes together in gossip about the towering figures of those tremulous days. Amanda especially liked Andrew's Howard Baker impression: a thundering Tennessee twang that boomed, "What did the president know, and when did he know it?"

This afternoon, he had caught sight of her in the galleries. They'd left the floor in the middle of the Philippines debate: risky for both of them, since they were supposed to be in the cloakrooms fighting each other on foreign aid appropriations. "What the hell," Amanda had said in the corridor, laughing. "We'll just cancel each other out."

It had been horribly hot and sweaty in her perennially unkempt apartment. Suddenly it had been time to rush back to the Hill, to hike all the way to the House chamber before doubling back down the elevators to the subway. He shouldn't have escorted her all the way, but he felt dirty asking her to make all those circuitous double entrances.

The first night, oddly enough, had been easy. At 2:30 A.M., he'd dragged himself out of Amanda's warm covers and dressed for the frigid air. As the taxi rattled to a halt, his house blazed warning, spilling yellow pools onto Georgetown's brick streets. Andrew was mentally prepared to do battle. He was determined not to apologize by making up a plausible excuse. Besides which, he couldn't think of one. By the time he mounted the steps, he was furious with Tricia for denying him the simple bliss he had nearly forgotten.

When she hurled the door open with an icy, "Where the hell have you been?" Andrew told his wife the stupidest story he could imagine, a silly account of a secret briefing with the CIA about a Castroite conspiracy in Nicaragua. He waited, his eyes daring her

133

to see through the idiotic lie. Instead, bafflingly, she lit into him for not making a bigger effort to locate her at the party. Listening to Tricia pour out her anger, how she'd not had the car keys and had to beg a ride home with Kitty and Bob, Andrew realized she actually believed the silly tale. As though men in trench coats routinely dropped into embassy parties, whisking junior congressmen away to some underground war room with a big map on the wall.

As the affair wore through the summer, Andrew became as reckless with Tricia as he was cautious with his staff. It was ironic. The affair seemed not to threaten his marriage, which he no longer valued. But it was a dagger to the throat of his career, about which he cared a great deal and which seemed ready to go right down the tubes.

Leaning back in the huge burgundy leather chair behind the big black desk, Andrew forced himself to tune in to Juan Cadillo's steady monotone. Juan was always giving a speech, whether ordering a Pepsi from the receptionist or restating the entire past history of their political relationship. Andrew could have done it in twenty seconds. You promised to endorse me over Masters, then you screwed me over so you could be his heir. Only Masters died without a will, and Brackler took you to court and wiped you out.

"My father is very old-fashioned," Cadillo droned on unapologetically. Andrew kept his Listening Intently mask firmly in place. "He felt we had to give the Old Guard one last chance on the Masters thing."

"I appreciate your frankness," Andrew said. At least, he thought, the little snake isn't going to pretend his betrayal was anything but pure, naked self-interest. "You know I support the general goal of electing a minority congressman from Dallas," he continued slowly. "But your 'Old Guard' has split you up into three different districts."

"They'll never cut us in," Cadillo said, shaking his head in mock embarrassment. "The Fourth is not for us, Andy. But our people could decide which way it goes."

"I agree," Andrew said, a shade too quickly. "The Fourth will never elect a minority. But the Seventeenth?" His voice trailed off as he watched Cadillo's face to determine whether he was really planning to move over into the adjacent district and take on Buck Drake.

134

"The Seventeenth would be difficult." Julian Mendoza spoke for the first time. "But not impossible."

Mendoza's eyes roved around the office, such a striking contrast to John Masters's old inner sanctum. There was no photo gallery, just rich mahogany paneling that smelled faintly of lemon oil. Sebastian's got the right idea, Julian thought: no pictures, nobody gets left out. He was amazed; Andrew's credenza bore not even the inevitable smiling portrait of the Wife.

Mendoza drew a deep breath. "We think Drake can be taken."

"I'll say," agreed Callahan. "Christ, he's just a TV weatherman." Andrew shot Callahan a cold look that said he shouldn't bad-mouth other members, even while plotting against them. My, thought Callahan, aren't we getting clubby?

"Let's cut the horseshit," Cadillo interrupted. The pompous bland monotone was gone. "Just between the four of us, okay?" He leaned forward intently. "Nobody knows about this, not even my father. He doesn't understand modern politics, you know?"

Andrew nodded his understanding. He had a father, too.

Cadillo hurried on, "I'm not willing to wait the rest of my life on the off chance Buck Drake and his poker pals might decide to let the waiters run the restaurant. We're gonna move in now. A lot of people know how stupid that guy is. We can do it, with your help."

"You've got it, Juan." Andrew added cannily, "If I'm around to give it. I've got problems of my own."

"I'd love to help you crush that motherfucker, Andy." Julian looked back coolly at his contemporary. "Trouble is, I'd be dead if I came out for a Republican now, with Nixon and all. You should hear what they're saying back home."

"So Ron tells me," Andrew said dryly. "Juan, Nixon's finished. Any day now, we'll have a new president."

Mendoza shook his head vigorously, spraying flecks of white dandruff on the shiny black wood in front of him. "With all due respect, you don't understand our community, Congressman," he said firmly. "They would never accept Juan's endorsement of you under the current circumstances. They would see you as just another Washington bigshot, taking our votes for granted and giving nothing in return."

There it is! Andrew thought exultantly. The open window! "We want this to be a two-way street," he enunciated slowly. "We don't want something for nothing. Anything we can do? To, ah, advance your, ah, advancement?" Come on, Juan, Andrew thought. What do you want?

"I need a victory." Cadillo was as impatient as Andrew. "I can't go into another campaign with nothing but two losing congressional races on my résumé. Andrew, I need a job."

Andrew breathed an inward sigh of relief. A job. No slush fund, nothing illegal or unethical. Just a job to provide cash and respectability, something to look good in a newspaper story: "Businessman Juan Cadillo today announced his candidacy for (fill in the blank)." Andrew would just call Dad, create some big-title bogus PR job with one of the Senanco subsidiaries. What would you like, sir? Land? Hotels? Air freight? Chocolate mint or pistachio?

Simple, easy to deliver, aboveboard. So why come to me? Andrew thought warily. "We'd love to help. My father can talk to some people."

"Juan has his own father," Mendoza said wryly. "We had a specific thing in mind, actually."

Cadillo jumped in. "Regional director of HEW, for the seven states of the Southwest," he said proudly, a child reciting a poem. "I'm very qualified," he added earnestly. "I chair the city's Human Services Commission."

"He'd be the first Hispanic ever to serve in that post," Mendoza said, selling hard now. "It's a big presidential appointment. No one could blame the Cadillos for supporting the congressman who made such a breakthrough for us."

The HEW job was a huge political plum, Andrew knew. It was currently being contested by some twenty congressmen from Arizona to Louisiana, all infinitely better connected at the White House than Andrew.

"I'll do what I can," Andrew assured the two Mexican-Americans as they walked out of his office. "If not HEW, maybe Labor or Commerce."

"HEW," Cadillo said abruptly. Andrew's respect for him went up another notch. Cadillo extended his hand: "Sorry, Andrew. That's the one we need."

Andrew smiled good-bye. He nodded as Darla handed him a fistful of messages. There were two from a colleague on his Asian Affairs Subcommittee: "Where were you today?" A dozen from

136

constituents. Seven from Tricia, marked in frustrated progression from "Please Call" to "ASAP" to "Urgent."

Andrew sighed and crinkled the whole stack of pink slips into a little ball. He hooked it cockily into his wastebasket. Two points, he thought. Now, who the hell can I call at the White House?

Three hours later, Tricia still sat in her kitchen cranny. For the thousandth time that day, she wondered where exactly her husband was at that moment.

The front door slammed an answer. "Hell-o!" came his usual call from the front hallway.

Tricia wiped her eyes and shoved the huge volume into the drawer. She picked up the postcard and slipped it into the long open pocket of her bright yellow sundress.

"Hey!" Andrew whisked into the kitchen. He stooped to deliver the obligatory peck on her stony cheek. "You're not dressed."

"I'm not going," Tricia said dully. "I've had enough embassy parties."

"Very funny," Andrew said sharply, pulling her to her feet. He marched her unwillingly toward the main hallway. "Come on, hon," he cajoled. "Haig may be there tonight. Somebody will know what's gonna happen, and this boy needs to know. Bad. You'll never believe what Juan Cadillo wants in exchange for his Mexicans."

Andrew practically stumbled into her as she whirled on the parquet floor. Tricia yanked the leering postcard from her dress.

"Who is she?" she cried. A single tear leaked helplessly down her cheeks. "Are you still seeing her?"

The hollow clichés tumbled out in a pleading whine that sounded nothing like the militant tone in her brain. Damn, she thought, I sound like *Days of Our Lives*. Next my lower lip will be quivering a mealy-mouthed, Do you love her?

Tricia repeated the question firmly, loudly: "Well? Are you?"

"What?" Andrew stammered. He backed away, as if to get a better view. "Who? What's wrong?"

"Good God," Tricia said as the realization flooded through her. "I knew! I've known all along. What a pathetic idiot you must think I am!" Andrew looked back at her dumbly, dabbing a thin sheen of sweat from his forehead. "There must be something wrong with me." Tricia shook her head in wonderment. "I knew. The minute

137

you walked in the door that night. The minute I realized you'd left the party. I mean, how obvious could you be? And all the times you've rubbed my nose in it. Good Christ, no wonder Kitty was looking at me funny yesterday."

She looked up at him, panic freezing her blood. "Does everyone know?" she sobbed. "What's it been, six months? Seven? Do you and she celebrate your month anniversaries, like we used to? You bastard!"

The tears were gone now, steamed out by anger, and she was glad. She was not, not, not going to lose control.

"Tricia . . ." Andrew's voice petered out inconclusively.

For once, she saw with satisfaction, Andrew Sebastian was at a loss for words. Usually he treated her like a loud-mouthed heckler at the back of the crowd: "Yes, well, thank you for your views, ma'am, I'll carry those thoughts back to Washington." Tricia let him stew. She wobbled backward into a soft chair, fumbling vaguely for the armrest.

Andrew stood in the hallway, frozen and a bit green about the gills, hands on his hips, blue jacket dangling from one finger. He stared at the center of the red Persian carpet on the parlor floor. Denials racketed wildly through his head, but beneath it all was a steady resounding boom that told him to tell her the truth. He opened his mouth and tried.

"I did meet someone," he said haltingly. "That is what this is all about?" His defiant gaze rose to meet hers. "I'm not pleading guilty to the wrong crime? You want to know about Amanda."

"Amanda," Tricia said softly, pronouncing each syllable like a new word she'd never heard before. Her throat was dry and swollen, and it hurt her to talk. "Who is she? Have I met her? I'm sure her photo doesn't half do her justice," she said, flipping the offending snapshot onto the coffee table.

"She's just somebody I met," Andrew said limply, his courage slipping as he saw the pathetic curiosity in Tricia's eyes. He glanced down at Herr Rettmer's postcard. Now that the moment was here, he wished it had never come. "I met her at a party," he said, voice shuddering a bit. "That party."

"And you're still—seeing her, of course," Tricia stated matter-of-factly, trying to keep the plaintive note out of her voice. "Today?"

"Yes, I did," Andrew said, adding, "We—Tricia, I never meant to hurt you."

"No. Of course not," she said. God, that hurt, hearing him call the two of them "we."

"Let's see, have we covered all the bases?" She ticked off the high points in clipped fragile sentences that teetered at the fine edge of hysteria. "What's her name? Amanda." A scathing flash of scorn. "Do I know her? No. You never wanted to hurt me. Very kind. What else is there? Frankly, Andrew, I refuse to ask."

"I don't know whether I love her."

"I don't give a shit." There was pity and wonder in her voice as she said, "You don't know what you want, do you?"

Andrew paused. He realized she was right. He simply had nothing to say.

The shrill of the hallway phone shattered the thick silence between them.

"Saved by the bell?" Tricia said sardonically.

He turned to answer it.

"Let it ring," she commanded.

"I can't," he mumbled, and bent to pick it up. "Might be the office."

"Oh, heavens, yes, of course!" she bit back. "The office. How stupid of me!"

Andrew ignored her, listening intently to the barking male tones she recognized all the way across the room. Callahan, she thought. Andrew's other girl.

Andrew's end of the conversation was worthless: "When? What time tomorrow? Well, this takes care of the other. No way I can go back to Dallas now. It's official? That is great news. 'Bye."

Andrew turned to her, his heart hammering in his chest. What could he possibly say to her? Hating himself, he ducked the issue. "He's calling it quits," he reported. "Tomorrow, at noon. Nixon's resigning."

"Great," Tricia replied dispiritedly. Possibly the greatest crisis of my life, right up there with being raped on a street corner. And he wants to talk shop.

Andrew stared off into the space over her left shoulder, as if she weren't there. "This isn't the time," he said slowly, dissecting each word with a politician's scalpel skill. "There's a lot I want to say. A lot I want to hear." As always, he was fluid and articulate under pressure. "I want to think about it first. You should, too," he advised solicitously, feeling the worst kind of coward.

139

"I am sorry. I know that doesn't solve anything. But I just can't deal with it right now," he emphasized, glancing down at the phone. She knew he itched to snatch it up and call everyone he knew and spend all night talking about Nixon and Ford and What Would Happen Now.

"I gotta go," he said abruptly, words tumbling out in a rush. "Things are happening too fast."

Her gaze followed wordlessly as his tall, angular back disappeared out the front door, jacket whipping up and over the right shoulder to cover the Rorschach splotch of sweat down his back.

Tricia's eyes blurred and crossed; she saw two and four and eight doors as they slammed shut in his wake. She wiped her nose and lurched to her feet, sandals slapping down the hall, through the bright white swinging door of her spick-and-span kitchen. Her legs felt rubbery, unstable. She went directly to the little nook to look up the number for Braniff Airways, making one quick detour to step up on her toes and reach inside the cabinet above the refrigerator, where Andrew kept the Chivas.

"It was bound to happen." Amanda's voice faltered as she poured the Soave Bolla, her mind racing for the right words. "Is it a relief?"

"Yeah," he acknowledged. He leaned his head against the back of her sofa in exhaustion. "I should have stayed and talked it out," he said, suddenly wishing he had. "I just couldn't. I needed time to think. Talk to you."

"Oh, no!" Amanda said resolutely. She crossed the short distance between them and handed him a huge goblet filled to the brim with pale liquid and crushed ice.

She shoved a stack of newsprint off the couch and sat beside him, cross-legged and tomboyish. She spelled things out. "This happens to lots of people in this town, and now it's happened to us. I don't know what you should do. But I'm not going to do anything," she said firmly. "What do you want?"

"Tricia asked me the same thing," he confessed. "I don't know. Keep seeing you, that's for sure."

"What about her?" Amanda interrogated briskly.

"There's been so much there," he replied. "I can't imagine what things would be like without her. Better, probably. More complicated."

"Now you're talking politics," Amanda said, glad to move to their sure and steady common ground. "Reelection."

"Why not?" Andrew's eyes shone with defiance. "It's what I am. I'm going for it all, Amanda."

"Doesn't everybody?" she interjected dryly. "Everyone who's ever run for dogcatcher thinks he can be president."

"Why else bother?" Andrew let the wine sluice down his sandy throat. It was strange. Twenty minutes ago he couldn't wait to flee here. Now that he'd reached the haven of Amanda's apartment, he wished he were at home, talking this out with Tricia.

"What about this Nixon resignation?" Amanda burst out, unraveling the gift-wrapped conversation piece they'd both been dying to open.

They squatted on the couch and drank wine, and chattered into the night. She made linguine with clam sauce, and they watched the late news. They made love and talked politics until the small hours of the morning. Then, thinking of the beautiful, broken woman he had deserted in Georgetown, Andrew lay awake until dawn, wondering if he and Amanda had anything else to share.

After the fall, Congress was a gang of unruly school kids with a substitute teacher. The floor was suddenly raucous. Resolutions sailed toward the Speaker's rostrum like paper airplanes at a blackboard.

Before the mob could separate the sagging jowls from his slumping shoulders, Nixon choppered off the White House lawn with a quick wave and a few feeble tears, leaving behind a caretaker to guard the tyrant's retreat. Congress, incensed over the new president's pardon of the old one, moved quickly to pass a flurry of new laws to strip the imperial presidency of its grandeur. Facing a November bloodbath, House Republicans fell all over themselves to explain how they had been one of the very first to call for Nixon's resignation.

But Andrew had it on the record, in writing, in the pages of *Time* and *Newsweek*. Suddenly he had lots of friends.

On the crowded House floor that September afternoon, Andrew prowled the busy aisles with a single object in mind: the HEW job for Juan Cadillo. His latest poll showed him thirty points behind Brackler. Brackler was concentrating everything on an anti-Watergate tidal wave. Andrew was desperate to get "Big Jim" off his back by launching a big counteroffensive in the barrio. For that, he needed Juan Cadillo.

"Sorry, Andrew," said Telmar of Arizona, shaking his head sadly. "I'd love to help, but Goldwater's already got somebody up for that. Hopi Indian from Flagstaff. Love to help you, but my whole district is one damn big reservation." Andrew nodded and worried, scratching his signature absently on the latest amendment for the new War Powers Act. He wondered if Callahan had heard back from Mark Latham at the White House.

Their only big break had come a month ago, just after the new president took office, when the White House had decided to keep Mark Latham on as the White House personnel director, in charge of all presidential appointments. Latham was a Texan. A fierce Nixon backer, he disliked Andrew intensely. But Latham wanted the party to hold Andrew's seat and was enough a politician to realize the Cadillo nomination was the only way to do it. Besides, Latham was said to have his own political ambitions and was inclined to do big favors for important Mexican-Americans. There had been a string of warm, inconclusive meetings; Latham seemed impressed by the growing list of Cadillo backers Andrew had gathered on the floor.

Andrew glanced down at the petition: 214 members! No one had ever worked this hard for an appointment. He punched his card into the slot to vote "yea" on a procedural vote, watching his light flash green behind the Speaker's rostrum. He always liked to check, not trusting the electronics.

Ron Callahan met him outside the cloakroom door, breathless from his long run through the tunnel.

"Sorry!" he wheezed, coughing his hacking smoker's rumble. "Subway's out. Wanted to let you know right away."

"What now?" Andrew snapped.

"Latham's been sacked." Callahan cleared his throat and spit into an antique brass spittoon that had once held the expectorant of Webster and Clay. I've always wondered who spits into those, Andrew thought. Now I know: Callahan.

"So who's in charge now?" Andrew's voice was frantic.

"I don't know," Callahan said simply. He followed Andrew back down the statue-lined hallway. "They may not fill Latham's job for weeks. In the meantime, they'll just leave all the appointments open."

142

"That's just great," Andrew whispered in disgust. Elbowing aside a middle-aged Scoutmaster, he yanked his administrative assistant aboard. The tourist-packed elevator lurched downward.

Andrew and Callahan sprang free in the basement, sprinted down the tunnel catwalk toward the Rayburn Building. Callahan's pudgy legs pumped to match Andrew's long strides.

"We can't afford to wait," Andrew addressed the empty air in front of him. "We have to do something. Dad's pulled every string he's got, but most of them left with Nixon. And now we've lost Latham. Surely there must be someone in charge."

"Maybe we should just call Latham's old extension, and see who picks up the phone," Callahan piped up from behind him.

Andrew halted and turned to face his aide. His face rearranged itself into a twisted smile. "You're a genius, Ron," he said genuinely. "Can't you walk any faster?"

They felt like teenagers making prank phone calls. Hello, do you have Prince Albert in a can? Let him out! Do you have pig's feet? Better wear shoes!

"This is how Woodward and Bernstein figured out E. Howard Hunt was the burglars' contact," Callahan explained, punching the new push-button phone he found so incredibly annoying. What was wrong with dials? "They found a phone number among the suspect's effects, called it, and it rang at the White House—It's ringing."

"White House, Mr. Stuart's office," came the secretary's languorous whine over the speakerphone.

Andrew's stomach gave a peculiar lurch. Why did he know that name?

"Ah, yes," Callahan barked an absurd southern drawl. "I'm ad-dressin' some, ah, correspondence to Mistah Stuart. Could you please spell his name for me, honey?"

"Yes, sir," the voice said politely. "S-t-u-a-r-t."

Callahan rolled his eyes. "How 'bout that first name?"

"It's just P-h-i-l-i-p, sir." The secretary's tone became clipped; she worked for the White House and had more important things to do. "Anything else, sir?"

"No, ah, just sending these nominations over to Stuart for that slot at Interior," Callahan said casually, his disguise slipping a bit. He husked a little deeper, "That is right, darlin'? Stuart gets all this personnel stuff, now Latham's gone?"

"That's right, sir," she replied. "It's only temporary, until they replace Mr. Latham."

"Fine, fine," Callahan boomed. "Stuart usually handles congressional relations, isn't that right?"

"Yes, sir," the woman said proudly. "We'll be doing both for a while."

Callahan hung up just as Andrew pegged the familiar name that was butterflying around in his head. "Phil Stuart," he said. "Isn't he a young guy, blondish hair, dresses like a banker?"

"Youngest special assistant in the White House," Callahan said with a trace of envy. "Guy's only twenty-seven years old. Read a profile on him in the *Post* last week."

"Twenty-six," Andrew said absently. He picked up the receiver so he would sound better on the other end: these speakerphones could be maddening.

"White House, Mr. Stuart's office," soothed the same secretary.

"This is Andrew Sebastian."

"Yes, Congressman," she said quickly, ten degrees warmer. The lady knew the difference between her anonymous callers and her congressional relations. "Can I help you?"

"Is Phil there?" he breezed with easy familiarity.

"Let me check, sir."

A short pause, then Stuart's voice oozed cautiously, "Congressman?"

"Phil?" he barked jovially, as though they were old college roommates. "Andrew Sebastian! I understand you're taking over for Mark Latham."

"For a while, yes," Stuart said smoothly. "Along with my regular duties. Like trying to stop you guys from reducing us to ashes."

"Got to get it out of our systems, I guess." Andrew laughed sheepishly.

"Speaking of which"—Stuart launched a rather obvious segue into serious horse trading—"can you help us out on this Philippines thing? The president agrees with you in principle. He's death on government spending. He wants big cuts in foreign aid next year. But we can't accept another bill limiting the president's authority, not after the War Powers Act. Your Philippines ban is the worst of the lot."

"Pride of authorship aside, I think it's a pretty good bill," Andrew said evenly, trying to cover his wounded pride. "There's some room for constructive compromise," he added hastily. "I want to help the president, not hurt him. If he's ready to cut aid to Manila, maybe we can work it out."

"Great, Congressman," Stuart said, his natural eager-beaverness showing through. "The president will be thrilled. He really wants to pull everything together again. After all, there's the congressional elections to think about. How are things looking at home?"

"Pretty bleak," Andrew admitted. He decided to play it straight with Stuart, who seemed to bear him no grudge. "I've got a lot of ground to make up before November."

"Anything we can do for you from here?" Stuart offered. As if he didn't know, Andrew thought. The White House aide continued, "Fly the president in for a dinner or something?"

"Well . . ." Andrew hemmed.

"I know, it would do more harm than good." Stuart chuckled. "I like to offer, just to see how you guys will turn me down. You won't believe some of the excuses."

"There is one thing," Andrew said. "The Cadillo appointment. I've collected two hundred and fourteen signatures, but it seems to be stalled over there."

"I might as well tell you, Congressman"—Stuart's tone turned cool—"we've filled that slot."

"What?" Andrew shouted into the mouthpiece. "With who?"

"Mark Latham, actually," Stuart replied, a bit taken aback. "He put his own name down before he left. The packet just went down to the Senate. Sorry."

Andrew's mind reeled. Latham! That double-crossing bastard! He listened in silent fury to Stuart's faint apologies. "Latham's still a Texan at heart, I guess. He wanted to go back home. Maybe run for Congress someday."

Andrew got his gist. Andrew Sebastian was on his way out, and the party knew it. They would throw him to the wolves, let an unsavory cur like Brackler steal the seat for one term, then come back in 1976 with a new Republican candidate: Latham.

"I hope what we talked about can still go forward," Stuart said halfheartedly. "On the Philippines."

"Not goddamn likely!" Andrew exploded.

Callahan's eyes grew wide. "What's going on?" he whispered.

Andrew tore recklessly into Stuart. "I'm gonna ram that Philippines bill straight up your ass, pal. We're voting first thing tomorrow morning. Then I'm going back to Dallas and stomp all over Jim Brackler. And then I'll be back," he hastened on belligerently. "What do you think of that?"

"I think," Stuart said slowly, "that if you were more of a team player, you never would have gotten into this situation. I tried to help you, but you didn't listen."

"You're giving me advice?" Andrew roared. Callahan, appalled, shook his head in reproof.

"Just stating the obvious," Stuart said coldly. "You have to get along to go along, you know?"

"Yeah, well," Andrew said, trading clichés, "what goes around, comes around." He hung up the phone with a futile bang.

Six weeks before, Andrew had returned to the looming dark town house on O Street to find Tricia packed and gone back to Dallas. He hadn't seen her since. Nobody but Amanda knew of their estrangement, not even Callahan. Andrew had ordered the staff not to call him at home anymore; he was spending most nights at Amanda's.

Now, as he hunted under her squeaky queen-size brass bed for a second black sock, he wondered if he was suiting up for his last day on the bruising playing field of the House floor. "My plane leaves at two," he called to Amanda, who was bustling together some eggs in the kitchen. He sniffed the aroma of burning bacon. She knows I hate black bacon, he thought irritably.

Little things about Amanda bothered him now, like the martyring way she insisted on cooking these elaborate feasts at ungodly hours of the morning. Amanda ate voraciously, constantly; it seemed to have no effect upon her long, leggy figure.

Her body, that was another strange thing. At first those long skinny legs arrowing up into her tight rear had driven him into a frenzy, her pert breasts a taut invitation to the palms of his hands. Lately, though, she seemed simply bony, awkward, insubstantial.

And frivolous. There was no denying it: Amanda was shallow. Andrew couldn't seem to focus her attention on anything serious, anything long-term; she was consumed with today's rumor, tomorrow's floor calendar.

As a total human being, Amanda couldn't compare with Tricia. Tricia seemed to grow more stunning even as she got more frigid; with Amanda, the first time had been the best. Andrew and Tricia had shared everything; with Amanda, there was only politics and sex.

Andrew straightened his blue-and-red rep tie in the mirror.

"Need a ride to the airport?" Amanda's voice tinkled gaily from the kitchen. "Once we beat you on the Philippines, I have nothing else to do."

"I'll get a cab," Andrew shot back. "You'll have a lot of explaining to do to the generals. They'll probably put you up against the wall and shoot you."

"Bacon's ready," Amanda said firmly.

Andrew made a face in the mirror and strode quickly to the small dining room table.

"Andrew," she said softly, sipping her orange juice as he sopped his toast in egg yolk and crumbly fried bacon, "I need some help."

"Sure," he said automatically, surprised. Amanda never asked anything of him. She was terribly independent. It was one of the many personality traits that were starting to irritate him. Amanda was like her furry white housecat, Dr. Giles: all over you while you were there, never seeming to miss you while you were gone.

"What can I do for ya, ma'am?" he drawled with a smile, wanting to give her something in return for showing him how to lust again.

"This is serious, cowboy." She drilled the words into him. "I haven't said anything because . . . well, just because. I'm in real trouble on the Philippines. We didn't see things getting this far. Who would dream Congress would take away the president's power over emergency appropriations? The situation down there is an emergency, Andy. I've been there. The poverty, the Communists in the mountains. Your bill would be a disaster. An open invitation to the Chinese and the Russians. What's worse," she confessed in a rush, "if I can't beat or water down your bill today, the Marcos government will fire my firm. Then my firm will fire me," she added simply, folding her hands. She lowered her brown eyes to her orange juice and awaited his reply.

Andrew sat stunned. He pushed his plate across the glass-topped round table and dabbed at his mouth with a paper napkin. "I can't believe this," he said almost inaudibly. For the first time in years, he wanted to cry. He felt sick and alone and betrayed. And, in some strange way, relieved. "Is that what this is?" he cried. "I must be an idiot."

147

"Hey!" Amanda's head jerked up angrily. "I'm a lobbyist, Andrew. This is what I do!"

"Yeah," he said, crushed. "You do it very well."

"You son of a bitch," Amanda hissed. "You think I'd sleep with some hotshot congressman to buy his vote? I'm good, and I do my job, and it just so happens I'd be working on you this morning whether or not we were—"

"I thought I loved you, for a while," Andrew interrupted dispiritedly. "I just can't seem to learn how all this works."

"Don't give me that *Mr. Smith Goes to Washington* shit!" Amanda shouted. "You're trying to make me feel like a whore, so you can justify walking out on me today. Aren't you? You think I haven't been around long enough to know when something's over? You weren't coming back!"

"No." Andrew spoke softly, though he hadn't realized it until that second.

"You don't like this much, do you?" Amanda's eyes reddened, but her chin was firm. "Hysterical women. Tough choices. You always find a way to just walk out. Damn it, you'd listen to me about the bill if we weren't sleeping together. If I didn't ask, I'd be screwing the people who pay me. I can't do that. I'm a professional."

"So am I," Andrew said curtly, "even if Washington doesn't think so. I can't screw the people who pay me."

"Aw, Andy, get off your high horse!" she cried. "Who made you pope? You think anybody in Texas gives a rat's ass about presidential appropriation authority in the Philippines? You think anyone in your district even knows where the Philippines are?"

"They damn sure expect me to," Andrew mumbled. He stood up and grabbed his jacket. "I'm sorry," he lied, not wanting to end on this note. "I didn't mean to imply—hell, Amanda, I loved you."

"You didn't even know me," she said, blinking rapidly. "Get out. It's what you want. Please! I'm going to cry. I don't do that in front of men."

Andrew went into the bedroom. He hurled the rest of his clothes into his Louis Vuitton suitcase and snapped the locks home. To the left, her bathroom door was shut. Locked, probably. He put his ear to the door.

Silence. Amanda even sobbed in private.

"Hey," he said gently. "Just one question, okay? Did you ever love me?"

Nothing came for a full minute. Then a small voice said, "No."

Andrew walked out into the rainy street, wondering if his wife would be home when he got there. A taxi splashed into view. "Airport!" he shouted. "National!"

Amanda was right: nobody in Dallas had thought about the Philippines since MacArthur made good on his promise to return. The resolution would die stillborn without its sponsor, but who cared? It was time to get back to Dallas and find out what was left of his life there.

9

orry," Andrew mumbled to the ring of shadowy men seated around the huge black granite conference table in the oval corporate boardroom. At regular intervals around the austere gray fabric of the room's single curved wall rested massive Lucite-encased photographs of the corporation's landmarks: an awesome ground-up view of the sleek bronze International MarketPlace in Dallas; InfoComplex, an exact replica of Victorian London's white wedding cake Crystal Palace built in San Jose; a dizzying aerial of the twenty-square-mile Worldport Project in Osaka; the tangled off-shore derrick city of the North Sea's Shell Centre. At one end of the oval was a blank screen; the huge photos paced the distance on either wall to the room's centerpiece, an enormous curved black Mercator projection headlined "The World of Senanco." Across the map's twenty-foot breadth, small yellow lights twinkled in Hong Kong and Houston, Copenhagen and Caracas.

Andrew had sat through hundreds of his father's meetings, though this was the first time he had ever dared arrive late.

Roger Sebastian was a dangerous man on any terrain; here in his own lair, surrounded by the flayed pelts of his forty-year safari for the world's Ultimate Deal, Roger was the undisputed King of the Jungle. Saudi princes had come here, and Cabinet secretaries, and AFL-CIO presidents and Japanese economic ministers, and Back Bay financiers who traced their ancestry to the *Mayflower*. Framed by his own worldview, ensconced comfortably in his vast head-of-the-table chair of Milan doeskin, Roger had intimidated them, sweet-talked them, browbeat them, charmed them, threatened them. Andrew had seen men leave fuming in anger; breathless with new wealth; sneering and haughty; bewildered and bankrupt. But he had yet to see Roger walk out of this room with less than what he wanted.

Andrew fumbled for a seat in the gloom shrouding the men brought here from New York City to rescue Roger's favorite Senanco property. Andrew hadn't met them yet. Apparently that wasn't necessary. He could see his father glaring at him through the darkness. So I'm half an hour late, he thought sullenly. I could hardly announce it to the Elks Father 'n Son Pancake Breakfast: "Ciao, boys. Gotta go see what the Madison Avenue boys have whipped up with Dad's money."

"That's all right, Congressman," said a silky voice at the far end of the table. A tall figure in impeccable Brooks Brothers swiveled up out of one of the form-fitted conference chairs. "We know how busy you must be right now, eh?" He gave a tiny wave to the projectionist's window.

On cue, the massive silver rear-projected screen came alive with a splash of scarlet. In white letters the slide promised: ANALYSIS.

"James Brackler, or Big Jim, as he calls himself"—red light from the screen reflected in the ad man's gold-rimmed aviator spectacles— "is running the textbook anti-incumbent campaign. On one hand, he's tied the Watergate can to your tail. He's linked you with everything wrong in America today: dishonesty in government, air pollution, tax loopholes for the rich, inflation, too much welfare, not enough welfare. He's got you for being part of the system—the same rotten system that gave us Watergate and Vietnam. On the other hand, he says you're a bumbling incompetent who can't work within the system, who hasn't passed a single bill. Got you coming and going, eh?"

"Sounds like we need a change," Andrew grumbled, his voice petulant.

"I didn't say he was right," the ad man said mildly, adjusting his glasses. "Just effective."

Andrew was glad to see his father fidget in the pink wash of light that illuminated his seat.

"We know what's happening," Roger Sebastian barked. "We've got a month to go and we're losing our asses. So what's next?"

"Television, of course," replied the media strategist. "There are two options."

On cue, the screen flashed to cobalt blue with bold white letters: ATTACK.

"The first is to go after Brackler." Brooks Brothers' words brought Andrew's head forward with a jerk of interest. This was what he had come to hear. His spirits drooped as the media whiz added, "But we don't recommend that. An incumbent never attacks his challenger. Gives him credibility, eh?"

"What if the incumbent's twenty-five points behind?" Callahan spoke up laconically from where he sat to the ad man's left, his frown barely visible in the sickly bluish reflection. Andrew nodded agreement, though he did wish they wouldn't talk about him as though he weren't sitting right there. Even Callahan had slipped into the habit.

"Twenty-six, according to your latest numbers," piped up a new voice from the deep blue void to Brooks Brothers' right. "You're up four points from September, which we attribute to the interim radio campaign we put up two weeks ago."

"I've been campaigning a little, too," Andrew said. "I don't suppose that helped."

"Of course. Person-to-person campaigning certainly can't hurt," the main presenter added generously. "But we don't have time for you to meet everyone in the district. Nor do we have the time to change voter perceptions of Brackler. His appeal is negative: they want him because they don't want you. Or at least," the tall man added lamely, remembering the candidate's feelings, "they don't want people of your type. Republicans. Officeholders. That's what we have to change."

The screen flickered to a soothing forest green with the words: REPOSITION CANDIDATE.

"Our task is to redefine your image with a new positioning," the man gurgled in a volley of Madison Avenuese. "The campaign will focus on three key points. We talk about nothing else until election day."

The screen flashed red again. Andrew thought, They're running out of colors. Three words blazed white: COURAGE. COMMITMENT. INTEGRITY.

"I hope you don't mind," the man continued blithely. "But we've gone ahead and assembled a spot, using file footage. We think you'll like it. Best we've ever done, eh, Clampton?" A bespectacled ad head bobbed vigorously in the gloom. "Let's take a look, eh?"

The conference room came alive with a crossfire of explosions and ack-ack noises. The screen flashed battle-action footage from the jungles of Southeast Asia. "Vietnam," the announcer boomed ominously. Then the screen cut abruptly to a congressional hearing, young John Dean bent low over a battery of microphones. "Watergate," the voice tolled. Then a grocery store, where a vaguely Hispanic-looking woman blanched at the total on the cash register. "Inflation," the announcer said solemnly.

Then Andrew was surprised to hear his own voice saying, "These are tough times." The screen switched to a dramatic view of him speaking down to the camera from a flag-draped podium. "They call for tough leadership," Andrew's voice resounded, jacked up by some kind of woofer or tweeter that made him sound like Charlton Heston addressing the Israelites from Mount Sinai.

The announcer's voice rendered a twenty-second synopsis of Andrew's congressional career, extolling his COURAGE (drumbeat) and COMMITMENT (cymbal crash) and INTEGRITY (trumpet blast). Images flashed across the glistening screen. The *Time* photo of Andrew nose to nose with Nixon: "Leading the fight for honesty in government against impossible odds." Andrew walking down the Capitol steps into a crowd of reporters: "Fighting for Dallas in the halls of Congress." A shot of four olive-green army tanks rolling over a hill at the viewer: "Working to rebuild our country's defenses." Finally, Andrew's bronzed features, hair ruffled by a breeze, as he strode down an airplane ramp onto the tarmac at Love Field: the battle-scarred veteran returning to a hero's welcome. The camera zoomed from behind a shouting group carrying placards to frame Andrew's stern face. The announcer boomed soberly, "Sebastian. Courage. Commitment. Integrity."

Music up. A trill of flutes. Fade to black.

Andrew rubbed his eyes as domed fluorescents lit the table. He stared in amazement at the six grim faces surrounding the long oblong table.

"You can't be serious," he said, laughing. "You can't air that. It has nothing to do with me! Where'd you get those tanks? That shot at the airport. Those people were protesting, for Christ's sake!"

"We found a shot from behind," said an effete creative type with carefully trimmed black mutton-chop sideburns. He wore a melon-colored shirt and purple tie under his gray vest. "We inspected it very carefully in the editing room," he lisped. "You can't read a single sign. Looks just like one of those shots on the evening news. POWs back from 'Nam, hail the conquering hero, that sort of thing."

"I wasn't in Vietnam," Andrew said crossly. "I don't mean to be difficult, but this is just too—far out. I've got a good record. Why can't we talk about that?"

"We don't have time," Callahan jumped in. "Andy, we've got to go for the Hail Mary. I know it's slick," he admitted. "But we have to get their attention. We can fix that last shot, if you insist," he added, looking to Roger for help.

The old man looked thoughtfully at the tall media genius at the end of the table, whom he had hired because he was the best in the business. "Jensen," he said deliberately, "you're supposed to know what you're doing. By the way, what's this gonna cost?"

"Half a million," came a happy chirp from the small, bespectacled numbers gnome to Jensen's left. "Four hundred eighty thousand. Including our commission."

"Of course," Andrew muttered. Then he spoke louder, addressing himself to Callahan and Roger, "We can't do that."

"I don't care what it costs," his father assured him.

"That's not the point," Andrew complained. "Congress is working right now on a Campaign Finance Reform Act to ban contributions over one thousand dollars. I'm a co-sponsor."

"That'll never fly," Roger snorted.

"Don't be so sure," Andrew said. "In any case, spending half a million of my dad's money may be legal, but Brackler will crucify us. Accuse us of trying to buy the election. Which is exactly what we're trying to do."

"There's no choice," Callahan broke in bluntly. "It's this or lose."

"That's it, then," Roger said summarily in his best chairman-of-the-board fashion. He rose from the smooth granite that had held a lifetime of Roger Sebastian decisions. "We go with it."

Jensen looked toward Andrew, clearly uncomfortable at not having the candidate's imprimatur.

Andrew rolled his chair back and stood. "What do you need me for?" he said without rancor. And left.

With a start, Big Jim realized the girl was staring at him.

After a decade of practice, Jim Brackler knew how to work a room. He scanned the dimly lit faces for his next priority, stroking each contributor carefully, never letting the pet he was currently fondling know his time with the master was nearly up. It was then, as he prepared to ever-so-gently disengage himself from the elderly managing partner of Jarrett Hart's Big Eight accounting firm, that he noticed the girl.

Quickly, delightedly, in the heady campaign march of the past few months, Jim Brackler had grown accustomed to being recognized. It still startled him, from time to time, when a tollgate attendant leaned out of his booth and cried, "Hey, aren't you somebody? On TV? I know, you're running for mayor!" Out here on the campaign trail, virtually everyone knew him, and gathered about him, and turned their heads to nudge and whisper and wink at him across the room. It was all he had ever dreamed and more, but after six months of round-the-clock campaigning, it had become routine.

This girl was different.

Now, as her eyes riveted onto him again, he was sure. Despite a decade of virtually monastic devotion to his ambition, even Jim knew a come-hither glance when it reached out and grabbed him by the balls.

She was the unlikeliest-possible conquest for Big Jim Brackler. Suddenly, with that one spark of interest from her deep-set eyes, she excited Jim unlike anything since—he thought of Tricia Sebastian's cool beauty, her layered skirts swirling down the long staircase, the slender chin raised carefully above bare, tanned shoulders.

This girl was like that, cool and composed and Highland Park perfect. Yet she radiated a barely suppressed sexuality. Her poised breasts strained to be unleashed beneath the stiff taffeta. The coquettish figure was out of place at the banquet: she looked young. Younger even than Tricia had been; she belonged not at a Jarrett Hart fund-raiser, but at a Hockaday School tea dance.

155

Then, bold and alone, she came to him.

"Hello," she said simply, unblinking.

Up close, she affected him physically, and he was afraid she would notice. "I'm Jim Brackler," he said. He thrust his hand in her direction, careful not to touch her pale lavender cocktail dress.

She made no move to shake it. "I know."

Jim had never experienced anything like it. Her voice was sneering, contemptuous. She stood in a lopsided way that said she was bored; snatched a glass of white wine from a passing tray with practiced expertise. Yet she hardly seemed eighteen. She moved terribly close to him, her breasts nearly brushing the lapels of the dull gray suit Jarrett's secretary, Penny, had ordered for him from Mr. Hart's personal shopper at Neiman-Marcus.

"I'm Melissa," she said. Her eyes closed sleepily, then opened wide again. There was something intimate in the way she paused before supplying the rest. "Melissa Thomasson. Do you know my father?"

Normally he would have pretended the name sounded familiar. "No," Jim replied simply.

"Good," she smirked.

She was coming on to him! Jim cared not at all whether she was really attracted to him or merely drawn to the fact he was running for public office, that he had been on television, that his burly features adorned the huge posters plastered around this red-brocaded banquet room of the Fairmont Hotel. Who cares? he thought. He felt like he was floating on a cloud. She wants me!

This happened to other people. They met, at bars and church socials and library stacks, and they ogled each other and sparked and smiled, and struck up casual conversations. He had thought of it many times, in the halls of Congress, in the streets of Dallas, when a pretty girl like this walked by. But they never looked back. Now, one had dropped into his lap—literally, because this Melissa stood not two inches from the hard knot below his belt.

He had not the slightest idea what to say. Then he remembered who he was and why she had been drawn to him.

"Are you a contributor?"

"Daddy is," she said in a tone that mocked. "You really ought to meet him. He paid five hundred dollars for a dinner he's not going to eat."

"Where is he?"

156

"Dubai, I think," the Thomasson girl replied. There was a jaded wisdom in that languorous voice that belied her looks; Jim realized now that Melissa was not the teenager she seemed from a distance. "Or Yemen. One of those oil places. I came instead."

"Why?" He was surprised at how easily he could talk to this girl.

"I wanted to meet you," she said. She placed one dainty foot between his enormous black wingtips, then brought to his left ear her lips, full and slick with wet, clear gloss. At first he was sure he had misheard.

Then she repeated it. "Do you want me?"

Her breath was frightfully hot, even in the warmth of this crowded room. Just two feet away, contributors were queuing up to receive the two minutes of candidate cocktail chatter they had paid five hundred dollars apiece to receive.

Then, as suddenly as she had arrived, Melissa was gone.

The dinner was an agony. Jim's speech was turgid, incoherent; his eyes kept drifting from the podium, searching the dark audience for her table—center left, two rows back, in the roped-off area Jarrett reserved for his softest touches. She would raise her eyebrows in invitation, part her lips wide, feign a yawn; grin crookedly at his flustered scramble to regain control. As he limped to the conclusion, smiling weakly at the polite applause, he watched with dismay as she rose from her table and walked out.

Then came more speeches: scripted words of warmth from local Democrats; the longest prayer of benediction Jim had ever endured. Finally the houselights came up. Jim literally burst through the tangled crowd at the dais. Ignoring Jarrett Hart's glare of reproach, he brushed past the departing herd, a billion dollars of net worth on the hoof. Had it been just a tease? Searching for her in vain, he bolted for the revolving door. Perhaps the valet had not yet brought up her car.

"Mr. Brackler?"

The bell captain, faintly preposterous in a medieval costume that belonged in front of Buckingham Palace, touched gently at his shoulder.

"Yes?"

"I was asked to give this to you." He held out a tiny cream-colored envelope with the hotel's scrolled "F" in the corner and waited in vain for a tip.

The elevator was new and shiny. But to Jim, fever-hot with

157

anticipation, it seemed terribly slow. He sallied forth on the eleventh floor, following the arrows to the room number: 1134. He checked the small brass plate that swung from the key he had found in the envelope. Hands trembling, he inserted the key into the doorknob, embarrassed at the way it rattled in the deserted hallway.

He swung the door inward. It would only open halfway. He shoved his bulk through the aperture. Inside, every lamp was lit, the curtains flung wide as if the room were an empty stage, its audience the twinkling lights of skyscrapers surrounding the Fairmont.

The door slammed shut.

"Big Jim!" Melissa's bare buttock slapped loudly against the door. She had been crouched behind the door for ten minutes, naked and cold in the icy hotel air-conditioning. Her hard, swollen breasts jutted wildly as she sprung at him. "It's party time!"

Jim stood dumbfounded. He stared between her legs, at the dark, curly hair exposed there. Between his own, all desire dwindled and then died.

Melissa bounded toward him. Grinning good-naturedly, she wrapped her long legs about his baggy trousers, fumbled wildly at his belt.

Brackler gave a small cry of surprise. He pushed her away, confused. Seconds before he had been flush, straining with lust. Now, her bawdy flesh repulsed him.

"You wanna play rough, huh?" Melissa rebounded quickly, a feisty lust in her eyes. She grappled at his shoulders, tumbling him playfully to the bed.

"Get your hands off me!" Brackler shouted, shivering with fear and a sudden, inexplicable rage.

The Thomasson girl, taking it all as part of the game, ripped at his belt. With remarkable speed, she jerked Jim's gray slacks and white jockey shorts to his knees, trapping him on the bed, a temporarily helpless water buffalo roaring in the mud.

"Goddammit!" Brackler raged. She dove toward his limp organ. He slapped softly at her curly brown head. Then, before he could stop her, he sensed the ooze of her saliva. "Please," he whimpered, mortified by this horrid invasion of his most intimate territory. She ignored him, kneading roughly what was left beyond her lips, until Jim felt sick with physical pain.

Why did it have to be like this? Was he cursed? Why couldn't she have just met him afterward, shared a drink, even seduced him in whatever way normal women did such things? Jim liked to be in control, *had* to be in control, to take what was not meant to be his; this sudden onslaught, lewd and frightening in the hard light of the hotel room, reminded him of his cackling mother and those hideous nights in his bedroom, listening to her simpering laughter through paper-thin plasterboard, imagining what revolting things she did to the surly, hairy men who came there.

His lust, stiff and trembling moments ago, shriveled to nothing in the oily murk of that sucking, slurping mouth. Jim was terrified, repelled, enraged.

"Stop it!" he bellowed. He seized her shoulders and hurled her away from him, wobbling to his feet beside the queen-size bed.

She yelped as her head struck the flocked wallpaper. "That hurt," she said, nonchalant. Then she grinned and slithered to her feet, crouching like a judo artist. "Ready for—ooh, look at the poor little guy!" She pouted her lips in sympathy, shaking her head at Brackler's sad, shriveled member. "We'll have to do something about that, won't we?"

Tears of frustration welled in Jim's eyes. He backed away warily, fumbling his pants over his hips. She cooed and giggled, chasing him across the room with measured, threatening paces, until he felt the cool glass of the window against his broad shoulders.

Then, without warning, he bolted past her with a sideswipe block that might have earned him a spot on Coach Chamberlain's varsity squad. Knocked aside, Melissa tripped across a low coffee table and crashed backward onto the bed. She raised herself slowly on one elbow, curling one long, silken leg behind her naked flank to dab a single drop of blood from her ankle. Brackler saw a grimace of pain wipe the unrelenting lust from those dreamy, half-lidded eyes. He could almost feel himself stirring again.

"Ooh, I *like* you!" Melissa soothed, and rose again. Watching in disgust as her breasts wobbled toward him, Brackler dodged awkwardly to the door.

"Where are you going?" Melissa demanded. Her attitude shifted abruptly. She stood in that bored position again, one hand on her hip. "We just got started."

"You're—weird," Brackler hissed.

"*I'm* weird?" she scoffed. "You're some big macho politician, and you can't even get it up?"

"Do you screw everyone who runs for office?" Brackler, his rage

159

and his fear replaced by wonder, edged cautiously to the door. "Or do you just give to Democrats?"

"I'm what you might call a star-fucker, Big Jim." She grinned salaciously. "Astronauts, rock stars, anchormen. Come on, huh? After all, Daddy did buy a whole table." She started toward him again.

Jim fled for the lobby and the safety of the world he knew.

Tricia groped fuzzily under the den couch for the remote control. "You make me sick," she told the ten o'clock news. She switched to another channel and focused her slightly blurry vision. Jim Brackler's features reappeared. God, the man was positively ubiquitous—a word she had learned from Andrew in happier times. "You—bick—witus," she pronounced aloud.

Tricia talked to herself often these days. To drown out the silence. To sense the liquor better. The booze chewed up the endless hours while he was out campaigning; helped ensure that she was sound asleep by the time he crept in at night. But drink as she might, Tricia was unable to close out completely the cacophonous whine of her husband's political career as the day of reckoning approached. Especially since his new TV commercials had invaded her last preserve with an incessant two-week barrage of Andrew, Andrew, Andrew.

Andrew's face popped up on the news program. "The Sebastian forces have released a new survey," the reporter's voice said. A dim corner of Tricia's memory tuned in. She hadn't heard about this. "The incumbent Republican has now pulled within five percentage points of his challenger." The set now showed Andrew and Brackler debating in a high school auditorium. "All eyes are on Texas's Fourth District to see if this maverick Republican can separate himself from the herd, and keep his ship afloat amidst the tidal wave that threatens to sink his party at the polls this November," noted the self-anointed analyst. He added a final mixed metaphor: "The race is neck and neck as they head for the finish line, but Big Jim plans to pull the rug out from under Sebastian at a news conference tomorrow. For Channel Eight, I'm Bernie Zollars."

Great, thought Tricia. Just when I thought we were home free, Andrew rebounds with the biggest political comeback since Harry Truman. She flicked the channel to an old Doris Day movie on Channel 11. It was the one where Rock Hudson played a hypochondriac. She watched until Tony Randall showed up as the alcoholic next-door neighbor. She got up abruptly, swaying a bit as she strolled into the kitchen for some more ice and another nip.

Then she heard Andrew's voice from the den. In spite of herself, her heart leapt. Was he finally coming home at a decent hour so they could have this out?

Then she heard the sound effects, the gunfire and the cannons, and realized it was only another bloody commercial. "These are tough times," her husband's voice caromed eerily around the empty walls of her lonely house. "They call for tough leadership."

Tricia poured the amber liquid to the brim and hustled back to the den to catch the tail end, with that absurd picture of his stern-jawed face on the airplane ramp.

"You tell 'em!" Tricia raised her glass in toast. Her high-pitched cheerleader's yell chimed with the announcer's stentorian bass: "Sebastian. Courage! Commitment! Integrity!"

Brackler's gut punch came the next morning, just fifteen days before election day, when candidates with uneasy five-point leads called press conferences to unload whatever truckload of dirt they had saved for the final days of a hard-fought campaign.

Andrew was having lunch at Herrera's with Julian Mendoza when it happened. Herrera's was a shabby little hole with lipstick-red walls and a curtain of limp emerald beads hanging inside the metal front door. It was stuck on a no-name street between the northbound and southbound lanes of Harry Hines Boulevard, next to a tortilla factory where Julian's people worked, scraping fifty cents an hour from the pasty corn dough so they could pay it right back to one of the three great Mexican restaurant families who owned the neighborhood's discount stores and tortilla factories and Affiliated Supermarket franchises. And Herrera's, which served the best puffed tacos and worst iced tea in the city.

"Beer for me, too," Julian told the sour Mexican waitress. She waddled to the stainless-steel cooler three feet away from the cluster of cafeteria tables that composed Herrera's dining room. She slapped two bottles of Budweiser on the table. As an afterthought, she flipped an elderly metal bottle opener on the table.

"To the new numbers," Andrew said, raising his bottle. "We have you to thank, Julian."

"That's not what Jensen says." Mendoza smiled, his big teeth clasping the beer bottle as he sucked down a swallow.

161

"Bull," Andrew said doggedly. He was determined not to give the New York ad whiz an inch, even if the commercials did seem to be working. "Since you signed on, Brackler's spent all his time trying to hold us off in the barrio."

"Too bad Juan Cadillo doesn't hate that sumbitch like I do," Mendoza lamented. "There was just no way Juan could give you an outright endorsement after the appointment fell through."

"He gave us you," Andrew said warmly. "That's better." *If I get reelected, I'll offer Julian a permanent job,* he thought resolutely.

"Hey, Ron!" Andrew signaled to his campaign manager, whose ever-widening girth loomed in the bright rays of noon sun piercing the perpetual dimness of Herrera's.

"Brackler just hit us," Callahan said without preamble, eyeing the waitress with suspicion as he lowered himself onto a chair. "Hard. I just got off the phone with Sam at the *Morning News.*"

Callahan looked furtively over at Mendoza, wondering how freely he could speak before the newest member of Andrew's inner circle. "He released copies of a letter written by your father. Allegedly," he corrected morosely. "Signed by Roger, sent to Senator Longley back in 1962."

"So?" Andrew demanded.

"It's a request to have you deferred from the draft," Callahan blurted, his eyes begging Andrew to dispute his words. "Brackler says you didn't want to go to Vietnam. That you got your father to pull strings in Washington to get you exempted. You were, you know. Exempted."

"That's an outright lie," Andrew protested. "I never requested a deferment, or anything else. I was deferred during college. So was everybody back then. My number just never came up."

"Brackler's got documentation from the Pentagon to back it up," Callahan insisted. "Sam says he's got you cold." He ticked off the documents on one hand: "Letter from Roger to the senator, requesting that you be exempted on the grounds that your work for Senanco's international subsidiaries was 'essential to the maintenance of the civilian economy.' Correspondence from Longley to the Selective Service Administration, officially requesting same. He's got a notice from the Pentagon, declaring you a Class two-A, exempt from military service on the basis of essential nature of civilian employment. Sam says it's locked up tighter than a virgin's knees." Callahan looked at his boss sympathetically. "By the way, Sam is interested in hearing your response."

Andrew was in shock. Understanding seeped in slowly. His father! While his friends were off in Southeast Asia, getting blown to bits by land mines, Andrew had sat home safe and sound, protected by the strangling force of his father's embrace. His innards lurched as an image streaked unbidden through his mind. Tommy's body, what was left of it, rolling down the luggage rack off an air force DC-3 in a long line of steel caskets. He and Tricia offering condolences to a stricken Elma, black-clad and weeping.

"Oh, God," he cried, thinking of another airplane ramp, another gathering. "Our TV spots! No wonder Brackler hasn't ripped them. He *wants* them on the air. Courage, commitment—God! We've gotta call Jensen. Get them off the air!"

"Hold on, Andrew," Callahan said, picking at the silver label of his beer bottle. "Let's not overreact. Those spots have brought us within five points."

"Listen, Ron!" Andrew said tersely. "My father's not running this show anymore. I want those spots off. Now! I'll turn on the TV set tonight, and if I see one second of me walking down that airplane ramp like Johnny come marching home, you're fired. You read me?"

"Sure, boss," Callahan said, cowed. "But—"

"No buts," Andrew cut him off in midprotest. "Here's a dime." He slapped the coin on the table, pointing to the pay phone in the dark far corner of the tiny restaurant. "Call them now. I'm going to see my father."

Roger could barely keep his mind on golf. Even Chubb Howard was trouncing him; to his experience, Chubb couldn't hit a golf ball to save his ass. They were out with two fellows from Republic Bank who wanted Roger's business but knew they'd never get it. Still, it was a perfectly acceptable reason to play golf on a cool Tuesday afternoon in mid-October. Roger mentally added up what he had lost so far. A thousand, at least. He wished he could just pay up and quit. He wanted to call Andrew and find out how things were going today. The aging multimillionaire squinted under his white-billed visor at the misshapen black clouds that threatened from the south. Maybe it would rain, and he could honorably forsake the final six holes.

"Rog," Chubb called from the yellowing Bermuda grass of the fairway. "Isn't that your boy?"

"Sure enough," Roger replied coolly, feeling the familiar chill of parent panic, like the time Andy's school had called his office and told him his son had appendicitis. It was just a bad stomachache, of course. Andrew never seemed to get very sick, just as he never seemed to get very angry or sad or jubilant; just the content happy medium that most parents only dream about. Somehow that always made Roger uneasy, like a gardener who knows the winter will be a cold one because the summer has been so balmy.

Andrew strode purposefully toward the twelfth hole, dressed in his uniform navy-blue campaign suit and an angry red expression more thunderous than any Roger had ever seen on that unlined visage. His son stalked within inches of Roger's weatherbeaten, eternally sunburned nose. When he spoke, his voice was deathly pale and still.

"I want to talk to you," Andrew said hoarsely. "Now."

"Sure," Roger said, his blue eyes open wide with concern. "Chubb, fellas . . . do you mind? Y'all go on ahead. I'm not doing squat, anyway."

Andrew ignored them, mutely steering Roger's steely elbow toward the faded, old-rich-dowdy clubhouse of Dallas Country Club. They reached the white wrought-iron chairs on the flagstone patio. Andrew literally shoved his father onto a padded chaise lounge.

"You just lost me the campaign," Andrew barked the terse words he had rehearsed on the way over. "You and Jack Longley got me exempted from the draft. Brackler's got the proof. I've made a fool of myself! Courage, commitment, integrity. How could you let me do it? You didn't even tell me!"

"Oh, Lord," Roger said under his breath, feeling his heart tumble deep into his groin. Suddenly he felt a thousand years old. "I had honestly forgotten about that." His voice was simple and sincere. "Hell, Andy, I only did it for you! They were starting to kill all those kids in that shitty war. What was I supposed to do? When I had the power to prevent it? You can't expect a father to do that."

"What about the other fathers?" Andrew cried. "What about George Butler? He's got friends in Washington. You didn't see Tommy hiding behind his daddy's skirts!"

"Don't you wish he had?" Roger snapped, brutally honest as always.

164

"Tommy wouldn't have!" Andrew responded hotly. "But I never had a choice, did I? You decided for me, like always. From now on, stay out of my life, okay?"

"Andrew, everything I've done was for the love of you," Roger said, feeling suddenly weepy and bone-tired.

"That's no excuse," Andrew said bitterly. "You smother me, Dad! I'm tired of being your puppet. Buy a fucking dog. Don't arrange things for me anymore, understand? You've done enough." He turned from his father's broken face and began to walk away.

"That's easy to say now," Roger croaked as his son's broad shoulders receded toward the sliding glass door. "You're alive and well and a success, thanks to me."

Andrew slacked his pace, then stepped into the clubhouse. Roger watched him go in silence, feeling something like pride pierce the agonizing pain in his chest. For the first time in his life, Andrew had stood up to him.

Andrew sat in the Lakewood Landing for hours, watching the sky darken unnaturally. From time to time he got up to pump more quarters in the jukebox and annoy the other customers with yet another rendition of Van Morrison's "Tupelo Honey." He drank beer and then tequila and eavesdropped as one regular after another banged in from the gusty outside world: "Looks like rain, don't it?" By the time the clouds cracked open and poured sheets of black on the evening rush hour, he was quietly smashed.

A still small voice tapped at the far corner of his mind, telling him to call it quits, clean out his trust fund, pack up and leave. Maybe he and Tricia could go to an island somewhere and sort things out, discover how to love each other again. I want her, Andrew thought, hoping the men in the corner were too busy playing darts to notice the drunk politician crying in his beer. There's no one else to love, he thought bleakly. And no one left to love me.

He knew he would lose the election, the way only a candidate can know. Hell, would I vote for me? Especially since I know what I am. A coward.

Because he had known all along.

Everyone he knew in those days had been drafted. Those were the Kennedy years, the "meet any hardship, pay any price" years. They all had gone; many came back in plastic bags. But not Andrew, despite his ominously low lottery number. Roger had seen to that,

165

doing the dirty work without soiling his son's lily-white hands. Deep inside, Andrew knew now that he had known then. I'm a coward, he thought as he stared blindly at the fifty-odd beer placques adorning the Landing's walls. Just as Tricia had chosen to ignore his affair, he had known all along but had never wanted to face the facts. Because I like things easy. Because I was afraid to go to Vietnam.

With a sick, sudden lurch of alcoholic clarity, Andrew saw himself as others soon would. A pampered dilettante. The creature of another man's arrogance. A coward.

For the first time since the day they met on the Ownby practice field, Andrew understood why Jim Brackler despised him. Just now, Andrew agreed.

He lurched out of the bar and seesawed into the pouring rain. Andrew drove home with insane caution, windshield wipers going full blast, shoulders hunched over the console, hands gripping the wheel at ten and two. He pulled into the sweeping circular driveway with relief, ignoring the scratch of thorny hedges on the silver paint of the passenger side. I never wanted the damn Chinese holly, Andrew thought rebelliously. Give me a nice soft photinia any day.

"Well!" Tricia sniped as he slammed the front door shut and shook the rain from his shaggy brown hair. "Hello."

"No need for a haircut tomorrow," he said gleefully, crystalline blue eyes glittering nonsensically. Peter O'Toole eyes, Tricia thought with a start, glancing over her shoulder at the ABC Movie of the Week, *Lawrence of Arabia*. She shrank from him. "You're drunk."

"Join the crowd, huh?" Andrew's eyes leered knowingly. "Where d'you keep the stuff?"

Tricia wished she could slip back to the coffee table and hide her Scotch glass. "What are you doing here?" she asked, upset at having her evening ritual disturbed. "The office has been calling. You've got a reception."

"No point," Andrew said wearily. He steered unsteadily to the gleaming black lacquer bar and began hunting for something to mix with the Stolichnaya. "Do we keep anything wet in this wet bar?" he grumbled.

"Shouldn't you be downtown?" Tricia had sat here for weeks waiting for him to come home at a normal hour and talk to her. Now he was here, and she couldn't wait for him to leave. So she could drink more Scotch and find out how Lawrence was going to make it across the desert.

"Don't you get the news on that box?" Andrew gestured wildly across the vast emptiness of the house, then held a bottle aloft in victory. "Vermouth! The very thing. I lost today, dear," he elaborated, enunciating each syllable with precision. "Didn't you hear?"

"I heard," she said softly. She had never seen Andrew like this, hurt and alone and out of control. It went right to her gut.

He hasn't earned my forgiveness, she reminded herself. Only my pity. "Andrew, it'll blow over," she said only half-scornfully, the faintest hint of conciliation in her voice. "One-day wonder, that's what you always say." Actually, the evening newscasts had been terrible; Tricia had been glued to the set in horror as her husband was slowly ripped to shreds.

"You think so?" he replied, a piteous note of hope creeping in. He took a long sip. "I don't."

Tricia crossed the broad expanse of thick carpet. "You don't need this." Gently she took the rocks glass from his trembling hand and set it on the mirror-smooth top of the bar. This is as far as I go, she resolved. He's got to meet me halfway.

"You're one t' talk," Andrew slurred, nodding sadly at the empty half-gallon of Scotch.

"I know when to quit," Tricia said. She reached out her hand with surprising steadiness. This is it, something inside her warned. No farther.

Then, dreamlike, she heard her voice say, "Let's go upstairs and talk."

Dutifully, he followed her up the long spiral staircase. As they reached the landing he stumbled, leaning heavily against her.

"Tricia," he said, trying to shuffle the mess of his thoughts into coherence. "About Washington. That's what it was. Washington. It was my fault," he said with a drunk's painful slow sincerity. "It wasn't about you, I promise. You're, you're just—it wasn't your fault."

His voice sounded tinny and small as he clutched her close. "I'll make it up to you, I swear." How stupid and hollow that sounds, he thought, wishing he could kiss her and make the whole nightmare go away.

"Ssh," she said. "Let's talk about it tomorrow." She smiled self-consciously. "When we're sober."

Clumsily Andrew grabbed her even closer, cramming her hips into his pelvis. He closed his lips roughly around the surprised little

167

"O" of her mouth. He could hear the phone in his study ringing insistently. It was his private hotline for political business.

"Let it ring," Andrew murmured, breathing vodka fumes in her face.

Tricia's head pulled back. "It's Callahan," she said, glad for a break in the action. She wasn't about to swoon into his arms like the lovesick heroines in the fifteen old movies she had watched that week. "He's frantic. You have to talk to him."

Andrew considered her, eyes liquidly studious. "'Kay," he said, starting for the study.

"Where have you been?" Callahan was beside himself. "I've got sixty people here! Do you know what time it is?"

"Rats off a sinking ship," Andrew said despondently. "I'm not goin' anywhere tonight, Ron."

"You're drunk," Callahan accused in a disappointed tone.

"You're right," Andrew said. "I'm goin' to bed now."

"What about Brackler?" Callahan protested. "The campaign? He's having a big rally in Casa Linda tonight to premiere some new TV spots. Julian's going. Don't worry, Brackler doesn't know Mendoza's—"

"G'night, Ron," Andrew said with finality. "Don't call again." He hung up without a good-bye and weaved purposefully into the darkened bedroom.

Tricia lay on her back in a grandmotherly blue flannel nightgown, covers pulled up to her chin, eyes stark and staring in the shallow shafts of street lamp streaking in through rain-ribboned windows. He undressed quickly, stumbling out of his pants and socks and underwear all at the same time. When he fell to his knees in a tangle of pinstripes, she had to laugh.

"Whazzo funny?" he exclaimed in a mock-drunk slur. "Whajoolookinat?" He grinned playfully as he extricated himself from one last black sock and crawled the four feet to his side of the bed.

"Go to sleep, will you?" Tricia said lightly, trying to ignore the prowling hands creeping toward her breasts.

Andrew snuggled closer.

"Really," she said crossly, thinking, It's not going to be that easy, buster. "This is not the time. I'm not about to just—"

With a sudden roar, Andrew was on top of her, his nakedness dangling in her face. Wordlessly he pinned her hands behind her pillow and clamped his thighs on her legs, smothering her mouth with his tongue, wriggling her nightgown up over her hips.

"Hey!" She struggled, too late, and realized she was trapped. "This is not funny!"

Andrew slackened his grip but kept on, maneuvering himself between her legs, kissing and licking and loving even as he used his limbs to keep her loosely caged beneath him. If I can just show her! he thought wildly. Just once, if she could feel it! I know it's there!

Tricia fought him bitterly, even as she felt herself caving in below. She bit at his nose, clawed his back, rammed her legs up at his groin. He drove on relentlessly, as if booze or lust made him insensible to pain. She could taste warm blood from his torn lips as he speared into her, deep at first into her rough, barren insides, then shallow and caring. He moaned and shoved deeper, which made her furious and hot and wet.

She was being raped again. This time, no one would come to the rescue; her hero was right here on top of her. Excited and angry and scared, Tricia struggled like a feral leopard snared in a net, ripping at his eyes, pulling hair from his head, jamming her butt downward in the bed in a vain effort to snap off his prick.

Andrew was oblivious. All he could feel was the two of them coupling madly in the snarl of sheets and blue flannel. It was working! Tricia's hips gyrated madly below his. It was a sensation unlike anything he'd ever felt before, even with Amanda. They tore at each other's bodies for what seemed like forever, the booze reining him in until he exploded and she blew up inside, the fury and fear gushing out of her in a flood of bliss unlike anything she had ever felt. They gripped each other silently, pressed their cheeks tightly to one another, mingled tears of joy and relief. Then, lying exhausted and spent in a pool of sweat-slick linen, they slept.

Half a mile away across White Rock Lake, the puddle-strewn parking lot of Casa Linda Bank swelled with the shiny black Cadillacs and battered white pickup trucks of the coalition Jim Brackler had built in the Fourth Congressional District of Texas. Inside, talking loud to make themselves heard over the sky-splitting thunder, Jarrett Hart and his bankers smiled and chatted with goateed black radicals who would be arrested just for cruising past the bankers' opulent Highland Park homes. Union wives blew up balloons; their children mingled with the Mexican kids by the punch bowl, which was commanded by a battalion of Baptist ladies who knew God was a Democrat, just like Daddy.

Over it all presided their man of the hour, Big Jim Brackler. The crowd ignited as he walked through their midst. Big Jim pumped hands and slapped backs, his enormous calf head cracking open with great brays of laughter. It wasn't charisma, exactly, but it sure as hell was power. Jim Brackler was even more impressive in real life than on the ten-foot photos plastered behind the stage in the center of the bank lobby's burnt-orange carpet. When Brackler grabbed your elbow, he gripped you so hard it hurt. But you felt the ache for twenty minutes, and you were damn glad he had grabbed you and not that idiot shop steward from the plant.

The loyalists swarmed around their candidate as he how-yewed his way through the masses. Brackler noted Julian Mendoza cowering at the far edge of the crowd. Big Jim smirked. Good. Sebastian's new token Mexican can toddle back to Little Lord Fauntleroy and tell him all about our big bad new commercials.

"This thang workin'?" Brackler bellowed into the microphone, beefing up the Texas twang the way he always did on the stump. He tapped the steely mesh of the mike head, the way they had forbidden him to do in the Zig Ziglar public-speaking course Jarrett Hart had made him take. Big Jim thumped the microphone again and watched the technician wince.

"Harley hates it when I do this. Don'tcha, Harl?" Brackler thumped the mike again. The crowd roared with laughter. "Sorry, Harley, but you know what happens when somebody tells me what to do. Right, Dan?" His bearded law partner cum campaign manager nodded with mock weariness. The crowd chuckled with appreciation; he and Mullins did this number all the time.

"Guess I'm jes' bullheaded," Brackler said with pretended shame. "After all, they tole me a poor redneck from East Dallas would never go anywhere against a rich boy like Andrew Sebastian"—he hissed the name with exquisite prissiness—"but here . . . we . . . are!"

Brackler's resonant voice boomed over the whine of microphone feedback and lit up the crowd. They stomped their feet and whistled and cheered, until he stretched out his stocky arms for quiet, hairy elbows jutting out from his short-sleeved tan polyester shirt.

"Lessee, there must be two thousand of y'all out there," Jim

170

hollered as he mimed a head count. "Nineteen hunnerd one, nineteen hunnerd two— Yep, two thousand exactly!"

The crowd roared again, to let him know they were there. He was talking about them, right in front of the TV cameras! They hooted and waved to their relatives as the minicams panned the crowd.

"How many y'all are Democrats?" he cried. The masses jumped up and down to demonstrate their affiliations. "Any Republicans here?" he asked scornfully. Suddenly you could hear a pin drop. Brackler loved this, the sensual thrill of controlling the crowd, manipulating their emotions; inciting their anger, fueling their ego, basking in their love. Once you got them going, it was so *easy*.

"Well, least y'all know how to answer that question," he continued. "If Andrew Sebastian were with us, how you think he'd face it?"

From the back of the room came a shout: "Depends on which face you ask!"

The crowd tittered with amusement. Good boy, Denny, Brackler thought, beaming with pride at his stepbrother, whose eyes shone with devotion at the far corner of the bank lobby.

Brackler opened his arms and waved to the bank of ten identical television sets in a row above his head. "We got Harley's boss to donate a couple TVs so y'all could see this," he said, nodding grandly at their applause for all his trouble on their behalf. "You're gonna like what you see!"

On cue, the lights dimmed. Ten television sets lit up with the multicolored bars of a test pattern. "Looks good so far, Jim!" someone bellowed spontaneously from the center of the crowd.

"Better'n my homely face, that's for sure, Ed," Big Jim shot back, and the crowd broke up again.

Then they hissed quietly as Andrew Sebastian's tanned face filled the screens. They watched him descend the airplane ramp as the announcer's voice began ominously, "Andrew Sebastian talks about courage. But what about the record?" The screens filled with battle-action shots taped straight from the Sebastian commercials: tanks cresting a hilltop, American soldiers in the jungles of Vietnam.

"When his country called, Andrew Sebastian ran for cover," the announcer said sadly as a photostat of Roger's letter appeared on the screens. "He dodged the draft. Not like Jim Brackler!"

The music zoomed up as a photo of Brackler flashed through the room, wearing his army uniform and silver captain's bars. "Jim

171

Brackler answered his country's call as a U.S. Army officer during the Vietnam War," the announcer continued, adroitly ducking the fact that Captain Brackler had never set foot outside Arlington, Virginia. "Jim Brackler is a patriotic veteran who fights for his country, right or wrong. As our congressman, he'll fight for what's right in Washington!" A combative Big Jim mounted the steps of the Capitol, lifting his eyes reverently to the flag.

"Big Jim Brackler for Congress," the voice concluded with a twang. "Real courage, Texas style!"

The applause rang again and again as they played the rest of them, a battery of eight different commercials attacking Andrew from every possible angle. One used an old newspaper quote from Sebastian's 1972 campaign against Masters: "The *Dallas Morning News* calls Sebastian 'the draft dodger's best friend.' Now we know why!" Another showed a cash register ringing up one sale after another: "Sebastian thinks his daddy can buy anything. He bought his way out of the draft. He bought his way into Congress. Now he thinks he can buy your vote. Big Jim Brackler for Congress. Real courage, Texas style!"

The lights came up, and the people thundered and cheered. James watched Dan Mullins and Denny Frawley pump up the crowd. He cast a sidelong glance at Jarrett Hart and the coterie of well-dressed bankers and lawyers who were financing the last-minute TV blitz with half a million in cold cash. Hart beamed back a contented smile that knew he had aced out a rival and bought himself a congressman. So he thinks, Brackler thought elatedly.

Feeling a thrill up his spine, he seized the microphone with both hands. "Whaddya say, folks?" bellowed Big Jim. "Wanna see 'em again?"

The cheers drowned out the drumming of rain on the rooftop, and Big Jim Brackler knew it in his heart. They were his people forever.

10

In the dream, Andrew was trying desperately to get to the House floor to vote on his bill. The final bell was ringing. All six lights blinked red above the clocks in the subway tunnel. But he couldn't make his legs work right, because he was drunk. People shouted at him, telling him to hurry: his father, Callahan, Amanda, Tricia. Tricia most of all. Her shriek sent shafts of pain into the impacted molar of his brain.

"Andrew!" Tricia shook him awake, her eyes glued shut against the rude morning-after sunlight.

Andrew grappled at his bedside table, one hand fumbling for the phone. He knocked it to the floor. When he picked it up, there was only the dial tone. So how could it be ringing? His head ached horribly.

Tricia lay next to him, wide awake but feigning sleep, every muscle in her body tensed. How do I feel? she wondered. Should I purr like a kitten or scream like a banshee? She dug inside for an answer.

Andrew finally located the ringing noise. He mashed his fist down on the alarm clock. "Tricia?" he called softly.

She eased one eye open and was taken aback by the raw red scratches crosshatched across his chest.

"My God!" She sat up with a start. "Did I do that?"

"Throes of passion?" he said sheepishly, trying as always for the laugh to relieve the discomfort in the stuffy room.

It was the wrong thing to say.

"You bastard!" she hissed, anger incinerating inside. "You raped me!"

"Come on, Tricia," Andrew pleaded. "I made love to you. And you liked it. You're supposed to! What's so hard about admitting it?"

"That's not the point," she said, holding her ground. "You used force. Who do you think you are, Rhett Butler? You're stronger and meaner and you held me down, and then we did it. That doesn't make you a lover. Just a rapist. You're a coward, Andrew."

"Yeah," he said. He felt husked out, empty. "So they tell me."

Eight days later, Tricia balanced her red Gucci clutch purse precariously, propping it between her scarlet silk-sheathed thigh and the crook of her left elbow. She leaned against the silver door of her Buick, her right hand ransacking the purse. How could they be missing again?

Several years ago, when they still gave each other little joke presents, Andrew had gifted her with an enormous sunflower key chain. "You'll never miss that," he'd assured her. Now, when she needed it most, the damn thing was nowhere to be found.

Her too-high heels clicked sharply on the bricks of the circular drive as she backed awkwardly up to their front door. She glared through its round window. They weren't on the coffee table, where she usually left them. Did I lock myself out of the house again? she asked herself. Surely I haven't had that much to drink.

She crouched down on her knees, careful not to run her last pair of nylons. She dumped the whole rotten mess on the front porch: wallet, aspirin, tampons, mascara, credit cards, an almost empty box of breath mints, more aspirin, credit card receipts—aha! The goddamn keys. She ran back to the Buick. Gunning the engine, she vaulted out onto Lakewood Boulevard. Swerving slightly to avoid a child on a bright blue bicycle, she aimed the car into the setting sun. She cursed the small white hands of the dashboard clock.

The biggest rally of the campaign, and it had started five minutes ago. Without her.

Politicians can be late. It is expected, even relished. Their supporters take a perverse pleasure in seeing how important and in demand their candidate is.

But a politician's wife is never late. She shows up on time, or half an hour early, to check the sign-in sheets and fuss with the crepe-paper streamers, so the troops know she is working harder than anyone for her husband's victory.

Tricia plummeted down Live Oak, a broad avenue whose stately Georgian mansions had mostly been replaced with auto parts stores and discount furniture shops. They flashed by unseen in the Buick's gray-tinted side windows. Damn, damn, damn. He had made such an effort this past week, and so had she. Now it was all spoiled because of the stupid keys, and those electric curlers that wouldn't heat, and the hundred and one other gremlins that had conspired to keep her from Andrew's side on this crucial Wednesday night before next Tuesday's election. Tricia fumbled again in her purse for the breath mints, to chase away the odor of Chivas.

This past weekend, when she was up at headquarters for the first time in this campaign, Ron Callahan had taken her aside. "If we all pull together, I think we can do it," Callahan had whispered, holding a small scrap of yellow legal paper between his pudgy fingers. Andrew's father spends thousands of dollars on that Houston polling wizard, Tricia thought wryly, and it comes down to a coffee-stained scrap of yellow paper with three letters and three matching numbers:

B   51
S   34
U   15

"We've dropped eleven points since they hit us on the draft thing," Callahan had allowed. "But that's not near as bad as I thought. If we can pull the undecideds . . ." His voice had trailed off on a high note as he'd bobbed his head back and forth in speculation. Tricia had felt a warm ray of hope pierce the damp atmosphere of the deserted late-night headquarters. Seventeen points behind! Could they cover that in little more than a week?

Now, she swung the Buick right on Peak, cruising quickly through a slum neighborhood she only braved when she was in a hurry. Just a few blocks to go. Maybe Andrew will be late, she prayed, and won't even notice.

Tricia could not, would not, lose her husband. She needed him. And now, maybe for the first time in his life, he needed her. As she headed underneath the rush-hour traffic on the elevated lanes of Central Expressway, Tricia mused that Andrew's career had become the child she had never borne him. It united them, gave them a common undertaking in which each played a vital role.

So she had cut down some on her drinking and stopped taking sleeping pills and started getting up early with Andrew every morning and making his coffee. They would talk for a few minutes, with the daybreak dancing gay patterns on the round green breakfast table. And they talked in bed, like they used to, sacrificing precious hours of sleep on the altar of a marriage they now knew to be a jealous and volatile god. Little by little they began to thaw a bit, even made love again in a cautious fashion, like two reluctant combatants, neither of whom wanted to strike the first blow nor back away from the fight.

Tricia changed lanes smoothly, accelerating down the home stretch toward headquarters. Damn, damn, damn, she thought again. She swerved to pass a slow-moving plumber's van, then stomped hard on the gas.

Suddenly, red and blue revolving lights filled her rearview mirror, and the quick dark growl of a police siren drove her foot to the brake.

"Where the hell is Tricia?" Callahan hissed through clenched teeth, his scruffy mop of fast-graying curly hair bent close to Andrew's ear. Worn by the past two weeks, he was past caring whether his words offended.

Andrew looked up in surprise from the floor, where he had crouched to meet a blond toddler belonging to his most loyal precinct chairman.

"She's not here?" said the candidate with pretended nonchalance, smiling weakly to cover his disappointment. He had been so sure things were getting better. He shrugged imperceptibly. "Hi there, cutie!" he cried. He boosted the child to his shoulder with the overarching enthusiasm of one who aches to be a father but isn't.

176

"What's your name?" he asked with genuine interest. "Let's go find Mommy."

Andrew offered one last backward glance toward his campaign manager, his cold candidate's eye appraising the swelling crowd. Tricia had spent all weekend on the telephone with Ron and Julian to get them here. It had paid off: there must be six hundred volunteers here. So where the hell was she?

As Andrew stepped wifeless to the makeshift podium, Tricia stood meekly in her stocking feet on a stark, cold gray linoleum floor, clinging to her purse with one hand, a pair of ivory pumps in the other. The drab institutional-buff walls of Dallas County Jail were dotted with signs. ALL VISITORS MUST WEAR ID. ARRESTING OFFICERS: STAY WITH YOUR PRISONERS. CHECK FIREARMS OUTSIDE. NO LOUD TALKING OR SINGING. Tricia had a bizarre vision of the prisoner in front of her, a heavyset black-bearded monster with a brutally bloodied nose, breaking into a chorus from "The Sound of Music."

"Move along, ma'am," her arresting officer ordered crisply. Only a police officer can make "ma'am" sound like an insult, Tricia thought. She wanted to scream in frustration, but a tiny voice in her head quieted her. She shuffled forward to the gunmetal-gray desk, her toes curled up tightly, as if to keep the filth of the jail's human flotsam and jetsam from defiling the soles of her nylons. God, the smell!

She raised her head, looking hopefully at the disinterested young sheriff's deputy who sat picking crumbs out of his mustache behind the square steel block of his desk. Can you help me? her blue-green eyes pleaded. The deputy blinked impassively, extracted one last morsel from the bristly red fuzz beneath his thin nose, and extended his hand palm up.

"ID," the deputy said tonelessly, accepting her driver's license from the policeman who had pulled her over on Lemmon Avenue.

"Please—" Tricia turned urgently to the police officer who had arrested her, a nice-looking young man with blow-dried hair and a jaw that jutted proudly to a dimpled point. "My husband is—"

"A congressman," the handsome policeman replied, his careful icy-blue eyes expressing neither awe nor anger, only that alert boredom peculiar to policemen everywhere. "I hear you, ma'am," he said tonelessly. "If you'll cooperate, we'll get through this much quicker. Okay?" It was not a request.

The mustached deputy looked up briefly from the green booking sheet. "Offense?" He pronounced it like any good southern lawman, accenting the first syllable: *aw*-fense.

"DWI," Officer Jut-Jaw replied flatly.

"But I . . ." Tricia fumbled for words. It wasn't the Scotch that slurred her tongue, she felt sure. She was just nervous. Christ, how many had she downed this afternoon? Three? Four, maybe, at the most. Surely that had oxidized or whatever by now. Tricia found the tongue in her cotton-dry mouth: "Officer, I am not intoxicated." She took the words slowly, careful not to blur her consonants. "I did touch my finger to my nose," she pointed out hotly.

"You did, ma'am," the young blond policeman said. "But just now, down the hall, that machine you breathed into? It showed a blood alcohol level of oh-point-two. So we have to book you. You can try the Breathalyzer again in a few minutes. Do you understand what I am saying to you?" he asked slowly, as though speaking to a very small child.

"Of course," she snapped, thinking, Careful, Tricia, let's play it cool, let's do whatever the Man says until we can get to a pay phone and call our husband. Let's not cause a scene and let every street lizard in the Dallas County Jail know that the congressman's wife just got picked up for drunk driving. She shut her mouth and surrendered her decorative gold belt and ivory shoes to the box held out by the deputy. Why do they want my shoes? she wondered bleakly. They're afraid I'll bludgeon a guard with a Bruno Magli?

Tricia stood red-faced and mute while they rolled her fingertips in ink and pressed them onto five marked spaces on a small white card. The deputy pawed through the contents of her purse in a loud monotone: "One bottle aspirin, Bayer. One comb, black. Two earrings, gold. One bottle aspirin, Tylenol. Four credit cards, Mastercharge, American Express, Texaco, Neiman-Marcus." They led her in front of a big box camera, where she instinctively froze her face in a smile as the flash popped.

"May I use the phone now?" she asked frostily, cringing to avoid the vomity smell of a drunken prostitute lurching past on the steady arm of a blue-shirted deputy. "My phone call," she reminded him. "May I have that now?" It was like playing Simon Says.

"Yes, ma'am," he said with an elaborate politeness just this side of sarcasm. He nodded toward the gaggle of policemen, deputies, and felons surrounding a waist-high shelf of phones marked: PRIS-

ONERS. TWO MINUTES ONLY. "I'll wait 'til the husband gets here," the officer told Deputy Mustache Picker. "No need for her to go to the cells."

"Yeah." The deputy jerked his head back down the hall toward the crowded admitting area on the left. "It's a zoo tonight already." The mustached deputy turned and headed back down the hall.

Tricia and her arresting officer pushed in next to the beefy black-bearded pugilist from the admitting line. Neither of them saw the young deputy with the reddish mustache as he turned into a doorway marked SHERIFF'S OFFICE. NO PRISONERS ALLOWED.

"I don't know, Jim." Dan Mullins shook his head slowly, his left hand stroking his close-cropped black beard. "We just can't seem to put him away."

Brackler nodded heavily. "We're what, fifteen points ahead? Big deal. With all we've dumped on him, he should be dead in the water."

They were cloistered with Jarrett Hart in the paneled law-firm conference room where Brackler had first met Dan a year and a half ago. But now the brass-plated sign on the front door read MULLINS & BRACKLER, ATTORNEYS-AT-LAW.

"Goddammit, boys," Hart said without rancor. He arched back in his chair. His leonine shock of white hair nearly brushed the Robert F. Kennedy portrait on the paneling behind him. Mullins's political sympathies were no secret to his clients. "Are we in trouble?"

"No, sir," Mullins replied quickly.

Lay it on the line, Brackler thought. Don't try to con this old guy.

Mullins obviously knew their sugar-daddy well. "There's been too much movement back and forth," he lamented. "First Watergate. Bang, we're thirty points ahead. Then Sebastian comes on with the big bucks, and he's right on our tail. Three weeks before election day, boom, the draft-dodging deal. The voters are over-loaded— Yeah, come in!"

Dan's secretary entered, waving a message slip like a white flag before her. "Mr. Brackler, Bill Wood is on the line for you," she said primly. She handed Brackler the slip of paper and turned to Dan. "It's six-thirty, Mr. Mullins," she said softly.

"Yeah, sure, go on home," Brackler said, flopping one hand

179

generously. He used the other to seize the telephone. "Sheriff, how you?" he shouted in his best Big Jim style. "Great, great. Whatya-know good?" There was a long pause. Hart and Mullins looked on curiously as Jim's thick dark eyebrows knit in a troubled frown. "Well, that's just terrible, Bill." His broad face cracked open in a huge guffaw. "Terrible! Hold on. I gotta couple guys here wanna hear this." Jim punched the red Hold button and turned excitedly to Dan: "How do you work this thing?"

Seconds later the conference room filled with the gravelly twang of Dallas County Sheriff Bill Wood, a legendary Texas lawman and Democrat, though not necessarily in that order. Bill Wood believed a good sheriff never let politics affect the way he enforced the law. Unless it was election time, and Republican fat cats like Roger Sebastian had recruited some young buck ex-deputy to run against him, which, even if it didn't worry Sheriff Bill Wood, mightily pissed him off.

"What was that, Bill?" Hart stood up and perched his tall heavy frame against the table, bracing himself forward by slapping one big palm on the slippery polished brown wood.

"—that you, Jarrett?" Wood's voice growled foggily through the speaker. The speaker worked like a swinging door. The first bit of every sentence seemed to get slammed off.

"—just picked up Andrew Sebastian's wife," Wood said, a dis-embodied bark of laughter jolting through the speaker. "On a DWI. She's out in the holding tank."

"You're kidding!" Mullins cried. His sharp teeth flashed a vicious grin. "Can you hold her overnight?"

"—ell no," Woods boomed. "You know what goes on in those cells? I don't even go down there at night, son. Sebastian'd sue my ass from here to the Supreme Court! Somebody's already here to pick her up. Name of Callahan."

"Okay," Brackler put in. "Can we get our hands on the arrest report?"

"—here in front of me. You wanna send somebody down?"

"I'm on my way!" Mullins shouted over his shoulder. He banged out the rear exit door and into the hallway, leaving Big Jim pounding on the table in ecstasy.

Jarrett Hart cast a troubled look at his candidate. Then he cleared his throat and thanked the good sheriff for his conscientious attention to duty.

11

A sudden hush descended over the election-night crowd at Sebastian headquarters. Maudie Phillips, proud veteran of two previous such events, climbed up on a rickety brown metal folding chair to chalk the first numbers of the night. Under Andrew's column, she wrote "192." Under Brackler's, "15."

An excited babble rose behind her, sparked with scattered applause. Maudie wheeled precariously on her perch, puzzled. Looking back at the blackboard, the elderly volunteer flushed red. She snatched up the big black eraser from the runner at the foot of the huge slate board. It had a series of precinct numbers running down the left. Spaces on the right would hold totals from each precinct. Scrubbing quickly at the slots, Maudie reversed the totals under their proper headings. She nodded primly at the results of her handiwork and accepted old Mr. Horton's hand to help her down, oblivious to the audible moan of disappointment.

Tricia turned away from the scene and walked back to the punch bowl, enduring a long look from Maudie's old biddy friends as they doled out a cup of exceedingly nonalcoholic punch. No spirits at this party, Callahan had decreed yesterday, gazing at Tricia levelly. Standing in front of the purse-lipped Guardians of the Punch, Tricia reflected that Andrew was the only one who hadn't reproached her.

"A one-day wonder," Andrew said jovially on that dreadful morning after, spreading out the newspapers on the breakfast table. "The *News* barely mentions it. And who reads the *Times Herald?*"

Every time she shut her eyes, Tricia could see the hard black Helvetica type: CANDIDATE'S WIFE FACES DWI CHARGES. And that hideous picture of her, grinning like the village drunk on a four-day bender, her tight swept-up bun of hair knocked askew in a way that made her head look like a trapezoid, all slanted off to the left. Not the sort of clipping you put in the scrapbook. And those nasty last-minute Brackler commercials, with her police mugshots up on the screen for everyone in Dallas to see.

"Too late in the game," Andrew had said, dismissing them. "Besides, people look at that and say, 'There but for the grace of God . . .'" She accepted the reprieve at face value: it was pure gold on occasions like tonight. Even Andrew's father, who usually treated her like a princess, stood cold and aloof across the room, staring at her like the village tramp. He should be so smug, thought Tricia, after that draft business. With friends like us, Andrew hardly needs enemies. She threw a surreptitious gaze at the blackboard, where Maudie was hammering a few more nails into Andrew's coffin.

Andrew bounded through the sweaty crowd, loosening his tie out of respect for the too-warm-for-November humidity that swirled through the plate-glass doors. Tricia had propped them open earlier with a pair of bricks. "Hi!" Andrew said boisterously. He surprised her by ignoring the Blue Hairs and sidling up to her directly.

He nuzzled her cheek quickly. "How's my girl?"

Tricia felt herself go uncontrollably cold. "If you mean have I been drinking"—she spoke slowly—"the answer is no. Though I may start."

Andrew looked hurt. "Maybe I'll join you," he whispered. "I bet Big Jim is throwing a hell of a party."

She smiled tightly, conscious of a TV camera pointed in their direction. "Go talk to your fans," she trilled hollowly, thinking for one quick second that maybe the score was even between them. One way or another, they could start a new life tomorrow. Andrew smiled a big puppy-dog grin, planted a slobbery kiss on each of her cheeks, and padded off to make everyone feel better. Tricia sipped at the sickly-sweet red punch and watched his sweat-darkened white shirt disappear among the colored print dresses of Andy's Army. She decided it was time to go and find a drink.

Brackler had wanted the election-night party downtown at the Adolphus, where Congressman Masters and the other big Democrats had always celebrated. Mullins had overruled him. "You're the man of the people," he'd said flatly. After their usual two-hour wrangle, they settled on a UAW union hall in East Dallas.

"We got some more numbers!" Big Jim shouted into the microphone from the podium they had positioned at stage right, next to a massive white billboard covered with columns of black figures. The crowd roared, waving huge green-and-white Brackler placards and poster-size pictures of Big Jim himself.

"With thirty-five percent of the vote in, it's lookin' pretty bad, folks," Jim admitted, pausing slightly. "*For Andrew Sebastian!*" His supporters cheered, a wave of hurrahs and laughter pocked with whistles and catcalls.

"We—you, really..." Brackler paused, letting the crowd pat itself on the back. "You have racked up an in-*credible* sixty"—he paused again for drama—"*sixty-three percent of the vote!*"

He paused one last time, then launched forward with gusto, voice stair-stepping louder and louder: "What a night. What a night! *What a night!*" Over the thunderous echo of the foot-stomping, rafter-raising ovation, Jim could barely hear Dan's words as he whispered frantically into his ear.

"I need to see you!" Mullins hissed, the bristles of his beard stabbing into Jim's earlobe. "Alone." His tone was foreboding. "Something's wrong with these numbers."

"There's something wrong with these numbers," Callahan said to himself, not looking up from his thin black-bound spiral notebook.

"You got that right," Andrew put in mildly. "Forty-five percent of the vote counted, and he's beating the crap out of us."

As the totals grew bleaker, Andrew had given up rallying Andy's Army and retreated to Callahan's bunker, buried well behind the lines at the rear of what had once been a string of car salesmen's offices. His father was there, too, in defiance of the unwritten rule

183

that had kept Roger out of all the locker rooms and election-night backrooms of Andrew's paternally guided career. Andrew would have said something, but the two of them weren't speaking. He ignored the iron-faced patriarch crouched on the metal folding chair in the corner.

Callahan's abode was in the old used-car manager's office, the place where customers had once been led to "see if the boss can do anything for you on the price." The little black notebook, the frantic answering of phones and scribbling down of numbers, Callahan's relentless chain-smoking: despite the presence of Roger's ghost at the feast, the entire tableau had a familiarity that Andrew knew was more than déjà-vu. Right now, Andrew felt he'd spent his whole life sitting across from Callahan's desk, trying to read his sloppy upside-down writing in that cursed book.

"That's not what I mean," Callahan said, looking at Andrew with a puzzled face. "It may not be as bad as it looks."

"How's that?" Andrew asked guardedly, feeling like *Dragnet*'s Joe Friday, the TV hero of his youth. Just the facts, ma'am.

"I've just run a cross-comparison of Brackler's best precincts," Callahan said cautiously. "The ones we predicted he'd be strongest in. Then I matched them against the precincts reported in so far. They're the same boxes."

"Which leaves us where?" Andrew's face was blank.

"With a chance," Callahan asserted carefully. "The only Democrat areas we don't have in yet are the Mexican boxes. Julian's downtown checking those right now."

"We all know how that works," Roger croaked from his corner perch. He rambled on, telling them what they already knew. "The party bosses won't report the totals from Little Mexico 'til they figure out how many votes they need."

"Another thing," Callahan persisted. "Brackler's precincts are coming in awfully early. The cumulative total in those areas, your votes and Brackler's added together, isn't really that high."

Andrew was starting to comprehend. His father, quick as always with numbers, spelled it out. "Our precincts aren't in yet because they aren't done counting the votes yet," the elder Sebastian said slowly, his bony, age-spotted fingers pulling idly at the leathery, dark-tanned folds of his turkey neck. A stray thought streaked through Andrew's head: Will I look like him when I get old? Will I butt into my son's life like he does? Remembering that he had no son, Andrew tried to focus as the other two dissected the remains of his political career.

"I think a lot more people in our precincts voted," Callahan finished. "I've been doing some calculations. If the other half of the precincts voted at thirty percent higher levels overall, and if we could take fifty-five percent of the vote in those boxes—Andy, we could still be in this."

Andrew felt a surge of adrenaline sear through his chest. Smiling broadly at his campaign manager, and grimly at his father, he stood suddenly and walked out of the room. He couldn't pretend to follow all of Callahan's arithmetic, but it awoke in him a need to find his wife. He had to go tell Tricia the news.

"I've had calls from the people we placed in Sebastian's best precincts," Mullins began without preamble. "And from Denny down at the county courthouse. This thing is going to be closer than we thought."

The three of them sat next to the large metal sink in the union hall's enormous kitchen. Dan's dog-eared precinct map was spread out on a wooden cutting board. Mullins picked up a long curved carving knife and pointed toward the northeast section of the blue-lined map.

"Sebastian's good boxes haven't come in yet," he reported. "Our people say they're voting at record levels."

"Maybe they're voting for us?" Brackler spoke first, ignoring the gruff way Jarrett Hart was clearing his throat. "Maybe even Republicans are fed up with Andy, what with the draft thing. And this business with his wife."

"Maybe they're fed up with you," Hart cut in with distaste. "It's one thing for that to hit the papers, or even to help it get there." He glanced sharply at Mullins, then jabbed his finger into Big Jim's shoulder. "But those commercials?" The rough old gentleman banker shook his head. "Folks don't like that, Jim. I don't like that."

"The issue was dying, Jarrett. Uh, Mr. Hart," Brackler fumbled nervously, his eyes focused on the map. "We had to keep it alive."

"Now it's gone and backfired on you," Hart growled.

"We don't know that," Mullins placated. "It's going to be tight, that's all. We're way ahead. But it's going to be a long night." He shot Brackler a warning glance. "It's too early to be out there claiming victory, Jim. We may not know until tomorrow."

185

"That close?" Brackler cried incredulously. "What about those nursing homes? The barrio?" In the final weeks of the campaign, Mullins had concocted a brilliant scheme to send Brackler operatives to local nursing homes and "help" the elderly residents, many comatose, to vote absentee.

"I've added our extra absentee votes into the count," Mullins said. "Nobody knows what the Mexicans are going to do. Julian Mendoza's been awful busy down there."

"Okay, so it's a little closer than we thought," Jim summarized shortly. "We're still kicking ass. Keep me posted, guys."

Jarrett Hart was clearly offended. Big Jim, secretly terrified that his coach was about to turn into a pumpkin, really didn't care.

"I'm gonna go enjoy my party," he mumbled. He pushed through the rubber-lined swinging kitchen doors, into the enveloping raucous warmth of the crowd.

At two o'clock in the morning, even Maudie Phillips tottered out of the empty headquarters, waving her treasured eraser through the plate glass at Andrew's weary frame. "You call Maudie the minute you know, hear!" she rasped, her voice ragged from chalk dust. "The very second!"

Andrew nodded weakly. A few stragglers from the press sat drinking warm punch. Vultures, he thought with unaccustomed rancor. Waiting for the body to drop, so they can get footage of me conceding for tomorrow's wake-up news.

His legs ached from standing. His eyes smarted from too much of Callahan's smoke and too little sleep. He dragged himself to one of the thirty telephone cubicles that circled the room. He dialed the house again. No answer.

Andrew was seriously worried. But after Tricia's encounter with the local gendarmerie last week, the last thing he wanted to do was call the police. Finally, listening to the rhythmic buzz in his ear, he decided to drive to the house. He took a deep breath and strode down the hallway, where Callahan was still scribbling numbers under his father's taut, red-rimmed eyes.

The candidate poked his head through the campaign manager's door. "Have you seen Tricia?"

"Is Julian out there?" Callahan barked.

"I asked you first," Andrew said impatiently, concern rising in his voice. "Her car's gone. Has she been back here lately?"

186

"Who?"

"Tricia, damn it."

"Tricia Dammit has not been here," Callahan said with a harassed smile. "And neither has Julian."

"You called?" Julian pushed past Andrew into the cramped, messy office, holding a long sheet of white paper with tallies scrawled in a splatter of ink and pencil. He nodded respectfully to Andrew's father, hunched on an uncomfortable-looking chair to Julian's right.

"The barrio," Mendoza announced, one tawny hand dropping the sheet on Callahan's cluttered blotter. Callahan scowled at him and ran one ink-stained finger down the figures. Andrew, torn between concern about his wife and curiosity about the Hispanic vote, compromised by remaining in the doorway and scanning the dwindling crowd down the hall.

"Julian," Callahan said with genuine warmth. "Are these for real?"

"I drove personally to every precinct and checked the counter," Mendoza confessed with pride. "It was Juan Cadillo, man. He put the word out. His father paid lip service to the bosses, but even the old man was impressed with how hard Andy worked for Juan's appointment."

"The turnout wasn't much down there, Andrew," Callahan said, snatching up a ringing phone. "But it looks like we split the barrio. Fifty-fifty." He barked into the receiver, "Yeah, Callahan here!"

"Great," Andrew said quietly. "I'm going home." He felt strangely indifferent to what his two aides were doing, as though they were balancing someone else's checking account. "Call me and tell me how it turned out."

"Wait a second," Callahan said hoarsely into the mouthpiece of the phone cradled in his shoulder. "Where do you think you're going?"

"Home," Andrew said simply.

"No, you don't," Callahan shot back. "Sit down! We're only two thousand votes behind, and there's not much left uncounted. It's still mathematically possible."

"Fine," Andrew said, dispirited. "Call me at the house. Tricia's missing." Do I have to spell it out, Ron? My wife is an alcoholic, and it's past bar-closing time, and she's nowhere to be found. Happens in the best of families.

187

"Tricia," Callahan said absently, turning his attention back to the voice on the other end of the line. "Right."

"I'll go with you, if that's okay." Roger spoke in a plaintive tone Andrew had never heard from his father. A strange thought occurred to him. Does my father need me? When it came right down to it, he was probably the closest thing to a real friend Roger Sebastian had ever known. Andrew stared at the skinny folded-up old man in the corner. He hadn't noticed how small his father had become in the last few years. Just in the past couple weeks, since the draft-exemption scandal, he seemed to have aged a decade. Roger's skin looked pale and unhealthy, the way a sixty-nine-year-old man's face looks at that hour of the night-morning. His gray-blue eyes held real concern. The elder Sebastian cleared his throat and added dryly, "I sent your mother home. You're the only ride I've got."

"Okay," Andrew said abruptly. He really wanted to do this alone. What if he found Tricia passed out on the front porch?

But he didn't want to hurt his father anymore. He didn't want to hurt anyone anymore. All he wanted was find his wife and go to bed. He flicked his thumb toward the door. "Let's get this show on the road."

It's over, Brackler thought exultantly. And I won!

At a quarter to two in the morning, Dan Mullins had railed at the slowness of the vote-counting process. On the phone to Denny, he fumed, "Are they using an abacus down there?" Angrily he had pulled a much abused blue blazer over his narrow shoulders. "I'm going down to the county." He stormed out the back door of the union hall. "Back in twenty minutes."

Now, good as his word, here Dan stood. Brackler's best friend in the world grinned like a monkey with the world's biggest banana.

"I now pronounce you United States congressman," Mullins said with mock solemnity. "An historic landslide. We won by eight hundred votes."

"You're kidding!" Jim said, breathing out the billow of air he had held tight in his chest since the moment Dan had banged back into the room. "Only eight hundred votes! Are you sure?" He hesitated. "Are we safe?"

"Absolutely," Mullins said. "They won't certify the count until tomorrow. The Sebastian people don't even know yet. But I got it straight from the elections administrator. It's yours, Jim."

188

"Good night, boys," Jarrett Hart said curtly, sliding his line-backer's frame off of a tall silver stool. He hooked his suit jacket over one shoulder. "Good work."

"You're not disappointed?" Mullins queried the old man confidently. "About the margin?"

"A win's a win." Hart shrugged. "We got our money's worth. I just gotta git. I been married fifty-two years, boys. Margic can't go to sleep unless her back's against mine. And vice versa. Give me a call next week, Danny," he added. "We can talk about Jim's committee assignments."

"Right," Brackler cut in. "I'll call next week."

Hart looked slowly from one young man to the other and sighed. "You all work that out between you. I'm goin' to bed, where old men belong this hour of the night."

"Me, too, Jim," Dan said suddenly, quick to follow the powerful banker out the door for one last parking-lot chat. "Congratulations, Jim. See you at the office?"

"Sure," Brackler said with false nonchalance, realizing abruptly that he was the last one left in the union hall. "At the office, fine." Even Denny was still downtown. Was this all there was?

"We can order a new nameplate." Dan laughed as he edged out the back door. "Brackler and Mullins, Attorneys-at-Law."

"You're kidding," Brackler said.

"No," Dan said, smiling with a new father's irrepressible pride. "You're a congressman now, Jim. We've gotta cash in."

He held his hand face up, waiting for the gimme-five hand slap that was trendy these days. Big Jim, shell-shocked and unaccountably sad, dutifully smacked his partner's palm. He watched the young lawyer scramble after Hart, a big clumsy puppy falling over his paws to keep up with his master.

Now, Jim was alone. Which, he reflected, is the way it always has been. It used to be all right, being alone. But tonight? He'd thought it would be different. The way it had been earlier, with people cheering and the big boys suddenly sucking up to him like never before, and the television lights searing his eyes.

Instead, here he stood, in the gleaming metallic kitchen of an empty banquet hall. He looked at his wavy reflection in the tinted windows of the kitchen's swinging silver doors: a tall, bulky, round-faced young man who at thirty had everything he had ever wanted, but only once had been inside a girl who hadn't been paid for the privilege. And let's face it, Brackler thought bleakly, that one was a tad unwilling. Sometimes, late at night, he thought about those days with something like remorse and wondered if it could have been different.

Imbued with a sudden soaring inspiration, Big Jim lumbered across the red-tiled kitchen floor to a grease-smudged white phone on the wall. The Fourth District's new congressman-elect seized the receiver and pressed it to his ear, punching urgently at the buttons.

"H'lo?" Even slurred and sleep-irritated, her voice brought a sharp pain to Jim's chest. This is a mistake, he realized.

"Ma?" Brackler said cautiously. "That you?"

"Huh?" The voice at the other line came groggily awake. "Who's this?"

"It's me, Ma," Jim explained patiently, desperate to cut through the haze. "Jimmy. Your son."

"Jimmy?" His mother's wheedling saccharine tone raised hackles up and down Brackler's spine. He gritted his teeth, gripped the phone. "It's me, Ma," he repeated. "Jimmy."

"Shh!" Patty Brackler whispered loudly. "Mac uz out late, and he's sleepin'. You goin' get me in trouble!"

"Did you see me on TV, Ma?"

"TV?" she replied, confused. "I didn't get no TV from you, Jimmy."

"Me," he replied dejectedly. "Me, on television. In the election, you know? I won tonight!"

"On TV!" she exclaimed with sudden victory. "Yes! Ah saw you, Jimmy. Two, three times. Mac saw it, too! On the commercials. I was proud, Jimmy! Mac was proud. Can you lend me fifty dollars, Jimmy? I got an operation—"

Jim hung up the phone quickly. He rested his broad, feverish forehead against the dewy gray wall of the kitchen. Pressing his hands flat on the stucco wall, he ground his skull painfully into the prickly gray paint points, feeling the stomach-racking sobs well up within him. His eyes bulged with the hot shame of tears. Then he cried, because he had everything he had ever wanted, and there wasn't a single human being in the world with whom he could share it.

*   *   *

190

"Go away!" Callahan shouted at the pounding on his office door.

The door swung open in response. A dark, bespectacled reporter from Channel 8 stuck his curly black head through the crack.

"Come on, Callahan, what gives?" complained the journalist, an aggressive Los Angeles import Callahan had grown to despise. "Our guys just got Brackler in the parking lot. He says it's all over."

"Our count shows us two hundred behind," Callahan insisted doggedly, looking at the white adding-machine tape that scrolled steadily from his desktop calculator. "So don't get your panties in a wad."

"Either way, you lose," replied Bernie Zollars, anxious to get his footage and go home. "Where's Sebastian?"

"Gone home," Callahan said casually, making a snap decision. Nothing wrong in admitting that. Maybe it even looked confident.

"Without calling Big Jim to concede?" the reporter persisted.

"There's nothing to concede," Julian Mendoza snapped from his seat opposite Callahan.

"Never say die, right?" Zollars's sarcasm was wearing thin. "Where's Sebastian live, anyway? Assignments says we gotta stay on this until we get both victory and concession. Usual rules. How 'bout an address, Ron?"

"Look it up in the phone book." Callahan grimaced. "You need help finding one?"

"Screw you, Callahan."

"Oh, Bernie," Callahan drawled as the TV man backed out of the office, "we might have a story for you."

"I know." Zollars nodded wearily. "'Sebastian Challenges Election Results, Demands Recount.' Standard form."

"What would you say about vote fraud?"

The reporter sighed, holding up his hands in surrender. "Notice how the winning team never hollers foul?" Zollars shook his head. Then he paused, peering at Callahan through the pall of white cigarette haze. It wasn't like Ron to bullshit, the reporter mused. "You got any evidence?"

"Nothing I can talk about."

"Screw you," the reporter responded automatically, then added the reporter's standard sign-off. "Keep me posted." The door swung shut behind him.

"They stole it," Mendoza said quietly, staring at the long curlicues

191

of calculator tape strewed across the campaign manager's desk. "Nursing homes. Oldest scam in the books." He shook his head. "Look at Precinct 4411: Brackler 971, Sebastian 51."

"Not too subtle," Callahan agreed, pushing to his feet. The campaign manager dug in the pocket of his crumpled gray flannel slacks for his car keys. "There's not a thousand literate people in that whole neighborhood."

"They could at least have spread the phony stuff around," Mendoza huffed, his professional standards offended by the crudity of the vote scam.

"It's better this way," Callahan said, baring his teeth in a ferretlike smile. He bustled toward the door. "Pick up that phone and start trying to call Andrew's house," he ordered brusquely. "Keep dialing until you get him. Tell him we're within a few hundred votes, and explain about the nursing homes. Be sure and warn him the TV crews are on their way." Mendoza nodded and snatched up the phone.

Callahan finished: "I'm gonna drive like hell, but I may not beat them there. Tell him not to say a damn thing to the press until I get there. Make damn sure he doesn't concede! Got it?"

"Got it," Mendoza said, listening to the phone as it began to ring. And ring. And ring.

They drove in silence. Roger Sebastian stared out the passenger window at the greens of Lakewood Country Club, reminding him that Andrew hadn't smiled at him since the day he had stormed into Dallas Country Club and interrupted his golf foursome. The real estate tycoon leaned his head against the Cadillac's plush headrest and took a deep breath that rattled in his chest.

"Nice car," he commented lightly, watching the yellow-lit speedometer crawl toward fifty as Andrew took the deep curve on Gaston Avenue.

"I liked the Mercedes." Andrew was tight-lipped, unforgiving. "Politics," he explained briefly.

"Right." Roger sighed, regretting the paternal habit of turning even the blandest small talk into advice. "That was a nice car, the Mercedes," he added weakly.

Andrew said nothing, his eyes scanning the dark, winding road.

Roger cleared his throat. "Son," he began ponderously, "Tricia has a problem. You know that, don't you?"

"Thanks, Dad," Andrew snapped. "I'll handle this, okay?" He paused and gulped for breath. "Turning my wife into an alcoholic is the one thing in life I've managed to do all by myself."

"I didn't say she was—"

"Nobody ever says, Dad," Andrew interrupted. "That's part of the problem. My problem, okay?"

"Of course."

They were silent again, listening to the quiet, distant squeal of the big automobile's tires. As Andrew turned into their neighborhood, it leapt into his headlights: Tricia's smashed silver Buick, front end brutally accordioned around the trunk of the huge live-oak tree that marked the corner. Roger's head snapped forward as his son slammed on the brakes. The big black Caddy jittered to a sudden stop behind the glowing red brake lights of the wrecked Buick.

"Oh, my God!" Roger said in horror. Andrew kicked his car door open before the Cadillac had come to a full stop. As the old man reached over to ram the Cadillac's gearshift into park, Andrew ran to the left side of his wife's car, black wingtip shoes pounding hollowly on the tarry street.

The Buick's white interior light spilled out onto the street, the driver's door gaping open like a crooked pull tab on a tin can. Andrew leaned forward into the car seat, his ears filling with the loud, wasplike buzz of the open car door. As his father's image peered eerily into the Buick's passenger window, Andrew reached inside and yanked the keys out of the ignition.

Tricia was nowhere in sight.

A single blow from inside had starred the windshield, shattering a cobweb of cracks. Andrew's eyes took in the blood-soaked vinyl of the white dashboard and realized his wife's head had hammered into the safety glass.

"Oh, Lord," Roger said as he opened the passenger door. The bent door frame protested the abuse with a piercing screech of metal. "Where is she?" he gasped.

A shiny blue van turned into the street and circled wide, slowing as it began the right-hand turn on Lakewood. A man's voice called from the van's dark window: "Need any help?" Roger looked toward his son, then waved the van on, not sure what to do.

Andrew knelt frozen on the street. He fingered the sticky red blood that soaked garish inkblot patterns on the slick alabaster upholstery. Dangling uselessly from the dash, the ridiculous sunflower key chain he'd bought Tricia was stained a deep rust.

Andrew snapped his head up and looked out at the street through the glass of the open car door. Roger followed his son's gaze. Andrew stared at the cross-eyed pools of light cast by the Buick's tree-crumpled headlights. A low moan escaped unheard through his lips.

In the whitewash of light across the sidewalk, an uneven trail of blood-red spatters led into the darkness down Lakewood Boulevard.

Tricia stumbled and fell to her skinned knees again. The gritty sidewalk bit into tender flesh, a shock of new pain that jarred her from kneecaps to shoulders. This time she lay down on her side and sobbed, cocking her throbbing head sideways to feel the cool hard cement against the hot gummy hair above her forehead.

Rolling over on her stomach, she pushed herself upright and tried to straighten out her legs. She breathed in. Her stomach and breasts burned where the steering wheel had pummeled her midsection. Am I bleeding down there, too? she wondered. Alarmed, she used both hands to pull awkwardly at the front of her blood-soaked plaid pinafore. She felt the zipper on the back gaping open as she hauled the fabric away from her pink-stained white brassiere. Nothing, she saw with relief, squinting her blood-encrusted right eye in the glaring white light from the street lamp. Just the first few reddish marks that would soon bruise her stomach solid black. Feeling very sick and torn up down there, she wondered if there could be anything internal.

Careful not to place weight on her battered knees, Tricia lurched to her feet and staggered weakly toward their circular drive. It was a nice house. The thought comforted her. She focused on moving toward the brass-plated sconces that cast twin beacons of yellow light from either side of the oval-topped front door of the big brick colonial.

It wasn't easy, placing one foot in front of the other without falling. Her head was dizzy, booming inside with dull thunder, like the worst hangover of her life. The heavy thud of pain inside drove out all sensation of the stinging at her knees, the gash on her forehead. It didn't hurt at all on the outside, she realized, tapping curiously at the two-inch scalp cut with her finger. She dabbed the

194

blood away from her eyes. In fact, there was precious little external pain to account for all the carnage: just the booming in her head and the dizziness that scrambled her thoughts.

It was impossible to keep her feet moving without stumbling and swaying and falling, down, down, down, until the wicked Chinese holly reached out to grab her, keeping her from slamming her knees into the red bricks of the driveway.

"Thanks," Tricia told the shrubbery stupidly. Angling to her feet, she plucked a jagged leaf from the torn shoulder of her now crooked dress. She swayed unevenly on the slanting drive, then stumbled toward the door.

Not fair, she thought, not fair at all. She hadn't had a drop to drink. She had done what any good woman would do on a night like this: taken a long drive, had a good cry. That she had chosen to do so at forty miles an hour on Gaston Avenue was just bad luck. The chest-racking sobs of a really good lung-whooping, eye-burning, saliva-down-her-chin crying jag had been more than the Buick could take. She'd swept into Avalon a little too wide: the Electra had bounced up over the curb and hurled itself into the big shady tree on the corner at Lakewood Boulevard, just two lousy blocks from home.

"Goddamn car," Tricia muttered with a loony laugh, thinking of all the automotive tragedies she had suffered recently. I was born for mass transit, she thought crazily. Staggering up the driveway, she dug in the purse she had instinctively dragged by its strap all the way down Lakewood Boulevard. A lady never goes anywhere without her purse, Tricia thought proudly.

"Not again!" she cried, tears welling up in frustration. Those goddamn keys! Sighing audibly, she held the purse over her woozy head, scattering the contents on the cheery doormat that read THE SEBASTIANS. WELCOME! She sank against the door, sobbing in great anguished heaves.

Seconds later, that was how Channel 8's bright blue van found her, trapping her in a blaze of headlights like a frightened doe caught by poachers of the night.

"I'm okay, really," Tricia insisted woozily, shrugging off Bernie Zollars's patronizing hands. The reporter and his cameraman hauled her to her feet. "It's just my keys. I left them. Locked them. In my car." She turned unsteadily toward the door and twisted at the knob, feeling their questioning eyes on her naked back.

195

"Roll tape, Lippett," Zollars whispered in a voice as light as feathers on wind.

"What?" the cameraman replied incredulously.

"Roll tape!" the reporter hissed.

Shrugging, the cameraman complied. Unobtrusively the heavyset photographer clicked on the minicam and angled it upward in Tricia's general direction.

Zollars leaned forward again and put his hand on the woman's shoulder, pulling it back when he felt the moist blood. "You've had a wreck, Mrs. Sebastian," he said soothingly, eyes roving down her bared torso. "I saw the car. Can we take you to the hospital?"

"No, really," Tricia said, smiling weakly. "I'm fine. Please, I just need my keys. I was upset, not paying attention. I'm fine."

"You're bleeding, Mrs. Sebastian." Zollars emphasized the last name ever so slightly in the direction of the remote microphone on the camera's head. The minicam now rested in the cameraman's arms, its autofocus lens swiveling slightly. Zollars offered, "Are you sure we can't—"

"What the *hell* is going on here?" a thunderous voice demanded from beside the van.

Running footsteps clapped on the brick driveway. Andrew's tall, angular frame loomed into view.

"Your wife is, uh, hurt," Zollars said slowly. The reporter backed away from the candidate, caught in the act.

"You're *interviewing* her?" Andrew raged. He tossed Zollars into his cameraman. The minicam clattered to the driveway. Andrew burst forward to catch Tricia gently by the arm.

"Jesus Christ," he said softly, his voice tinged with a jagged edge of emotion. "You look awful," he said helplessly. "Are you okay?"

Tricia nodded apologetically and let herself collide with the warm comfort of his sweat-soaked shirt.

The Cadillac eased to a shaky stop along the curb. Andrew had run all the way up the street, following the paint-spatter trail of blood as his father idled along beside him, illuminating the sidewalk. Now Roger brushed past the men from Channel 8 and joined the tableau on Andrew's front porch.

"Give me your keys," Roger commanded briefly. Andrew handed him the bloody sunflower ring, indicating the bronze key that fit the door. The older Sebastian worked it into the lock and eased open the door. He reached out and took his wobbly daughter-in-law by one slender wrist.

A third pair of tires screeched into the driveway. As Roger helped Tricia inside, Ron Callahan exploded up the walkway.

"What happened, Andrew? I saw Tricia's—" Callahan halted, spotting the Channel 8 van. Two more cars pulled in behind them: more press from the headquarters, mopping up their election-night coverage.

"She's had an accident," Andrew said in a trembling voice, eyes bloodshot and angry. "I don't know how bad. I've got to go," he said shortly. "Dad's inside. We have to call an ambulance."

"Mr. Sebastian, could we just get one quick statement on the election?" Zollars shouted, his sardonic voice rasping over Callahan's shoulder.

The campaign manager reacted automatically, leaning forward into Andrew's ear. "Don't give 'em anything yet," he whispered quickly. "We're only a couple hundred behind, and we can challenge—"

Andrew backed away in horror. "What the hell are you talking about?" he screamed, incredulous. "That's my wife in there! And you want to talk about an election?"

Callahan, who didn't have a wife, who'd never even had a real girlfriend, looked as if he had been slapped. "Yeah, sure," he mumbled. "Sorry, I just—forget it."

"And you!" Andrew stepped forward toward Zollars. He suddenly felt belligerent. "What do you want? A comment on the election?"

Red-faced, voice cracking with tears, Andrew lunged at the cameraman, grabbing the minicam from his shoulder. "How's this?" He whirled the camera in a half-circle and crashed it into the side of the van, denting the blue door, sending the lens shattering to the bricks.

Callahan put one hand helplessly to his head, leaning brokenly against the house. Zollars and the photographer stepped back as the infuriated candidate battered the van with the heavy camera, until the minicam's side vent popped open and a large black videotape cartridge fell to the driveway. Andrew reached over and scooped up the plastic cartridge. He dug at one side of the tape, ripping yards of black ribbon out of the slender box. The spools sung a high whine in the startled silence.

"You're not gonna fuck with her any more!" Andrew breathed angrily. Tears spilled down his flushed cheeks. His voice rose in a strangled shout. "Nobody rapes her again, you understand? Not you. Not Brackler. I'm out. That's my statement, okay? Screw you all!"

Andrew whirled to face Callahan, mouth quivering. "Get these bloodsuckers off my lawn," he said loudly, so the press could hear each measured word. "And call Brackler. Tell him he can have the goddamn seat. I'm through."

The door banged shut behind him.

"You can say that again," snickered Zollars, looking around for support.

Callahan walked forward menacingly. "You heard the man," said the beefy campaign manager. "Get out of here! Before Andy comes out here and takes your head off." He turned and retreated inside.

Zollars turned to the small gathering of journalists in the Sebastians' front yard. Two pointed television cameras at the front door.

"Did somebody get that, at least?" Zollars whined, heavy-browed brown eyes imploring the little group.

"We got it," said Zollars's colleague from Channel 5, a pretty young blond woman who gazed at Bad Bernie with an undisguised mixture of admiration and disgust. "Every word."

December
1987

12

A thin restless carpet of leaves skittered across the dull yellow lawn of the campus mall. As usual, autumn had struck Texas without warning. Overnight, the long rows of spreading oaks had dropped their dusty gray foliage; the weather turned sharply from a springlike mid-November to the chill that always grips Dallas the week after Thanksgiving.

Andrew paused to hunch the big armful of books farther up on his ribs. He ignored the persistent wind that crept through the layers of his English tweed sports coat, blue-and-pink Shetland crew neck, and blue Oxford button-down shirt, his neck kept warm by the soft wine-colored wool tie Sean had given him last Father's Day.

Andrew liked the cold. It allowed him to dress like a college professor.

Remembering the time, he quickened his pace. His cordovan loafers crunched on the scattered twigs on the sidewalk leading to his last class of the day. If he didn't hurry, the kids would ignore the statutory ten-minute waiting period and consider the class canceled. It had happened be-

201

fore. He would show up a few minutes late, only to find a message scrawled on the blackboard: SORRY, DR. SEBASTIAN. WE WAITED AS LONG AS WE COULD.

Last time, some rat-fink colleague had snitched on him. The dean had called Andrew in for one of his famous little heart-to-hearts, greeting him with a sarcastic, "Ah, the late Andrew Sebastian!"

Andrew scurried up the wash of cement steps pouring out between Dallas Hall's Doric columns. Though he had been out of the whirl of politics for fourteen years, he still couldn't seem to master the fine art of being on time.

"Ah, ah, ah!" Andrew shouted exultantly, halting the parade of nineteen-year-olds as they marched out into the rotunda from the direction of room 103. "Got you!" he gasped, flush with victory. "About-face!"

The herd of collegians lowed a gentle moan and reversed direction, filing slowly into the classroom. Andrew glanced at the scrawl on the chalkboard. He consulted his watch, analyzed the handwriting, and glared out from the lectern.

"Pinkston, you only gave me six minutes. Just for that, we'll all do a little pop quiz," announced the gently graying professor. The class groaned as one. All heads turned bitterly toward the flush-faced redhead in the back row. "I hope you all read your Hofstadter over Thanksgiving," Andrew drawled. "Please summarize, in one paragraph, his thoughts on Hamilton and the Federalists. You have ten minutes." As the notebooks flopped open and scribbling sounds filled the room, he couldn't resist a final shot.

"Except Pinkston," he added, throwing the freckled sophomore an evil smile. "He gets six."

"About time," Tricia muttered without malice as her husband's battered Jaguar purred beneath the kitchen window. She heard the car door squeak open, imagining the awkward gymnastics Andrew endured to wrest his long frame from the British racing-green XJS. Not for the first time, she wondered, Why do tall men like small cars?

The screen door between her and the leaf-strewn pool slid open noiselessly. Andrew appeared, a pile of books under his arm.

"Work tonight?" Tricia asked, disappointed. "Sean's been waiting to tell you about school. And you're late, as usual. I thought maybe we could all go out to eat and a movie." This came in a quick rush as she mopped her hands on a dishtowel. "Hi," she added simply.

"Hi." He embraced her. It still amazed him, even after so many years, how easy it was between them now, how different from the way it once had been. "Sorry," he added routinely. "Had to keep the little swine late, to teach them about not doing their assigned reading over Thanksgiving."

Tricia shuddered. "Glad I'm not one of your students." She reached up on tiptoe to kiss him once, twice; smoothly, wetly. She helped him unload the books on the bleached pine of the kitchen table. "Why all the work?" she asked, trying not to whine. She hated to sound like one of those naggy women who have nothing to do all day.

"I didn't get to it in Colorado," Andrew admitted, scraping out a wicker kitchen chair and rotating it backward. "That article on Wilson? It's got to be at the Southwestern by Friday, or you know what," he explained grimly, drawing one finger across his throat.

"Publish or perish," Tricia joined in as they chimed the despised code of academia.

"Dad!" The distant thunder of tennis shoes hammered down the hallway of the brick North Dallas ranch-style they had bought after Sean was born. Their son burst into the den, a tumble of crisp new blue jeans and the long-sleeved rugby shirt he wore six days out of seven. Tricia washed the damn thing in hot water every night, hoping it would shrink enough so she could throw it away.

Sean screeched to a rubber-soled halt on the soft white kitchen floor, leaving double-furrowed black marks.

"Socks in the kitchen," Tricia said automatically.

"Okay," moaned the eleven-year-old. He kicked off his shoes in one swift practiced motion and hockey-pucked them back onto the den's tasteful gray carpet. He clambered into the chair next to his father's, straddling it backward, as Andrew always did. Sean's gawky little-boy legs jutted in all directions, long white athletic tube socks dangling from the ends of his toes. Tricia watched her husband notice the slavish imitation and revel in it.

"So Mr. Sean," Andrew began, reaching out to ruffle his son's dirty-blond hair. It was now starting to turn brown, as had Andrew's in the sixth grade.

"So Mr. Dad," Sean rejoined, pale blue eyes glowing.

"What did you learn in school today?" All three of them spoke as one and burst into laughter at the ritual.

"We had a guest speaker," Sean said, chipper. "A senator," he added, knowing this would please his father. "A U.S. senator, not a state senator," anxious to let Dad know he understood these fine distinctions.

A small, familiar ache passed through Andrew's chest, the one he got whenever talk turned to politics. In his classes he was careful to focus on the past.

"A senator," he replied, summoning the proper awe for his son's brush with greatness. "Jack Longley?" he probed, sure it wasn't. The state's aging senior senator wouldn't be out making speeches to elementary schools, with his retirement coming up next year. It was an old rule of Ron Callahan's: Never waste time on people who will never be old enough to vote for you.

"Nope." Sean smiled, tight-lipped. Andrew thought, It's to be a pop quiz.

"Ted Kennedy?" he guessed, wanting to give his son a few.

"No," Sean said, his disdain acute.

"Buck Drake, then," Andrew said, naming the state's junior U.S. senator. Sean didn't like to let him win too easy.

"Nope!" Sean beamed victoriously. "You shoulda heard him, Dad. He was a great speaker. I got to shake his hand. I told him you used to be a congressman. He knew you!"

"Yeah?" Andrew leaned forward and hung his chin over the chair, his interest no longer feigned. "Who was this spellbinding orator?"

"What's that?" Sean asked innocently.

"It means a good speaker," Tricia cut in. "Who was he?"

"Jim Brackler," Sean announced, grinning beneath the snub nose he had inherited from his father. "I got his autograph on my history book."

Tricia sucked in her breath involuntarily. Her lean, angular little boy flipped the book over so his father could see his prize, inked in heavy black on the brown paper cover, beneath the printed red letters urging mothers to shop at Minyard's Grocery. Sean held out the book that way for what seemed like a full minute, oblivious to his father's stare.

Tricia was reminded of one Easter Sunday when Sean was two, back when Andrew was working day and night on his Ph.D. and she was scrambling around trying to potty-train the baby. At dinnertime, all the relatives were just sitting down to her fancy ham dinner when towheaded Sean appeared in the doorway of the dining room, hands outstretched before him, bearing his proud offering in the palms of his hands. "Look, Mommy!" he enthused as she froze in horror, and the whole room exploded in laughter. "Potty!" Sean never lived it down.

Tricia blinked away a little tear as Andrew reached out for the book, reacting just as he had to Sean's proud potty on that Easter Sunday.

"That's great, Sean!" Andrew took the book, holding it by the edges as if not to defile his hands with the autograph. "What else happened at school today?"

Later that night, after they'd gone for pizza and sat through three hours of the latest George Lucas space epic, Andrew sat staring at the blank yellow legal pad between his books on the smooth mellow wood of the butcher-block kitchen table. He had wasted a good hour rearranging Wilson biographies and arcane monographs on trust busting. He just couldn't seem to concentrate on the nation's past, what with his own sitting right there on the kitchen cabinet.

Looking to his right, he could see the nasty scrawl profaning the cover of his son's textbook. "Say hello to your father!" read the autograph, its hearty tone belying the snide intent. "Big Jim Brackler."

What kind of asshole, Andrew wondered, signs his own name "Big" anything? He imagined signing his article for the *Southwestern Journal of Political History* with a broad flourish: "Big Andrew Sebastian."

SMU had been thrilled to have Andrew back in the mid-1970s, after he had gotten his degrees and Tricia had gotten out from under the bottle. Andrew Sebastian was quite a plum for a school whose academic standing had never been quite top rank: a former U.S. congressman whose role in rooting out the Watergate scandal had earned him a couple of footnotes in the Woodward and Bernstein books. Even Schlesinger mentioned Andrew's fleeting year in the Capitol spotlight, going on to note the "palpable irony" of his scandalous debacle in the post-Watergate congressional elections.

Strange, Andrew thought, how the events of intervening years made the scandals of his 1974 debacle innocuous, even quaint. A draft dodger? Carter pardoned them in 1977. Drinking problems in the family? Talk to Betty Ford.

"Come to bed," a soft voice said behind him.

"In a bit," Andrew replied. Embarrassed, he hid the letters he had written across the top of the pad: BIG JIM BRACKLER.

"Still thinking about him?" Tricia asked. This was the first they had spoken of him in years.

"I guess so," Andrew said dully, thinking that his son had been half-right: Brackler was still in the House. But soon he would be a U.S. senator.

Brackler was a latter-day Rasputin whom the assembled nobility of Texas politics could not seem to kill. There had been scandals, rumors, even an indictment. Somehow the brass-knuckled populist always came out on top, proof of some black-magic political juju whose precedent Andrew had yet to find in any poli-sci textbook.

With more than a touch of envy, most Texas pols agreed with the assessment of former Brackler opponent Mark Latham. "Brackler doesn't just beat you," the two-time Brackler victim had commiserated to Andrew some years back. "He mangles you, like a pit bull with a rat in his teeth."

Which is why, Andrew reflected as his wife's bed-warm arms slipped around his neck, Jim Brackler will be a U.S. senator by this time next year. "Nobody wants to be the next rat," he commented aloud.

"Huh?" Tricia's sleepy voice tickled his right ear with a hot, breathy intimacy he couldn't have imagined fifteen years ago.

"Never mind," he said, his mind suddenly on other things. "Let's go to bed."

The dull buzz of the intercom bored slowly into her consciousness, a dentist's drill whining away at the stubborn enamel of her brain. Finally the bit pierced the shell of sleep and hit a nerve.

"Yeah, yeah, yeah!" she cried in agony, lifting the covers with one trembling hand. There, his liver-spotted bald dome collapsed between her thighs, lay an eight-term congressman from Ohio— or was it Iowa?—whose name escaped Amanda.

She knew his party affiliation, though, by the white rime of powder dusting his nose, her vagina, and—she ran her tongue over her lips—the outer edges of her memory. Democrats always seemed to have better drugs.

Amanda slid one leg out beneath the somnolent old legislator. His head plopped onto a pink cotton sheet that was stiff with his semen. Randy old goat, she thought as she drew on a flimsy black satin nightgown. She slipped the covers over his slack, fish-belly face, thinking that the congressman looked dead. Wouldn't that be ironic, she thought. I spend all night boffing his brains out to get his vote against House Bill 7720, and he croaks on me. An involuntary shiver ran up her spine at the specter of the headlines.

Any day now, she thought. Too many people know, and too many are talking. Maybe I should get out of town, before the whole fucking city blows up again. Amanda stumbled unsteadily through her thousand-dollar-a-month high rise and fell against the button marked Talk.

"Yeah?" she said dispiritedly, wondering who the hell wanted up here on a bleak Washington Monday. Most members were already home for Christmas break. Besides, they knew better than to drop by unannounced. It was too easy to run into a colleague like Old Baldy back in the bedroom.

"Miz Roberts?" The doorman's fat-man bellow boomed out of the speaker, inflaming the raw wound in her head.

"What time is it, Curtis?" she snapped. See if I slip him fifty bucks this Christmas.

"Two twenty-three, Miz Roberts." The voice echoed around the tapestry-hung walls of the penthouse. "There's this guy says he has to see you. His name is Parker Worthington." Amanda felt a sudden roll of dread in her stomach. "He's got a plastic ID from the Justice Department. Want me to tell him to go away?" Curtis asked doubtfully.

Amanda could envision some attorney standing impassively next to the rotund doorman, rolling his eyes ever so slightly as he eaves-dropped. "He's for real." She sighed. "Only Justice hires guys named Parker. Give me five minutes," she ordered.

Within four, Congressman Hankins was on his feet and down the garage elevator. Amanda had to give him credit: the old guy really knew how to get his shit together. Unfortunately that included the congressman's furtive gesture to sweep four lines of the good stuff off her glass bedside table, into his brass business-card holder emblazoned with the angry eagle of the congressional seal.

"'Bye, honey!" said the disheveled representative, blowing her a

207

kiss as he licked coke off his lips. "You can count on me," he added, making her feel the worst kind of whore.

Just for that, she thought, I won't tell you your nose is still smeared with cocaine. Explain that to the boys on Armed Services.

Sixty seconds later Amanda opened the door to Worthington's knock.

The Justice lawyer's WASP name hid a black face. "Mrs. Roberts?" The attorney's ebony features were immobile, his broad lips barely parting. He held out his wallet to expose the white ID card with the faint blue eagle.

"Miss, or Miz," she corrected with a faint smile, somehow sure the slip had been intentional. She hadn't kept a single souvenir from her brief marriage to Arnie Zurawik, least of all his name. "I'm sorry, Mr. Worthington. I'm not feeling very well."

"I just need to give you this," he intoned. He handed her a thin white envelope with a congressional frank. "Can I ask you to sign this receipt?"

They're using lawyers to deliver subpoenas, Amanda thought bleakly. I must be more important than I thought. "Sure," she responded. Her knees wobbled as she took the government-issue ballpoint from his coffee-colored fingers and scratched her name on the miniature clipboard. Handing it back through the crack in the door, she put her hand to her forehead. She was sweating like a pig. She leaned against the door until she felt the latch snap shut.

No need to open the envelope. The congressional eagle in the corner told her all she needed to know. Amanda rushed quickly to the lavender master bathroom, feeling her small breasts jiggle, an uncomfortable reminder that gravity was having its way with her. Surrounded by fifteen feet of mirror-topped marble sinks, she pushed open the swinging doors and fell to her knees in front of the pale purple porcelain. She coughed and spat for a minute, but nothing came rolling up her throat.

Leaning her spreading rump against barefoot heels, she stared balefully at the blue-swirled congressional signature: Michael Rodszinsky, M.C. In case you had any doubt, dear, it's spelled out in black letters across the bottom, beneath the improbable Polish name of the chairman of the House Ethics Committee. OPEN IMMEDIATELY. SUBPOENA.

An image flashed through her head: hot TV lights; wan-faced witnesses with defense lawyers whispering in their ears.

Amanda dragged limply across the carpet, into the small study adjoining her bedroom. She had known this was coming. Her sources were still good, though an uncomfortable number were already running for cover: unreturned phone calls, unreturned glances. A few were sticking by her, like Old Baldy the White-Nosed Reindeer. Enough to let her know the hurricane would soon blow her way.

Amanda spooned up some of her own private stash. Shoving aside stacks of unpaid bills, she spread the fine powder in two short rows on the custom-made mauve laminate desk. Just a tad up each nostril, so the buzzards would stop circling her brain.

"Damn." She spoke aloud, whirling in her purple Herman Miller swivel chair. Her long satin nightgown caught beneath one wheel as she pushed close to the terminal and clicked on the word processor. Awash in the green glow that pulsed from its screen, Amanda reached down to yank the pale blue fabric free. She adjusted the bodice of her gown to cover her exposed breasts, which, she thought, when you examined them from the right angle, were not so goddamn bad for a woman of forty-one who had lived a lot these twenty years in Washington.

"I thought I had weeks left," she complained bitterly to the screen. "Months!"

She ransacked her mind to think of anyone she knew on the House Ethics Committee, at the big magazines; anyone, anywhere she could ask for help. She pecked slowly at the keys. Her father had been right, in her high school days. She should have taken that typing course.

Big Jim Brackler eased out of the wide first-class seat as the 707 banked for the final descent into DFW International. He lumbered up the aisle toward the bathroom. Brackler's eyes swung pugnaciously from side to side, roving purposefully to meet dirty looks from the other first-class passengers. They were angry because the plane had sat on the ground for forty minutes, waiting for Congressman Jim Brackler to arrive.

Fuck them, thought the congressman. He knew he abused National Airport's congressional privilege more than he should, but he just couldn't help himself.

He wedged his way into the tiny toilet closet, thinking, Despite all my grand New Year's resolutions, it's been months since I have jogged a block. He'd written them down last week, doodling during an Ethics Committee hearing:

1. Run 2 mi/day.
2. No liq. until Elec. Nt.
3. No—

Alarmed at nearly committing this last to paper, he had crumpled the whole mess into the nearest spittoon.

Now, as he slid back into the aisle seat Denny had requested for him, he looked sharply at his stepbrother. "Have you got me on Turtle Creek?"

Back in 1975, over Dan's strenuous objections, Brackler had given Denny a fat salary as his administrative assistant. "He's only twenty years old!" Mullins had cried. "We've got a dozen more qualified supporters to choose from." Brackler's reply was curt: "Denny was there first."

"We've moved up in the world," Denny Frawley replied. "Mr. Hart's giving us the penthouse."

Jim grunted, unimpressed.

"You should see it, Congressman." Denny used the title, careful as always to keep his place. "Hot tub, VCR, compact-disc player. The whole nine yards."

"Just so it's on the Creek," Brackler said with a mollified air. "I need to start jogging again." He liked to tell people when he planned a new regimen. It made him feel honor-bound to follow through, even if it was only goofy old Denny.

Denny nodded with a bit more vehemence than Brackler liked. Am I that fat? the congressman worried. "Long session." Brackler winked. "Know what I mean, Den?"

Denny, assuming his lord and master was referring to all the wenching that went on while congressional court was in session, grinned back: "Yes, sir!" Denny's incisors looked as if they had been filed to fang points. "The Hill's loaded with 'em," he bantered knowingly.

Big Jim appraised his stepbrother coolly. He was glad he didn't share the same DNA pool as Denny, who was dumb as a post. He marveled that Denny could work so closely with him for fifteen years and still not know his most protected secret.

210

"Yeah," Jim replied tonelessly. If someone wanted to kill the ten dumbest guys in Washington, he thought, they'd have to hide Denny Frawley quick.

The compartment jolted abruptly. The wheels bounced on the runway. They heard the high thunder of landing noise.

In the next fifteen minutes Brackler remembered why he kept Denny Frawley around. Denny whisked him faultlessly down the landing ramp: "Congressman has an urgent appointment, 'scuse us, ma'am!" Past the luggage claim: "Here's the tags, hold 'em for me!" Into the backseat of an idling Lincoln Continental limousine: "Driver, here's the address. Hi, Dan. Sir, I'm going back for the bags, Dan's going with you to SMU, I'll see you after the speech!"

Off went Brackler and Mullins, sailing through the twists and turns of the massive airport's interminable ramps. Soon they were blasting at eighty miles per hour through the limitless brown prairie northwest of town. The driver eased up the thick curtain of sound-proof glass.

"You've put on some weight," Dan noted, a small smile playing around his lips.

"Fuck you," Brackler said casually. "So what's new?" The eternal politician's question.

Dan replied, "The Republicans still haven't found anybody."

"That's good, I guess," Brackler said moodily. He wanted to win but hated to win without a fight.

"It's making fund-raising a little tough," Dan acknowledged. "Everybody likes a sure thing. But nobody likes to give money when you don't need it."

"We need it," Big Jim said irritably. "There's plenty of people in Lubbock and San Antone who don't know diddly about Jim Brackler."

Dan grimaced. He hated the way politicians always referred to themselves in the third person. "Jarrett's been making his calls," he said. "We're just not getting the checks."

"Tell 'em we think the governor may get into the race against me," Jim said with sudden inspiration.

"That's good!" Dan looked at his law partner with respect. "Ridiculous, but good. Austin will eat it up."

Brackler smiled beatifically and watched the prairie disappear in the limousine's gray-smoked rear window.

Andrew wasn't sure what impulse made him wander into the back of Bryan Hall to catch Big Jim's act. Sadomasochism, probably. Or curiosity, a delayed reaction to his son's praise for Brackler last December.

Now, it was too late to back out. Bloody little Pinkston had spotted him from across the room. The boy immediately zeroed in for what the kids called a "brown-nosing session."

"This should be interesting, huh?" Pinkston said with a cloying grin, despite the fact Andrew had given him a C— last fall. Andrew had been gratified to find his spring course rolls empty of Pinkston, Robert E.

"This will tie right into this semester's reading," Pinkston carried on primly. "Oh, can you sign this add-drop slip for me?" The sophomore thrust out a precarboned registrar's form in a flurry of yellow, pink, and white paper.

I should have flunked him, Andrew thought ruefully.

The bustle died slowly. A door opened behind the small stage. The beefy congressman stomped up the back steps and sat on a folding chair behind a long table draped with a university banner in Mustang red and blue.

Pinkston chirped hoarsely into Andrew's ear: "Fat sucker, isn't he?"

Andrew, gazing in surprise at the white flecks of sideburn hair sprouting from behind Brackler's bulbous cheeks, nodded with satisfaction. On second thought, Pinkston wasn't such a bad kid after all.

"I don't give a rat's ass what you think, Denny!" Brackler raged in the privacy of the eighteenth-floor penthouse. "Just get me the fucking information, okay?"

"Yessir," Denny said shakily. He wished Big Jim wouldn't do this to him in front of other people.

"Denny's got a point," Dan put in mildly from his seat on a high black-and-silver barstool. The lawyer scrubbed one hand at his wiry black hair. "The guy's a professor there."

"I'm sorry, Dan, but you don't know what you're talking about," Big Jim thundered. He paced wide circles around the huge leather-furnished apartment, like an angry lion in a circus spotlight. "And

212

you!" Denny winced as the congressman jabbed one stubby finger in accusation. "This comes of letting up on your reports!"

Denny gulped and fiddled with his tie. "I didn't think that—"

"When'd you start thinking, Denny?" Brackler demanded.

"They got so repetitive," Denny said lamely. "Nothing ever happened."

"Well, *something* happened," Brackler said suspiciously.

A guilty snatch of memory sneaked through his mind, something he'd done last fall on a whim. Surely it took more than that to rattle the bastard's cage. Still, there Sebastian had been today, cowering gutlessly in the back row, ducking his lean, smug patrician face from his view. How did he get a tan like that in the middle of winter? Big Jim wondered. Ski trips, probably. Rich shit.

Now, Brackler stared at his own pasty countenance in the gray-flecked mirror behind the long black-topped bar and made a decision. "Follow him," he ordered curtly. "And everyone around him."

"What?" Dan interjected, incredulous.

"Don't let them see you. But find out everything there is to know about him. Who he sees. Check his business affairs. Where's his money coming from? Follow his kids, his wife. Especially the wife— she's a weak link. Somewhere, there's something we can kill him with. A crooked loan fixed by his father. A kid on drugs. A country club that doesn't accept Negroes. Whatever it is, I want it found. Now! Before this thing gets out of hand."

Brackler ignored the reflection as Dan's eyes rolled in the mirror. "The Republicans are scraping the bottom of the barrel," he explained quickly. "And I lay eyes on him for the first time in fourteen years? That ain't no fucking coincidence, Dan!"

Feeling unaccountably nervous, Brackler strode behind the bar and threw three ice cubes into the end of at least one New Year's resolution. He aimed one last glance at Denny. "What are you standing here for?" he barked.

"For God's sake, be discreet," added Mullins.

Brackler nodded his irritation. "Yeah, discreet, fine. Just hop to it!"

The long, slack-jawed face topping Denny's spindly neck bobbed agreeably. Big Jim listened to the aide's footsteps scurry down the hall to the elevator. Then he gazed down from the massive floor-to-ceiling window at the winding path along the dead black water of Turtle Creek, wondering how many miles he had to run to burn off the calories in a jigger of bourbon.

Andrew pressed "44" on the sleek illuminated panel. It beeped loudly and began to speak.

"Going up," intoned the elevator's androgynous voice. Seconds later the doors slid open on his father's floor. There, his thick-set features obscured in a cumulus of cigarette smoke, slumped Andrew's best friend.

"About time," said Ron Callahan, consulting without asperity the shiny gold Rolex Roger gave all Senanco employees on their tenth anniversary. Callahan rammed his hand in front of the doors. They bounced back apologetically as the untidy Irishman stepped aboard, followed by a middle-aged man in a dapper Bill Blass suit. Callahan exhaled a billow of tobacco exhaust. The stranger stared fixedly at a small, tasteful brass plate that read NO SMOKING, PLEASE.

"Thought we'd go to the club," proposed the transplanted Bostonian. The elevator doors slithered open to reveal the Spire Club's stunning top-of-the-world view of downtown Dallas. Andrew nodded without enthusiasm. He didn't relish the prospect of his father horning in with some Spire Club colleague. Things were pretty good between him and Roger, but today, for no particular reason, he wanted to talk to Callahan alone.

As they returned from the salad bar, Andrew said casually, "My department's putting on a distinguished lecture series." Andrew noticed Callahan's plate: a topsy-turvy stockpile of German potato salad, banana-and-strawberry ambrosia, and three little stacks of grated cheddar cheese, garlic-bread croutons, and bacon bits. Only Ron Callahan, Andrew noted with satisfaction, could mine fifteen hundred calories out of a salad bar. He chewed and swallowed a lettuce leaf and resumed, "You'll never guess who was our first speaker."

"Not the Honorable Big Jim?" Callahan asked, probing with his fork to find the deviled eggs he'd cached at the bottom of the heap.

Andrew nodded. "Our next U.S. senator."

"Not if our guys in Austin have anything to say," Callahan said through a mouthful of food. Part of his job was to keep up on the state's political affairs, particularly those regarding Jim Brackler. Roger had helped recruit half a dozen fair-haired Republicans to challenge the leftish congressman from the Fourth District. "The party's still looking," he continued dispiritedly. "They've got to hurry. They moved the primary up to be part of Super Tuesday."

"How's the vice-president looking?" Andrew interrogated eagerly, a political castaway desperate for news from the outside world. They didn't get much good political gossip in the faculty lounge.

"He could be vulnerable in Iowa." Callahan pulled at his tie to unbutton his shirt. "But he'll come back in New Hampshire."

Over bloody prime rib from the buffet, the conversation lagged. Callahan nodded at a few familiar faces among the high and mighty. One in particular nagged at him, a tall, skinny drink of water with a pockmarked face who hovered obsequiously in the outer lobby: a latecomer looking to join his party. With his awkward stoop and hangdog expression, the man looked terribly out of place among the proud bankers and oil barons of the Spire Club. Callahan recognized the face but couldn't place the fellow. He hated that. Putting the right names with the right faces was key to the Game.

The skinny man caught Ron's eye. Seconds later, just as a name was breaststroking toward the surface of Callahan's mind, the fellow disappeared. His attention swiveled to the dessert cart.

"You gonna join me?" Andrew said, blue eyes twinkling above high-boned, Aspen-reddened cheeks.

Nonchalant, Callahan pointed at the chocolate mousse cake. "I'll take a slice of that."

"On second thought"—Andrew's gaze narrowed—"I pass."

"Bastard," Callahan muttered. They laughed, and for a minute it was like old times.

Then the staleness of the years got between them. Apropos of nothing, Andrew resurrected the subject of Big Jim. "He's flat dangerous," Andrew advised. "After his speech, a little creep from my classes told me Brackler ought to be president."

"He's not alone," Callahan said slowly. What was Andrew's sudden interest in all of this? "Evans and Novak wrote him up last week. Called him the Texas populist. A tougher Jimmy Carter. Some people think he could go all the way to the top."

"You're not serious?" Andrew said in disbelief.

"Brackler's failing upward." Callahan shrugged. "He survived that mail fraud thing. No matter what comes at him, he's got this uncanny ability to turn it his way."

Andrew remembered when Callahan used to say the same kind

of thing about Andrew Sebastian. The college professor felt a chill through his bones that had nothing to do with the subfreezing January temperatures on the other side of the big glass pane. "Surely someone will oppose him."

Callahan nodded. "The party may let the Reverend Billy Anderson do it, just to get Anderson out of the way."

Andrew frowned. The self-righteous, squeaky-clean TV preacher wouldn't stand a guppy's chance against a shark like Jim Brackler. "He wouldn't have a prayer."

"Very funny," said Callahan, who despised puns. "It's a good strategy. These leftovers from the Moral Majority days are an embarrassment, what with all the sex scandals."

"Why not put up a real candidate?" Andrew protested.

"Nobody will do it," Callahan said. He joked, "Unless you'd like to take another kiss at the pig."

Andrew made a wry face. Callahan always mangled Texas aphorisms with his harsh Boston accent. But what really rankled Andrew was the harsher reality in his friend's facetious tone.

"No thanks," he said, suddenly off guard. "I'm out for good. Not even if they begged me."

So who's begging? Callahan thought. It occurred to him that Andrew protested rather too much.

"Besides, that's not an option for me," Andrew added needlessly, an oblique reference to his highly publicized outburst on that long-ago election night. "The only office I'm after is department chairman, in a couple of years," he said with a grin. "Then dean. You should meet the prick we have now."

"Yeah?"

As much as Callahan tried to enjoy the bittersweet morsels melting in his mouth, there had been a strange look in Andrew's eye. A memory blinked unbidden through his brain: Andrew's tear-streaked face on television, the tendons in his neck distorted with rage, as he raved madly into the lens, slamming a minicam unit into the side of a blue van. Not your basic campaign commercial, Callahan thought, shuddering at the thought of Andrew Sebastian ever setting foot in elective politics again.

The moment passed, but there was a sour aftertaste of things unresolved. Callahan signed his name and membership number across the lunch check and wondered uneasily whether he should mention any of this to Roger.

216

Andrew often let his afternoon class go a little early. If he drove like hell, he could just beat the schoolbus and surprise Sean with a ride home.

The shiny green Jaguar slid to the curb in front of Arthur Kramer Elementary. A yellow line of schoolbuses idled patiently across the street, awaiting the pandemonium that would explode with the final bell.

Like the bus drivers, Andrew kept his windows rolled up tight, the heater up full blast. The other parents did the same. Virtually all were women much younger than he: anxious wool-bundled housewives in Volvos and Jeep Wagoneers, ready to whisk their children off to ballet practice and Cub Scouts. Andrew spotted only one other father in the lot, parked directly in front of him in a white Chevrolet. He hated being hemmed in in this long line of parents. But it was worth it, just to glimpse that reliable burst of delight on Sean's face as he heard the discreet British beep of the Jag's horn.

The bell pronounced schoolday's end with a jarring buzz. The brightly variegated foliage of a thousand schoolchildren blossomed forth. Andrew scanned the tumbling crowd for Sean's dark blue jacket. Great, he thought, his gaze flicking from one identically attired four-foot-six blonde to the next. Clearly, navy-blue down jackets were in vogue at Kramer Elementary.

Just as he was about to get out and call Sean's name, Andrew spotted his son climbing aboard the front bus. He slipped the low-slung coupé into reverse, ignoring the tooting cherry-red Wagoneer behind him.

"Yeah, lady, I see you," he muttered, impatiently backing his car out of the line.

Fortunately, the father in front of him was doing the same thing. The white Chevrolet snapped free and bolted toward the buses. Andrew gunned the engine.

The Jaguar followed the Chevy through a quick U-turn.

"Sean!" Andrew shouted. He eased down the Jag's window, admitting a blast of icy wind, and hooted the horn.

"Sean!" He cursed as the Chevrolet halted just behind the bus Sean had boarded. It was maddening, watching his son chatter away with his friends behind the thick fog on the bus windows.

Andrew started to climb out.

"I can't do that," he said to himself. It would embarrass Sean to

217

have his dad haul him off the schoolbus. He sighed. There had been a time, not so long ago, when Sean wouldn't have minded.

The bus started off with a loud *whoosh* of air brakes. The Chevrolet took off, escorting the schoolbus like a white tugboat pushing a massive yellow freighter. Andrew followed the procession obligingly as it wound through the perpendicular streets between the school and their neighborhood. The bus eased to a stop at the corner of Preston and Joyce Way, one street from their house.

Sean was the only one off at this stop; he was forever lamenting the "long" two-block walk home alone. "Sometimes," he'd confided to Andrew on one of their father-son rides home, "I get off one stop early, so I can walk partway with Jimmy and Austin. Do you think that's dumb?" No, Andrew had assured him. Wanting to be with your friends was not dumb. At least, he thought, no dumber than what he and Daddy Chevrolet were doing, tailing a schoolbus across the city so they could spend ninety extra seconds with their kids on a bleak winter afternoon.

The bright metal doors swung open. Sean leaped to the pavement. The schoolbus huffed off down Preston Road.

Andrew was about to honk for Sean's attention when a curious thing happened. Instead of following the schoolbus into the busy traffic on Preston, the Chevrolet turned right and began creeping ever so slowly along Joyce Way.

Following Sean.

Denny's heart leapt into his throat as the green car door flew open. Two long arms in rough gray wool grabbed the lapels of his nondescript blue suit coat and hauled him sideways. His skinny, horse-like head snapped downward toward the ice-encrusted gutter.

His attacker, grunting with the effort, hurled the frightened congressional aide onto the hard brown Bermuda grass. Denny tumbled uncontrollably across the lawn, an unwieldy log cast into a rushing river by a tall, angry lumberjack.

"Who the hell are you?" screamed Andrew. A dozen years of pent-up rich man's paranoia burst out at this anonymous kidnapper. He had been warning Tricia about this since Sean's birth. Andrew hurled himself on top of the defenseless Denny, pinning the skinny man's wrists painfully to the ground.

"I, I—" Denny gasped for air. What was Sebastian doing home?

In the two weeks he had been researching the family, his main subject never had left campus before five-thirty. "I wasn't—"

Then a rare inspiration struck Denny's mind.

"Who are *you?*" the aide snapped, managing a hint of indignation.

A tiny sliver of doubt pricked at Andrew. "Let's see some ID."

Denny glared at him in response.

Andrew released one of the man's wrists and dug in the pocket of the blue suit coat crumpled beneath him. Denny began to stammer incoherent explanations as Andrew flipped open a black imitation-leather wallet.

"Let's see," Andrew pronounced grimly, ignoring the squirming jellyfish beneath his rump. "Maryland driver's license, Dennis P. Frawley. What's that, P for pervert?" Andrew grunted, feeling a new burst of anger and suspicion. There had been several child disappearances in Dallas lately; most had been found later, molested and knifed, abandoned in a ditch. Is that what you're up to? Was my little boy supposed to end up on the back of a milk carton?

"American Express, Mobil," Andrew read quickly, "Bethesda Public Library. Aha!" A chill knifed down his wool-clad back. He dug his knees into the snooper's bony shoulders. "Congressional ID card," he said bitterly. "Don't leave home without it."

He hurled the wallet onto the grass and seized Denny's jaw, grinding the young man's head into the dead turf. "Why did Brackler send you?" he hissed, spewing a spray of spittle and venom into Denny's fluttering eyelids.

"To check on you!" Denny stammered, feeling the adrenaline pounding uselessly through his veins. Damn Big Jim and his lunatic obsession with this obscure has-been. All he wanted now was to flee.

Then another thought occurred to him. That made two in one day: a land-office business for the meager general store of Denny Frawley's brain.

"I wasn't following the boy," he added dully. "I was, uh, with you."

Andrew contemplated the trembling young man for a full thirty seconds. Brackler really is crazy, he thought. And dangerous. Still, he felt a little sorry for the pawn trapped beneath him. Which reminded him: he needed to get up, before Sean and Tricia spotted the man of the house wrestling with some acne-scarred half-wit on their front lawn.

Anger flared inside him again, burning deep and hot in his stomach. "If I ever see you here again," Andrew said slowly, evenly, his voice quivering slightly as he sucked in a deep breath, "if I ever see you anywhere near my family, I will kill you." He knew it sounded phony and melodramatic, but Frawley seemed to take him at his word.

Just to make sure, Andrew went on, "I have a message for you to take to the congressman." He sneered slightly at the title. Watching Frawley's face intently, he relaxed his pressure on the man's shoulders.

Then he balled up his fist and hit the aide in the nose, hammering Frawley's lanky equine cartilage with all the pent-up rage of fourteen years.

"Something happened," Tricia said flatly, lying next to him in their big king-size bed. Her hand crept across the down comforter, fingers playing warmly around the cold, tense muscles of his shoulder.

Andrew sighed and rolled to face her. He couldn't keep it from her. It didn't fit the new rules, the ones they had honored through the good years of what they jokingly called their "second marriage."

Rule number one: Honesty in all things. "I went to pick up Sean today," Andrew began.

Tricia drummed her fingers on the cool sheets, stifling her impatience. Andrew had spent the entire evening locked up in his study. When she'd brought in hot cocoa, there were no history books on the big antique partner's desk, just a pile of scrapbooks, four big white vinyl volumes full of old newspaper clippings from his political campaigns.

"I couldn't get to him before he got on the bus," Andrew explained. "I followed him home." He paused again. "So did someone else."

He told her the whole story.

"Jim Brackler was having our son followed?" Tricia's voice rose in a blend of horror and incredulity. "Why would he do that?" she cried, feeling herself freeze up. "Why haven't you called the police?"

"Brackler's crazy," Andrew said blandly, trying to sound at ease. "This guy swore he was just following me."

220

"What can we do?" Tricia panicked. "Should I drive Sean to school tomorrow?"

So like a mother. Andrew felt a sudden fierce glow of love. Give her a crisis, she makes a list of errands.

"I don't think he'll be back," Andrew said soberly, feeling a gentle throb in his right knuckles. "If it makes you feel any better, you can run him over there and back for a while. As for the police, what could I tell them?" He faced her squarely. "That a United States congressman is having his people follow my eleven-year-old boy?" Andrew drew her stiff torso toward him, sheltering her with the dark bulk of his chest.

"Why?" Tricia persisted. Andrew's hands sent cold prickles down her back, up between her breasts. "Andrew, this is serious," she remonstrated, running her hands down his steely forearms in a gesture that said: Okay, but give me a minute.

Andrew picked at the stray hairs that fell across his wife's frowning eyebrows. "I don't think there's any danger," he said with sincerity. "Or I'd have done more. Brackler's no threat."

Tricia knew he didn't believe it. Jim Brackler was the distant hawk that hovered always above the tiny shadow of their lives. If they tried, they could imagine him a tiny flyspeck in the sky and ignore him. But in the end, he always swooped in for the kill.

Andrew drew her close, easing her on top, which she liked better. Tricia leaned over and kissed him, pulling his tongue deep into the cavern of her mouth, rolling it over inside her. His hands kneaded rough circles into her breasts, sending hot spears down her thighs. Her knees gripped his hips. He broke his lips from hers and slipped them around her right areola. He oiled her taut, firm-for-forty breasts with his liquid mouth. Then he wet his fingers with his tongue. He smiled in the dark at her giggle. Tricia couldn't help it: the gesture was quick and efficient, as though he were licking his fingers to turn a page in one of his history books. Andrew's wet fingers mingled with her breasts and set her on fire, pulling at her with an intensity that verged on a sweet, almost scary pain.

Tricia groaned and arched backward. His hands followed her skyward. She brushed slowly at the pulsating organ beneath her, stroking it with her moisture, until it was a little more than either could stand. Then she eased forward with a sigh and plunged down on top of him. He inhaled a huge gasp of air. She slicked up and down, holding it until she realized that it would happen tonight, which was rare for her.

She held on even tighter, until he arched his shoulders back into the pillow and cried out gruffly in a half groan, voice carefully strangled to keep from waking Sean down the hall. Then she let go, and they shuddered together in the cold room. She slid free and laid her head across the cool strong width of his chest, matted in recent years with a small, patchy field of curly brown-gray hair that she adored. Especially at this moment, when the little death was on him and he lay completely in her possession.

It was her favorite time for truth; his, for sleep.

"You want to run, don't you?" Tricia said softly.

Not a question; it seemed almost, to Andrew's drowsy ears, a suggestion. The thought excited him a little, nearly piercing the fuzzy gray wall of sleep falling like gentle warm rain on his head.

"Yes," he uttered quietly, hypnotized. This was the first time he had actually pieced it all together. "That's exactly what I want."

There was silence from the taut figure beside him.

Andrew laughed and patted Tricia's back, beginning the finger stroke she craved in the first minutes after. "Just kidding," he assured her.

"No." Tricia smiled. "You've been thinking about this. For months." Looking at his face in the dim half-light, she knew she was right. She broke free and struggled upright on one elbow. "This college life isn't forever, is it?" she asked a little wistfully. "You've been a good boy too long, Andy."

"Well—" He really didn't know what to say.

"I knew it was coming," she said, a determined set to her chin. "I just needed time. Now we've had it."

"Are you serious?" Andrew's shocked tone reverberated louder, bringing them both fully awake from what he felt sure was a sweet dream. "You want me to run?"

Unbidden, the engine of ambition lying ever dormant at the back of his mind whirred into action. The Republicans still hadn't found anyone but the Reverend Billy to run. The primary was just six weeks away. Had the filing deadline passed yet?

"You're going to run," Tricia corrected with an air of resignation. "Don't you think I know the difference between retirement and"— her mind groped quickly for the word—"a hiatus? I'm a big girl now, Andrew. It's time to move on."

Andrew was glad she couldn't see the thin haze of moisture filling his eyes. Perched there on one thin elbow, her jaw clenched in determination, lay the most wonderful woman in the world. He remembered how close he'd come to bailing out, during those long months of A.A. and marriage counselors and the therapists and the constant, argumentative introspection he despised. But we did it, he thought, and there she is.

"Just one thing," Tricia said, reaching to stroke his forehead.

"Anything," he promised, even as his mind reeled away to thoughts of party primaries and polls and campaign strategies.

"Let's do it one more time," she said. "Before you go call Callahan."

Later, after a slow, melodious symphony that left her sweaty and weak and slack on his chest, she whispered into his ear: "One more thing?"

"No way," he groaned, exhausted. They squealed together in laughter.

"Not that," she said. "A promise."

"What?"

"For God's sake, beat him!" she hissed with a bitter gall that made him want to roll out from beneath her, to shrink away from the icy hate.

Tricia's fingers dug into his forearms. In the voice of a woman Andrew did not know, she added a stern, unqualified command: "Whatever it takes."

13

Amanda leaned low over the microphone, ignoring the attorney's prim glare down her cleavage.

"Wear something subdued and professional," Harley Atkinson, Amanda's prissy white-haired barrister, had warned her at yesterday's rehearsal. "Grays. Dark blues. High necks. We are a respected Washington lawyer, not a party girl."

Just to spite him, Amanda had arrived in a slinky scoop-necked red Valentino worth more than the monthly salary of the fifteen House Ethics Committee members arrayed in a horseshoe around the long wooden witness table. Their official salary, that is: most supplemented their $89,500 annual government pittance with another half million in law firm earnings, stock dividends, oil royalties, and other "investment income" from profitable joint ventures with generous tycoons in the home district. In fact, Amanda's Valentino was a gift from one such legislator, a conservative Long Island Republican whom they had recently nailed on a securities technicality. Too bad Grieco got bounced from Ethics, Amanda thought bleakly, examining the hostile, self-righteous faces of the fifteen congressmen who stared resolutely down the front of her dress. She could use a friend right now.

Wishing she had controlled her emotions and worn the damn navy suit, Amanda cleared her throat and spoke with unaccustomed meekness. "Could you repeat the question, please?"

The chairman heaved an exaggerated sigh, glancing pointedly at the gold Rolex he had received from the emir of Muscat. "I think you understand the question, Miss Roberts," he said, adding pointedly, "It is Miss?"

"Is that a proposal, Congressman?" she asked coquettishly.

The florid Chicagoan literally huffed and puffed, his bulging cheeks red with consternation. "Most certainly not!" he stammered, glaring at a few snickers from the two long prongs of the hearing table.

"Mr. Chairman, a point of order," drawled a committee veteran Amanda knew only slightly. The bulky Texan never looked up from the batch of constituent mail he was signing diligently, one sheet at a time. "This is going nowhere," the congressman complained absently. "Don't we have better things to do with our time?"

Thank you, Mr. Brackler of Texas, Amanda thought. She remembered that Brackler had beaten Andy Sebastian, the weak-kneed son of a bitch. She whispered hoarsely into the neatly cropped hair above Atkinson's ear, "I wonder if he's trying to cover up for a colleague or just bored?"

"Never look a gift horse in the mouth," Atkinson snapped in the low smooth subwhisper peculiar to lawyers, diplomats, and narcotics dealers.

God help me, Amanda thought. The man is a walking cliché.

Brackler and the chairman bickered for a moment. Soon two or three others joined in. Amanda sat back and enjoyed the melee, smiling to herself at the wall clock's relentless progress toward lunch hour.

"That's enough," the chairman barked in a grouchy voice that brooked no further delay. "Miss Roberts, you will please answer the question we've been posing all morning."

"I'm sorry," she replied sweetly. "What exactly did you pose?"

"Mr. Stone?" The chairman barked at the committee counsel, a youngish lawyer who squinted through gold-rimmed glasses. The counsel consulted his notes for the exact wording.

"Did you form any personal relationship, or personal relationships"—Stone paused, accenting the plural with a lisp of disdain—"with any member or members of the House Appropriations Committee, or the Subcommittees on Central American or Asian Affairs"—out of the corner of her eye, Amanda saw Brackler's head leap up from his letter-signing with sudden interest—"during the time you were a registered lobbyist, paid to influence members of Congress to increase U.S. military aid to the Somoza government in Nicaragua and/or the Marcos government in the Philippines?"

"That's a lot of question," Amanda replied.

"Feel free," the chairman rejoined dryly, "to be just as loquacious in answering, Miss Roberts."

"It's Ms. Roberts, actually," Atkinson put in, leaning over Amanda's shoulder into the microphone. "For the record."

The stenographer in the corner nodded obligingly, tapping at her little keys.

Good old Harley, Amanda thought, watchdogging the trivial. "Mr. Chairman, Members, let me see if I understand Mr. Stone's query," she began. Clearly she was to be her own lawyer here. "You want to know whether I formed what you call 'personal relationships' with these legislators to influence the Congress during the time I was working on behalf of several loyal U.S. allies." She added an afterthought: "I should point out that Mr. Stone has rephrased the question since the first time it was posed."

"How's that?" The chairman's head jerked up in surprise.

"Earlier, you asked if I had formed any of these alleged relationships 'for the purpose of' influencing the Congress," Amanda stressed carefully. "Now, you ask whether I formed these alleged relationships 'during the time' I was working to influence the Congress. There's a difference. Legally, and morally. The first is an act intended to cause a result; the second, merely a coincidental or simultaneous coexistence of two conditions. For example, it is one thing for a corporation president to use his knowledge of inside information 'for the purpose of' insider stock trading: that is wrong and illegal. However, there is nothing improper with his possession of that knowledge, even 'during the time' he is enhancing his net worth by other means. As long as he does not use his knowledge 'for the purpose of' insider trading."

The chairman, whom Amanda knew to be a former bond lawyer, was impressed. "Neat point, Counselor." He smiled slightly. "Let's have both answers, shall we?" he said. "'For the purpose of' and 'during the time.'"

"Of course," Amanda agreed with a bright smile. "A lot depends on how you and your colleagues define the term 'personal relationship.'"

"I think the witness understands what we mean," sneered Stone. The committee counsel obviously didn't like being caught out on points of law. "Let us say a close relationship of an intimate nature."

"How do you define intimate, Mr. Stone?" Atkinson spoke into the slender microphone jutting up from the witness table.

Hi, Harley, Amanda thought. Glad you could join us.

"Sexual relations, for God's sake!" exploded the chairman. "Need we spell it out?"

"I don't see why not," Amanda whispered hoarsely into Atkinson's ear. "It's just us boys, after all."

Except for the stenographer, everyone in the room was a lawyer. Not a single reporter had been allowed to attend the *in camera* hearing. Amanda marveled at the absurdity: putting fifteen lawyers in charge of ethics was like hiring the Manson cult to baby-sit your five-year-old.

"Interesting, this secret session," Atkinson whispered back. "It wasn't even listed on the daily calendar. You'd think they would love all the publicity."

Amanda said, "Maybe they're afraid of what they'll find."

Atkinson examined her with sudden curiosity. "What will they find, Amanda? You are going to stick to plan?"

"Let's see," she murmured mysteriously. Let him sweat a little for three hundred bucks an hour. It occurred to her that she would have to give up her penthouse to pay his bill.

She resumed, "Mr. Chairman, my job for the past twelve years has involved government relations work." She noticed Jim Brackler's curiously small eyes, tiny dots in that broad face. He stared at her, his letter-signing forgotten. What a simian-looking guy, she thought. Despite a certain rough-and-tumble appeal, he really was a singularly unattractive person to be such a rising star. According to *USA Today*, he was a shoo-in as the next U.S. senator from Texas.

Why are you so interested all of a sudden, Congressman-future-Senator Brackler? If you think I'm sleeping with *you* for a vote,

227

you've got another thing coming. Although, she admitted, if he could get me out of this mess, I might be tempted to give the big boy a tumble. Amanda wished she could nip out to the ladies' room for a quick snort of the white dust packed into a thin scroll of tinfoil in her purse. Powder her nose, so to speak.

"Yes, we've established all that," the chairman droned irritably. "Please proceed."

"*During that time*"—Amanda emphasized the phrase—"I formed a variety of business and personal relationships here in Washington. Some intimate, others merely professional. Does that answer your question?"

"One of them," snapped Stone, pushing his spectacles against the bridge of his nose.

The chairman cut in, "Ms. Roberts, did you form any of these relationships with members of Congress 'for the purpose of' influencing their vote?"

Amanda wanted to shout, No!, and tell these witch-hunters what they could do with the stake at which they were trying to burn her. But she knew this was the moment to start taking Atkinson's expensive legal advice.

Besides, she was guilty as sin.

"I'm sorry, Congressman," Amanda said, adjusting the floppy, scooped neck of her dress. "On advice of counsel, and under the rights guaranteed me under the Fifth Amendment of the Constitution, I must refuse to answer that question, on the grounds that it might incriminate me."

It was a phrase she would recite again and again that morning, like a reluctant Hail Mary, until this band of gray-suited inquisitors took her off the rack in frustration and broke for a hearty lunch in the Members' Dining Room. Except one, the member from Texas. Jim Brackler lagged behind for a quick chat with Harley Atkinson about his client, a girl in need of a friend.

Andrew had never seen his father so angry.

"You can't!" Roger's taut cheeks streaked with red veins. "I won't allow it!"

"I can," Andrew said quietly, "and I have. Ron and I came straight from the press conference."

"You!" Roger shot Callahan a fierce look reserved for trusted executives who had betrayed him. He dismissed him with a quick, angry nod: "I'll deal with you later." Callahan backed out of the chairman's office and into the foyer.

"What gives you the right," Roger shouted, his voice quavering but steely, "to drag our family name through the mud again? Have you thought about anyone but yourself, Andrew? Your wife? Your son? Me?"

"It's not about you," Andrew said wearily. He had dreaded this moment ever since he'd made the decision. "It's not about Tricia or Sean. This is about me, Dad. My career."

"You had your chance. And you blew it." Roger spoke with a cold, cruel finality. "You'll be a laughingstock! And for what? You can't win!" he said flatly.

Andrew was tempted to remind his father who had written that infamous letter to Senator Longley. But that would be cowardice, he thought. Worse, a lie.

"You're dead right, Dad." He sighed, dropping his lanky frame onto the white leather couch. He could feel his heart hammering, like when he was eight and his father had caught him playing with matches in the attic of the Azalea House. "I did have my chance, and I blew it," he acknowledged. "My chance, my mistake. I let other people tell me what I wanted to do. I even let 'em do it for me. Especially you, Dad." Andrew's level voice held not a trace of malice. "But this time, it'll be different."

That's for sure, he added mentally. Last time he'd held a press conference, two dozen journalists had come. Today only three had showed up.

"You're damn right it'll be different!" Roger snapped. "You want to be Don Quixote? Dredge up all that crap? Fine," he said icily. "You'll do it alone."

Andrew rolled his eyes. "Don't you ever listen?" he said, smirking slightly. "That's how I want it!"

"Bullshit," Roger sneered, popping his top desk drawer open and slamming it shut again in a gesture of disgust. "You've always taken my money. And everything else!"

"Did I ever have any choice?"

"You will this time." The old man fidgeted in his brass-studded captain's swivel chair, averting his gaze toward the enormous LeRoy Neiman original on the opposite wall: a vividly hued sailboat of pinks and yellows and blues, plowing through a heavy froth. "You won't get a nickel from me," he said hoarsely through pursed lips.

"Fine," Andrew said, covering his surprise. He'd expected the old man to be upset. But not this bad.

"Nor from anyone I know," Roger continued fiercely. His eyes were still focused on the watercolor. "And that's everyone, son. You'll never make it to the primary!"

"Is that a threat or a dare?"

"It's a fact," Roger whispered intensely. Unwilling—or unable—to look his son in the eye, he pressed an intercom button on his sleek black marble desk. "Julie!" he barked.

"Yes, sir?" the secretary's voice squeaked from the speakerphone.

"Send Ron in here, will you?"

Callahan eased into the room and stood stiffly before his employer. Andrew noticed that his shirt collar was buttoned up, his navy-and-burgundy rep tie pulled snugly to his Adam's apple, perhaps for the first time since Andrew had known him. The sight of Ron Callahan neat made him uneasy.

"Ron, I want you to know how disappointed I am," Roger began with the phrase Andrew knew so well.

"Hold on!" Andrew objected, rising to his feet abruptly. "This is between you and me."

"Excuse me," the elder Sebastian said with mild sarcasm. "Ron works for Senanco, and his job"—he redirected his remarks toward Callahan—"is to keep me informed. We have discussed this possibility, Ron. Many times. You know my feelings," Roger accused coldly. "I can't believe you kept this from me."

"My fault, Dad," Andrew interjected quickly.

"I really don't give a shit, Andrew," Roger said loudly, his voice serene as his control over the meeting expanded. "What I really ought to do, Ron, is fire you."

"Now, hold on!" Andrew interjected.

Callahan literally ducked his head for the coup de grace. "It's okay, Andy."

"I understand your loyalty to Andrew," Roger said primly. "I appreciate it. But you need to understand that your involvement in this *campaign*"—the word in Roger's mouth was an expletive—"ends here and now, today. I will not be a party to it, nor will I pay someone who is. Understand?"

Callahan lifted his head and gazed levelly into the old man's red, wizened face. "With all due respect, sir, I've had my balls squeezed before." He sighed. "I don't much like it. You'll have my letter of resignation in an hour."

"This is for good, Ron," Roger said sadly.

"Yeah," Callahan said wistfully, glancing involuntarily around Roger's six hundred square feet of designer-furnished luxury. "I never really fit in here, sir. Anyway, I've got a job. Right?"

Andrew nodded dully as the hefty campaign manager strode across the mauve deep-pile carpet, head erect, closing the door softly behind him.

"You can't even pay him, Andrew," Roger said. "How long's that trust fund going to last you in a statewide campaign?"

Andrew examined his father in awe, shocked that he could ever have admired such a cruel, vindictive old man. "Ron spent the last week pushing me to tell you," he said curtly. "I didn't, because I knew you'd object."

"You knew I'd talk you out of it," Roger corrected. He added menacingly, "That was nothing, Andrew. Ron's just the first to get hurt. This is the real world we're talking about here. It's cold and it's hard, and you're all alone. No one's gonna come bail you out, boy."

"I'm not a boy," Andrew muttered.

"Oh, yes, you are!" Roger roared, and leapt to his feet, fists clenched. The sudden move sent adrenaline pumping involuntarily through Andrew's veins. "You are a spoiled little brat who doesn't care who gets hurt around him! You *will* call this off, Andrew! Right now!"

"Is that another threat?" Andrew's jaw jutted out combatively. His fingers curled into his palms.

"Get out of here," Roger rasped, grinding his knuckles into the cold black stone of his enormous desk.

"I guess we won't expect you for dinner this Sunday?"

Roger's spindly frame sagged back into the big captain's chair. One bony hand seized a fat file marked ACQUISITIONS. He did not look up as his son slammed the door.

"Dose dates check, Congrethman," Denny Frawley honked through the sticky mass of white tape that held the curved metal strip to his still-purple nose. "The bill came up Deshember eighth of theventy-four. And thith ith interethting: he dint even show up for the vote. It lotht on the floor. We hit him on that in your firtht campaign."

231

"Second," Brackler corrected, sliding onto the broad backseat of the limousine in front of Houston's Shamrock Hilton. Where old wounds were involved, Big Jim was always a stickler for detail. "We lost the first one," he reminded his stepbrother.

He grunted as the green-jacketed bellman closed the door behind him. "You didn't even ask how my speech went," he pouted.

"How wath it?" Denny asked obligingly. He wished he had been inside at the Homebuilders' Convention, so he could tell Big Jim how he had held them in the palm of his hand.

"Had 'em in the palm of my hand," Brackler announced triumphantly. "Andy doesn't have a chance. Most of those guys'r Republicans, and they gave me a standing ovation."

"Everybody loves a winner, I gueth," Denny said eagerly.

Brackler glared back. He preferred to think they liked him because he was the better man.

Big Jim returned to their original topic. "I remember that appropriations ban," he said. "Marcos was our big buddy back then, and Ford wanted to send more aid. Right after Watergate."

Denny nodded. "Sebathtian wath trying to look good by attacking the adminithtration."

"Only bill he ever authored," Brackler mused, smiling as the memories flooded him with vindictive warmth. "We cut Andy up on that. His first and only bill, and on the day of the vote he's nowhere to be found."

"He wath back in Dallath," Denny added, dabbing helplessly at a thin trail oozing from one shattered nostril. "He caught a flight that morning out of National. I got the expenth recordth."

Brackler winced as Denny gave a painful snort. "You oughta drive more careful," he said crossly, to cover his concern. "Was anyone else hurt?"

"Doe," Denny said nervously. "Jutht hit a curb."

Brackler wagged his head in wonder at his stepbrother's ineptitude. Denny's car wreck had put an end to his surveillance of Sebastian. But yesterday had verified all his worst fears, and most secret hopes, about facing Sebastian again.

"D'you see the Houston papers?" Brackler said jubilantly. "Not a word about Sebastian. Like he doesn't exist!"

He doesn't, Denny thought dully. Except in your paranoid mind. And in my broken face. A sudden throb brought tears to the corners of his black-rimmed eyes. The limousine swerved between the

232

chain-link fence of Hobby Airport, where Brackler's newly chartered "Victory Express" propjet was revved up for Midland.

"You want me to come with you?" Denny asked hopefully. The oil people threw a good party.

"Nope," Brackler said doggedly, climbing out onto the tarmac. "Stay on this Sebastian business. There's no smoking gun yet. I'm hearing all kinds of rumors, but his name hasn't gotten into it." He leaned back into the window, gathering his bland beige overcoat tight around his neck to ward off the early-March chill of the wind-swept runway. "And Denny . . ."

"Yeth?"

"That whistle-stop thing through the Valley? Postpone it," Brackler ordered. "Amanda Roberts has asked to testify before Ethics again. I need to be there."

The congressman turned toward the ramp leading up to the sleek, low-slung airplane. Then he touched his hand to his receding fore-lock and called back to the limousine. "Also," he said slowly as the aide finished jotting down his instructions on white three-by-five cards, "call Dan and ask him if he knows anyone at the national magazines."

"Like reporterth, editorth?" Denny inquired, curious. Media contacts were his job, not Dan's.

"No," Brackler said slowly, thinking. "Publishers. Owners. The guys who make money decisions, buy the articles. The big long articles. Exposés. *Esquire, Vanity Fair. Playboy,* maybe." Brackler ignored Denny's quizzical glance. "And tell Dan I need him in D.C. for a meeting next week."

"Magathine publisherth," Denny said, literally biting his lip as he drew a line on the card and scribbled below it.

"And Denny," Brackler said.

"Yeah?"

He stripped 10 hundred-dollar bills off the huge wad he always carried. "Take this." Big Jim wrinkled his face in mild revulsion, tapping his thumb against his own oversize proboscis. "Get the nose fixed, okay?"

"This," Andrew said, surveying the twenty careful arrangements of seafood salad and iced tea and raspberry mousse at the twenty empty places, "sucks."

Callahan grimaced, embarrassed. Tricia spoke up from Andrew's side, resplendent in a bright red spring suit with the nametag she had calligraphied the night before. "It's a busy time of the year," she offered lamely.

"With what?" Andrew said bitterly. "St. Patrick's Day?" He reached over and spun a chair around on one of its four legs. He plopped down dispiritedly, straddling the seat backward. "This is my father's doing," he announced.

Tricia ran her eyes morosely over the neat rows of hand-lettered lapel stickers on the small table near the room's front door. Each bore the name of one of Andrew's former contributors. How could they do this to him? she wondered.

"Well, it is now"—Andrew paused dramatically, making a big show of pulling back his blue pin-striped sleeve to reveal the face of his elegant black-faced Piaget—"twelve forty-nine. I think we can safely assume no one will be joining us for lunch."

Callahan felt a cold lurch in his stomach that was only partly hunger. The press conference had been a disaster; that, he had anticipated. At least he'd been able to convince Sam Dalton to do a little item in the *Morning News,* just to make Andrew feel better.

"Christ, Andrew *Sebastian?*" the veteran reporter had hooted over the phone. "The Vietnam War hero? The one with the crazy wife?"

"Come on, Sam!" Callahan had cajoled. "The guy is a former U.S. congressman who lost by a handful of votes. Which were stolen, if you recall."

"That's what they all say," Dalton had said. "Look, I'll come, but I can't do much with it. I mean, the guy hasn't got a prayer." There was the briefest of pauses, then Sam's voice had come back with sudden interest. "What's really behind this, Ron? Some kind of vendetta against Jim Brackler?"

Snubs from the press we can handle, thought Ron. This was different. Tricia's beautifully arrayed nametags spelled out the business and political leadership of Dallas: oilmen like Chubb Howard, party chieftains like Bill Crawford, CEOs of the city's ten biggest corporations. In the 1970s these men had backed Andrew through three tough, uphill campaigns. Now they wouldn't give him the time of day. Obviously Roger had put the word out.

"What do we do now?" Callahan said aloud, knowing it was a question Andrew should be asking him.

"I think," Andrew said quietly, an ironic smile twisting his lips, "we should eat."

And they did, three hungry people with the whole world against them. Soon they were laughing and stuffing shrimp and raspberry mousse in each other's faces, throwing out absurd campaign ideas— "We rent a pig," one began—and drinking so much sugary iced tea Tricia thought her bladder would burst. It was the perfect end to a terrible week, and it bred in all of them a stupid notion that things simply couldn't get any worse.

"The entire amount?" The young bank vice-president's eyes, already too large for his small round face, bugged out until the pupils became mere flyspecks in two round saucers of white. "Mr. Sebastian, there's two million three hundred fifty thousand dollars in those accounts!"

Andrew sighed inwardly. A fortune to some, two million dollars didn't go far in a state where U.S. Senate races routinely ran into eight digits. Thank God his house was paid for. He'd have to keep a little back for security and Sean's education. Was this what other people worried about all the time?

"Can't I just sign something?" he said calmly.

"It's not a question of signing, sir," the banker said respectfully, smoothing his hands over an expensive blond singles-bar haircut. "Of course you can have it. I mean, the trust fund is yours. It's just, you've been with the bank all your life. It's, uh, your father."

"I know, my father owns some stock here."

"He is our majority stockholder, Mr. Sebastian," the man announced proudly.

"Bully for him," Andrew replied. Watch it, warned an inner voice. Let's not air the family's laundry in front of the help.

"Mike, it's my money, and I need it." Andrew leaned forward confidentially. "It won't leave the bank. Not right away. I just need ready cash for my campaign."

"Your campaign?" said the earnest investments manager, who had surely been in high school when Andrew left Congress.

"I'm running for the U.S. Senate," Andrew said sadly.

"Oh, I'm sorry," the banker said, reddening from the gaffe. "I didn't—I hadn't heard."

"Exactly the problem!" Andrew said triumphantly. "No one has. That's why I need the money."

"You understand, the money is *invested*." The banker intoned the final word as though it were a state of grace.

"I know, substantial penalties for early withdrawal." Andrew waved a carefree hand. "Not to worry, Michael. It beats dying rich."

Michael Brooks, who had yet to get married, have children, buy a home, face a midlife crisis, or begin to tally how many years he had left to achieve his life's ambitions, clearly did not understand. He looked across a desk cluttered with computer printouts and said hopefully, "Maybe a loan, Mr. Sebastian? A line of credit, guaranteed against the principal? That way we don't disrupt your interest income, and we can avoid a big loss on the portfolio. You know what I mean?"

"Fine," said Andrew. Like many who came from money, he feigned indifference to the machinations of high finance but grasped its basic principles with ruthless precision. "How much?"

"Er, is this legal?" Brooks scratched at his ear nervously.

"It's legal," Andrew snapped. While federal candidates could accept no more than one thousand dollars from any one contributor, the so-called Rockefeller clause allowed them to spend as much of their own money as they pleased.

Which, Andrew thought, was either very good for him or very bad.

He repeated, "How much?"

"Five hundred thousand?"

"Seven fifty," Andrew countered. "You work out the interest schedule and deduct it from the line in advance. Figure we'll be spending all of that within the next few weeks. Start-up expenses, you know?" He smiled.

The figures whirred in Brooks's mind. The better part of a million dollars, a fortune he would kill for, and this guy was going to piss it away on an election. Surely he couldn't win. Michael Brooks read the Dallas papers every day, cover to cover, and the only Sebastians he'd ever seen were Roger, business page, once a week; and Nan, society columns, the socially correct once a month—not too often, not too rarely. Until today, Andrew Sebastian had been nothing to Brooks but a neat, upwardly marching set of figures chattering out of his dot matrix printer. Now here he was, trying to take all his money out of the bank.

"I'll take care of it," Brooks said, rising to meet Andrew's outstretched hand. "Best wishes on your, uh, campaign, sir."

The lanky college professor gave Michael an odd, wistful grin.

236

"I appreciate the thought," Andrew said. "But what I'd really like is your vote."

"S-sure," Michael said obligingly. He wasn't even registered, but it seemed to make the customer happy.

"Your client has a story to tell," Dan Mullins said simply, shuffling his polished wingtips in the sawdust.

"My conversation with the congressman was"—Harley Atkinson sipped briefly at his martini—"elliptical?"

"Let's keep it that way," Mullins answered softly, one lawyer to another. "You and I will deal directly."

"Understood." Atkinson smiled distantly, his cold blue eyes rifling the tables around them. He nodded imperceptibly to senators, lobbyists, generals—the usual luncheon crowd at the Washington Palm. A few of the faces matched the caricatures—scrawled in blazing color by the nation's great political cartoonists—that hung on the restaurant's walls.

Atkinson, landlord of one of the coveted private wine bins that stood just inside the restaurant's lobby, was a well-known personage in Washington, one of the city's most renowned power brokers. But his face would never take rank among the elected glitterati of the Palm's murals.

Harley Atkinson was in the discretion business. He had defended White House burglars, antiwar priests; journalists who stole Pentagon documents; zealous marine colonels who financed private revolutions. This case, like those, would be resolved not in the squalor of a noisy courtroom, but behind a dry martini in the sawdust-floored murmur of the Palm.

"This story . . ." Mullins began cautiously. "Is it actually written? In publishable form?"

"I am not a literary critic." Atkinson's mouth tucked upward, but his eyes never seemed to smile. "But the facts are all there. Typed and double-spaced."

"We'd like to buy the rights," Mullins said quickly.

"Magazine?" Atkinson sipped again at his drink, not looking up from the menu.

"Magazine, book, miniseries, whatever," said Mullins, dropping his voice low as a waiter in a green apron approached to take their order, "on one condition." They heard the specials; ordered the Maryland crab. Mullins explained, "We want to see the draft now."

237

"Impossible," Atkinson sniffed. "You're not a Hollywood agent. You're not interested in books or movies. You want access to the data. If we hand it to you now—"

"Nondisclosure agreement signed in advance," Mullins countered. "A nonrefundable deposit of ten thousand dollars for a twenty-four-hour review. If we like what we see, a hundred-thousand-dollar buyout, no royalties, and we have prior right of review before publication or broadcast."

Atkinson didn't miss a beat. "Fifteen for the deposit, you read it on site in my office and sign there, or she keeps the check. The rest is fine. But the package price is two fifty."

"One thirty," Mullins said, gulping at his Heineken.

"One seventy-five."

"Done," Mullins pounced. Too quickly, he realized, but what the hell? Jarrett Hart was paying to get this published. And Atkinson was buying lunch.

"As for Amanda," Atkinson said carefully, wondering why Texas's next senator was willing to pay such a price for a pile of dirty laundry on his House colleagues. It's not like Brackler is running for Speaker, he thought. "They're calling her again in March. What can we do on immunity?"

"The congressman is not involved, of course"—Mullins watched Atkinson's gentle nod—"but he had already planned to propose the subject for consideration."

Atkinson paused. This was the ticklish part, the definition of the unsaid: the reason clients paid him one-thousand-dollar-an-hour legal fees to eat soft-shelled crab at the Palm.

"Total immunity?" he persisted.

"No problem," Mullins replied, tucking a napkin properly under his pinpoint collar without hesitation. "But she's got to come clean. The whole story."

"It's quite a story," Atkinson warned.

"We'd like input on timing," Mullins said. "Especially on Sebastian. We don't want that out in April."

"Sebastian?" Atkinson was puzzled. A face from the past crawled slowly to mind. "Andrew Sebastian?"

"Hadn't you heard?" Mullins said. "He's announced against us in the Senate race."

So that's what this is all about! Atkinson's eyes showed no hint of his surprise. How did I miss that? Strange, it hadn't been reported in the *Post*. He felt more comfortable now that he understood Brackler's motives.

"The timing is up to you," he said. Once we've agreed on the dowry, he thought, who cares about the wedding date?

Mullins raised a slender crystal water goblet. "I think we have a deal."

Atkinson nodded his soulless smile, rattling the olive in his martini glass. Only one thing pricked at him: just this morning he had read every word of Amanda's explosive fifty-page article. Andrew Sebastian's name was nowhere to be found.

Well, he thought briskly, that can be fixed. Especially if there was any truth to it. After all, as he often advised his clients, honesty was always one of the alternatives.

"Where are you going?" Roger Sebastian growled to his wife, who was dressed in preposterous lime-green warm-ups and a white visor that read PEBBLE BEACH.

"To play golf," Nan said archly.

Roger had been a bear since his spat with Andrew, mooning around the house all day, pestering her instead of going into the office where he belonged. Nan dreaded the unlikely advent of her husband's retirement. She had her weekday routines. She hardly wanted him moping around the house all the time, complaining that there was no "real food" in the cupboards.

"It's raining," Roger pouted as she fumbled in the huge hall closet, trying to find her clubs. "And you don't play golf."

"It is not raining," Nan replied patiently. She unearthed the big leather bag, trembling under its weight. "And I've been playing for years. You just don't like to play with me, that's all."

Roger firmly believed that playing golf with women—who didn't bet, didn't tell dirty stories, and didn't drink beer—rather defeated the purpose. "Humph," he said.

"I'll be playing every Tuesday and Thursday," she insisted. "I'll be good enough to beat you by summer."

"That'll be the day!" he cried, leaning to help with the bag and giving one wrinkled cheek a peck in the process.

As she sped down the long curved driveway and shot out onto Lakeside Drive, Nan looked back wistfully in the rearview mirror of her big silver Rolls. Her last glimpse of Roger was painful: a frail man in his eighties, too old to command, too proud to step aside.

He stood slump-shouldered on the front porch in the gray overcast; fretful, confused, alone.

There is a point in some human contests when things are so unremittingly abysmal that the participants realize there is nothing they can do about them. It happens to football teams that are hopelessly overmatched; to poverty-stricken children who know there is nowhere to go but up. Sometimes this utter helplessness helps; liberates, even inspires. So it was with the fourth Sebastian campaign.

Nothing was expected of them. Thus, every tiny step forward was a stunning victory.

Like the day feeble old Maudie Phillips, one side of her body completely paralyzed from a stroke, tottered in on a nephew's arm, the first volunteer to arrive at the vast empty castle of their campaign headquarters near Love Field. Maudie stayed, and her nephew stayed, though Tricia had nothing for them to do.

"That's just fine, honey," Maudie assured her. "We'll start callin' some of the other girls, and get them on the phones to recruit some other folks, until we have forty people down here ever' day. And by then, Ron Callahan will have something for us to do. Or," she added sweetly, "we'll tell Andy to fire him."

When Sam Dalton did a Sunday piece on Andrew for the *Morning News*—OLD RIVALRY REKINDLED IN SENATE RACE—it was as though they had made the cover of *Time*. The article raked up all the old scandals and labeled Andrew's quest "quixotic." But Callahan sent photocopies to every small-town weekly in the state.

"Right now, any ink is good ink," he explained. "Besides, nobody in Lubbock knows what 'quixotic' means."

One day in February may have been the best. Andrew looked up from one of his interminable arguments with Callahan to see a smoothly coiffed, grandmotherly figure in a hideous green sweatsuit shove open the plate-glass front door.

"Well?" Nan said, blue eyes crinkling with mock belligerence. "Are you going to put me to work, or do I go help the Reverend Billy?"

Nan became a fixture at Sebastian headquarters, imploring on the telephones, stuffing and licking and stamping, slipping the occasional hundred-dollar bill into the wicker collection basket when she thought no one was looking. Andrew never asked what his father

240

thought. Tricia finally filled him in: "Only Tuesdays and Thursdays, and always in golf clothes? She's cheating on him, dummy."

According to their first poll, less than 10 percent of Texas voters knew Andrew's name. The same number also claimed to recognize Ron Callahan, whose name they had inserted into the identification series. Callahan called it a "placebo."

"It gives us a baseline," he explained. "There's a certain amount of people who always say, 'Yeah, I know who that is,' just so they don't look stupid."

"You mean nobody knows who I am?" Andrew said in anguish. "Ron, I was on *Meet the Press!*"

"In 1973," Callahan corrected brutally. "Anyway, not to worry. Look at it this way. You have what us Catholics call *tabula rasa*. A blank slate. All the voters will know is what we write on it. And what your opponents tell them."

For now, the bad guys were keeping mum.

Brackler was ominously quiet on the subject of Andrew Sebastian. "I welcome him, I truly do," Big Jim commented in Dalton's *Morning News* feature. And, unable to resist one small barb: "I am glad to see he has his personal problems worked out."

The Reverend Billy Anderson dealt with his new primary opponent in the classic fashion of heavy favorites: he ignored him. Anderson had a strong base in his hometown of Houston and a heavy following of evangelicals across the state. His campaign war chest ran into the millions, gathered in ten-dollar increments from little old ladies from every trailer park in Texas, who sat transfixed every week through all five hours of his TV show, *The 300 Minutes*, where the reverend attacked CBS, Ted Kennedy, Satan, Ted Kennedy, abortionists, *The New York Times*, Ted Kennedy, and Jim Brackler. At precise fifteen-minute intervals, a perpetually grinning Anderson issued hysterical calls for more cash; a superimposed red phone number flashed across his chest with a loud beep.

The primary race broke wide open for Andrew in early March. In a poll by the *Houston Post*, 40 percent of Texas Republicans said they would not vote for a television evangelist. In a sample match-up between Brackler and Anderson, the poll showed Big Jim at more than 70 percent.

Republicans began to worry. How bad a debacle would they face with a TV preacher at the head of the ticket? Would it hurt the

241

party in other races? Might Andrew Sebastian, skeletons and all, be the lesser of two evils?

Callahan capitalized with a flurry of radio commercials in the big cities. The ads stressed Andrew's "firm belief in the separation of church and state." Every spot began and ended with the same name booster: "I'm Andy Sebastian, *Republican* for U.S. Senate."

It was simple, and it was working. On March 10 Anderson's people leaked a poll that showed them ahead of Sebastian by a margin of 42 percent to 32 percent, the rest undecided.

"God, are they stupid!" exulted Callahan, dousing the morning *Herald* with his first cup of coffee. "Don't they realize how much credibility that gives us?"

"That's good, huh?" Andrew asked dubiously, though he knew it was. "Ten points behind?"

"We've got ten days, for Christ's sake!" Callahan shouted, hammering his fist gleefully against a carpeted partition.

At ten o'clock that same night, Callahan kicked open the door of his apartment, flopped a grease-spattered pizza box on his coffee table, and flipped on the evening news. There was a story about a fire in Mesquite; the inevitable piece on AIDS. Next, Channel 8 cut to the Capitol dome, "where our Washington correspondent, Bernie Zollars, is standing by with a live update on today's House Ethics Committee hearing."

"Mark, big news today in the widening congressional investigation of foreign influence peddling on Capitol Hill." Zollars squinted self-righteously into the camera. "Ethics Committee chairman Michael Rodszinsky allowed cameras in for the first time since these top-secret investigations began."

The image changed to a hearing room Callahan recognized. Rayburn basement, room B210, he guessed. "The committee's star witness was a strikingly beautiful young lobbyist—"

"Come on, Bernie, it's television!" Callahan critiqued. He always talked to the TV set. "Show us, don't tell us!"

Obligingly, the station cut to an extreme close-up of a haggard woman wearing tortoiseshell glasses and a severe navy-blue suit.

Zollars continued, "Amanda Roberts answered questions about alleged sexual misconduct in a 'sex for votes' scheme some claim goes back fifteen years."

"Fifteen years! That"—Callahan belched—"is a lot of fucking." He cackled aloud.

Zollars went on, "Roberts, a former lobbyist for various right-wing regimes, says she used her sexual relationships to trade sex for votes—"

"That's right, Bernie," Callahan commented. "Get the word *sex* in there as much as possible."

Amanda Roberts looked vaguely familiar to him, though she certainly had never tried to trade sex for his influence. "Too bad," he admitted aloud, wondering why he seemed to spend every night alone, watching political news on television and reading political magazines, until it was time to grab a few hours' sleep and get back to politics. Could it be, he thought, that I'm too wrapped up in my work?

"While no names were mentioned, there was discussion of specific incidents where members of Congress, particularly the House, changed their votes on appropriations bills in return for Roberts's sexual favors. One Ethics Committee member—"

Callahan lurched forward on his seat as Jim Brackler's face filled the screen. "Hot damn!" he said, rubbing his hands in glee. Could Brackler be wrapped up in all this?

"—proposed granting immunity to Roberts in exchange for further testimony in the sexual bribery scandal. Soon, sources say, Amanda will name names, including several members of the Central American and Asian Affairs Subcommittees."

Asian Affairs? Something rattled in the vast political engine of Ron Callahan's brain. A blonde who kept popping up at Andrew's subcommittee hearings. Those few months when Andrew was forever disappearing, hours at a time. Callahan pushed the thought from his mind. Andrew Sebastian? What a laugh. Mr. Family Man. The most beautiful wife in town. He's going to trade votes for sex with some old-hag lady lobbyist?

"By the way, Mark, they've got a name for this one already." Zollars was winding up, leering into the camera. "They're labeling it Amandascam. From Washington, I'm Bernie Zollars."

"You jerk," Callahan muttered nonchalantly. He cracked open another Budweiser and reached under the couch for his copy of *National Review.*

A rocket's red glare of fifty bright, patriotic campaign signs led the three of them up the church sidewalk. Tricia was pleased to see Andrew's among them, matching Billy Anderson sign for sign. The sign war halted at a small white marker declaring a demilitarized zone: NO ELECTIONEERING WITHIN 100 YARDS OF POLLING PLACE.

Inside, the Republican precinct chairman serving as election judge greeted them. "Hello, Senator!"

"He's not a senator yet," Sean corrected soberly. "This is just the primary." Everyone in line laughed. Andrew, ignoring the warning outside, shook hands all around. The election judge stamped the back of Sean's hand Republican, and they went to the small blue plastic voting booth. His son was just tall enough to reach up and snatch the voting punch.

"There it is," Andrew said proudly, flipping to his name. Sean's eyes sparkled appreciatively as he followed Andrew's finger, punching the hole by the vice-president's name, then rushing down to vote for his father.

Andrew had won the coin toss for top ballot position. "Worth five points in a primary," Callahan had pronounced. "Lots of folks just go to vote for president. Below that, if your name comes first, they figure you're the incumbent."

They walked out of the Sunday school classroom, smiling broadly for the camera crew Callahan had wheedled into meeting them here at 7:15 A.M.

"Did you see all those voters with the *Morning News* in their hands?" Tricia whispered excitedly. "They were punching straight off the list."

Gazing up at the huge cross on the sloping church lawn, Andrew thought, Thank you, Lord, for creating newspaper editorial boards. Virtually every daily paper in Texas had endorsed the former congressman over the TV preacher.

Andrew boosted Sean on his shoulders so he would get into the TV shot. "I'm worth votes," Sean had once explained to Andrew, with that shocking wisdom of the very young. "People like kids."

Headquarters was a madhouse, the way Callahan liked it on election day. Tricia manned the shortwave radio that controlled the drivers taking elderly voters to the polls; Callahan took the telephone hot line to key precincts around the state. Sean, liberated from school for the occasion, ferried Pepsi-Cola to volunteers on telephones.

Andrew, as usual, was in charge of fidgeting. The candidate was election day's most useless appendage. He was about to go shake some hands downtown when Callahan waved from his cubbyhole.

244

"Yoo-hoo!" Callahan's feline grin bespoke a healthy lunch of canary. He pushed Andrew down by his shoulders. "I just talked to Wendell down in Houston," he mumbled through a mouthful of taco-flavored Doritos. "Nobody's voting."

"No shit!" Andrew's voice broke into high register.

"Anderson's home base is deserting him. The whole Bible Belt. Waco, East Texas, Abilene," Callahan listed. "This Jimmy Swaggart deal was the last straw."

"Maybe they're voting late?" Andrew said, throwing cold water on the hot tingles up his spine.

"We marked twenty key precincts as indicators. Ten are Anderson's, ten are ours. As of"—Callahan consulted his watch—"ten o'clock, Anderson's boxes are reporting fifty percent less than their normal vote totals by this time of day." He tore the white tape out of his calculator and gave it to Andrew.

As though, Andrew thought, I can interpret these hieroglyphics. "Maybe they're just voting late?"

"Andrew, Anderson's people are farmers, oil field workers, blue-collar suburban commuters. They vote early, or they don't vote at all." Callahan shifted incessantly from one foot to another, as if he had to go to the bathroom. "Our precincts, on the other hand, are mostly urban or small town. Housewives, white-collar workers, older folks. They vote throughout the day. Andy, the total count in our boxes is *twice* what it normally is by this time of day."

"We're going to win," Andrew mouthed.

"We've already won!" Callahan assured him. Then his face fell. "Uh-oh."

"What?" Andrew said, afraid Callahan's mighty calculator had missed a zero somewhere.

"Look who's here." Callahan raised his eyebrows toward the front door.

Andrew wrenched his head around to see his father, back ramrod straight, ruffling Sean's dishwater-blond head.

"Not a word," Andrew warned quickly. "I'll handle it."

He walked to them in quick, jerky steps. "Go get Grandpa a drink, Sean," he ordered softly, not flinching his gaze from Roger's slate-blue eyes.

"What kind?" Sean asked.

"Any kind," Andrew barked. Sean knew the tone. He scuttled to the kitchen, knowing he was to take his time.

"What brings you here?" Andrew asked evenly.

"I couldn't stand it." Roger shrugged. He inclined his grizzled head to the phone bank. "Is your mother back there?" he asked bluntly.

Andrew nodded.

Roger said dryly, "She hasn't played golf in thirty years."

"No offense, Dad," Andrew hissed, "but I don't need your help. Or your money."

"Who said anything about money?" Roger said quietly. "I just want to be here."

Andrew saw what could have been tears in his father's rheumy eyes. His own throat grew tight. For some reason that made him angry. "You know I'm going to win," he accused, lowering his voice below the headquarters pandemonium. "So now, you're with me. Right behind me, until I need you."

"Son, you may get through this primary," Roger said through clenched teeth. "But you don't have a snowball's chance in hell against Jim Brackler next fall."

"Thanks for the pep talk, Dad," Andrew said sardonically. "See how much I need you?"

"You'll need me all right," the elder Sebastian predicted sadly. He dug in his pocket for a quarter. "Here. When you grow up, and learn how men resolve their differences"—he handed the coin to his son—"you call me."

"Don't hold your breath," Andrew advised.

"You call me," Roger repeated, unfazed.

Sean arrived, juggling soda cans. Cautiously he asked, "Pepsi, Seven-Up, or Dr Pepper?"

14

ndrew won the nomination.

They lay in their king-size bed, swathed in victory. "Listen to this!" Andrew licked the inky grime off his fingers. "'Sebastian seemed destined to win the chance for a rematch against Brackler, a former SMU classmate.' Destined? The *Chronicle* didn't mention us until three weeks ago."

Tricia watched her husband tear eagerly through the sections of every major newspaper in the state. He looked like Sean ripping open packages on Christmas morning. She arched her back languidly against the green silk headboard, realizing this was the first time since February they'd been able to sleep in. She cocked her head and listened for noise from Sean's room. Nothing. Good.

They luxuriated among the newspapers, savoring last night. The morning sun lit Tricia's thick, luscious hair, glinting with rare hints of silver.

"Hey," Andrew said softly, shoving the newspapers off the bed as he remembered something. "We forgot."

"You're big with the promises," Tricia taunted, drawing

his head toward her until his lips touched the stiffening areola of her left breast. Last night, as they'd stood before the cameras declaring victory, Andrew had breathed hot love boasts into her ear. Somehow, by four o'clock in the morning, after they'd thanked all the volunteers, accepted a congratulatory phone call from the vice-president, and crashed exhausted into bed, his ardor had ebbed to nothing.

Tricia planted her knees on either side of his firm buttocks, leaning back until her long, unpinned brown hair brushed his kneecaps. She kissed the red-gold skin where his forehead met his slightly receding hairline, running her fingers through the thick gray-flecked hair above his ears. They played that way for a good ten minutes, groping and fondling like kids in the backseat of a 1963 Impala.

Somewhere between there and the point when Tricia rolled off with sudden urgency and drew him inside her, Andrew forgot all about his 52–48 upset of the Reverend Billy Anderson. He even, for the first time in two weeks, forgot about the Damocles' sword of Amanda Roberts that had dangled over his head since news of the scandal began to seep out of Washington. Andrew knew full well that Brackler would use it, that he was just saving it for the right moment. He thought maybe Big Jim would save it a little longer. For now, Andrew told himself it didn't matter and lost consciousness in the sheer bliss of making love to his wife for the first time in weeks.

They barely heard the loud, insistent knock on the door, the squeaky tones of preadolescence.

"Mom? Dad? You awake?"

"No!" Andrew groaned, glad master bedroom doors came with locks. Tricia laughed silently behind the hand he had clamped over her mouth.

"Go watch Bugs Bunny!" Andrew ordered. "Your mother and I are sleeping!"

Tricia's giggles bubbled up through his fingers.

"Shh!" he whispered fiercely, feeling the passion fade with his own laughter.

"Aw, Dad . . ." Sean's scornful voice pierced whatever romance was left. "They don't have cartoons on the weekday."

Sean waited for a response; his father, for the patter of little footsteps retreating down the hall. Both waited in vain.

"When do you think you'll be up?" Sean persisted.

"Not for a while, son," Andrew said mournfully, staring down between his legs. Tricia exploded with mirth.

The respite was done. Within minutes Tricia was downstairs making breakfast; Sean, in the den blaring a *Star Wars* video at eardrum-shattering levels; Callahan, on the phone, informing Andrew that their new opponent planned an ugly new set of anti-Sebastian attack commercials later in the week.

"How are we gonna defend ourselves," Callahan complained, "when I don't know what's coming?"

Andrew was finally starting to understand Jim Brackler. It's not the Amanda thing, he prayed. Too early. That left only one possibility.

"Set up a press conference for tomorrow afternoon," Andrew said curtly. "Then come see me. There's something we've got to talk about." He glanced at the crumpled sheets beneath his naked torso. He wished he and Tricia had finished, while they'd had the chance. Cupping his hand over one ear to cut out the staccato roar from the TV, he added, "But not 'til four. I've got some business to take care of."

Andrew put down the phone and reached over to switch on the answering machine. Humming Darth Vader's battle hymn, he grabbed a red silk kimono and padded down the hall to help Sean eat some blueberry pancakes.

Dan Mullins's fist thundered on the door.

There was no answer. They stood impatiently in the small vestibule at the far end of the seventh-floor hallway of Austin's Four Seasons Hotel. Mullins and Jarrett Hart could hear shallow sounds of subterfuge within. The rustle of bedclothes. A scurry of footsteps. Soft, feminine speech.

"Didn't know Jimmy ever got himself laid," Hart said approvingly, despite the anger that had brought him to his candidate's doorstep on a Sunday morning. "Hope he's careful, what with all that up in Washington."

Mullins smiled nervously, his slightly simian features wrinkling under salt-and-pepper bristles. "He's careful," the happily married lawyer assured him. Thank God, he thought, that Hart doesn't know just how careful Jim Brackler needs to be. Not that it would matter;

big contributors like Hart didn't care if their Washington errand boys fucked sheepshit, as long as they voted for the oil depletion allowance.

"It's Dan!" Mullins bellowed, heedless of disturbing the well-heeled guests down the dimly lit corridor, Texas-elegant with mellow stone light sconces carved with the antlers of Hill Country deer. "Open up!"

The door cracked open. Brackler, his sweaty figure wrapped in a voluminous melon-colored sheet, peered out from behind the door chain.

"Oh!" Big Jim said in surprise. He clearly hadn't expected to find the ninth-richest man in the state pawing his doormat.

The door closed. There was a fumbling noise. It flew open again. Brackler was now resplendent in a white terry-cloth robe with a gold Four Seasons crest stitched on the chest.

"Come on in!" he said grandly, ignoring the firm set to Hart's jaw. "Wanna order breakfast? I can get room service."

"Ate hours ago," Hart said accusingly. The big banker settled his frame uneasily on an antique reproduction of a straight-backed prairie sofa. He glanced involuntarily at the closed bedroom door, then came straight to the point. "You seem awful cheery this morning," the elderly man barked. "How the hell could you let this happen?"

"What?" Jim said innocently. He knew perfectly well what the old man meant. "We won big last night, Jarrett!"

"We were unopposed last night," Mullins injected. "God damn, Jim, we shoulda hit Sebastian with the Roberts stuff."

"I'm spending a fortune having her damn article published," Hart muttered. "And you sit on it! I told you Sebastian was moving up!"

Mullins nodded. "Now we've gotta contend with Sebastian, instead of crazy old Anderson."

Big Jim shook his head stubbornly. "Sorry, fellas, you got it all backwards." He grinned toothily and picked a big green Granny Smith apple out of the fruit basket on the coffee table. He bit into it with a loud crack.

"Andy's the one we want," Brackler said confidently. "And he's the one we got. We got the goods on him! More than you know," he added with a small secret lilt that grated on them.

"Goddamn, boy, you don't have to pay for it!" Hart shouted. Then he lowered his voice, suddenly mindful that some bimbo had her ear cupped to the other side of the gilt-edged door opposite the bay window view of Town Lake. "Now Sebastian's won the primary, he'll be able to put some real cash together," the banker complained.

"Fine," Brackler replied with more confidence than he possessed.

Big Jim's morning-after mind, still shaken from this frightening invasion, raced furiously to uncover how he really felt about facing Sebastian. Good, he decided. Because I hold all the cards. "This little campaign will cost Andy a bit more, that's all. Maybe more than money."

"You arrogant little shit!" Hart hissed, now truly angry. "This is a personal vendetta, huh? With my money!"

"Aw, calm down, Jarrett," Brackler mumbled through a mouthful of apple. "You'll get your senator, don't worry. Besides, *Playboy*'s giving you something for the article, and you got Amanda's TV and movie rights. They'll be worth a fortune when she starts testifying, and we leak galleys to the press. I'll expect a cut, of course," he added with a grin, "since I was her agent, more or less."

Offended, Hart stomped toward the door. "I'm out!" he shouted, not caring who heard. "Dan, I'm sorry. I don't have to take this shit from some snot-nose politician."

Dan followed the old man out the door, his voice soothing. "Mr. Hart, please."

The door banged loudly behind them. Brackler collapsed against it, shaking. Would Jarrett Hart really pull out? If so, he thought, I could really be in the shitter.

He heard a muffled noise from the next room. Despite the pit of acid in his stomach, Big Jim felt himself uncoiling erect, trembling against the rough terry cloth of his robe.

That frightened him even more. Had Hart heard something? He ran quickly across the sitting room and flung open the double doors of the bedroom, half in fear, half in lust.

There was blood on the tousled sheets.

Suddenly aware of the chance he had taken, Brackler ran to the bathroom door. He twisted the knob. It was locked.

"Hey," he commanded. He pressed his ear to the smooth, creamy wood and heard her whimpering inside.

"Open the door," he said softly. "Please."

Images of last night streaked through his brain. Warming himself before the dying embers of his victory party. Drinking too much bourbon. Watching the good-looking young men leave with the good-looking young women, giggling up the elevators. Sitting here watching late returns on cable, playing with himself, wishing he had the courage to go downstairs and compete with the fray. Wandering up from the waterfront to Fourth Street, where pimps shopped their wares. Peeling off hundred-dollar bills until he'd heard the magic words: "Yeah, you can do whatever the fuck you want wid her, man."

Half an hour after that, a tiny knock at his door.

Had he gone too far? Why wouldn't she open the door?

"Please?" he repeated urgently. He pressed his warmth against the door, the urge rising in him as he recalled the squirming, almost invisible rise of her shallow breasts.

"Let me in!" Brackler roared. He stepped back and kicked the door with his bare foot. It shuddered in its frame. "Now!"

There was a stifled cry from inside, a babble of Spanish and tears. Jim heard the lock click. He wrenched the door open and gaped in dismay at what he had done.

The pretty little Mexican girl, surely no more than twelve, lay curled between the toilet and the bathtub, lithe brown shoulders squeezed impossibly between the shining white porcelain. Clasped tight between two frail, quivering arms, her bony knees poked up beneath her chin. One brown eye was swollen a sickly pink, the upper eyelid yanked inside-out. Her other eye was stark and staring, blinking rapidly; the lush black lashes, so alluring last night, now fluttered in what had to be a physical state of shock. She had not stopped bleeding below; he sensed her small, warm drops beneath his naked feet.

The tears welled up hot and shameful in Jim's eyes.

"I'm so sorry," he said. She stared uncomprehendingly at the towel rack above her head. Gently, awkwardly, he knelt beside her.

Ignoring her birdlike flinch, he drew her slowly to her feet. She covered her nudity helplessly with both hands. He examined her narrow, bruised child's body clinically. The fervor in his thighs died; in the sobering daylight, he could not imagine desiring this sexless infant.

Big Jim worried suddenly, How will I get her out of here? He carried her to the bed, laying her carefully clear of her own stains. He had gone over the line, worse than ever before.

He had known it even then. Her mute acquiescence had somehow enraged him; he had hit her, and finally she had struggled, until he'd struck her so hard that she'd fallen into a stupor. Then he'd savaged her, in front and behind, knowing he was over the edge, that she might be dead, even. The risk and the terror had driven him on; thrilled him, with that mad lust that lunged up within him from time to time, goading him to shatter all the barriers, break all the rules.

Now he had broken one of his own, the rule that said he never, ever did this in his home state, certainly not in a hotel full of campaign contributors. Jim left the shivering girl and walked to the parlor.

He would have to call Dan.

And Dan would be angry. Again.

Two days later, Denny peered across the perpetual gloom of Joe Miller's Bar, trying to etch out the faces of the Monday-night regulars.

Bernie was late. Probably stuck editing a story for the six o'clock, he thought. The aide sucked unhappily at his beer, glowering away advances from the reporters and lawyers and politicos who frequented Miller's. They understood: he had an assignation. They respected his business; Denny, in turn, would keep his distance the next time they wanted to meet a source or pass on a tip.

"Bernie!" Denny hopped off the barstool.

Zollars blinked his eyes rapidly, molelike behind the gold-rimmed Yves St. Laurent eyeglasses his wife made him wear on television. "They take ten years off you, Bern," Mona would scold. "God knows you need it, with all those good-looking kids after your job."

Entering Joe's place was like plunging into eternal damnation, one quick step from the sun-washed order of sleek, modern Dallas into a murky haze of cigarette smoke and character assassination. Though its furnishings were clean and spare, Joe Miller's was a dirty place. A perfect site, Zollars thought, to pick up the dump truck full of political muck Frawley would surely unload on him tonight.

"Denny, how are you?" Zollars asked without interest, his manner that of a picky apparel buyer inspecting a new line. The bespectacled reporter, his curly hair flecked with hair oil, ordered a gin and tonic with the confident air of one who knows his tab will be picked up by another.

"Great, Bernie, great," Denny mouthed quickly, anxious to get this done. He slurped quickly at his Coors. "I've got something for you."

"I figured," Zollars replied. His eyes strayed around the room, playing the Joe Miller's game of Who's with Whom.

"On Sebastian." Denny grinned, trying not to appear too much the eager beaver. He rubbed at his nose. It still hurt like a bitch when he blew it. "Remember that night back in seventy-four? When he freaked out and attacked you?"

"How could I forget?" said Zollars. Contrary to what Denny may have thought, Zollars bore Sebastian no grudge. "Best pictures I ever got," he mused dreamily, savoring the sweet newsman's memory of a prominent political figure gone berserk on camera. Sebastian screaming at Zollars, tears streaming down his eyes: sheer visual poetry. "Too bad it was Channel Five who shot 'em," he lamented. "I'd kill to have those on my reel, but goddamn if Bert Sanford'll ever give them to me."

"You'll never guess what happened next," Denny leered, hurrying forward to keep the man's interest. "Sebastian and his wife left three days later on a plane to California." He slid photocopies of two airline tickets across the bar. "Flight 261, DFW to Palm Springs."

"So?" Zollars said, eyes roving disinterestedly toward the big TV set suspended over the bar. "Excuse me, Denny. Hey, Joe!" he shouted.

"Hey, what?" cried the mustachioed, frizzy-haired proprietor, a Canadian transplant who served the best drinks and the worst jokes in the city.

"Can you turn it up?" Zollars said.

"What a ham," Miller muttered loudly. The gang around him laughed. *Channel 8 News* swept into the room in a rapid-fire burst of aerial helicopter views of the city's downtown skyscrapers.

"Anyway," said Denny, annoyed at the distractions, "they checked in, both of 'em—get this, Bernie—to the Palm Springs Center for Drug and Alcohol Treatment." He paused dramatically, eased several more photostats in front of Zollars's gin and tonic.

He waited in vain for a reaction. "Well?"

"Huh," Zollars grunted. He riffled vaguely through the smudged copies on the bar, illegible in the gloom. "Sorry, Denny," he said, adjusting his glasses on his beaky nose so he could see the television. "Old news."

"Old news?" Denny said incredulously. "It happened a long time

254

ago, but it's never been brought out. You could be the one to break the story!"

"Not unless you brought a time machine," Zollars said sarcastically. "Don't you listen to KRLD?" A Dallas radio station, KRLD's motto was, "All news, all the time." Zollars gestured with his drink toward the TV set.

"Sebastian and his wife held a press conference three hours ago," he said dryly. "It was all I could do to cut it in time."

"What?" Denny stared at the screen, dumbfounded.

"Shut up and see for yourself," Zollars said, smirking a bit. He didn't much like Andrew Sebastian, but he had to admit: today's press conference had been a masterstroke. Besides, he didn't much like Denny Frawley or Big Jim Brackler, either. He wasn't supposed to like these people: he was a reporter, a professional.

Zollars gestured to Joe Miller to turn the set louder and leaned back to listen to the sweet music of his own voice: "Senate candidate Andrew Sebastian, the former congressman who upset the Reverend Billy Anderson in Saturday's primary election, began his uphill battle against Representative Jim Brackler today with a surprisingly candid revelation."

Sebastian's face appeared amidst the balloons and confetti of last weekend's victory party. The image changed to a smiling Andrew and Tricia Sebastian, holding hands above their heads behind a podium.

"Sebastian held a news conference just hours ago with his wife, Patricia, to disclose that she became an alcoholic during the time he served in Congress." Zollars's voice accompanied file footage of the Sebastians campaigning together fifteen years ago, their clothes and hairstyles amusingly outdated.

"Following his narrow 1974 loss to Brackler, Sebastian took his wife to an exclusive clinic in southern California to treat her problem, which both say she has licked for good."

The set cut to an extreme close-up of Tricia's face, showing tiny wrinkles under the harsh glare of TV lights.

"I thank God my husband was there for me when I needed him. . . ." Tricia's voice echoed in Denny's ears. He winced. He thought in horror, Will the congressman blame me?

The soft female voice continued, "I have beaten this disease. But others do not have access to the care and treatment that got me through that awful time many years ago."

Denny noticed the careful emphasis on the final three words, "many years ago."

Tricia went on, "Andrew and I want to take this opportunity to encourage all those who need help to seek it, so we can put an end to the terrible scourge of substance abuse."

Denny groaned aloud. "Oh, come on!" he said hotly, accusing Zollars. "You didn't buy off on that?"

Zollars waved him to silence, so he could hear his wrap: "The Sebastians also called for more federal drug and alcohol treatment programs, stricter drunk-driving laws, and a new national drinking age of twenty-one." Zollars's voice resumed softly, matching the visage Mona called his "sensitive face": brown eyes soft and understanding, brows crumpled in a thoughtful expression.

"So far, the reaction has been resoundingly positive," Zollars's commentary continued. "Sebastian gets points for candor at a time when many are questioning the morality of top government officials. And, since statistics say nearly fifty percent of Americans face some type of drug or alcohol abuse within the family, Mrs. Sebastian's success in tackling her problem may win her husband sympathy at the polls. For *Channel 8 News*, I'm Bernie Zollars."

Zollars swiveled on his stool. He wanted to ride Denny Frawley a little more, but the pock-faced, skinny congressional aide was gone.

That made Zollars mad. Denny had forgotten to pay for his drink.

The twelve-cylinder engine throbbed quietly, eating up the endless miles of west Texas highway.

"You can't drive a Jaguar on a campaign swing of rural Texas," Callahan had howled as he'd pulled out of the headquarters parking lot in Dallas that morning: five hours, three receptions, and 231 miles ago. "It's just not done!"

"You find me the money for a plane, and I'll chuck it!" Andrew had shouted as the gravel spurted behind him.

Now, wheels humming along the highway, George Benson's jazz guitar on the Blaupunkt stereo, Andrew was glad he'd stuck to his guns. It was bad enough driving alone down the endless stretches of dusty high plains, the only break an occasional doughnut with the Mineral Wells Junior League or the Volunteer Firefighters of Wichita Falls. Where were the falls? Andrew wondered. All he saw was dirt, dust, and sand.

He was soothed by the eerie strains of Benson's "Masquerade," the copacetic sensation of fuel-injected horsepower. It helped him forget that he was driving from one dusty town to the next, sucking on Dairy Queen sodas, while his opponent streaked through the skies in a propjet, hitting five major media markets a day.

Andrew's day had started well enough, with a jubilant family reading of a *Good Housekeeping* profile on Tricia's triumph over alcohol.

Sean had seemed thoroughly untraumatized. "I wasn't born then, was I?" he'd asked matter-of-factly. No, Andrew and Tricia had explained. "Mm . . ." Their son had shrugged. "C'n I have some more sugar?"

"May I," Tricia had corrected absently, and raised her eyebrows. The conversation had moved on to whether Andrew would be home for the big soccer game against Greiner.

What Andrew really despised about these long drives was being alone. He had always been a son, a fraternity brother, a husband, a father: surrounded by people who knew and loved him and respected his place in their world. Now he was on his own, out of his element, campaigning in desolate, dying towns among strangers who were worlds apart from his urbane Dallas. Southwest Airlines didn't reach these places. That meant no one to meet him at the airport, no one to hold his briefcase; no one to introduce him to the old biddies and the Elks at the coffees. Just himself. Walking into schoolrooms and churches that were never hard to find: "Can't miss it, only one in town." Putting on a nametag stenciled by a Veteran of Foreign Wars: "Is that T-A-I-N or T-I-A-N?"

Andrew ejected the cassette tape. He punched the radio's electronic buttons in a useless attempt to find some rock and roll. "It is time," he pronounced aloud, "to stop feeling sorry for myself."

He glanced at his watch. He would make a short pit stop before he spoke to the Panhandle Savings & Loan Executives at the First State Bank in Seymour, at three. "Plenty of time," he muttered, humming to the Waylon Jennings tune on the AM dial.

Like every other county seat in West Texas, Seymour was nothing more than a few short brick streets off the interstate, with a bank and a diner and an M. E. Moses five-and-dime; the county courthouse, a jail. Wizened faces frowned as the foreign sports car careened down Center Street. Andrew wondered if it was true what

257

they said about West Texans: that they kept their mouths pursed shut like that to keep the dust from blowing in.

Enjoying the attention, he pulled into one of seven parking spaces slanting at odd angles from the curb in front of Sadie's Diner. Jamming a coin into what was surely the only nickel parking meter left in the hemisphere, Andrew sniffed. Chicken-fried steak. He hooked his blue blazer over his shoulder, glad Callahan had urged casual khaki slacks and a sports coat: "Andrew, you wear a pin-striped suit out there, they think you're with the IRS."

He slid onto a stool near the cash register. "What kin I git you, hon?" the waitress twanged nasally.

"Chicken-fried steak, iced tea, and a piece of pie." Andrew glanced briefly at the menu. "What kind do you have?"

"What kind of what?" she said snippily, her eyes wandering to the campaign button in his lapel.

"What kind of pie?" Andrew stretched out his hand. "I'm Andrew Sebastian, by the way," he added, smiling broadly.

"Pie," the waitress commented perishingly, making no move to accept his hand, "is pie. You want it or not?"

He picked at his food for a long time, drenching each forkful of the deep-fried cube steak in gobs of congealed whitish cream gravy. Looking at the notes he had scrawled on his sweat-soaked schedule, Andrew saw that he'd signed up maybe ten volunteers that day. Someone in Olney had given him a check for ten dollars, which might pay for half of the super-unleaded gasoline he had burned coming out the Jacksboro Highway. He hoped to get a few contributors out of his three o'clock speech to the savings and loan guys here in Seymour. But most of them were hurting from falling oil prices.

The campaign was flat broke. Andrew realized, as he dug in his pocket to pay his check, that this was the first time he could remember checking the price of a meal before ordering it. He savored his last bite of peach pie and thought of how he and his dad used to go to Brink's on Gaston Avenue every Saturday after the barber shop and eat chicken-fried steak and peach cobbler.

Andrew paid the waitress and walked briskly to the pay phone. He dug in his wallet for the special quarter he had cached there. He dropped it in the slot, dialing a zero. He would have to call collect.

15

oger's money, and that of his friends, helped.

Two months later the chartered King Air leveled off above the parched border town of Brownsville, banking north for the quick run along the blue-green Gulf of Mexico to Corpus Christi.

With an audible sigh, Andrew settled back to make a few notes for his next speech.

They had just finished a triumphant three-day swing through the Rio Grande Valley, an economic desert where ranchers, shopkeepers, and a rising Hispanic middle class thirsted for change. His plan called for radical tax reduction, expanded trade with Mexico, and an innovative "workfare" plan requiring welfare recipients to work in return for federal benefits.

Now Andrew prepared to give a similar pitch in Corpus, in Spanish. He flipped open the pocket dictionary from his graduate school days, searching the Spanish term for "national defense."

The smoking lamp *ping*ed from red to green. Callahan dug in the pocket of his blazer.

"Andy, we've got to talk about something." He exhaled a little spurt of smoke out of one side of his mouth. "Your father called."

Andrew stared back silently, not picking up the bait.

"He wants to join us out here on the road," Callahan continued carefully, knowing he was on rough ground. "He says he can help."

"He's helping enough," Andrew said shortly, one hand flapping loosely around the cabin. "Paying for all this." Thousand-dollar contributions were pouring in from all over the state, thanks to Roger's phone calls, Roger's mailings, Roger's dinners.

"Ron, my deal with my father was clear." Andrew slapped his hand on the handrest. "He stays in Dallas and raises money. We run the campaign. If we let that camel's nose under the tent, he'll be sleeping on top of us by morning."

Callahan smiled. "What am I supposed to tell him?" he persisted. "It's his plane."

"Wrong," Andrew corrected mildly. "It's our plane. Paid for by our contributors. Besides, he's too old for this grind. If he gives you any more crap, tell him to call me." Andrew's blue eyes were cold. He wanted no repeat of the 1974 campaign, when he had felt like a bystander at his own fatal car crash.

Callahan changed the subject, using the smoldering stub of his first cigarette to light a second. "Those new TV spots are really helping. Your name identification is up fifteen points across the board. And Brackler's negatives are way up. Some people don't like those nasty ads." As expected, Brackler's TV commercials used the Channel 5 footage of the camera-smashing incident from 1974.

"Super," Andrew said with finality. "Then you can cancel your trip to Washington. I don't want you involved in any skulduggery up there."

"You don't know what I'm finding," Callahan began eagerly.

Andrew cut him off. "I don't want to know," he snapped. "Drop it."

It was not a request. Andrew leaned back again in his seat, glad to be flying instead of driving.

By the end of August, the Sebastian campaign's fresh new ideas, along with Roger's fresh new money, had maneuvered Andrew within ten poll points of the opposition.

Then Damocles' sword dropped and split Andrew right in half.

The blow jerked him out of an exhausted sleep at 6:10 A.M. on Labor Day, the traditional launch date for the final two-month push of an American political campaign.

Normally Andrew was up by six. He never could sleep when his front lawn held a newspaper that might contain his name. But yesterday had seen him at seven different barbecues between El Paso and Dallas, a distance greater than the trip from Chicago to New York. Andrew slept through the first few rings, huddled shapelessly under the sheets.

Tricia grabbed the receiver and pressed it against the approximate location of her husband's ear.

"Andrew!" Callahan's voice squawked. "This is Ron."

As though anyone else calls me at this hour, Andrew thought bleakly. "What's up?" he rasped.

"Have you seen the papers yet?"

"Do I sound like I've read the papers?"

"No-o-o." Callahan spoke with slow sarcasm. "Why don't you do that little thing, Andy, then call me back," His voice had a raw edge. "Try the *Herald*," he recommended tartly. There was a sudden click, then the loud buzzing of the dial tone.

Andrew staggered to his feet, pulled on a pair of SMU Mustang gym shorts, and wobbled outside, feeling the old-man sensation of getting out of bed before his body was ready. A neighbor in a passing station wagon honked at the sight of the Republican nominee for U.S. Senate bending over, naked but for a scanty pair of red-and-blue gym shorts, to scoop up the heavy newspapers and scuttle back up the walk.

Andrew tore the red rubber band off the *Herald* and set it to one side, where he placed all the ad circulars and Labor Day sale inserts. The *Herald* was stripped, gutted, and ready to devour. He spread the front page flat and scanned the headlines with his face screwed up in a wince, a man at gunpoint awaiting the pull of a trigger.

SEBASTIAN LINKED TO AMANDASCAM

(Washington—AP) Senate candidate and former U.S. Congressman Andrew Sebastian (R-Dallas) allegedly dropped his support of a 1974 ban on military aid to the Philippines in return for the sexual favors of Washington lobbyist Amanda Roberts, according to a copyrighted article in next month's edition of *Playboy* magazine.

Roberts, the center of a growing Capitol Hill sex scandal, names Sebastian as the first of her "many, many" liaisons with key congressional figures. Segments of the article obtained by the Associated Press describe an incident in the fall of 1974, when Roberts claims she convinced Sebastian to leave Washington on the day his bill to ban aid to the Philippines came to the floor for a vote, effectively killing the legislation.

Roberts, who claims she was then "having an affair" with Sebastian, was employed at the time as a lobbyist for the government of former Philippines President Ferdinand Marcos.

Sebastian was unavailable for comment Sunday. His opponent, U.S. Rep. Jim Brackler (D-Dallas), called the allegations "disturbing" and promised renewed congressional probes into the sex-for-votes scandal.

Andrew, not lifting his eyes from the page, groped with one hand for the telephone on the kitchen wall. Like an accountant with fluid ten-key, he punched the digits of Callahan's home number by rote.

"Unavailable, hell!" Andrew hissed through clenched teeth, not waiting for a hello. "Our office was open."

"What would you have said?" Callahan said sharply, suspiciously. "They did call, by the way. There were two messages from the A.P. on my desk last night."

"Why didn't you tell me?" Andrew complained.

"It was late, and I thought we could return them this morning.

262

Besides"—Callahan bit deep—"I wasn't aware we were about to be linked to a sex scandal."

Andrew grunted meaninglessly. His eyes darted down the endless column inches on the inside page. "No details, anyway."

"How much is there?" Callahan said, silently cursing Andrew for making him come out and ask. "Is it true, Andy? Can they make it stick?"

Andrew was reminded of the story of Shoeless Joe Jackson, the baseball star implicated in the Black Sox scandal. According to legend, a young fan had approached his hero after a game and cried, "Say it ain't so, Joe, say it ain't so!"

"That's two different questions," Andrew said calmly. "Whether it's true, and whether they can make it stick."

"Don't be pedantic," Callahan barked.

There was a long silence on the line.

"Well, I guess that's my answer, huh?" Callahan's voice was soft, hurt.

Andrew took a deep breath. "Ron, I did have, ah, an affair with Amanda Roberts," he said slowly. "She's really a very—well, not the way they've made her out."

"That's just great," Callahan fumed. "She's a nice girl. I'll be sure and tell that to the Prestoncrest Republican Women's Club." The campaign manager zeroed in on the essential: "What about the vote, Andrew? On the Philippines?"

"That's pure bullshit! I came back because of the campaign," Andrew insisted, anxious that Ron understand this. "Don't you remember? Come on, Ron. You know me better than that. We've been friends a long time."

"Sure," Callahan said bitterly. "Like the way you opened up with me about all this?"

"I didn't want to worry you," Andrew said weakly. "Look, Ron, this can all be dealt with."

"Oh, really?" There was real asperity in the crack of Callahan's voice. "How?"

"You can put out our side of the story, for one thing," Andrew said hopefully. "Put this in context."

"Context?" Callahan cried. "God damn it, Andrew! Will you quit acting so cool? This is our ass on the line! You know what woke me up this morning? A call from your old pal Phil Stuart. Who, by the way, is now the vice-president's press secretary."

"I didn't know," Andrew said. "How did that horse's ass get hooked up with our party's presidential nominee?"

Callahan wasn't about to be sidetracked. "The veep wants to know whether there is any more," he went on. "Stuart's exact words were, 'Is there a smoking gun here?'"

"See?" Andrew tried to summon up his courage. "Even Stuart can see it. This story's pretty thin as it sits, Ron. All they've got is a coincidence of timing. It's got Brackler's fingerprints all over it. Unless they get more details, I think the story's gonna die." He wasn't sure if he was trying to convince his campaign manager or himself. "There is no smoking gun," he underlined.

"That's not exactly what he was saying," Callahan replied, his voice flat and cold. "He was doing a damage assessment, so they can decide whether to let us sink or try to salvage. The veep needs Texas. This thing could drag the whole party down here."

"Why?" Andrew said, glad to be on the safer ground of political gamesmanship. "I mean, the others who have been named . . ." He paused, more than a bit embarrassed at this callous political discussion about strange men who had lain with a woman he'd once thought he loved. "They're all from the other party."

"I'm sure the vice-president appreciates you making it a bipartisan effort." Callahan's words were rough, abrasive. He was hurt and angry, and he wanted his candidate to suffer. Particularly, he thought, since I'm the one who has to clean up the mess. "This is serious, Andrew," he added. "There's talk in Washington of a special prosecutor."

Andrew felt fear's adrenaline pumping through his limbs, thinking of the last time Washington was abuzz with talk of "special prosecutors" and "smoking guns."

He listened hollowly as Callahan went on, "There's something I gotta know, Andy." The campaign manager added pointedly, "And this time, I want you to be straight with me."

"Ron, I'm sorry about that," Andrew said earnestly. "I was wrong. Just couldn't bring myself. I just thought the whole thing might blow over."

"It won't," Callahan assured him curtly. "I have to know. Is there more? More women? Anything more about this than what's in the paper?"

"No," Andrew said. "That's it. And what's there is all twisted around. She did try to soften me up. I really don't think that's why

264

we got together. But I didn't throw the game, Ron," he insisted, thinking again of Shoeless Joe. "I want you to know that. I was wrong to be with that woman. But it didn't affect my vote."

"Okay," Callahan said. "You know what this means."

"What?"

"There's only one way out of this. If you're still in to win."

"More than ever," Andrew assured him with real heat in his voice, wondering how he would break this news to Tricia. And, help me, God, to my son.

"We've got to get tough." Callahan's voice was ominous. "Take the gloves off. I've done some things. Things I haven't told you about," the campaign manager added bluntly, letting Andrew know that he, too, had his secrets. "They're coming along," he added vaguely, "but I need more ammunition."

"Get it," Andrew said flatly, without hesitation.

"I may have to bend the rules a little," Callahan taunted, relishing his victory.

"Do what you have to do," Andrew growled, uncomfortable but resolute. He remembered what he had once told Phil Stuart: What goes around, comes around. It was time for Brackler to get some of his own. "And Ron," he said, "I really am sorry."

"Yeah," Callahan said huskily. "Unplug your phone for a while, then call me around eight."

"Sure," Andrew said meekly as the phone clicked in his ear. His stomach wrenched as he thought of the horrible morning stretched out in front of him. Explaining this to the people he loved. Fighting fires in the press. The confused look in Sean's eyes when he tried to prepare his son for what the kids would say in school. Thank you, Mr. Brackler, Andrew thought, wondering if twelve-year-olds knew what an "affair" was.

He looked at the clock over the microwave oven: 6:30 A.M. It was going to be a long day.

To Andrew's surprise, they survived the initial flashburn of the scandal.

It was a long and terrible month. Strained moments with Tricia, Sean, his parents. Brackler's hecklers in the crowds. An awful week in mid-September when a supermarket tabloid printed a blurry snapshot of Andrew "with party girl Amanda Roberts at a swank embassy reception in Washington." The tabloid was passed around at Sean's school, cause for another long father-son discussion: mute nods; unshed tears.

Tricia had been wonderful, though her reaction sent a shaft of pain: "Whatever hurt that caused, I felt long ago." She offered a frail smile. "F.I.P.O., that's what Ron says." Callahan told Andrew it stood for Fuck It, Push On.

Andrew dropped fifteen points in as many days and couldn't raise a nickel from a lemonade stand. But Callahan told him they weren't dead yet.

"In politics, an hour is a day, a day is a month, and a week is a fucking lifetime," he counseled. By that standard, November 5 was still five lifetimes away. "That's as long as a whole national campaign in England," said Callahan, who knew such things.

After a month of horrible publicity, the scandal faded for lack of new revelations, as a great huge log burns itself to glowing embers and, finally, to a pile of cold soot. Ever so slowly, Andrew's Amanda connection crept off the front pages, nestling back on A-27, among election reports from Venezuela and stories about pit bull dogs mauling postmen in central California. By the beginning of October the candidate was starting to believe his campaign manager's admonitions that things couldn't possibly get any worse.

Then, they did. This time it was Callahan's fault.

"How could you do this to me?" Andrew bellowed, hurling the half-rolled newspaper across Callahan's messy apartment. "After all I've been through? God damn it, Ron!"

"Would you mind closing the door?" Dallas's October night air already had a slight chill. Callahan ambled to the front door of his apartment. He was tempted to leave but shut the door instead.

His candidate snatched up the *Times Herald* again, brandishing it about. "I told you to be careful, you shit! All those trips. Who paid for it, my father? I knew! I knew you were up to something!"

"You're damn right you knew!" Callahan lashed back. "And you didn't care, Andrew! 'Do what you have to do, Ron.' Remember?" the campaign manager shouted. "You wanted to get that bastard, and you didn't care how old Callahan did it! You just wanted to win! No, excuse me," he corrected with a cutting sneer. "You just wanted to beat Brackler. That *is* what this is all about?"

"Let's not change the subject," Andrew snapped. "And I don't think we need to worry about beating Brackler. You've pretty well taken care of that."

Andrew unfurled the bold black headline: SEBASTIAN CAMPAIGN AUTHORIZED WIRETAPS ON BRACKLER. "I love the way they heard our side of it," he said caustically. "I suppose I have my campaign manager to thank for that?"

"They've all called," Callahan said quietly. "Our side will be in the morning editions. We didn't break the law, Andrew. It's another Brackler setup. We never tapped his phone. They were parabolic microphones, from across the street. All perfectly legal."

"Legal!" Andrew shouted, fists clenched. The candidate crossed the room with quick steps to thrust his jaw into Callahan's face.

Callahan, having seen his employer's famous temper in action, suddenly feared Andrew would hit him.

"We're not talking about legal," Andrew raged. "We're talking about stupid. And wrong. You hired *detectives?* Jesus Christ, Ron!"

"Don't you want to know what we found out?" Callahan cried. "It's big, Andrew. It'll kill him."

"I don't ever want to hear another word about it," Andrew said coldly, although Callahan could see a flicker of curiosity in those electric-blue eyes. "I don't need your dirty tricks to win this election."

Oh, yes, you do, Callahan thought. Still, he felt an icy spear of guilt shaft through his rib cage. He had gone too far, been too sloppy. Damn that gumshoe, letting Frawley spot the parabolic from Brackler's town house.

"Honestly, Andrew, everything was completely legal," he protested. "I checked it out with a lawyer before we started. We never did any real electronic wiretapping. Just listening. There's a difference," he explained, his ruddy Irish freckles flushing. "I know it looks bad. I'm sorry. I just got caught up. I never thought—"

"You never thought," Andrew said, repeating Callahan's words with the biting sarcasm he saved for mocking Sean's excuses. "Well, you've done it now. I'm dropping out. I just hope to God we don't have to go to jail for this."

Callahan waved one big hand. "Don't be so melodramatic," he said. "These things never go to trial. It's all political smoke, just for the press."

"That's comforting," Andrew mocked. "I won't go to jail, I'll just lose my reputation, and the election."

"No, you won't. You're not quitting. I am," Callahan announced without emotion. "I've already called all the papers, and the wire

267

services. You should leave now, Andy. We shouldn't even be talking. This is my fault, and you had nothing to do with it, okay? I'll take the heat."

"You should," Andrew said tentatively, running the scenario through his mind. Callahan could see the politician's wheels turn: Will they buy my campaign manager as a scapegoat?

"There's a famous painting," Andrew said wearily, dropping onto Callahan's couch among a sea of old newspapers and paper plates smeared with macaroni and cheese. "It's a Russian family, or Eskimos, I can't remember which. On a sled, being chased by wolves, and they're throwing their baby to the wolf pack to save themselves. I'm not that desperate, Ron." He smiled suddenly, and Callahan felt unaccountably warm.

"Besides, it wouldn't satisfy the pack," Andrew continued crisply. "They want red meat. Me. So," he said slowly, "I might as well keep the baby."

"No," Callahan said flatly. "Go with me on this, Andrew. You're in for five more weeks, and I'm out for good. It's done, Andrew. I've already called them."

"Call 'em back," Andrew ordered gruffly, shoving his way to his feet and heading for the door. "Then come to headquarters, and we'll put a statement together."

Callahan felt the beginning of tiny tears at the corners of his eyes and didn't know why. Andrew just wanted someone to blame in November, when the roof fell in.

16

Amanda Roberts picked her way across the slippery cobble-stone sidewalk. She peered miserably at the faded masonry of one looming Federalist town house after another, trying to find the right numbers. She was looking for 3310 P Street: an awfully tony Georgetown address, in her opinion, for the rough-hewn man she sought on this icy evening.

The late-afternoon October dusk shrouded the familiar wrought-iron gates of Washington's most exclusive neighborhood. Amanda clutched tightly at her scarf to keep the sleet out of her thick blond hair. She wore it swept back in a tight knot, clasped to her temples by two oversize decorative combs of blue lapis lazuli. Her fingers probed carefully: had things come undone up there? She didn't typically wear her hair up like this. But then, she thought wryly, this is not your typical night on the town.

Amanda waited to cross 33rd Street. At the stop sign, a black man nearly broke his neck eyeing her from the inside of a sleek blue BMW. She ignored him pointedly and wondered again if she had been right to wear the big tanuki coat. With all the rain and sleet, its matted, spiky fur made her look like a drowned yak. The BMW, its driver still ogling blatantly, eased slowly southward on 33rd, tires slithering as they encountered the ice-sheathed trolley lines buried in Georgetown's brick streets. Amanda cursed the black man silently as she tiptoed across the street, because he was safe and warm inside a German-engineered luxury car while her own had been repossessed two months ago.

She drew near what had to be her target: the shabbiest house on the block. It was a narrow white slab with no iron gate, no leaded-glass bay window full of expensive furniture. Just a short flight of steps up to the front porch and two slit windows with tiny shafts of light sneaking through drab baby-blue curtains. Why was he still in Washington, Amanda wondered, with the November elections barely two weeks away? She double-checked the address. Then she mounted the steps, not sure whether to be frightened or relieved that her source had been correct.

Amanda paused under the small awning and slipped the scarf carefully from her upswept coif. Brushing the water quickly from her fur, she reached into her alligator purse for a small gold compact. Snapping it open, she dipped one long, lavender-polished fingernail into the dwindling supply of white powder. She pressed it furtively to each nostril, inhaling two invigorating jolts of Colombian courage. It made her eyes water and gave her the strength to lift her hand to the tiny black doorbell. She pushed it twice, firmly.

There was the long pause of someone who does not expect guests. Footsteps pounded down wooden stairs. The door cracked open. Big Jim Brackler squinted through the unwelcoming sliver between door and jamb.

"Yes?" The congressman looked at her coolly.

"You know who I am," Amanda said starchily. "Every housewife in America knows who I am. Can I come in?"

"I didn't put you out in the cold, darlin'. You did that all by yourself." Brackler grinned, immensely pleased with himself. He made not the slightest move to open the door. "Why don't you go home?" he suggested. "This is the last place you ought to be seen."

"If you don't let me in, I will stand on your doorstep until the *National Enquirer* photographer I lost back in my parking garage catches up with me," Amanda announced slowly. "'AMANDA PAYS LATE NIGHT VISIT TO ETHICS COMMITTEE MEMBER.' How's that gonna play in Fort Worth, buster?"

Brackler sighed and pushed the door open, bowing low in mock welcome. "*Mi casa* is *su casa*, honey. But I only got a few minutes," he warned. "I got a plane to catch."

"I should think so," Amanda said, softening her tone. She stripped the floor-length fur languorously from her shoulders, arching her back to smooth her shimmering bronze blouse. She offered him the tanuki. He stared back, making no move to hang it up. This was going to be tough, she thought bleakly.

"You must be pretty sure of yourself, Big Jim," she teased. "How many days 'til the election? Ten?"

"I'm not too worried about ol' Andy Sebastian, darlin'." He grinned. "Thanks to you."

"Cut the darlin' crap, okay?" Amanda spat suddenly. "Who do you think you are, J. R. Ewing? I thought you were a feminist."

"I voted for the ERA, darlin'," Brackler said smoothly, evenly. "I just don't see any need to be polite to girls who come tramping to my door uninvited. No pun intended, of course."

Amanda let that pass. "I'll get to the point," she said, settling onto a small overstuffed settee next to a stone-cold fireplace in the tiny den.

"Please," Brackler said belligerently. "I've got that plane."

"I know we've barely met," she began.

"We've never met," Brackler corrected sharply. "Except in committee hearings."

"That's right." Amanda nodded. "But I've had some dealings with Dan Mullins."

Brackler cut in abruptly, "Now hold on! I want to make sure you understand. Whatever dealings you've done with Dan, that's nothin' to do with me."

"Of course." Amanda smiled pleasantly. Better to play by his rules. "Could I have a drink, do you suppose?" she asked sweetly. "A cup of coffee?"

"You want coffee, go to House of Pancakes."

His voice cut into her like a knife. She tried to remember when a man had spoken to her like that. Her father, perhaps. But he had been a policeman, a rough old cop who had taught his daughter to shoot straight, both figuratively and in the ballistics sense. Right

271

now, her mind skating high on coke, her throat tight and bitter, she wished her dad were here from Illinois, so he could beat the hell out of this cocky tub of lard for treating Sergeant Roberts's daughter like a 14th Street whore.

Amanda drew the air shallowly into her lungs in a way she knew made her smallish breasts stick out better. "Congressman," she said shakily, feeling tears spring easily to her eyes. They did that lately. "Jim," she corrected. "I'm in trouble. Bad trouble. I'm dead broke. They've taken my car, my apartment, everything. The deal with your—with Mullins. It's a rip-off. Not that I'm blaming you," she added quickly before he could protest again. "I know they arranged it all without your knowledge."

"That's right." Brackler nodded vigorously.

"I've got nowhere else to go," Amanda said plaintively. "I can't even pay my lawyer. And he tells me now that the committee may decide to deny my immunity. That I may have to go to jail."

Amanda sobbed. With a sick lurch, she realized she wasn't playacting. The thought of going to prison scared her to death. Not because of what it would do to her reputation, her parents in Glen Forest, her career. Those were all in ruins. But prison was, as the kids said these days, serious shit. People died in prison, and got raped by bull-dyke trustees, and lived in squalid gray cement rooms with squalid gray toilets in the corner, and never got to leave. Deep in her gut, she knew she would die in prison. And so, she had decided she would die before she would ever allow them to put her there. She would even sleep with this bloated pig of a congressman, if that's what it took. How could she have been stupid enough to look upon him, or any politician, as a savior?

"You may go to jail," Brackler acknowledged, trudging to a big La-Z-Boy chair. He plopped himself down. The chair's springs screamed in protest. He looked at her with bellicose eyes. "You know what they say: Don't do the crime if you can't do the time. I'm sorry, I just don't feel real sympathetic, Miss Roberts."

"Amanda," she put in quickly, dabbing at her eyes.

"I'm sorry, Amanda," he repeated, and for a moment he was. Amanda was a sad, lonely woman, as lonely as he was. And beautiful, in a drawn, willowy sort of way. His tone grew quiet, almost tender. "I hate to be the one to tell you. But it's been decided. That's why I'm still here. We spent all week discussing it."

"You promised!" Amanda shouted, real betrayal in her voice. "All of you! The whole committee!"

"You were never guaranteed immunity," Brackler said formally, brushing his hair down over his balding forehead. "We said we'd consider it. We did. We voted against it."

"You could bring it up again!" Amanda urged breathlessly. She leaned very close to the congressman's chair, clenching the fur coat tightly in her lap. "You're vice-chairman. They'd listen to you!"

"I made the motion to deny," he admitted flatly, not shrinking back from the tall, frankly sensuous woman whose enormous brown eyes spiked his interest. "How could I not?" Brackler asked, voice faintly mocking. "I'm running against one of the guys you screwed for a vote, Amanda."

Amanda's lips quivered. Her sources hadn't told her Brackler had been the one to shaft her. In spite of herself, Amanda admired the bastard for being man enough to tell her to her face.

"You're gonna send me to jail? After all I've done?" Amanda fell suddenly to her knees on the cold wooden floor, grasping his thighs through the brown polyester of the congressman's slacks. "I went along with you!" she cried. "The article, Brackler! I made it look just like you guys wanted! What about me, huh? What happens to me?"

"I'm sorry," he said quietly, in a creaking voice that fought to ignore the flushed feminine cheek pressed to the inside of his right thigh. A powerful tingle crept up toward his groin. "What you did, with Sebastian, with the rest. It was wrong. You gotta pay the price."

"God, I'll do anything!" Amanda cried in real anguish. Her hands dropped. She yanked her blouse over her head in one fluid gesture that knocked her hairdo askew. Brackler stared back at her blankly. But she saw the sudden bulge in his crotch, inches from her tear-streaked face. "Anything!" she hissed intensely. One long, bare arm stretched up to his fly. The other groped to find his big, thick hand and bring it to the taut flesh cupped tightly in the black lace of her French push-up brassiere.

"Please don't do this to me!" Her fingers fumbled at his zipper. Feeling him rise stiffly against her palm, she sensed victory.

"That's enough!" Brackler roared. He stood, knocking her to the floor with his knees. Her skull banged painfully against a coffee table full of newspapers. Her head filled with red mist and cocaine.

Through it, she heard him shouting at her. "Get out of my house! Now! You stupid bitch!" She felt his hands reach down to grab her by the hair. He hauled her roughly to her feet.

"You think I'm that stupid?" Brackler hissed. He ripped brutally at each side of her head, tearing the lapis combs from her tangled hair. He bent them backward before her large brown eyes, now wide and staring with terror.

"You wear a stinkin' wire to *my* house?" he howled in anger. "I'm a United States congressman, goddammit!" He snapped each comb in half, baring his crooked teeth in a wicked smile as the half-hidden silver microphone dropped from the second comb. It bounced on the scarred wood floor.

"Hello, FBI," he said with acid irony, crunching the tiny electronic bug with one brown shoe. He watched in disgust as Amanda, gagging on her knees, grabbed at her fur coat and wrapped it around her half-naked torso. Leaning over, Brackler ransacked through the coat with his two huge hands. He grabbed her bare ribs, pulling her to her feet.

"What else you got for me, huh?" he said viciously, running one hand down the front of her pants until his uncut fingernails jabbed up between her legs. "A tape recorder up your twat?"

"Nothing!" Amanda cried desperately, thinking that she had found something worse than prison. "They made me do it!"

"Not fucking likely," he snarled. He patted her down savagely until he was satisfied.

"Now, you were saying?" His voice rose in mocking falsetto: "Oh, please, I'll do anything! Anything? What'd you have in mind?"

Amanda, helpless in his brawny arms, looked toward the door.

"I wouldn't worry about them," Brackler said sardonically. He pushed her to the floor, tossing her coat to one side. He jerked the bra from her chest with one rough pull. "Nobody's gonna come busting in here to save you." Big Jim lowered himself on her, pulling at her zipper, forcing her hands to undo his. "You been watching too much TV, Amanda."

"I'll tell them," Amanda whispered fiercely as his raspy face bit at her neck and breasts, even as she felt her own hands, guided by his very strong fingers, stroking him onward. "I swear to God I'll tell them."

"Who's gonna believe you?" Brackler grunted. He laughed aloud as he slid inside her, feeling powerful, secure, in control. Amanda

274

lay back against the cold hard wood and bit her lip, crying and shuddering and trying to think of Glen Forest and all the things she should have been.

It was over very quickly.

"Thanks," Brackler grated, chest heaving. He clambered to his knees, pulled his pants over his big hips. "Now I've had it all. Everything he's ever had. Except maybe about five hundred million bucks. Now kindly fuck off, will you? I've got that plane to catch."

It was cold outside, with the sleet bulleting harder than ever. Amanda held the fur coat close against her bare, goose-pimpled breasts. She leaned back against the front door and stuffed her brassiere, blouse, and lapis combs into her purse. Then she staggered down the steps and walked blindly up P Street, unaware that one of her black Stuart Weitzman pumps still rested in Brackler's fireplace.

"Get in."

The BMW's door flew open. She climbed dumbly into the cheerless warmth of its backseat. Parker Worthington looked over the driver's headrest. "Good try, Amanda." His big teeth were all she could see of his black face in the darkness. They reflected the eerily familiar blue instrument lights of the BMW's dash.

"Not good enough, was it?" Amanda said bitterly. In a flash, she decided what she must do. What her father would do. "I'm still gonna do time, Parker," she said tonelessly.

"I think so." Above everyone else in this Amandascam mess, Worthington felt sorry for the sad, cynical woman at the center of it all. He felt especially bad about tonight. But that was the breaks.

"If it were up to me . . ." Worthington began.

"I know," Amanda said dispiritedly. "It's up to the committee."

She felt her mind skidding relentlessly in the backseat. Lately she had trouble telling whether it was the cocaine or the general shittiness of her life that was the only roller coaster in the world that plunged forever downhill. "You didn't tell me Brackler was the one who jerked my immunity," she added accusingly.

"It was a close vote," Worthington said. "Brackler was key. If it wasn't for him, you'd be in the clear."

Brackler. It all came down to him. Amanda felt an arrow of clear, cold hate pierce the oozy mist in her brain. It was one thing to shove her on the floor and rape her like an animal. Plenty of men had done that; most of them were still in Congress. But Brackler

275

had used her to do his dirty work, then hung her out to dry. Besides, she reflected, I really don't have much to lose, do I? What are they gonna do, put me in jail?

Amanda broke the long silence as the black man made another aimless circuit of the slippery, glazed back streets of Georgetown. "Parker, you should have told me."

"I couldn't," Worthington said, ashamed of his cowardice. "Orders. Besides, I didn't want you to think I had goaded you into this." The black attorney spoke with sudden force: "He really fucked you, Amanda."

"No kidding," she said dully. "You guys didn't get a thing?"

"Nothing," the Justice lawyer said sadly, still not sure how to act around this very beautiful and very dangerous woman. He wished he had brought one of the FBI agents from the Comm van with him, as a witness. "It was worth a try," he consoled her.

"Was it?" Amanda thought, nauseated at Brackler's strangely callused hands on her ribs, his slithery tongue on her collarbone. "I'm glad you thought so."

Worthington wanted to ask what happened after the microphone went dead, but he didn't. You didn't have to be J. Edgar Hoover to figure it out. "So what do you do now?"

"Go home, I guess. Will you take me there?" Amanda asked simply. He nodded and headed south, toward M Street. As the BMW drew near her shabby second-story walk-up, Amanda wondered if her Visa card could still stand a one-way airplane ticket to Texas.

Dawn broke cool and bright over the piney woods of east Texas, promising another glorious late-October day on the wide, unmoving waters of Cedar Creek Lake. Andrew stopped on a low promontory overlooking his father's ranch near Seven Points, glad the rain had stopped in the night. It was nice to be here, among the scrubby, heavily scented spruce: the perfect escape from the awful crush of the past few weeks.

Thankfully, his schedule had brought him to Longview last night, so he could sneak over here and sleep for a few hours and catch the daybreak over the water. Soon it would be time to rush back to the fifteen-bedroom mansion that his mother called "the lakehouse." He would throw off the red-and-green-plaid lumberjack shirt in favor of a dark gray suit and soothing gray tie and skid down the road to make his seven-thirty breakfast in Kaufman. Andrew breathed the crisp air shallowly into his lungs and spotted the first bass boat rippling across the far side of the lake.

"Excuse me!" Phil Stuart said miserably. "Could we do this back at the house? Say, over a cup of coffee?" His eyes were streaked with crimson. His tie flapped loosely in the brisk wind off the lake; muddy water oozed inside the ankles of his carefully polished wingtips.

"You asked for this meeting," Andrew snapped. "If you had any sense, you would be quiet and enjoy the view. It's pretty rare you see a sunrise like this."

"Not rare enough," Stuart commented dryly. "I thought you said this place was just outside of Dallas."

"You're in Texas," Andrew countered. "A hundred miles is just a hop, skip, and a jump."

He ambled down the slope to the water's edge, his lizard-skin boots squishing six inches deep into the black mud. Normally he would never think of walking into deep mud in eight-hundred-dollar boots. But it was worth a pair of Tony Lamas to see how far the Yankee would follow him.

Stuart grimaced and tiptoed beside him, cursing under his breath as one shoe came loose. The vice-president's campaign aide perched awkwardly there for a moment, one leg folded up like a flamingo, a gray argyle sock sopping wet and dangling from his toe.

"I get the point," Stuart whined. "This is the part where you take the city boy out on the farm, like when Johnson took Bobby Kennedy deer hunting. I didn't come here to play games, Andrew. I'm here at the orders of the vice-president of the United States, who will almost undoubtedly be elected president nine days from now. Unless you and Callahan have any more surprises for us," he added snidely.

Andrew whirled to face the smaller man. At forty Phil Stuart still looked like a prep school junior, his blond hair parted carefully in a short Ivy League brush.

"What's that supposed to mean?" Andrew snapped.

"I'll be frank," Stuart said soberly, as though this were a rare and momentous thing.

"Please do," Andrew replied. "You've come an awful long way to lie."

Stuart shook his head in annoyance. "You don't know what you're doing, do you?" he asked. "To the vice-president? To the country?"

277

Andrew was honestly perplexed. "What?"

"It's 1973 all over again," Stuart explained. "Scandals. Spying on the opposition. This time, you're on the other side. It's ironic, really. The whole time you were up there on your white horse, you were just like the rest. Down in the mud."

"Bad choice of words," Andrew said coolly, gesturing to Stuart's feet. "What's your point, Phil?"

"The point is, we want you out!" Stuart spoke with abrupt fierceness. "Drop out now, before the election. Before any further damage to the ticket. With this latest scandal, our polls show you thirty points behind Brackler. For Christ's sake. Thirty points! You can't win, Sebastian. And you're dragging everyone down with you!"

Stuart nearly shouted as he warmed to his message. "Ron Callahan won't tell you to your face, but he knows it, too. We're getting pleas from every congressional candidate and justice of the peace in Texas. They're afraid you'll sink us. Maybe hurt the vice-president. We can't afford to lose this state!"

"That's what this is all about, isn't it?" Andrew said, his jaw set stubbornly. He thumped his finger into Stuart's suit jacket, rocking the man backward with its force. "What's your offer, Stuart?" he asked suddenly, his voice cold and insinuating. "What's in it for me?"

Stuart exhaled a quiet burst of relief. Now it was just price. "The vice-president respects you, Andy," he said. "He sees a role for you in the next administration."

"An ambassadorship, maybe?" Andrew said hopefully.

"I don't know about that," Stuart hedged. "I can't make any promises at this stage."

"Of course," Andrew said remotely, his eyes traversing the dawn-dappled lake. "That would be illegal. Or at least unethical. And we wouldn't want that."

Stuart ignored both the mild sarcasm and the splendid view. "Quite frankly, with your background in academics, you could be a real help in some key policy areas," he oozed. "The vice-president has read some of your articles, Andrew. He thinks you have a real feel for the way the system works. Enough for a top sub-Cabinet role. OMB, even. Or EPA."

"Wouldn't he be worried about the confirmation hearings, with all this terrible scandal?" Andrew asked with mock innocence. "If

278

I'm so dangerous to the ticket, wouldn't I be"—he searched for the word—"problematic?"

Stuart had prepared for this. Sebastian was no fool. "It would be up to you to make it through the Senate," he said levelly, shivering a bit in the wind. "We know we'll take heat. Frankly, it's the lesser of two evils, and we would rather take the one that happens after we win. You know the first three rules of politics."

"Callahan taught them to me," Andrew said. "The first rule is: Winning is winning. Second rule: Losing is losing. Third rule: See rules one and two."

Stuart nodded. "You understand our position."

"Yep," Andrew said shortly. "I think it stinks. No deal, Stuart." He turned his wide, rangy back to the aide and took three big strides up the hill.

"Sebastian!" Stuart's shriek echoed off the water. "This is your last offer!"

Andrew turned to look down at Stuart, who was working his feet loose from the blackish-green muck as the wake from a passing speedboat lapped shallowly over his heels. "Oh, Stuart!" Andrew shouted into the wind.

"Yeah?" The aide frowned up at the man atop the hill.

"I'd be careful," Andrew hollered with a smile. "They like this time of morning, when the sun first comes out."

"Huh?"

"Snakes," Andrew shouted, feeling better already. "I think I saw a water moccasin on the way up."

According to Callahan's postgame analysis, they might have survived it all, if only the candidate had avoided the Big Debate Mistake.

Amandascam they had already weathered. The brief flurry of negative publicity over the surveillance episode died when the attorney general announced that no laws had been broken. Texas voters were beginning to be repelled by Brackler's relentlessly negative campaign: the terrible battery of Brackler attack spots on television; the daily sneak feeding to the press of dog-eared documents and ancient videotapes. In Callahan's view, they still had a distant chance—until the evening of October 27.

Political professionals despise any medium they cannot control. Debates are the worst of the lot. The candidate is alone, on stage in a high-stress situation, in the full glare of TV lights. Anything can happen, and usually does.

Callahan lectured his charge on the eve of that first big debate in San Antonio.

"Never try to win," he urged. "Nobody wins campaign debates. People lose them. They make a big gaffe everyone remembers, long after anyone remembers what was said about the issues. Like Ford telling Jimmy Carter Poland was a free country. Or Carter telling Reagan that Amy advised him on nuclear disarmament. That's what you've got to avoid, Andrew. The Big Mistake."

Andrew made his before the debate even began.

It all started in the cavernous front entry of San Antonio's ultra-modern Henry B. Gonzales Convention Center. Brackler arrived early, resplendent in a loud houndstooth sports coat. His on-the-road entourage had swelled in the headiness of the last few days. As the tall, portly congressman stumped across the bare concrete floor, a colony of fourteen coat holders swarmed around him, driven into a frenzy by the pollen of imminent victory. They ranged from queen bees like Dan Mullins to six or seven drones whose names Brackler never could quite remember. He glowered over his shoulder at the mass of blue-suited men behind him, shooting a smug glance at Mullins.

Mullins had opposed this debate; had managed to keep Brackler from making a single joint appearance with Andrew through the entire long summer of the campaign. In late August, just before Amandascam broke, the Sebastian camp had aired a series of hard-hitting TV spots featuring Andrew debating an empty chair in Houston. "Where is Jim Brackler?" the announcer's voice intoned. "Hiding from his record? Come on, Jim. You can run, but you cannot hide!"

The commercials incensed Brackler. There ensued a month of long-distance negotiations between Mullins, Callahan, and the League of Women Voters, involving everything from the height of the microphones to the size of the flags. Finally the dates had been set: San Antonio on October 27; Dallas two days later.

Mullins didn't like debates any more than Callahan, especially when his candidate was twenty-nine glorious points ahead. Thank God we pushed them back this late, Mullins thought. He bobbed along in the crowd that was Brackler's wake as the congressman veered suddenly to port, heading purposefully for a side door. The mob halted suddenly, aides in the rear running smack into the front phalanx of Brackler camp followers. The whole retinue milled awkwardly outside the men's room door. Mullins grinned at their discomfort. But even he wasn't about to follow their leader in to take a pee.

Inside, Brackler straddled the urinal, placing one hand flat against the cool burgundy tile wall.

"Ah!" He exhaled a huge burst of air. His head jerked up as he heard a familiar voice behind him.

"Scared the piss out of you, James?" Andrew Sebastian said cockily. Brackler's opponent reached over the sink and pumped quickly at the long, skinny soap dispenser. The room smelled suddenly of almonds.

"Primping?" Brackler snorted, discomfited. He couldn't twist his head around to face Sebastian, not without peeing all over his trousers. "It's not gonna help, buddy. Not this time." He stuffed himself into his pants and zipped up quickly, ignoring the warm drops on his thigh.

"Nice jacket, James," Andrew smirked, stressing the final *s* with a sibilant twang. He knew this was childish, but he couldn't resist. Besides, he thought, what an opportunity to psych the man out.

"I really like it," Andrew continued earnestly. "Reminds me of the upholstery of a sixty-five Corvette I once had. You're not going to wear it on TV? They'll think it's a test pattern."

"Haw, haw," Brackler said, walking pointedly to the sink farthest away from Andrew. He fumbled desperately for something witty to say in return. Andrew leaned against the tile wall and stared at him for a moment. Then he pushed off with one shoulder and sauntered toward the door.

"D'you bring ol' Tricia with you?" Brackler taunted. When all else failed, guys like Andrew Sebastian always got pissed when you talked about their women. "How 'bout Amanda? I bagged 'em both, you know," he added conversationally. "Of course, so has half of Washington. Amanda, anyway. I don't know about Tricia."

In the mirror, Andrew's face grew red and blustery, the veins in his neck stiffening into whipcords. I've got him, Brackler thought with glee. He reached down to mop his hands dry with a paper towel. Then he turned to face his nemesis.

The restroom was empty.

Moments later, in the tiny cubicle allotted to Andrew as a green room, Callahan bore the brunt of his candidate's fury.

"Goddammit, Ron, give me something!" Andrew thundered. "I need ammunition. The vice-president's polls show us thirty points behind. We've got nothing to lose."

"The Big Mistake," Callahan chanted doggedly. "You've got to avoid that, Andrew."

"Mistake? The only one I've made is not accepting your goddamn resignation!" As each new day brought another revelation, their relationship had grown increasingly rocky. "We can't go any lower in the polls. Let's do something out there tonight!" He spoke with a fierceness, a fire Callahan had never heard before. "I've got to win this, don't you understand?" Andrew grabbed him by the lapels. "I've got to beat that son of a bitch!"

"It depends how far you're willing to go. I've still got the stuff from Washington. The stuff you refused to look at," Callahan reminded him pointedly.

"Anything," the candidate snapped. "Whatever it takes!"

"Brackler doesn't know we have this, or they'd never have risked an investigation on that surveillance thing," Callahan said quickly, breathless with excitement. He reached over to the huge, locked briefcase he lugged about the state with him. Inserting the key, he hauled out a slim manila folder from a deep pocket.

"You've heard all the rumors about how Brackler gets his rocks off," Callahan began, enthusiastic. "Hookers, congressional pages, little boys."

Andrew waved his hand impatiently. "He's a bachelor. There are always rumors about bachelors."

"Yeah." Callahan wondered if Andrew remembered that he, too, was unmarried. "There's more than rumors," the campaign manager said. "I've got photos, Andrew! Known minor prostitutes, as the police reports put it. Slipping into the back door of his town house in Georgetown."

Callahan fanned a stack of grainy black-and-white photos across a table in the corner of the room. "Look how they come out."

Andrew leaned forward with interest, indulging the voyeuristic satisfaction of sneaking a peek at Jim Brackler's back door.

"Christ!" he said with real disgust. He felt suddenly sick, soiled; the spindly, swollen-faced girl in the picture, though dressed in the miniskirt and high white boots of a 14th Street whore, couldn't possibly be any older than Sean.

The door popped open, and Tricia stuck her head in. Caught in the act, Andrew spun to block her view. "Ten minutes, guys!" she said gaily. "Need anything?"

"No, thanks." He forced a weak smile. "Be out in a minute." The door pulled shut.

"Callahan," Andrew said slowly, feeling a burning sensation inside, "I can't. This is not what I meant." He shook his head sadly. "I can't go use this. It brings me down to his level. This is . . . well, sick."

The irony had not struck Andrew until that moment. Brackler's snooping had helped drive him into this race. Now here was his own campaign manager, showing him dirty pictures from his opponent's back door. How did I let things get this far out of hand? he wondered.

"Anything, you said. Whatever it takes." Callahan was sullen, lips pulled down in a pout. "I'm sorry, Andy, but this is what it takes. You've got to be tougher than him! Morally tougher. That means making some compromises."

"Sorry," Andrew said lightly. "Not this one."

"I've got it all, Andy." Callahan geysered forth a last-minute stream of salesmanship, waving pictures and police reports in front of the candidate's upturned nose. "Names, dates. Police reports. Brackler's never been arrested, but the girls have. Even the little ones. God, dozens of times!" He flapped photocopies of arrest reports, rifling through mug shots that matched the faces outside Brackler's door. "Andrew," he pleaded, "I'm not suggesting you go out there and wave these in his face. Just let me show them to Sam Dalton from the *Morning News*. Jesus, just think what it would do to him!"

"I was just thinking what it would do to me," Andrew said softly. He didn't mean to hurt Ron's feelings, but he felt himself backing toward the door, as though repulsed by some terrible smell. "Sorry, Ron. You know me better than that," he said, shaking his head. "I think I could kill him, you know?" Andrew said with sudden vehemence. "Just go out there and strangle the big shit, in front of the TV cameras. At least that would be honest. But not this way."

Andrew walked out. The door swung shut.

Crestfallen, Callahan flipped on the TV set. Maybe, the campaign manager thought whimsically, he'll really do it, just walk out there and throttle that oversize rag doll right there on live PBS television. Wouldn't that be a sight?

Callahan laughed aloud over his frustration, watching the commentators run through their predebate babble. The cameras zoomed in on an empty stage with two empty seats at two empty rostrums, each equipped with a goosenecked microphone and a full glass of water. Callahan watched his candidate mount the platform and take his place.

"Uh-oh," he said guiltily. "I pissed him off." Andrew's face was still taut and tense, which meant he wasn't concentrating. The campaign manager grimaced, mystified as ever when it came to Andrew. The man hated Brackler with unusual venom, for some ugly and personal reason that Callahan never had been able to uncover. Yet he was too white-gloved to throw a little political mud his way.

Then Callahan saw something that made him gasp, first with a flash of belligerent pride, then with horror.

Brackler came bounding on screen, his broad, flat face wreathed in smiles. The big congressman crossed the platform quickly, purposefully, passing behind his own rostrum. Then he stood simply before his opponent and thrust out one giant paw toward Andrew.

Taken by surprise, Andrew looked up at him with ill-concealed distaste. His hands remained folded around the microphone.

"Jesus, Andy, shake his hand!" Callahan shouted. "Shake his fucking hand! It's a setup, can't you see? The picture, for Christ's sake!"

On screen, Andrew just stared up arrogantly, his knuckles whitening on the smooth wood of the small rostrum. Brackler, affecting a sheepish visage, shrugged and grinned in a way that said: Okay, if you want to be that way, but I'm going to keep this gentlemanly.

Callahan groaned in agony. On the ten o'clock update, and tomorrow in the papers and probably next Monday in *Time* magazine, his candidate was going to look like an arrogant, stuck-up prig. Which, Callahan thought as he glowered at the TV set, Andrew most certainly was. He had offered him Jim Brackler on a silver platter. Instead, Andrew had gone out and made the Big Mistake.

* * *

284

Tricia was mystified. Why was everyone so upset? She thought Andrew had been wonderful. There goes gloomy old Ron Callahan, she thought in exasperation, scowling about that silly handshake business. Even Andrew's normally smooth features were wrinkled and pale behind his wan smile as he claimed debate victory in front of the reporters.

Ron himself had emphasized the importance of their own reactions in the first few minutes after: "That's when we get to put the right spin on debate coverage. The debate itself is nothing. It's the spin—how they cover it afterward, who they declare the winner."

Tricia edged toward the campaign manager to tell him how very bad his expression looked on camera. She reached out to touch one of his rolled-up, coffee-stained shirtsleeves. Then, distracted by a vaguely familiar face in the crowd, she drew her fingers back in surprise.

"What?" Callahan said irritably.

"Nothing." Tricia was distant. "I thought I—never mind."

For some odd reason, she felt a hot flash of adrenaline throb through her veins. She rubbed her palms softly over tired eyes, careful not to smear the mascara. She craned her head back and peered into the dark risers of the auditorium. Whatever it had been, it was gone, swallowed in the anonymous crowd surging out the back door.

Then she saw it again: the sudden flare of a hazily familiar face. It was a woman, and her hair was different from the last time Tricia had seen her. A volunteer, perhaps, or the wife of a big contributor—but she didn't think so, not with the warm sweat oozing between her fingers and that little alarm bell in her head clanging the way it did when she spotted Sean playing with Andrew's bandsaw in the backyard or doing those horrible flip dives off the bull-nosed brick surrounding the swimming pool.

"Tricia?" Callahan was looking at her strangely now. "Are you okay?"

She struggled visibly to clear her head. "I'm fine. It's—I thought I saw an old friend."

The woman's head dipped low behind a dozen members of the audience. They filed out the black-painted steps. Then, just as the head swiveled away behind its frizzy mop of long blond locks, it came to her.

"Ron, it's a little crowded in here," Tricia said. "I'll catch up with you guys later, okay? At the Hyatt?"

Callahan, absorbed, nodded absently. Tricia headed impulsively down the steps.

It was hard to tell, in the shallow red glow from the exit sign. After all, they had never actually met. But the closer she drew, the more certain she became. Those features had haunted too much of her life.

Then, as the crowd flowed outside, Tricia glimpsed the woman's profile in the flat orange halogen arc lamps. No doubt. It was she!

The cool autumn air felt good on Tricia's cheeks, which were flushed with a hot, possessive sense of outrage. How dare she come here? After all she had done to Andrew. To them.

She was up to something. Tricia knew it instinctively. Something hurtful and rotten. Without thinking it through, she felt very sure she needed to find out what.

Following her was absurdly easy. Andrew's former mistress walked slowly, with a wobbly gait that seesawed from one side of the broad walkway to another: now creeping along the newspaper boxes rimming the brick wall of the Convention Center; now veering lazily across the cement, stumbling one high-heeled shoe into the grass verge opposite the spotlighted Spanish mission church across the street.

Together, hunter and prey, they worked their way up to the crosswalk at the corner of Second and Presidio. The woman was quite drunk. Or high, Tricia corrected herself quickly. As she watched anxiously from behind one great square pillar of the plaza, Amanda Roberts leaned casually against a concrete streetlight base. Reaching inside her purse, the tall blond woman extracted a gold box and a tiny silver spoon, and snorted what had to be two hits of cocaine, one for each nostril—all in full view of a mounted police officer whose horse waited patiently at her side until given the signal to cross the street.

Shocked, Tricia almost missed her chance. The light changed. The patrolman clip-clopped across the crosswalk. Amanda, oblivious, wiped her nose and followed the mounted policeman, staggering slightly to avoid the horse droppings. It was all Tricia could do to get across without being spotted.

She hung back in a little knot of tourists, waiting for her quarry to wobble down the long flight of steps from Presidio Street to San Antonio's scenic Riverwalk, a mile-long canal lined with lush vegetation and a constant flow of sight-seeing barges. By the time it was safe to trot down the steps, Amanda had disappeared into the after-dinner crowds along the canal.

Damn, Tricia cursed silently. I've lost her. She sideslipped furtively through the tourists clogging the narrow, cobbled walkway, ducked past a big fountain, and walked briskly onward. Amanda was nowhere to be found.

Then, just as suddenly as she had lost her, Tricia spotted the tall woman. She was seated alone at a small cafe table by the water, her black leather purse slung on the canal railing. As Tricia eyed her from a secure post near the fountain, Amanda's hand reached into the bag and pulled out a wallet. She handed a good-looking young waiter a credit card in exchange for what looked like a glass of gin, or maybe vodka. He had barely set the drink on the table when Amanda snatched it up. Plucking the lime off the rim with disdain, she gulped at the clear liquid with an urgency that Tricia found disturbingly familiar.

A strange sensation spread inside her chest as she got her first good look at the woman's face, pale and hollow-eyed under the gay Chinese lanterns dangling from the huge willows. This was no femme fatale, Tricia realized with a flash of courage. Amanda Roberts was a drunk, a drug addict. She looked like a walking public service announcement against substance abuse. Although she tried to shove it away, all Tricia felt was pity. Or empathy, perhaps.

"Takes one to know one," Tricia muttered. Abruptly she squared her shoulders, sucked in a deep breath, and marched over to the cafe.

"Ms. Roberts?" she asked peremptorily. Awkwardly, she extended her right hand.

Amanda, head down, sighed. She didn't respond, hoping the anonymous autograph hound would go away.

"Amanda?" Tricia said loudly. "I'm Tricia Sebastian. May I sit down?"

Amanda's head snapped to attention. Her eyes focused blearily on the tasteful dove-gray raw-silk suit and expert coif of the still-beautiful fortyish woman standing above her. There were gray streaks at the temples, masked with just the right amount of highlight tint. Amanda had always envied the oh-so-pretty, almost Mediterranean face.

"Sure," Amanda said uncivilly. Her long jaw jutted out belligerently.

"I won't be but a minute," Tricia said in a brisk, businesslike tone. "I want to ask you something."

"Shoot." Amanda's head wagged sardonically, her smile mocking the ice cubes as she twirled the empty rocks glass.

"You're making this very difficult," Tricia scolded. Nervously she smoothed the textured hem of her gray skirt, waving the waiter away with a frown.

"I should make it easy?" Amanda scoffed. "What is this? Wronged wife, confronting the mistress? You're a little late, dearie."

Amanda signaled the waiter back to the table: "Tequila rocks, but skip the lime, okay?" She turned back to Tricia, wanting to hurt this prim, self-righteous Junior Leaguer. "Know who taught me the virtues of tequila?" she asked with a leer.

Tricia blinked back coldly, knowing the answer.

Amanda laughed at her discomfort. "Only decent thing he ever did for me," she snapped. "It's a comfort to me now, in my golden years." She pushed self-consciously at her hair. "You had some burning question?"

"What are you doing here?" Tricia blurted.

"Drinking."

"You know exactly what I mean," Tricia replied frostily, as though speaking to a child. "Here, in San Antonio. And back there. How did you get in, anyway?"

"I called Sebastian headquarters this morning," Amanda bit back. "They had plenty of tickets left, and would I please bring a friend? Not a good sign, Mrs. Sebastian."

"Tricia," she corrected automatically. First names were the lingua franca of politics, even among enemies.

"So, Trish, it's a crime to attend a campaign debate?" Amanda said, raising her pale, unpenciled eyebrows. She wore little makeup. Her face looked washed out, haggard, as though she had just woken up. "I have as big a stake in this election as any of these folks." She flapped her hand wildly at the tourists beaming at them from a passing barge. "I may change my registration."

"You've done enough," Tricia said, coolly persistent. "What are you up to?"

288

Amanda's drink arrived. "Maybe I'm here to help," she said slyly. Then she spoke quietly, as if to herself. "Not you. Andrew, maybe. Myself, for sure."

Tricia shook her head in irritation. The woman was drunk, rambling. She tried a new tack.

"Amanda . . ." She dropped her voice confidentially, a just-us-girls tone. "Why don't you set the record straight?" She spoke with urgency as the idea swept over her. "Hold a press conference. Right here, tomorrow, with all the media still in town! They'd come. You're famous!"

"Infamous," Amanda said sourly. Swallowing the last of her liquor, she gestured for another. Tricia couldn't remember ever drinking that fast, even at her own personal worst. "They'd come," Amanda agreed glumly. "But why should I? Huh, Trish? I mean, what would that do to the legend of Amanda, the Washington whore?" She cursed herself for signing away the TV and movie rights to Mullins. How could a streetwise girl like me have been so stupid?

"Your lies have ruined Andrew," Tricia spat. "And a lot of other people. It's sick."

"Isn't it?" Amanda leered ironically. Then she leaned close to Tricia's ear and whispered seriously, slowly. "By the way, those other guys ruined themselves, okay? I dint hafta lie about them."

"But what about Andrew?"

Amanda stared at the pious, angelic, upturned nose. With that honey-dripped southern drawl, Tricia made her feel like some vain, spiteful Scarlett O'Hara. She wanted to scream at this snotty woman, to let her know her Ashley Wilkes was just as horny and wicked as all the rest. Something in Tricia's eyes made her tell the truth, instead.

"Trish, your boy's as clean as Ivory Soap. Damn him." Amanda's eyes drooped until they were nearly closed. "Ninety-nine and forty-four one-hundredths percent pure. What a pity!" she murmured. "Things could have been different."

"Then why won't you tell the world?" Tricia hissed.

"The world," Amanda pronounced, staggering to her feet, "doesn't give a shit. And neither do I, really. An' pretty soon, it'll all be over, okay?"

Amanda stared at Andrew's wife. The lobbyist's wide brown eyes

289

gleamed with a flash of sobriety that had not been there a moment ago.

"You'll like the way this turns out," Amanda said with smug mystery, squinting hard at the smaller, more delicate woman seated by the rail. "I promise. An' I won't be around for you to fret over, Melanie." She added wistfully, "You're awfully pretty, you know?"

"Thank you." Tricia didn't know what else to say. She sat perplexed, not knowing what to make of this eerie woman and her promises. Or threats? Why didn't she say what she meant? Tricia started to ask.

Amanda wobbled off abruptly, into the stream of passers-by.

"Take care of that man," she called from the crowd. She stumbled down the Riverwalk pathway and wheeled to the right, into the enormous atrium lobby of the Hyatt.

Tricia paid for Amanda's last two drinks. She waited impatiently for her change, wondering what this strange, reckless woman was doing in their hotel.

17

You're imagining things," Andrew said wearily, looping his tie around the starched collar of the fresh white Oxford button-down Tricia had bought in the hotel store.

"You weren't there," Tricia said stubbornly, tossing his razor and shaving cream into the zippered compartment of his garment bag.

"Thank God," Andrew replied, his words vehement. "You shouldn't have been, either. We can't have anything to do with that bitch." He glanced balefully at his watch.

"She's really not such a bad person," Tricia said mildly, turning over last night in her mind. It was like a scene in a movie; now, she couldn't quite remember how the lines had gone.

"She's poison," Andrew ordered flatly. "I don't want anything to do with her. Really, Tricia"—he shook his head in annoyance—"following her around!"

He changed the subject. "Did you see the papers?" His voice trembled with new anger. "They crucified me!"

"Ron said they would," Tricia commented softly. Is he

291

really so obsessed with his own problems? she wondered. Or does he have something to hide? Maybe it just makes him uncomfortable, even after all these years, to talk with his wife about his mistress.

"Great," Andrew snapped. "That's what I need today, Ron Callahan's I-told-you-so's." He yanked hard on his shirt cuffs to pop them out of the jacket sleeves.

"You're not listening to me," Tricia said slowly. She had lain awake half the night thinking about this, and she knew she was right. "She's a victim, Andrew," she insisted. "She's drinking and strung out on drugs, and I think she's about to go over the edge."

Tricia shuddered, remembering the sudden hard, cold clarity of Amanda's words as she'd left their table by the canal. There but for the grace of God, thought Tricia, remembering a hideous night in her own life years ago. She had sprawled on the cold tile of the bathroom in the Lakewood house for hours, examining the collection of pill bottles in her medicine chest; it had seemed the only way out. That was how Amanda Roberts had struck her: a frightened gazelle pursued by lions, whose only escape was to plunge off a rocky cliff. "Amanda's thinking about suicide," Tricia pronounced stubbornly. "She all but said so."

"What are you, her psychiatrist?" Andrew, now terribly annoyed, scooped up his speech notes from the bedside table. He ignored the six-by-eight-inch photo on the front page of the *San Antonio Light*, below the two-deck headline: SEBASTIAN SNUBS OPPONENT. GAFFE OVERSHADOWS FIRST DEBATE.

"Promise you'll leave this alone, Tricia," he commanded, his mouth set in a firm line. "Things are bad enough as it is. After last night, it's going to take a miracle to pull this off. The last thing I need is some reporter spotting the two of you together!"

Tricia felt an odd, funny premonition crawling over her. "What if she's down there right now in her bathtub, with her wrists cut?" She zipped his garment bag and handed it to him. "Never mind the woman's life," she said, voice suddenly cold and cutting. "How would it look in the papers?"

"I've got to go," Andrew said curtly. "You better get a move on. Ron's back in Dallas. My speech is at seven-thirty. The plane leaves at a quarter to nine. With you or without you," he added, a slam at her for delaying him last week in Houston. She'd had the cramps

292

and gotten behind schedule, forcing him to wait at the airport for an hour and miss a big dinner in El Paso.

Andrew took the garment bag from her hands and drew her fingers into his big palm. "Promise me you'll drop this, Tricia."

She nodded sullenly. He patted her arm absently and left.

She showered, dressed, and packed in a record thirty minutes. By seven-thirty she had left her bags with the porter in the hotel's fourteen-story garden atrium. She had plenty of time before the chartered King Air left for Lubbock or Laredo or Lampasas or wherever they were going for lunch. She got back on the glass-walled elevator and punched the button for the eighth floor.

"I just came down from my sister-in-law's room," she had told the clerk, playacting the ditzy socialite. "Now I can't remember the room number."

Clutching a slip of paper with the number "815" penciled large in the center, she rode upward, feeling unaccountably guilty. The elevator pinged. Tricia stepped off on the eighth floor and peered down the hall at the woman's room, unsure what to do next.

As if by some horrible magic, the door to 815 swung inward. An overnight bag slid into the hall, followed by a pale, tousled Amanda Roberts.

Tricia gasped and turned the other way. As she rounded the corner, she resisted a powerful urge to turn her head and find out if she had been spotted.

Obviously not. She heard the soft electronic whine as the elevator doors shut behind the female lawyer. Tricia waited an impatient ninety seconds, then slipped back to the elevator. It *whooshed* swiftly to the lobby. Looking down through the elevator glass into the atrium, she spotted Amanda at the desk, gesticulating in what looked like an argument over her hotel bill.

As Tricia got off the elevator and took cover behind a big wooden Indian in front of the gift shop, she knew with all her soul that she should stop. Now, before Amanda caught her and made a scene, before some reporter realized her husband's worst fears. But she couldn't.

Part of it was just maddening, idle feminine curiosity, the itch that prompts one woman to explore a friend's medicine chest during a dinner party. But together with curiosity, there was that undeniable sense of dread.

Feeling like a compulsive, melodramatic shrew, Tricia followed Amanda Roberts into the street, out of the Riverwalk's oasis, into the shabby, crumbling bricks of San Antonio's downtown business district.

Amanda's steps were brisk and direct. She crisscrossed past discount department stores crowded with Mexican families; walked twice past the ancient Spanish adobe walls of the Alamo, a tiny structure wedged improbably among ugly urban drugstores built in the 1950s. She appeared to be seeking something in particular; she would peer down one street, then walk on to the next. Probably looking for a decent pair of nylons, Tricia thought disgustedly. Maybe I ought to just go back to the hotel.

Then Amanda found it: a pawnshop. The long-legged blond window-shopped for a few seconds, peering in at what appeared to be a drum set and a row of typewriters. Tricia ducked into a McDonald's across the street.

Amanda entered the pawnshop. Tricia waited for what seemed an eternity. She drank two cups of coffee, watching anxiously as Ronald McDonald's big hand swept past eight-thirty on the wall opposite her tiny orange-topped table.

Finally Amanda reappeared and hailed a taxi. As she climbed into the cab's backseat, her face was bitter, angry. A decorative comb hung loose from one side of her disarrayed hair. The haggard blond woman carried nothing but the overnight bag she had lugged across two miles of downtown sidewalk. When the taxi signaled right and turned the corner, Tricia hustled across the street.

The owner of the pawnshop was an enormously fat, elderly Mexican. No part of his massive body moved when he spoke, not even his eerily thin lips.

"You just missed her, lady," he answered without interest. "She dint say nothing about meeting no sister."

"Sister-in-law," Tricia said absently. "Did she buy anything?"

"Just the pistol," the man said phlegmatically. "Thirty-eight police special."

"You sold a gun to some woman who just walked in off the street?" Tricia exploded, forgetting herself. "Couldn't you see she was upset?"

"You bet she was upset." The owner grinned ever so slightly, exposing a few crooked, blackened teeth. "She was mad about having to come back tomorrow and pick it up." A thought disturbed the man's immobile face. "Hey, I thought you was her sister." His eyes were black with suspicion.

"Sister-in-law," Tricia explained impatiently.

"I tole her she could take the ammunition, but I can't sell nobody a gun without the twenty-four-hour waiting period. It's a new city law in San Antonio. Sorry about your sister's prollems, but I got my license to think about."

"Problems?" Tricia chose her words carefully. "She, uh, told you?"

"Yeah." His eyes leered at the expensive sapphires around Tricia's long, sensual neck. "Her ex bugging her like that, I don't blame her wanting some protection," the obese man acknowledged. "Nothing to be ashamed of. Lots of ladies come in here with that kinda thing. Not too many know about guns like her, though," he said admiringly. "Usually they just want a little piece of shit like this."

He held up a small .22 revolver. "How bout you, lady? You need something to carry in your purse?"

"No, thank you." Tricia backed out of the store. She looked at her slim Cartier watch in despair. She had missed the plane. Within the hour, Andrew could be anywhere from Brownsville to Amarillo, and she was stuck here with an infamous Washington seductress about to blow her own head off. Andrew would be furious.

Tricia looked about frantically for a phone booth. At times like these, you called Ron Callahan.

"You put them on like this, ma'am."

At two o'clock the following afternoon, the man at the Waco Pistol & Rifle Range spoke patronizingly, adjusting the padded gray headphones over her ears. "See?"

"Thanks. I know what I'm doing," Amanda said with a touch of defiant professionalism.

"Okay, now we load, pointing the business end toward the ground," the wiry young man continued blithely, unhearing in the deafening crash of gunfire. He rambled on, showing her how to slot the rounds into the chamber, how to move the target back and forth on its electronically controlled wire, how to cock the pistol, how to flip the safety off, and—he put his arms around her white lamb's-wool sweater, so his knotty biceps could brush the subtle swell of each breast—how to hold the big gun in both hands and gently squeeze, not jerk, the trigger.

"Damn!" The instructor gave a low whistle. The target came back with eight small holes punched tightly together in the center, clustered at the heart of the black burglar silhouette.

"I wouldn't want to mess with you, lady," he said vigorously, eyeing the tangled hair and puffy jowls of the expensively dressed woman who stood before him, expertly jacking another eight-round load into the pistol. The blonde had probably been a real looker when she was younger, the instructor thought. But the pallid skin, the dead, half-closed eyes: she made him uneasy. He flinched as she reached out and lifted his earphone away from his head.

"Go away now!" she shouted brusquely. "I like to do this alone."

"Sure." He grinned nervously, suddenly sorry he had felt her up, the way he always did with these women.

Amanda turned back to her work. Snapping the chamber into place, she grasped the warm black steel of the pistol butt in her right palm.

It had been a couple of years since she'd practiced, though she always kept a pistol at her bedside. Washington was a dangerous city. Too bad she couldn't have brought her own; that was impossible, what with airport security. She hadn't worried about it. After all, John Hinckley had picked his up in a pawnshop in Dallas. Amanda hadn't counted on the new San Antonio city ordinance requiring a twenty-four-hour cooling-off period before handing over a lethal weapon. The delay had given her a chance to stay in San Antonio another day and pick up a few things she would need tonight.

Amanda's aching head screamed for cocaine, but her stash was stone empty. She had no idea where to score coke in Waco, a town so dry she couldn't even buy beer in the convenience store across the street.

She felt giddy with adrenaline, with the bittersweet pain of anticipation. As she loaded and fired, loaded and fired, her thoughts jumped around uncontrollably. Visions flashed through her brain: Brackler rutting away on top of her; Andrew Sebastian jumping her bones, protesting his love; Harley Atkinson, raving about the great deal Dan Mullins had for her. Then, inexplicably, an image from her midwestern childhood: Professor Harold Hill from the musical *The Music Man*, extolling the virtues of a good billiards player.

"A cool head and a keen eye," Amanda chanted whimsically. Then she put eight more rounds in the bull's-eye.

Outside, Ron Callahan's irritation turned to alarm.

The campaign manager was stuffed into the front seat of a rented Honda. After the long, slow drive up from San Antonio, Callahan had parked near a 7-Eleven store, watching Amanda Roberts enter the gun range across the street. Then he had rushed inside to use the phone, annoyed at this ridiculous waste of a day to satisfy the paranoid delusions of the candidate's wife. He heated a couple of burritos in the microwave and grabbed a root beer, cursing Tricia for this fool's errand. Then it hit him, with a force that sent the hefty campaign manager tumbling out to the tiny economy car. For the next thirty minutes he kept his pale green eyes glued on the long, low building across the gravel road.

Amanda Roberts hadn't bought a gun to commit suicide. He had never bought that idea, anyway.

"You don't understand, Ron!" Tricia had argued on the phone yesterday morning, after pulling him out of a critical GOTV meeting. "None of it makes sense! She's whacked out on drugs, booze, God knows what. Andrew won't listen, but I know! She's ready to pull that trigger."

But not on herself, Callahan thought worriedly, licking chili sauce from his lips. You don't practice at a gun range to kill yourself. You just hold the pistol in your mouth and blow your brains out. Besides, he had never heard of a woman committing suicide with a firearm. They took pills, like Marilyn Monroe.

The second big debate was only five hours away. Tossing what was left of the wax-papered burrito into the brown paper sack, Callahan gunned the whining four-cylinder engine to life and shot across the gravel lane. The spot next to Amanda's pale blue rented Chevrolet was empty. He nibbled on a Snickers bar and waited. He had washed a lot of dirty laundry in his time: kept candidate's peccadillos out of the paper; cut a few corners on campaign finance; bent the Texas wiretap law a little. But averting assassination attempts was a little out of his league.

"First thing is, you're out of it," Callahan had barked over the phone to Tricia yesterday. "Get the first Southwest flight back. If what you say is right, she can't pick up the damn thing 'til tomorrow. I'll catch an early plane down."

Tricia was not to be put off. "Then what, Ron? Wrestle it away from her? She'll just find another way. Can't we report it?"

He had been curt. "I'll take care of it."

Now, waiting in front of a gun range for an armed, deranged woman who was probably planning to shoot his boss, Callahan didn't feel quite so authoritative. Maybe Tricia was right, he thought. Maybe I ought to just drive back over to 7-Eleven and call the cops.

The plate-glass door with the big red-lettered OPEN sign tinkled ajar. Amanda Roberts appeared in the doorway, zipping her over-night bag. Good, Callahan thought miserably. At least she doesn't wear it in a holster under her arm, so she can whip it out and gun me down here in the parking lot.

"Miss Roberts?" His car door popped open. Callahan tussled briefly with the steering wheel, then climbed to his feet.

"Get lost," Amanda said gruffly. "No autographs, creep." She opened the door of her Chevrolet.

"I work for Andrew Sebastian."

Amanda paused, making no move to slide into the car seat.

Callahan bustled quickly around his little Japanese car and leaned across the Chevy's open door. "My name is Ron Callahan," he said. "I'd like to talk to you."

"Yeah?"

"Yeah." Callahan nodded, feeling a burst of courage as she tossed the overnight bag into the safety of the backseat. Her hand trembled a bit, he noticed. "Tricia Sebastian asked me to find you," he explained. "She thinks you could use some help."

"That's a laugh," Amanda snorted. "From what I've heard, it's you guys need the help. You're his campaign manager, aren't you?"

"I'm his campaign staff," Callahan said ruefully, hoping to strike some warmth. "We're a little underfunded."

"I really am in a hurry." Shaking her head to slide her long, tangled blond hair over her shoulders, Amanda eased nonchalantly behind the steering wheel.

"To get to Dallas?" Callahan inquired suspiciously. "Come on, lady. I know what you're thinking. It's crazy." He spoke in a flat, logical monotone. "You can't possibly get away with it. I know, and Tricia knows. Pretty soon the cops will know." He smiled nervously. "What's Andrew ever done to you, anyway?"

"Is that what you think?" Amanda cried. She erupted in an explosive cackle. "Oh, man, that's really crazy." She paused suddenly. "How'd you find me here? Was that you following me on the highway?"

"Amanda, I know everything," Callahan said. "Where you bought the gun. Where you're headed. But think about it. It's nuts, and I can stop you. Go back to Washington, okay?"

"You're bluffing," Amanda said slyly. His sheepish reaction told her all she needed to know. "You can't go to the police. I bought the gun legally, even if I don't have a carrier permit. That's no big deal. Half the women in America walk around with pistols in their purses."

"Half the women in America don't carry a gun to a political debate," Callahan snapped, watching her face carefully. Now he was sure; Amanda Roberts was headed to the Loews Anatole Hotel.

"Give it up, Amanda," he barked. "Catch the night flight back to D.C. Get drunk. Have a few laughs. You'll wake up and thank me." The campaign manager groped in his pocket. "Here's a few hundred for the flight back, okay? I'd go put you on the plane myself, but we got a big debate tonight." He extended a handful of big bills, part of the stash he always kept handy for emergencies.

Amanda's shoulders sagged beneath the headrest. When she spoke again, she sounded like a petulant little girl. "It was never Andy," she said dispiritedly. For some reason it was suddenly important to her that he understand. "It's Brackler. He's a real shit, you know?" Tears welled in her bloodshot eyes.

"I know," Callahan said softly. He placed the bills on the dashboard and held out his hand. "The gun?"

She reached back and unzipped the bag, withdrawing a large Styrofoam box strapped tight with two green plastic bands. Gently Callahan took it from her shivering hands. He slipped off the bands. The pistol lay there, black and looming and lethal, with a dozen spare bullets studded into grooved holes in the Styrofoam. He stifled an urge to hand it back to her and tell her to shoot the fat bastard.

Callahan's curiosity got the better of him. "Why Jim Brackler?"

"It's a long story." She sighed shakily. "You should have left me alone," she accused without heat. "Your man would have been a senator." She shivered as if bitterly cold and scratched in her purse for the car keys.

"You gonna be okay?" Callahan said. He now knew how Tricia must have felt about this sad, desperate woman. The drawn, hollow face he saw through the Chevy's window didn't sync with the Washington harpie you saw on *Nightline*.

"It's all right," Amanda said quietly, wiping huge tears from her cheeks. "I'm okay. Really. I just have to go now, okay?" Her voice was strained, raspy.

"Sure." He watched the blue Chevrolet spurt a thin double trail of gravel. It crossed below the overpass and joined the steady stream of traffic on the elevated lanes headed south, away from Dallas.

Callahan breathed a sigh of relief. He tossed the revolver in the back of the Honda and headed north, cursing his watch and the loss of a precious day. He would be lucky to get back in time to give Andrew a few tips on how to handle Big Jim tonight.

"What I really wanted was to let her go ahead and do it," he said two hours later, tired and only half joking.

"You should have," Andrew said sourly.

Tricia, sitting across the small fifth-floor hotel suite, was surprised at how much all of this had upset her husband. Ron was right. They should have waited until after the debate to tell him.

"I honestly think you mean that," Callahan said in a shocked tone.

"You're damn right I mean it!" Andrew's voice rose unexpectedly, echoing off the step-and-repeat Chinese rose pattern of the hotel wallpaper. "How dare you meddle in this, Ron! And you!"

The candidate rounded on Tricia. She flinched from the raw edge in his tone. "I expressly told you to stay out of this!" he shouted. "I can't believe you two! Sneaking back and forth across the state, following a madwoman with a gun. How could you get mixed up in this?"

"If we hadn't gotten mixed up in this"—Tricia hissed the last four words back at her angry, pacing husband—"that madwoman would be downstairs, ready to cause a very ugly scene. Maybe shoot somebody."

"Jim Brackler would be such a loss to society," Andrew scoffed. "It was worth disobeying my orders, risking a very messy scandal, to protect that bag of wind? What's going on here, folks? Whose side are you on?"

Callahan examined his candidate carefully and found something he didn't like. "You're mad because you're going to lose," he said slowly, with something like awe. "You'd rather see Jim Brackler dead than have him beat you again."

"Don't be ridiculous," Andrew rasped huskily. "I just . . ." His voice trailed off lamely. "I don't want us involved in anything."

The candidate tried to compose himself, to force a grim smile. But Callahan could see the wheels spinning behind the candidate's glacier-blue eyes. *What if? What if Brackler were dead and I won the Senate seat?*

Andrew spat a small bark of laughter and dropped onto a big, overstuffed green chair. "I don't think I'd send flowers," he admitted. The voice was cold and remote, as though it were not connected to his brain. "But that's all done. Of course you did the right thing." Andrew looked sharply at the two of them. "But next time I tell you to do something, I wish you would just do it."

The matter thus concluded, Andrew leaned over the small coffee table. He opened the big black briefing book Callahan had prepared for him.

"What does Big Jim have in store for us tonight?" he asked jovially. Andrew never could stand to have anyone mad at him for long, Tricia noted. "And what have we got for him?"

"What do you think Sebastian's planning tonight, Dan?" Brackler asked anxiously.

"Who cares?" Mullins replied airily, pouring whiskey from one of the tiny bottles in the minibar. They were on the tenth floor of the sixteen-thousand-room Loews Anatole Hotel, in the tower that loomed high over the Sebastian Freeway west of Dallas's huge apparel market.

"It's public TV, for Christ's sake," Mullins gloated. "Most people'll be mad we bumped Jacques Cousteau."

"Don't take him for granted," Jarrett Hart warned, nodding to Mullins's offer. "Scotch is fine."

The big banker leaned back on the small sofa and eased off his black wingtips with his toes. "Andy'll come out swinging tonight," he counseled.

"He'll come out shaking hands, that's for sure," Denny piped up from his seat at the desk in the corner.

Brackler's eyes narrowed, surprised. "Did you guys hear that?" the congressman announced. "Denny made a joke. How about that?"

Mullins chuckled. "I'll bet you're right, Den. That's okay, let him shake, Jim. It'll remind the press."

"It was on CBS national last night," Denny chirped from his Bob Cratchit stool in the corner. No one had offered him a drink, but he was glad just to be there. "A friend of mine told me the picture's gonna be in Sunday's *New York Times.*"

"To hell with that." Brackler grinned. "I'd rather have it in the *National Enquirer.*" Big Jim always remembered where his votes were.

"What, and knock Amanda Roberts's picture off the cover?" Mullins said. "I forgot to tell you. I could have sworn I saw her at that debate in San Antonio. Her hair was different, but I'd know her anywhere."

"What?" Brackler said. His bonhomie evaporated. The idea of Amanda Roberts skulking around Texas made him terribly uneasy.

"Denny, why don't you go downstairs and check around?" the congressman suggested. "I don't want that bitch pulling some publicity stunt. If you spot her, get the hotel people to kick her out."

"Sure," Denny said, hopping off the wooden chair. "I'll check it out."

"You do that," Brackler said dourly. "Another drink, Jarrett?"

In her bathroom on the Anatole's seventh floor, Amanda Roberts gave one last tug to the frightful black wig perched on her head. She slipped another stray blond lock underneath its tight-fitting mesh. A few bobby pins later, the wig was secure.

She stuck her contact lens case in her purse and put on her glasses. She never wore them out in public, preferring to wear the contacts or just squint a little. The ugly, black-rimmed spectacles made her look like a bug-eyed toad. With the application of far too much eyeliner and a big Sebastian button sagging from the bosom of the shapeless frock she had bought at a discount maternity store in San Antonio, she looked like a frumpy, no-class housewife volunteer.

Perfect, she thought.

She stood and walked into her hotel room, practicing the gingerly seesaw gait of a woman eight months pregnant. Amanda had never had the pleasure, thanks to the Pill and, once, a safe, kindly abortionist at a clinic in Bethesda. But she knew the walk and emulated

302

it rather well. The two shallow pillows duct-taped to her waist didn't bother her, as long as she thrust her hips forward a little.

Now that the time was really here, Amanda wondered if the pregnancy ploy would be good enough to get her out of the room afterward. She stifled another powerful urge to forget the whole thing and escape back to Washington. Escape? That was a laugh. To what? Shaky, she collapsed on the bed, glad of the bottle of Cuervo she'd picked up on the way into town.

The timing had been awfully close. She'd driven nearly twenty miles south of Waco before she could be sure Callahan wasn't dogging her trail. Then she'd doubled back to the gun range. Scooping up the cash Callahan had left on her dash, she'd gone inside and bought another Smith & Wesson. The twenty-four-hour waiting period had not yet found its way to Waco, Texas.

The .38 lay on the bed in front of her, fully loaded, the tiny red-rimmed safety catch flicked on carefully. Amanda checked the load again. She slotted the chamber back into place and slid the hefty revolver inside the big pocket centered over the front of her dress. Her fingers probed for the long slit she had cut on the inside. Then she nestled the pistol between the pillows. She stood, parading back and forth in front of the mirror above the chest of drawers, smoothing the cheap cotton fabric over the hump at her stomach. It looked good. Amanda drew out the pistol quickly, careful not to snag the hammer.

"Time to go," she whispered, humming eerily in the empty room. She recognized the tune, from *The Music Man*. Something about bells on a hill. She wondered if she really were cracking up. She decided it must be nothing more than forty-eight hours cocaine free.

Plus the normal stress and strain of planning a political assassination.

Amanda exhaled shakily, the breath coming in halting shivers. She took one last look in the mirror, then walked quickly down the hall. It was important to be early. She needed a good seat.

"Wouldn't you rather be in back, dear?" The soft lines of the old woman's mouth crinkled in understanding. "It's nearer the ladies' room."

"No, thank you," Amanda said nervously. "I already went." She offered a knowing, confidential smile.

"All right." The small, round-shouldered woman seated behind the table grinned. "I don't blame you for wanting a front-row seat. You deserve it, getting here so early." Nan Sebastian's age-spotted fingers rippled decisively through the ticket envelopes. She came to one marked BARBARA HASKINS.

"That's it!" Amanda yelped. Slow down, she thought. Take it easy. She felt the first wet sheen of perspiration on her forehead.

"Yes, right," Nan said, carefully checking the name off the list. Then she handed over the ticket envelope. "The seats aren't numbered. It's first come, first served."

"I know," Amanda said pleasantly. "I called ahead."

As she walked inside the big auditorium marked "Monte Carlo Theater," Amanda glanced at the sole security guard, an aging man in a gray uniform armed only with a flashlight. With satisfaction, she noted the way he averted his head slightly upon spotting the pregnant bulge of her stomach.

It was just as she had planned. Men always did that.

Denny Frawley was bored. He had been sitting in the deserted auditorium for forty minutes. The crowd was just starting to filter in, dotting around the plush orange seats. There were four hundred and twelve seats. He had just finished counting them.

Brackler's side of the auditorium was filling up faster, Denny noted with the smug satisfaction of the professional advance man. The left half already held at least fifty people, while the first rows on the right still stood empty.

A dark-haired, oversize pregnant woman lumbered down the center aisle and took her place on the front row, toward the far right. Instinctively Denny looked away.

Pregnant ladies always made him mildly uncomfortable. He didn't like to stare.

Andrew shooed them from his room.

"Go on!" he said, propelling his wife and campaign manager out into the dark, vase-lined hallway. The hotel's owner, a contemporary of Andrew's father, was mad for Oriental art. "I need a few minutes alone, okay?"

"He's in a funny mood tonight," Callahan remarked as they rode down to the vast, cavernous elegance of the hotel's extraordinary atrium lobby, festooned at each corner with a tapestry as large as a windjammer sail.

"He knows he's going to lose," Tricia said sharply.

Callahan stopped and gripped her by the arm, his lips moving close to her ear. "I was right, wasn't I? He'd rather see Brackler dead than lose this."

She hesitated. "It's not the Senate," she said softly, wondering if he could ever understand how her husband felt about that man. "You don't know all the facts, Ron. A lot of water under the bridge. Besides, wouldn't you? If it could just happen, without your lifting a finger?"

"No," Callahan said doggedly, his sad hound-dog eyes doubting and anxious. He straightened and waved. "Roger! Hi, Sean. You all set?"

By a quarter to seven both candidates were seated at a safe distance from each other. Each sat on an identical folding chair in tiny identical rooms at each end of the backstage area. Makeup experts hired by each campaign dabbed cotton swabs at sweaty faces, sprayed stray strands of graying hair behind their ears.

Dan Mullins entered the rear of the auditorium just a few feet behind Tricia Sebastian and Ron Callahan. He lagged back to avoid them and waved across the room at Denny. The aide puffed up the aisle importantly.

"No sign of her?" Mullins asked. They took seats in the back, near the aisle.

"She's not here," Denny reported. "I watched everyone come in. Everybody was told to be in their seats by six forty-five."

Mullins breathed a sigh of relief. He hardly wanted to face any complaints from that uppity call girl about the rotten deal he and Jarrett Hart had given her.

Hart took a seat behind Mullins. He whispered, "Any problems?"

"None," Mullins said, smiling wolfishly. "Everything's under control."

Tricia deposited Callahan in one of the seats roped off for them on the front row. She gave Andrew's parents a little squeeze and winked at Sean.

"I'll be right back," she said. "I want to give Daddy a kiss for luck."

"Good idea," Callahan interjected. "Give him a nice glow for the cameras."

Tricia shook her head in resignation; Callahan could turn the deepest human emotions into mere shards of his campaign strategy. She slipped up the steps at the far side of the stage and walked unsurely down a dark, narrow hallway.

Coming to a door marked Makeup, she tapped and eased it open.

"Oh!" Tricia gasped, taking in Jim Brackler's shiny, balding pate, his small, round eyes. "Sorry!"

She pulled the door shut and pressed her hot forehead against it, hearing the man's nasty guffaw. How humiliating! She circled quickly behind the stage, afraid she would run out of time. The slim gold Cartier watch at her wrist said it was nearly seven o'clock.

"Hi!" Andrew beamed when she walked into his room. "I hope you don't think I was too terrible upstairs," he said abruptly, ever anxious to make amends. "I'm sorry."

Tricia kissed one cheek. The young makeup woman smiled.

"I love you," Tricia offered softly, brushing at the damp skin-toned pancake on his face. "You look great," she assured him. "Break a leg!"

"Thanks." Andrew grinned. "I'd rather break his neck."

Tricia skipped down the stage steps, circumnavigated the apron. She was about to take her seat when something caught her eye. A black-haired woman, hugely pregnant, sat at the far end of the row, near the orange-carpeted wall. Her eyes seemed riveted to the slim figure of the moderator as he settled behind a podium.

As she settled onto her own seat at the other end of the row, Tricia looked at the pregnant woman with the natural interest of a fellow veteran. The woman was in her forties; a little old to be having children. But then, Tricia reflected, I was thirty-four when Sean was born. People were having children later these days, what with women's liberation and the two-career couple. Still, she didn't look at all like a yuppie working-woman Republican. More the Pleasant Grove housewife-volunteer type.

Then, as the houselights blinked and the murmur subsided, Tricia realized that the face seemed familiar. She remembered another auditorium, another hauntingly familiar face in the crowd. And it all fell together in her brain.

The houselights began their final long, slow slide toward semidarkness.

Tricia froze stock still, her temples hammering with fear. "Ron?" she said hoarsely. Her eyes never flickered from the oddly immobile form huddled at the end of the aisle. It was as though Amanda Roberts were a coiled rattlesnake, ready to strike if her prey so much as flinched.

She was wearing a horrid black wig and enormous tortoiseshell glasses. But there could be no mistake. Tricia watched as Amanda— it *was* Amanda; even now, in the darkness, there was no mistaking the angular nose, the wide mouth, that worried brow—lifted her right hand from her armrest and slipped it casually into the folds of her voluminous dress.

Then it all flooded over Tricia. The pawnshop. The scene with Callahan at the gun range. Her eerie threats. Those desperate eyes, glinting now even through the gloom, magnified by the Coke-bottle glasses as Amanda stared fixedly at the stage.

At my husband.

Blood roared in Tricia's ears. She could hear the P.A. system only dimly. "Ladies and gentlemen," the moderator was saying. "The Republican candidate for the United States Senate, Andrew Sebastian."

The crowd around her jumped to its feet. Ron Callahan. Her in-laws. Sean. Everyone, except the barely visible bulk at the end of the row.

Oh, my God, Tricia thought in horror. Sean!

"Ron!" Tricia tugged at the stocky campaign manager's jacket sleeve. She spoke loudly, oblivious to the stares from applauding volunteers behind them. "Look, there! At the end of the row!"

"Ssh," Callahan soothed. He peered down the line of Sebastian supporters, pulling Tricia back down to her seat. Andrew, up on the stage, took his seat at a small table to their right. Callahan's eyes roved to the pregnant lady at the end, then jerked blankly to the candidate's wife.

"What's wrong?" he hissed.

Tricia twisted forward in her seat. She looked one more time, to make sure. There was no doubt: the long jaw, the wide brown eyes beneath the shallow disguise. She half rose and reached across Callahan's wide girth to seize her son's arm.

On the stage, Andrew squinted past the footlights, scanning the rows for his family. Tricia saw his brow wrinkle in confusion; he

307

spotted her wrestling his son away from his grandparents and onto another seat, next to the center aisle.

She caught her husband's eye. They were only twenty feet apart. She flipped her head twice, viciously, in Amanda's direction.

"Hey," Callahan whispered. "What's going on?"

Tricia rasped a one-word explanation: "Amanda!"

Brackler appeared on the left side of the stage. He made his way to his seat.

How could she stop this? Everything was happening so quickly! Tricia felt as though she were in a dream, her feet and arms fighting to move through the leaden weight of too much gravity.

As she watched in horror, her husband's eyes moved with glacial slowness in the direction of her nod, until they came to rest on his former mistress. There! Andrew's cool blue eyes flashed with instant recognition. His gaze jerked back to Tricia in alarm.

"Where?" Callahan said stupidly. Following Tricia's finger, he searched the row, until, slowly, it began to sink in. "Jesus," he gasped.

"Take Sean!" Tricia thrust the protesting child at Callahan, ignoring the hushing noises of the audience around them. Callahan moved as though he were underwater. "Go!" Tricia hissed. "Go tell someone. Get her out of here!"

The campaign manager nodded mutely. Bending low, he led the boy rapidly up the center aisle. As the cameras whirred into action above their heads, Tricia breathed a half sigh of relief. At least one of her men was safe.

Amanda's attention was utterly absorbed with Andrew. The candidate stared back at the crazed woman, transfixed. Later, when she had time to play it back in her mind, Tricia would lie awake nights, trying to determine exactly what passed between those two in that split second before pandemonium broke loose in the Monte Carlo Theater.

"Mr. Sebastian?" the moderator's voice questioned. "Are you ready?"

With difficulty, Andrew broke off his gaze and focused on the man across the stage.

"Mr. Sebastian?" the moderator repeated.

"I'm ready," Andrew said, clearing his throat into the microphone. Tricia leaned forward, wondering if Callahan had found a policeman.

Her husband glanced back in Amanda's direction, then rose abruptly from his chair. "There's one thing I'd like to do first," he said loudly, his voice echoing in the hall as he walked away from the microphone.

He walked resolutely past the moderator. His long legs faltered only once before he reached Brackler's table. The heavyset congressman glowered up suspiciously.

"Put her there, Jim!" Andrew shouted nervously in a voice that mocked ever so faintly. The audience tittered knowingly. Brackler rose and extended his hand.

A sudden rustle to Tricia's left brought her to her feet. There, in the gloomy shadow of the harsh white television lights, Amanda Roberts leaped up from her seat and took two rapid steps toward the stage.

"Andrew!" Tricia screamed as the pistol swung free in the woman's trembling right hand. Tricia ran stumbling toward her.

On stage, Andrew pumped the bigger man's hand viciously, jerking it up and down for what seemed like forever. Brackler snarled, struggling to free his hand from Andrew's clutch.

His left hand clasped over Brackler's elbow, Andrew took one last look in Amanda's direction. Then he stepped unwaveringly between Jim Brackler and a .38 caliber bullet.

The gunshot's boom echoed off the dark acoustical tile of the high black ceiling. Amanda went down in a crash under the force of Tricia's attack. As the room exploded around them, both women saw Andrew clutch at his neck in agony. He collapsed on the smooth blond wood of the stage, the powder-blue collar of his cotton shirt soaked with crimson.

Epilogue

The candidate lay carefully on starched white sheets.

Normally, visiting hours would have been over. But the patient was a VIP; a hero, even. So the nurses bent the rules a little. They allowed his son into the room and the young paramedic who had saved his life. After all, it was election night.

He was confused through much of the evening. He fell asleep a good many times, from the drugs they gave him to deaden the awful pain tearing at his collarbone. The doctors said he would recover full use of his voice. But for now he could not speak, not even when the single pool camera came to film his reaction to the results. All he could do was smile at Callahan's jokes, Tricia's concern, his parents' pride. And reach out his right hand very, very gently, to ruffle the soft brown hair above his son's worried little eyes and try to keep the tears from spilling out of his own. The drugs made him weepy.

He caught large swatches of the coverage on the big television set angled downward above his bed. That, too, fatigued him, but he insisted with a steely glare that the bossy nurse, the tall one with the severe knot in her red hair, leave the television set on. He had trouble following it at times, but that was all right. They kept repeating the same things.

There was endless footage of the shooting, depicting again and again how he had stepped into the path of the bullet to save a man everyone in Texas knew he despised.

"They've been showing that over and over, on every newscast, all week long." Callahan beamed, impervious to the daggers in Tricia's eyes. "Great political theater."

Andrew knew Tricia thought Ron callous, but he could see the tracks of sleepless nights in the brown-black bags under the campaign manager's eyes. He wished he could tell his wife to lighten up.

The election-night coverage included clips from Amanda's news conference last Saturday, after she was released from custody. By a curious sort of unspoken, long-distance agreement, Amanda set the record straight on Andrew Sebastian and the Philippines and said nothing of Tricia or Callahan, of pawnshops in San Antonio or gun ranges in Waco. For his part, Andrew wrote his refusal to press charges on a police detective's long spiral notebook and accepted Callahan's assurances that Amanda would get the help she needed. In the usual Callahan manner, it had all been arranged.

The candidate's favorite part of the coverage was the Interview, the postmortem shouting match between Bernie Zollars and Big Jim Brackler, where Brackler had self-destructed.

"Do you believe Andrew Sebastian saved your life?" Zollars cried from the screaming mass of reporters jostling around the congressman as he walked toward a big black limousine in the Anatole's parking lot.

"Hell, no!" Brackler shouted back, scowling into the lens with disdain. Over the past week, that harsh screen image had burned its way into the subconscious of every voter in Texas.

It was strange that he did not relish Brackler's downfall as much as his own victory. In the end, it wasn't even close: Sebastian 54 percent, Brackler 46 percent. Callahan said his picture would be on the cover of every newsmagazine in America next Monday. With the lightning-quick speed of the modern electronic media, Ted Koppel was already there on the screen, reclassifying him as "future presidential material."

Andrew looked up at the people he loved best. They stared back at him, proud tears in their eyes. Tricia's husband, Sean's father, Roger's son: he was a hero to them now. Maybe to millions of others, for a day, at least, until some other tragedy or celebrity or scandal became America's flavor of the month.

Andrew wondered how they would feel if they knew the whole truth. The same, he hoped. Does it take more courage to react instinctively to danger, he wondered, than to walk knowingly into a bullet?

The phone rang. It was the vice-president, now the president-elect, calling to congratulate the new senator. Andrew groaned and rolled his eyes. Tricia frowned down at him. Her eyes sparkled giddily as she chatted her thanks to the nation's new chief executive. Andrew decided that he could live with his doubts, and slept.